THE COLOR

MATTHEW WARREN BOATNER

First paperback edition October 2019

Book design by Robin Vuchnich; mycustombookcover.com

Map by Amanda Kennedy

ISBN 978-0-578-59855-0 (paperback)

Published by Matthew Boatner

www.matthewwarrenboatner.com

For my Pops—the very best man I know

"…Let me look into a human eye;

…it is better than to gaze into sea or sky;

…better than to gaze upon god."

–Herman Melville

Contents

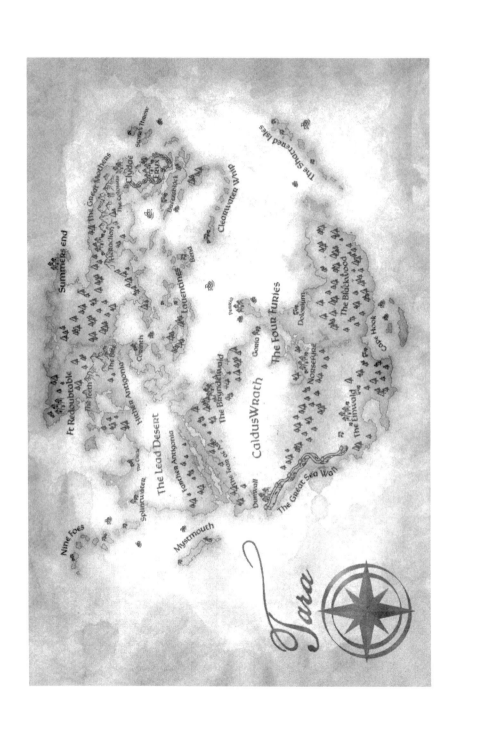

HOPE IN THE DARKEST OF DAYS

Cyrus the Raven

The Raven pushed his barrel deep into a cleric's cheek. He whispered his words, deep and low, and squeezed the trigger. *No quarter.* The hammer fell to flaring powder at mouth and muzzle, and the bishop's head lurched, his lifeless body careening back into the blackest corner of a broken carriage. The splat of brains and muck on the far window echoed across wintered trees as the man in white robes slumped to the buggy's floor. Delicate lines of smoke piped out in the cold, rising in cloudy strands from the priest's cheek and mouth, as well as the Raven's revolver. The bishop's hands—once cowering and raised—fell to his lap and rested together, as if praying.

He caught a glimpse of the face in fading moonlight, now propped against the carriage door beneath a reddened window, tinting the beams a rosy red like cathedral stained glass. The Raven eyed the shilling-sized hole that sullied the man's cheek just under the eye, odious like the barrel of Cyrus's smoldering revolver, now snug again in its holster.

"What'd ye say to him?" Deimos asked, making his way to one of the horses—the last of the living.

"Something I need not repeat," he said.

Deimos's horse looked an ominous ebony, tinted scarlet after the crossfire. It brayed and kicked in the shallowing snow, pulling and bucking under the ties at the terret and hame, stuck in the drive and weighed down by a line of dead nags. Deimos stepped through drift and debris—broken barrels, strewn luggage, and a few corpses resting in meager pools of soggy red.

The smoke from Cyrus's revolver emanated behind him as he moved along. The fog of his tempered breaths thickened with the black powder that stung his nose and hung in the air. "Gather supplies and make haste," he said. "We've a long way back. What are you—"

"You'd leave this beautiful beast to the wolves?" Deimos interrupted. "Shh, thatta girl." He gripped the bridle and stroked the mare's head as her stamping waned. "A proper horse, she is."

"A noisy one," Cyrus said, "and half the fuckin' country will 'ave heard us already."

"Let them hear, brother. Mere sheep they are….You worry like a woman." Deimos unhooked the horse from the pole straps and bearing buckles and led her out of the drive by bit and mane, clucking and ticking at her as he trudged. "There's a beauty. That's it, good girl."

"You'd sooner fuck the horse, it would seem."

"Ha! To be sure, brother. I like them shapely."

Cyrus knelt, reaching for the jacket of a dead man face down in the snow. He loosened the man's belt and snatched a box of rounds and a powder horn. A steel gorget rested over a clean collar, inlaid with gold and silver acanthus leaves etched delicately into the metal. *Captain of the guard, by his looks.* His coat was navy on gold with ornate blue-brass buttons and seam-lined pockets, and a crinkled sash lay draped from shoulder to hip over a mess of hempen *fourragère* cord anchored at one shoulder and looping down under the arm. The gloves were a pristine white but blackened by reins and errant sinew after the poor devil's last long ride.

He snatched a handful of the man's jacket and rolled him to his back. With numbing fingertips, the Raven sluggishly unhitched the raiment, ripping it from the neck and raising it high to the luminous moonlight, better for Cyrus's scrupulous eye. *This'll sell,* he thought.

The poor captain's skin neared a pale blue, with blood pooling a sickly purple in his face and forehead. Cyrus rolled the luckless bastard back to his icy respite. The dead man wore a fine saber, too, with the curve of a cavalryman and similar inlay on both the hilt and handguard to that of the gorget. The sword shone half-exposed amidst snow and coattail, sheathed in a scabbard likely worth more than the Raven's horse. Cyrus worked his fingers through webbing and belt loop, easing the scabbard from the leather as the body bounced and jerked with his yanking. *Dead before he could draw his pretty sword*, he thought.

Atop the new mare, Deimos trotted her over to a foraging Cyrus. Frightened, she seemed, but steady—steady enough to ride, which was more than Cyrus might've expected. The horse's head bowed deeply with each gait, as if to avoid Cyrus's stares. He smiled, knocking the saber loose from the belt, and he held it up to Deimos as he rode by. The Sage astride the mare gripped the sword's handle and yanked—the sword stayed sheathed.

"Frozen," he laughed.

The Raven reached out, gripping the scabbard more tightly than before. He widened his stance as Deimos wrenched the handle. The leather creaked under Deimos's gloved hand, and the saber slid cleanly from the spathe, offering a sharp ring to the still night air as his painted horse nervously jerked away.

"Sing to me, Goddess," Deimos muttered. He held the blade toward the stars while closing one eyelid in order to inspect the weapon more faithfully. The Sage swung and sliced and stabbed at the darkness, with sounds of whipping wind and steel sharp enough to pierce the very air.

Immaculate, Cyrus thought. The sword sang a tune to the moon and her stars, the weight of her plunges resounding through the cool wind that rustled the trees and shivered the hearts of the living. With a final plunge, she froze in place, outstretched to the Raven.

"A beauty," Deimos said. He played with it delightedly, like a new toy to be hurled into the air and caught mid-turn or twirled between dexterous hands as the old Furii found the sword's balance.

Balance, Cyrus thought. The Sage threw the sword high, suspending it in the stillness before catching the flat edge delicately across his fingertip. *Perfect.* The sword itself beamed, balancing and bathing in the bountiful moonlight. She shimmered like the snow and stars and the greens of Deimos's eyes, still ogling the piece from hilt to head. The unspoiled blade began to fog in the cold, and the Sage let out a cloud of smoky breath, scouring her in a misty white hue. Every hair was carved with careful precision—branches curled between steel leaves of acanthus, rolling in the intricate metalwork without so much as an etch out of place. A piece of fine art to Cyrus's eyes, but with the duality that lives in such tools of destruction, where the rolling, artful sincerities of a craftsman meet the harsh truth of the razor's edge.

"Absolutely marvelous…a work of art, to be sure," Deimos said.

"Looks like the poor bastard never used it. It'll fetch a fine price, but not in these parts." Cyrus handed Deimos the scabbard and turned for the wood line.

"No qualms here—too cold for the likes of me." Deimos flourished the sword for a final time before sliding it back into the scabbard with a last haunting note that echoed through the trees.

"Hurry," Cyrus urged. "We haven't much time."

Deimos followed on his new crimson-black steed, marching up the ridge through dead pine and snowfall toward the horses they'd rode in on, still hitched patiently beyond the clearing.

"What will you call your new mare?" Cyrus asked.

"Didn't think it just yet," he said. "Maybe…Shadow?"

Cyrus's eyes lingered on the bloodied horse for a moment but fell away. "Tis a fine name," he admitted.

Deimos frowned. "What's wrong with 'Shadow'?"

"No, earnest—it is a fine name for a fine horse. I just expected *less* from you is all."

Deimos snorted. "Like most, I daresay. I imagine our dearly departed cleric might've said the same."

The Raven let out a laugh. "To be sure, brother. How about that pretty sword of yours? What shall her name be?"

"I should think…Moonlight?"

"Ah, there it is! A terrible name, if ever there was one."

Deimos smirked. "Envy doesn't suit you, my friend."

Cyrus ignored the Sage, focusing on the hill ahead. It was steeper, buried in thick nesting snow and foliage blocking the path. Cyrus wrenched himself up with handfuls of slick limbs and paltry branches. Deimos the Sage found a path across the small clearing for Shadow to step through while he wiped some residual blood from the beast's mane, but with little success. A mess of dry, frozen sludge stayed knotted in the stranded reeds of her hair. *Unbecoming for such a horse*, Cyrus thought.

"I s'pose this should be some of your aged, sagely wisdom?" Cyrus called out.

"What's that?"

"Make them underestimate you, right up until you cut their throats."

"Or blow their brains out," said Deimos.

Cyrus laughed heartily. "Indeed."

The shadowy silhouettes of the pair's horses emerged from the tree line, still as the night air and tied faithfully to the same fallen log at the crest of the ridge. Their hay was a salty white and the water bucket frozen solid. Muzzle prints dotted the surrounding embankment.

Horses eat snow? Cyrus marveled as he snatched a last glance at the carnage at the mouth of the trail they'd left to freeze in the dark. The men moved quietly and quickly, re-holstering long guns and tying down powder horns to their overflowing goatskin knapsacks and leathery saddlebags for the long night's ride to Norsefyre. Muted shouts resounded faintly in the distance, accompanied by flickers of lamplight that twinkled through the crags of the wilderness they'd put behind them. The wind whistled quietly, undercut by the soft padding of horse hooves trudging through the drift. According to the Sage's plan, the men would head west before cutting north with the dawn, away from the main road and the inevitable highwaymen that patrolled it. The ride was enveloped by the quiet of the early morn, the tedium broken by crunching twigs underfoot and the snorts and whinnies of cold and tired nags in need of a deep rest.

A long while passed before the stubborn sun rose to melt the frost and warm the bones of the men and the horses that plodded through the whitened wood. A rhythmic fog smoldered from nostrils and mouths, giving way to rays of sunlight that burned the cold and warmed their hearts as the trees grew thinner with each passing mile. *We're hardly out of the woods*, Cyrus thought, an idle thumb itching at the hammer of a rust-colored six-gun cresting his stomach, snug in its holster but eager to be drawn. The hilt of an estoc longsword jutted from a tie-down on the lower saddle, well within arm's reach, and a repeating rifle nestled just beneath.

The Sage repeatedly unsheathed his new blade, swinging aimlessly at wayward branches like a boy might do with a particularly sword-like stick. He treated the blade with the deference of a simple stick, hacking and chopping at things indiscriminately along the path. Cyrus insisted he sheathe it more than a time or two, and only once the sun was up, broadening the risk of newfound onlookers, did the old Furii agree, but at the cost of his usual smile.

Deimos the Sage looked more pauper than Furii, this much was true. His robes were held together by hemp and straw cord that draped from each shoulder and across a broad chest. The coiling rope was frayed and tattered like the other piecemeal layers of his garb—mud-brown burlaps stained and faded and old as Tara. Cyrus would have thought him a beggar could he not see the steel gauntlets distended from tattered sleeves—antiquated metal gloves and vambraces that portended a grave robber far more than a Furii. Deimos commanded a kind of secret violence that proved a strange bedfellow for his pleasant demeanor. He was a Furii, after all, ignoble as it made him. A veteran, he was perhaps the oldest living of the elite warrior caste he shared so little resemblance to. Deimos the Sage wore no standard, wielded no familial great sword, and donned no illustrious vultus warpaint, but a Furii he remained, unlikely as it looked.

Cyrus the Raven was no Furii. A man he was born, and a mortal man he always would be, cursed with the failings of age and time, which Deimos and his Furii brothers and sisters never need fear. Cyrus ascended no ancient rite, met no friend or foe in the arenas of the Forge, and his blood remained untainted—just like the day of his birth—by the ilk that corrupted so many before. *The Furii's Burden,* he remembered it was called. The ritual blood, the unnatural ooze that beset the potential of honest men. *The Furii are not men,* Cyrus thought. *Full of madness and rage, those ones, pumping some witch's brew through their veins like the Devil himself.* They signed their souls to him, Cyrus believed, for the shallow price of boundless power and immeasurable strength next to mortal men, but the price was steep. Their minds slowly waned to the cosmos or bent the knee to the humors and ill will of spiteful gods. *For that is what the Furii are and always will be,* he had decided long ago, *servants of deities long abandoned, vicars of petty cosmic squabbles and puny endeavors gone awry.*

Nay, Cyrus was only a man—a cursed man, troubled and doomed to boot, but mortal and nearly free, as all men truly are. And yet, he had more in common with the Furii than he might've wished for—much, much more.

"Tis a midday, my feathery friend," Deimos said. "We're making good time."

Cyrus looked down to the tattered frayed ends—*the feathers*—of his duster hanging loosely over his back and shoulders. He shook his head, but smiled, too. "Agreed," he said, "and I can finally feel my fingers again."

"A problem I rarely suffer these days, I'm thankful."

Cyrus smirked. "That sludge that courses through your veins poses another problem altogether, brother."

"Aye, and bloody welcomed. The madder I go, the better, I say. Is a madman not truly the most content? Ignorant of all that ails this world?"

"I daresay he is," Cyrus said. "Blissful, but more fool than friend...but you know as well as I that the mind makes fools of us all—a prison without walls, and so on."

Deimos's lips curled.

Some distance up the trail, a signpost appeared, decrepit and worn and missing a placard. The top piece held a poorly cut arrow that read '*NORSFYR*,' and they turned their horses to the trail. Trickling water rained down from melting branches as birch and spruce and oak shone in the midday sun. The endless white made way for brown and hints of emerald. Weary travelers crossed the path, too, from time to time—paupers, pilgrims, even the occasional stagecoach rumbling and rocking through ruddy slush. *A crowd rife for robbing*, Cyrus thought.

The last of Deimos's childish mood left with the sun and the strangers. The man's stoic temperament returned, but with a crooked smile somewhere just beneath the surface. Cyrus was accustomed to the cosmic shifts of Deimos's disposition, as was accepted for most Furii, given the Burden. The Sage's face hid the truth of him well, but his hands were tied up between knotted reins, rending the leather under a creaky grip. Cyrus thought to speak, but swallowed his words. *The Sage steadies himself*, he thought. *We all must steady ourselves, time and again.* But Cyrus felt a doleful sadness for his friend, fearing that the demon's inside may one day demand too great a toll. He wrenched and wrung his reins under a slackless grip. *Steady, brother.*

"Your horse looks like the Devil," Cyrus said, pointing at the nag's crimson mane.

"Aye, I'd nearly forgotten." The Sage unplugged a canteen draped over his shoulder and upended it on the horse's neck. Shadow squirmed and brayed with the dousing while Deimos shushed her and rubbed the hair with a stray rag. "I'm not sure this will do."

"Perhaps it is best to leave her here," said Cyrus.

"I'd sooner die," Deimos said flatly.

"Perhaps you will if you keep riding a bloodied horse into town and the wrong people ask the right questions."

"More of the worrying, my dear Cyrus," Deimos said. "What can the likes of them do to us? To you, even?"

The Raven glared, unamused. "Arrogance invites injury."

"Aye, and a bloodied horse inspires fear." The Sage gulped a few last drops from his canteen and plugged it up, stowing it over his shoulder. "I reckon this crimson steed dissuades more highwaymen than a pistol or sword ever may."

His eyes rolled, but Cyrus offered no reply. *No need.*

Cyrus ignored the looks after a while, finding small comfort in a saddle and the Sage's company. His mind began to wander beyond the onlooker plebs that either scowled or shied away from his gaze. The footmen and the pilgrims grew scarce as the midday doldrums set in, and the rolling trees that lined the path passed by each minute as if they were miles. He was bored by the quiet redundancies of snow drifts and saddle sores. The Raven ached for an ale, above all.

Cyrus grazed on hardtack and a few last bites of saltfish he'd been saving. He handed his own mount a few helpings of dry oats as he brushed the horse's neck and ticked quiet comforts into soft, welcoming ears. *A good horse,* he thought. *I hope you survive all of this.* He meant the words but remembered the likely end to this poor beast. He'd never named him, for that reason. *I've named a few horses before.*

And with mild mid-afternoon, the boredom took him from the ride and the saddle. Cyrus combed the corners and cracks of his unyielding imagination. He returned to the comforting nostalgia of childhood, despite his will to forget. *Clydae,* he thought. *What I would give to see my city one last time.* But with the momentary solace came the creeping dark, clinging to the cold truth of what came next. He thought of Aura then, as he always would. He wondered where she might be and with whom, and what her opinion of him must be after all these years gone by. *No matter,* the Raven reminded, *I have work to do.*

The sun shone for most of the day on a green wood patched in white and weeping well into the early evening as the frost from branches had all but gone. The sunset welcomed Cyrus as it had from his earliest days, and he smiled with a radiance to match the setting sky. The land grew colder with the departing rays of sunlight, but the color—*oh, the color,* thought Cyrus—as vibrant as any he'd seen. *A promise made by the celestials that the sun may set, only to rise. Balance,* he mouthed.

But the ambush of the night before hung in his head and squandered the perfect sunset he wished to take in. The violence bled through, with splicing portraits of crossfire and shrieks and a kneeling man's plight falling on Cyrus's deaf ears. *I hate the violence,* he lied to himself. *We are punished enough with the savagery that plagues our beloved Tara, her lands ripe for slaughter.* He said he wanted no part of it, this cruel life of savagery and rage, but he knew the lie, deep down. He coveted it—*craved it.* The bloodlust comes for all men, after all, and he was no exception. He yearned for another fight, to end more lives like he had done in the wee hours. It played like music in his ears, the deep reverberating echoes of gunfire in the still night air, the shouts of men and the neighing of frightened horses, small steel hammers falling on gunpowder anvils, igniting the sky and the hearts of mortal men. *The stuff of dreams,* he vied, but Cyrus gulped hard, quelling his thirst but a while longer.

Twenty men, he mused. *We must've killed twenty men.* A seamless ambush, it opened with a swivel gun, even, like those of the man-o-wars that prowl for pirates among the Laurentines and the Breezeblock. Small, but wide, the gun rested atop fortified logs and was staked deep. *The damned thing tore the axle off the front of the carriage, and a good piece of the rear horses, too.* He'd put bullets in men and horses all the same, for which he felt an earnest guilt. He never reloaded, only dropped the empties to retrieve a few third-full cylinders from the dead. His uncurbed appetite sprang from the guns themselves. He knew he'd killed nary a man with the blades, only the bullets and bombs of cowards and cutthroats.

Shameful, he thought. *A poetry to swordplay, there is—a jig danced with a willing partner…graceful creatures enraptured in mortal sacrifice, as only one prevails.* Cyrus might yearn for peace, but the Raven *adored* a fight, for the fight was all he knew.

And so, the Raven gripped tightly to the ankles of Cyrus's shattered mind, pulling him deeper and deeper through darkness and void as the Prison called to him. The humble Cyrus feared this deepest of darks, so full of malice and pain, as he tried so oft to forget. The Raven thrived in such a place, built in the quiet respites of the underworld, full of violence and the will to do so. The Raven was born of a darkened heart, and so he brought the darkness with him. But so, too, came the Furii—old gods to Cyrus's kind. A waning pantheon with little power over steel and heat.

But gods and their power run loose in the land of Tara. The newest, and perhaps the greatest god to grace Tara's lands was the fiery birth of industry, cutting away the meager flesh and bone of a bygone yesteryear. The Furii caste ruled mankind for a millennium. The supposed demigods of mortal men, they were vicars of an old blood in need of decay, only to be outmatched by the cold machines of a callous future.

"What are you on about?" interrupted the Sage.

"Pardon?" asked Cyrus.

"Your eyes dance like an Antigonian whore," he said. "What ails you, brother?"

"Nothing," Cyrus said, tersely. "I—I just—"

"I'm itching for a fight, if not to cure the boredom alone," Deimos answered for him, his eyes raking across rolling, forested hills far and wide. "I forget how vast the Bryndelwald can be."

"I don't invite it," Cyrus said, "but it certainly would be *fun*. How much farther, Deimos?"

"Too far, brother," he said. "We won't make it 'fore nightfall."

Cyrus eyed a rat trail diverging from the road up the way. "Perhaps we can find a place to camp off the road a bit. My mortal belly could afford a fill. What say you, Sage?"

"Aye, I'll starve before long."

"You call yourself immortal."

"In age only…and perhaps, in the bedroom." The Sage laughed.

"Aye," chuckled Cyrus, "aye, a camp with ale will do nicely."

The men turned for the trail just as the setting sun peaked its last rays through naked branches. Cyrus spotted a clearing beyond the mouth—a patch of open sky, blazing orange and red in the heart of the deepening sunset. The path meandered a few feet more, etching into a scant hillside as the break in the trees widened away from the road. The cold air returned, met with the same billowing fog that steamed from warm horse nostrils and the sloppy drool that dangled from their bits.

"A fantastic spot—under the stars even," Deimos said, gleefully hurling one leg over the saddle and plunging into ankle-deep snow.

"How far do you reckon we've come?" asked Cyrus.

"No less than fifty miles, I expect," Deimos hollered over his shoulder, slogging toward the tree line.

"We should push farther in, brother," Cyrus said.

"More worrying…." Deimos kicked at a few low-hanging branches and snagged them under his arm.

His horse stamped in place with Cyrus still seated defiantly in the saddle. "You know as well as I—they'll come for us."

"If we go any longer tonight, brother, we'll kill these poor horses, and you might freeze to death yourself. Besides, we'll be off at daybreak."

Cyrus sighed deeply, looking to the horizon one last time—red, far redder than it ought to be this time of year, with cool blues deepening under the advent of nightfall. A steady breath clouded in front of his mouth, and he lifted a kerchief to the bridge of his nose, trapping the heat of his breaths over the singeing cold of his ears and cheeks. *A fire might do.* ...

"Fill your hands, if it suits you. Doubt we'll see a soul tonight." Deimos moved back into the open and dumped the kindling clumsily into the snow. Shadow startled at the sound.

"Easy, girl," he hushed. "Maybe not the warhorse we thought, eh?"

"We should leave 'fore sun-up," Cyrus said.

"Huh?"

"*Before* sunrise," Cyrus ordered, dismounting. "No need to take any chances."

"Dare I say it, Cyrus? I don't believe I've ever seen you so...on edge. You don't believe the old tales, do you? Those pesky Wolves of the Wald come to get us?"

There it is, the patronizing whoreson.

"I fear not the wolves," he said, "but if we can ambush them, they can return the favor."

"'Tis true," Deimos replied, clacking logs together in a modest stack, "but we've done our due diligence—fifty miles, deep in the Bryndelwald. Not a Patrian trapper alive that could—or would— track us that far, and on the road, mind you?"

Cyrus's lip twitched. "What world do you live in to think us so protected? That sorry Bishop makes thirteen—a baker's dozen, that is—and the League will come for the blood of the Church, Sage. *Think.* The Acolyte and his Tattered Banner, his Furii arbiters with all their loathsome titles....We should be ready."

The Sage rustled the dry leaves and kindling in open pockets of the pile and fetched his flint from Shadow's newly donned saddle-bags. "You speak as if I am unaware," said the Sage.

"Of course, I don't mean—"

"Please, friend, peace," Deimos said. His words were warm and welcoming, but Cyrus felt the stern finger someplace behind the smile. "The Patrian League is not what it was, brother, but I understand your concern. By mid-morn, we'll be mere miles from Norsefyre and the Four Furies. By nightfall, we'll be supping at a Brynjari hearth. The time for killing clerics is nearly at an end."

"Nearly," Cyrus aped.

"Why the melodrama, Cyrus?" asked the Sage, spewing sparks from flint and dagger into the dry heap. "We approach our goal, same as planned. What sod has since pissed in your porridge?"

"Do you trust him?" Cyrus asked, "the Brynjar, I mean." He fished deep into his saddlebag with a blind fingertip, working at the cleaning kit that seemed glued to the bottom. Cyrus snatched it free, the other hand untying the rifle bundle draped on the side of the saddle. He hoisted his repeater and breechloader from their buckskin covers. He secured the small deerskin cinch-bag of cleaning supplies under the other arm as he hiked toward the Sage and a pitiful fire aching to breathe.

The Sage blew gently into the pile. "Careful," he said. Small tufts of smoke snaked out of lesser embers, and he smiled wide. His face froze there for a time, watching patiently as the delicate flames caught the tinder. The flares redoubled with each of the Sage's puffs, where crackling timber and smoky fumes gave Cyrus the go-ahead. He laid his arms against the wood stack and unclasped two worn leathery buckles, producing a splotched rag and swathing it across the snow as he lined his tools in rank and file. He kicked a log, sat on it, and drew his six-gun from the holster with a flamboyant twirl around his trigger finger. The Sage looked away, still smiling, aimlessly.

"You didn't answer my question, brother," said Cyrus.

The frays of Deimos's garb lined through the flames as he buried the light with a thick branch. "It would be wrong to speak ill of my noble patron, even here," he said. "I'm a Furii, dear Cyrus, and nearly always have been. Speaking ill of a master is poor form, no matter the master. Besides, I can't trust myself, let alone anybody else," he said. "And especially not you, there, Ghost of Clydae...."

"Not that," Cyrus said tersely. "*Never* that."

"Worried someone will hear?"

Cyrus's wolf-like eyes beamed through the firelight. "Aye," he nodded, "a card we shan't play…at least until the time comes."

Deimos leaned back. "Have I not kept your secret safe to this end?"

"Safe?" the Raven asked, astonished. "A madman, like all the rest of your Furian brothers and sisters? Secrets are safe only with the dead."

The Sage chortled, "Oh, of course, I'd nearly forgotten…."

The two sat in silence as dark blue heavens turned to black. Cyrus avoided the Sage's gaze, focusing on the fire and his revolver. The night was quieting, the sounds and stirrings of the early evening faded away into lonely, muted starlight. Cracks of the wood and Cyrus's metal brush scraping gristle and grime from his disassembled pistol were all the sound that pierced the air, and each was deafening. Deimos chewed heartily on a ragged piece of jerked aurochs from a shady tin of his own hardtack he produced from someplace between sleeve and pocket. The snow around the fire was melting as the concealed dirt beneath turned to milky mud. The fire grew, whipping in a vibrant, menacing splendor as soundless cracks turned to roaring welcomed warmth.

"What would bring you happiness?" Deimos asked, breaking the silence.

"Huh?"

"Or rather, solace more like?" he said. "Happiness, after all, may be a stretch for the likes of us."

Cyrus raised his brow but offered no reply.

Deimos persisted. "If tomorrow, dear brother, we could wake up kings of Tara and all our struggles would be at an end—all the goals and deeds met, services rendered, and enemies conquered in one fell swoop, what would you do? Who might you be? Where might you go?"

"First, I'd hang every Patrian I could find—"

"Please, Master Raven," Deimos softly interrupted. "No need for all that. Indulge me, as you might yourself."

Cyrus shook his head and chewed his cheek, relenting. *Another of his tricks? Likely.*....His jaw ached once he loosened it, relinquishing the words as they came to him, giving in to Deimos's childish inquisitions. *Wise and old, yet young and foolish*, he thought.

"I suppose I'd hang up my guns and find solitude some place—a dairy farm in the Great Mothers perhaps, or a cottage in Nine Foes, or a Caravel at sea, even? I hear the Clearwater Whip is nice—"

"*You*, a sailor? Or a fuckin' dairy farmer?! Ha!"

Cyrus let the Sage laugh but continued, albeit in a different direction. "I...no, I have a much better game, sir. Why don't you tell me what *my* solace might be? You know me so well, it would seem."

Deimos sat up with another surge of boyish excitement, swallowing a bit of jerky as he clapped his hands together. "Cyrus!" he shouted. "These are my favorite sorts!"

"What sorts?"

"Games, of course," he said. "I love games."

Cyrus held up a hand. "No, no, no—first, sir, ground rules. You may make your statement. I need only confirm or deny."

Deimos's smile only widened. "That sounds...*fair*. But, you must promise to be genuine. No lies, nor tricks—only truth."

"Agreed," said Cyrus.

"Aye, this is exciting! I've always fancied myself good at these things. Let me think for a moment, brother. This will require a delicate strategy."

Cyrus chuckled with another shake of his head. "You haven't the faintest idea, Deimos—even if you are a *Sage*."

"I...reckon otherwise," he said, Deimos's eyes focused, fixed and scintillating with the flames.

The Sage moved to his knees with hands cupped together and index fingers aligned over a pair of curled lips. Cyrus felt the Furii's narrow gaze bounce about his face and features. The Raven's every curve, crevice, and silver hair shrank under the Sage's unblinking, paralyzing stare. *I'm young to his eyes*, Cyrus thought, but the Raven's age beneath the skin was far beyond the score and change he'd spent in human lifetimes. A young man's face marred by scars and a striking silver mane, brow, and beard, all quite out of place—it wouldn't take the Sage to tell him. His eyes—blue like the Devil, as they had been described—were an unnatural, bright glowing sapphire that might pierce the very soul of a weaker man, or so he liked to think.

"I already know of your genteel past life—"

"I thought this was supposed to be about my future, not my past, brother," Cyrus interrupted impatiently.

"Surely, I must know who you were before I can tell you who you will be?" Deimos protested. "Please, honor my process."

"Aye," Cyrus groaned.

"You jest about fishing and farming because, truthfully, you've never considered a life outside of this one—"

"Nay, I've considered many things," Cyrus said, crossing his arms.

"Of course," Deimos said. "Let me make myself perfectly clear: though not a Furii, you carry with you your own sort of burden, don't you? Why is that, I wonder?"

"Confirm or deny, Deimos, nothing more."

Deimos held up a hand. "Of course you carry the burden. Tis the burden of every man, not just the Furii—a burden of Ares herself and all her dear children."

"What burden?" Cyrus asked, as if he didn't know.

Deimos's smile widened, baring teeth. "Oh, dear Cyrus, you said it yourself. You desire the bloodshed—you crave it, as I do. You're as much the blood-drunk as I—"

"I'm no madman," Cyrus interrupted.

"That, brother, is a lie." Deimos's smile disappeared. "You find comfort in your supposed mortality, but you're a Furii in all but title. As if I haven't seen you all this time? Cutting through soldiers and guardsmen like piss through the snow. I've seen you thrashed to pieces by bullets and blades alike, only to fight on like the *god* that you are...."

Deimos composed himself. His gaze broke, and the redness from his face faded along with the thumping vein in his forehead. "Nay,

Ghost of Clydae, there's much more to you than meets the eye, a resonance that escapes me, deeper than the flesh. If I didn't know better, I'd think you cursed—sold your soul to the Devil, or something…but for what, I wonder? Where? Or, for *whom*?"

"That's enough," Cyrus said.

"I do believe it's high time you told us how it is you managed to escape the Prison Without Walls."

The cadence in Deimos's voice was like a nursery rhyme, bouncing up and down as the words itched under Cyrus's skin and prodded the dark corners of his mind. They unsettled him, chewing, biting, ripping like rabid dogs might do a carcass.

"Have I struck a chord, dear Cyrus?" Deimos asked.

The Raven didn't answer, reverting his gaze to the fiery comforts of the hearth, the blaze illuminating a pair of darkened, unrecognizable eyes.

"Please, brother, put my curiosity at ease. What did you say to that poor cleric back there?"

"The man begged for his life," Cyrus said, "offered me riches and wealth in his last moments."

"I say again, what did *you* say?"

"*No quarter*," he replied. The wind howled then, resigning the men to their lonesome wilderness. Cyrus wiped snot from his pouring nostrils as the sting of cold burned his skin. *Even Cyrus is no more, you fiend,* he told himself. *The cursed Ghost of Clydae remains, despite me.* It was an enemy he sought to stifle but with nary the strength. An old life rooted in the new violence of ancient villainy, truly—living as the beast that could put a bullet in an unarmed and feeble old man. *No pause…no fear…no quarter….*

"That's the one thing you don't seem to understand, *brother*," Cyrus purred. "I've escaped nothing."

The Sage's eyes stared blankly into the fire, but something tore them away. "There's a measure of untrustworthiness in every man, I think, not just the Furii," he said, nodding to Cyrus. "A sickness that lives deep inside—the animal that survives, angry and untamable. It's the monster, the madman—the price of entry for the blood that courses through our veins. The madness plagues the psyche of any and all. I wish for deliverance from such trifles, but alas, my own demons haunt me just the same. But you paid a different price, Cyrus—a steeper price, I grant."

"For that's all it is," Cyrus agreed. "A *price*. And the thing you speak of, a cost there is that sleeps inside us all—a debt beyond our means but owed all the more. Unyielding evil, our master is, one that yearns to be set free, to collect from our beholden souls. A demon of old, beyond our reckonings…like the primordial destructions of pestilence and famine and an undying sorrow that ravages the mind like it does our hearts. The King comes to reclaim what is owed…."

Deimos sat for a time without sound or movement, his gaze settling faithfully in the light. "Have you heard of the Battle of the Running Roost?"

"Come again?"

"Never?"

Cyrus rolled his eyes. "Pray tell."

"I s'pose I shan't be surprised," he said. "Still, a tale of a tale—"

"Please."

"The farther Antigonia holds rolling hills of bountiful crops as far as the eye could see. Hillsides of thick green bowled over shallow valley floors and river deltas ripe for buckwheat and rye grain—"

"Sage, please, I don't wish to hear—"

"And *beans!*" he shouted over him. "Oh, the beans! The peasants ate their fills of beans and onions and peas from local gardens, and fresh raspberries came with the autumn—the makings of a bountiful life."

The Raven leaned forward.

"But then came the Patrians—conquerors and slavers with all their fervor—to the enriched laymen of the river valley. They burned their crops and stole their stores, raped their women and enslaved their sons." He picked up another piece of jerky and wrenched it between his back teeth. "And so, this proconsul, what was his name? Ah, Cnaeus Decima, I do believe—"

"The Nighthawk," Cyrus supplied, playing along.

"Aye, the Nighthawk!" Deimos smiled. "The Nighthawk's march to the sea proved most vile—burning and pillaging with reckless abandon. And so came the last bastion of the last free state of the last remnant of an Antigonia that no longer thrives as it once did—Fort Redoubtable."

Cyrus's stomach sank out from under him. "Fort Redoubtable?" he gulped.

"Aye, Fort Redoubtable! Who's tellin' this story?"

"Sorry," Cyrus retreated. "continue."

"A holdout far beyond the edge of the earth, in the smallest, secret corner of Tara where gods and men rarely venture...."

"Aye."

"The peasants made their final stand in the mountain shadows of the Great Mothers' jagged peaks. A stranger stood above the rest, a furtive, nameless monk—a nobody. The Nighthawk and his legions crowded 'round the redoubt, ten deep for every scared peasant standing among them. 'The soil is rich in these parts and the people pious,' the monk said in parlay. 'Are you not a pious man? Do you not serve the Summer God, same as us?'"

Cyrus felt cold.

"'I do,' the Nighthawk admitted. 'Then let our gods decide our fates,' the monk decried, removing his humble medallions from a scrawny neck. 'A god you are to these creatures,' he said, pointing to a rooster plucking mindlessly about. 'Surely the mandate of heaven might give you strength over them?' The monk fixed the medallions around the cock's neck. 'If you are a champion of gods and men, then kill this modest chicken, and I shall name you our newfound god.' 'You mock me,' quoth the Nighthawk. 'I dare not, gracious knight. What power do we have here? Simpletons we are—the gravel beneath your

maniple's boot.' The Nighthawk saw among them haggard faces of
the worn elderly and starving young. 'Agreed,' he said with a shot of
his flintlock. He missed, of course, with such aimless ball. His lieutenants missed, too, and his triarii sharpshooters missed their marks by
more, and the velites hurled their spears and bombardiers threw their
bomblets and chased the rooster, even—"

"Oh, come now, Sage."

"But, the monk was keen, as only laymen are. His best men lay in
wait in the hills just beyond, wielding humble workman's hammers,
scythes, and pitchforks between them. They stormed the scattered
legionnaires, rending their arms away from their swords as hungry
farmers dragged their daggers across soft Patrian necks. Though not
a shot was fired by paltry peasants, the Nighthawk ran with his horde
like a horse from a snake."

"They beat him?" Cyrus asked.

"Not quite," the Sage said, "delayed, more like. They came back,
of course, and what men didn't scatter were rounded right up...cru-
cified, of course."

"*What?*"

"What?" the Sage parroted.

"Was there a point, just then?"

"Of course," said the Sage. "Never underestimate a Patrian's love
of chasing cock."

Cyrus howled, despite himself, and the Sage did the same. They
hooted and horned, and Cyrus wiped the tears from his eyes, nodding
and smiling at a joke well-told. "I underestimated you, Sage," he
laughed, "as always."

"Your estimations are apt, I'm sure," the Sage said, sipping from
a canteen. "But I offer only a smile before the frown."

"Frown?" Cyrus asked, sinking once more.

"We must speak plainly, brother, unlike any time before. Real,
this is, too real for jests and gentleness."

"Real?"

"Like the trees and the stars and the gods themselves, this must be true now. You know of what I speak."

"I don't." *I do.*

"Antigonus, Agathe, Ariston, Ares—these are not our gods. Tis the legends of old we must see to over these four pillar gods—the two that came before."

His heart had become his stomach—low in his belly and sinking still. Cyrus clenched a fist and closed his eyes, but the voices pried open his ears and wriggled their way in. He felt the barbs plucking at thoughts and feelings as he winced, the pressure ever building. *Shut it out, damn you. Shut this evil out.*

"One of hate, and fear," Deimos whispered, "the lord of the dead and King of Battle. But, the other, born of his own flesh, his opposite…."

"Life and love," Cyrus groaned.

"Aye," Deimos nodded, "life and love and the bright beautiful hope of paradise—his champion. Twin devils, they were, each one another's match and measure."

"And so they battled…"

"And so they battled to the ends of the earth." Deimos's eyes blazed a turbulent emerald as the words dripped from his mouth.

"Ah," croaked the Raven, "where has my dear Sage gone?"

Deimos's head lowered, his brow overhanging a piercing gaze. "The prophecy continues, Cyrus. Be wary…the King of Battle comes, and he comes for you."

"Comes?" asked the Raven. "He is *here*, brother, among us…in the wind and the stars, and the mind all the more. He stares at me from close and afar," he said, pointing, "with those wretched green eyes…."

"Where he must remain," said the Sage. "For the sake of our beloved Tara and her people, among *us* he must remain."

"I've escaped nothing, Sage. This—all of it—it's the Prison Without Walls, as it always was, figments in my tortured mind where

I am ceaselessly shackled, crying into ashen dirt like a powerless child in the farthest reaches of the cosmos."

"Hmm," the Sage sighed. "You may be right, Master Raven, but so convincing, is it not? This dream of ours, as you say?" His frayed sleeve followed the arch of his arm, motioning vastly across forest, sky, and snow. "We wade through brush and thorns along the path. Why not wade a little further? It could be no worse than what came before."

"Aye," he agreed. "This fire warms my hands like my heart. What more should I want?"

"Aura," said the Sage, smile curling, "but where might she be, I wonder?"

"Nay, Sage."

"No?"

"Whatever man I might've been for Aura all those years ago, he lives no more. The Prison killed him in the earliest hours."

"Now, Cyrus," said Deimos, "we can all come back."

Cyrus shook his head. "We can't. I will keep my distance, if only for her sake."

"Then perhaps you *are* lost."

"Oh, I am lost, dear Sage. As lost as lost can be. *IN FACT,*" he began to shout, "*WHY NOT? Why not* give *myself to the King of Battle here and now? He's almost here, ha!*" Cyrus laughed a deep, sickening laugh, full of hacking coughs as green began to glow through the brightening blue of his eyes.

"Cyrus—Cyrus, please," the Sage hushed, "remember yourself. Keep the devil out, damn you!"

The Raven shook violently under his cape, hair and strands bouncing between spasmodic convulsions. "*The Devil...and chaos... saint of despair...destroyer of worlds....*"

"Balance, brother, please," pleaded the Sage.

"*The*"—he coughed—"*the Prison knows no walls....*"

II

TRIALS BY FIRE

Marcus—The Prison Without Walls

Colors...these colors. These perfect colors. Exquisite....No, I can do better. Elegant...ethereal...impeccable....These words won't do! No, I don't want them to. There are no words—fuck the words, even. Needless and wasteful sounds, pithy grunts and careless noise—little justice they could do. A man might spend a thousand lifetimes searching for this hand-painted sky and miss it by a thousand years, but not me, not here, and most certainly not now.

I dangle by one arm as I often do, gazing out across a steep cliffside blanketed by setting sun. The Fire Falls shimmer in the deepening red that pierces the sky and stains the sunset with layered palettes of vibrant warmth. The silhouettes of the mountains darken under radiant heavens as the thundering water smashes atop the ancient rocks below. A flaming, fleeting heaven kisses the world goodbye as Tara and her colors extend across landscape and mountaintop, with the blood-orange and crimson of a vehement summer nearing the autumn—the brushstrokes of the gods, with a beauty to match the color.

I look behind to find a distant storm cloud saturated by sunset, and my worries drift away with the same gust that cools my brow. "This is it," I say, closing my eyes as the thick water droplets bead across my arms and back, drenching my hair and tickling the corners of my face with the life essence I seek, disguised as the mist that fans the rocks in perpetuity. My venerable soul smiles. I open my eyes to find the next slimy handhold, full of moss and decaying flora, as I climb and clamber with a quickening pace. Aura waits for me, I remind myself, near the top of the falls, and it would feel quite wrong to experience this without her.

My grip is careful and strong, rending full weight over the meager cracks and shallow holes that ladder beneath the raining mist. I reach the cave behind the falls that Aura described in her letter. I jump higher to get there and pull harder than ever as I ascend above a peaceful Clydae below, searching for my rightful place next to hers. I draw strength from the falls, from the mountains, and from Aura—the pinnacle of my worldly hopes and desires. She waits for me atop this formidable peak, and so I climb.

Aura is strong and steadfast like the very best of them. "She climbs the falls, too," I say aloud. She is every bit the warrior I am—more so, even. Her plebeian parentage matters only to my father, not me. She earns the right each day—the right to be called a candidate, a competitor—a warrior in the arena. She fights, she does—she vies for the Forge, and the Furii, and she bleeds, too, and we've cried together in the thralls of ascension as the others did, patricians and plebs—men and women all alike. My struggle has been hers for the better part of a decade, and hers has been mine. Tis our achievement—one we earned together—and I won't have it cheapened by the caste or anything else. She is my paragon, and she always will be.

"Took you long enough," comes a familiar voice.

"I was merely admiring the view," I say. The wet hair drips in my eyes, and I wipe it back and out of my face. I can't catch my breath. The cave is a vacuous black, but the gentle lines of her smile shine in the darkness, ever comforting me. She takes two echoing steps out of the shadows, and the sun loyally illuminates her. Her chestnut hair glows in the light, unkempt and bouncing in the draft of the cave as my palpable stare hovers over glowing white teeth and a pair of fine hazel eyes that steal away the last rays of a dying sunset.

"And how do you like the view now?" she asks, grinning even wider than before.

I laugh. "I couldn't say." I'm paralyzed.

Her smile fades a bit. A concerned look replaces the endearing one, contorting her brow as the light in her eyes disappears. Her gaze breaks away from me, woefully finding the floor. She takes a few halting steps to the edge of the cave, but I step further back, wishing I hadn't.

She lifts her gaze back to mine. Her eyes are piercing, fixed someplace between heaven and hell, and my heart pounds in my chest like a smith's smashing hammer, my ribcage the anvil. Those eyes—they're glassy and far away, and her voice trips between a whisper and a choke. "You do know why I asked you here, don't you?"

I take four wide steps toward her but stop short again, wishing I hadn't.

"You do feel it, too, don't you? I thought it was nothing at first—weakness—my head getting the better of me, a cruel joke. But, that isn't true, is it?" She turns, pacing back and forth without me, a finger resting gently on her ripe lower lip.

"Aura, I—"

"But then there was that moment," she says, turning toward me, "the moment. A moment like all the others, one among thousands that just… changed things. A moment that I can't ignore, no matter how hard I try."

Aura's eyes abandon the floor to find mine—burning glass amid amber sunset, a place between space and time. A dream of a dream, they are windows to a tortured soul, where swelling oceans roll and toil with the abyss, glowing, shining, mesmerizing proof of two kindred souls aching to be joined. Another chasm of creation, but one that is entirely mine.

In my looking, I see the truth in her eyes—pure, unsullied, and absolute. Her warmth, her radiance—she is a goddess to me, then like always, my guiding moonlight through the dawnless dark. I'll never be alone, I feel, in body and mind. She is here with me—haunting with those exquisite brown eyes. The very blood that pumps through my veins does so only at her command, my mortal self wholly hers, and no other's. I need no breath, nor sustenance, nor sleep, nor shelter, so long as those eyes stay fixed in mine, forever.…

III

AWAKENING

Aura—Past

Sister Gertrude couldn't just open Aura's door. That would be too peaceful for the likes of her. In her off-white robes, she felt the need to kick the door after quietly unlocking it. *How childish.*

In the dear Sister's eyes, Aura knew herself to be no better than a harlot or a sinner, but she found a simple kind of pleasure in rebellion. She was a threat to Sister Gertrude's overzealous faith—a badge she wore with honor.

Aura could hear the swine coming most nights, lumbering down the hall like an ogress sneaking into the chicken coup. Although Sister Gertrude did her damnedest to quiet herself whilst sneaking down the corridors or turning old iron latchkeys, Aura could always tell. *She's a swine, after all,* Aura thought—a stocky, ugly woman with saggy breasts and wrinkled skin from forehead to feet. She wore glasses so thick they reminded Aura of the seeping window panes in the old church quarter at home in Clydae. *I'll knock those lenses right off her smug face,* she fantasized.

This morning was like all the other mornings this week. Gertrude's sly steps might as well have been those of a horse clopping toward Aura's door. She slipped the key into the hole with a few tiny clinks and hums from the rusted iron, but Aura could hear every misshapen edge grinding inside the mechanism as the key slowly turned. This morning had a single difference, however, for Aura was wide awake, dressed in the same tired smock donned by the other Vestals in the priory, but holding the broken end of a bed frame as she crouched in the corner behind the door.

Aura held her makeshift club with both hands. Her palms were sweaty, dampening the wood under her ceaseless hold as she wrenched it between both hands in anxious anticipation. Her ribs felt tight, bruised by Gertrude's penitence from the day before. The shooting tightness seared with each of her practice swings. Her lip was split, too, accompanied by the yellowing bruise that stretched all the way from the corner of her mouth to the lobe of her left ear—a token Sister Gertrude had graced her with on the very first night.

The keyhole quieted, and the door burst open to Sister Gertrude, who barreled across the threshold, her trusty horsewhip in one hand and an iron lantern in the other. "Rise, Sinner. Stand and—"

Aura swung hard and low. The wood cracked in her hands, prickling her palms. The pain nearly disarmed her, but her fingers clutched the wood in eager desperation. The sound was sickening, like the noise a mallet makes whilst tenderizing a prized loin in a butcher shop. The woman sprawled to the floor in a heap of fatty flesh, the skin of her leg opened wide for all the world to see.

"Ah! Gods help me!" she cried.

"Shut your mouth, swine," Aura hissed, reaching for the door. She pushed it shut with one hand as she turned back to Gertrude, now cowering with one arm raised as she failed to crawl with the other.

"Help! HELP!" Gertrude wailed.

Aura closed the distance. She towered over the woman. The faint candlelight inside the broken lantern illuminated Aura's impossibly dark eyes.

A sharp grimace etched the lines of Aura's face. *One knock to the knee, and she's a blubbering fool,* she thought. *Her voice is shrill enough when it isn't yelping like a stuck pig.*

"Quit your bawling, filth." Aura raised the club once more and brought it down on the woman's shoulder. *Thwack.*

Sister Gertrude screeched, crying out again, "Mercy! MERCY! I beg you!"

Aura leaned in and pressed the wood up to the woman's mouth. "The key, Sister. Where's the key?"

She fiddled for a moment with her robes, patting and fumbling through the layers of white garb, her enormous breasts and belly jiggling away as she went. She favored one arm as she searched.

"Here, here it is!" She sniffled, raising the keyring on her finger.

Aura snatched the keys and stood up. "Are these all of them?" she asked, squinting.

"Yes, yes, those are all, I swear it."

Aura turned for the door but stopped just beyond. Without looking back, she said, "Don't make a sound, or I'll kill you."

Sister Gertrude let out another pitiful whimper as Aura moved down the hallway toward Lucy's room. Her bare feet glided along the cold wood floor. She looked over her shoulder as she made her way down the hall. *Someone must've heard.*

Knocking on the door that read *VII*, Aura whispered, "Lucy? *Lucy.*"

A groggy voice came from the other side, "Who...who is it?"

"It's Aura," she whispered, fiddling with the keys in the keyhole. Her heart was racing, the keyhole eluding her jittering fingers as she tried to fit the key in. She still gripped her club in one hand as the other rattled away at the doorknob. *Stop shaking, damn you.*

Lucy unlatched the door. Aura could see her standing in the darkness, the beige of her smock pale in the foreground, identical to Aura's.

"Ready?" Aura whispered.

"For what?" Lucy replied.

A shrill shout came echoing down the hallway. *Gertrude*—she'd dragged her *fat arse* down the corridor with her broken lantern and whip, calling in her fury to the other Sisters.

I should've flogged her while I had the chance.

"Grab your things," Aura snapped, turning back toward the flickering from her old room. She ran toward the light, the wood underfoot creaking as she steadied her club.

Sister Gertrude's eyes flickered, catching Aura on approach. The old woman shrieked, turning and limping furiously in the other direction.

Too late, Sister. Aura caught her in the back with a tremulous *thwack*. The Sister collapsed to the floor once more, the wooden planks wheezing as the boards shifted under her weight. She lay there for a moment, heaving, her screams muffled by robe and wood as she tried to crawl away from her assailant.

"I said *shut up!*" Aura reared and swung harder this time.

CRACK.

Oh, no. The blow was like lightning cracking in her hands as the wood bludgeoned the Sister's skull. *Too hard—far too hard.* The rigid edge of the bedpost had smashed squarely across her temple, and the muffled screams swiftly ceased as the body toppled to the floor, strangely loose.

Oh—oh, no.

Gertrude's head rolled sideways. The blood oozed in beating spurts from a gray crown, pooling red and loathsome black under the lantern's glow. Aura stood there, flatfooted and frozen, the bedpost trembling in her hands. The smell of copper turned her stomach. She eyed the weapon and saw the warped tip stained red.

"What have you done?" Lucy breathed.

Aura swung around and saw Lucy standing behind her holding a canvas sack. "I...we need to go," she said.

"Aura, did you...did you *kill* her?" Lucy's eyes mirrored the spilt lantern, glowing in the dark.

"*We need to go,*" she pleaded.

...

Hours went by with neither speaking a word. Aura's gaze had scarcely moved from her shoes as the girls marched along ruts and cobblestone. They walked a long way—or perhaps not long at all, but the minutes slowed and the distance ached along with her mounting guilt. They'd barely made it outside of town, pushing into the old growth that did little to welcome them. The amalgam of dense black thatch blotted out the moon and the stars all at once. The night was cool and getting cooler, thickening the breath that steamed from Aura's lips as she plodded along like the mules before her. She looked around from time to time, seeing signposts, pine trees, the cobblestones beneath her feet, and even Lucy, but her gaze promptly fell to the mud as her ponderings slowly suffocated.

For hours, she relived that moment, over, and over...*and over.* The nauseating thud resounded in her ears. Her fingers tingled as the wood met bone. The sounds frightened her, but more the sudden silence, lingering in the darkness of her place and mind. *Did I kill her?* The words clawed at her inside, an incessant line of them playing backward and forward, over and over, the events replaying in her head eternally. She felt the weight of the club she still carried—felt it smash into the old woman's head again. She hit her so hard that her hands still hurt. *What does that tell you?* she asked herself. *She's dead, and you murdered her.*

Aura caught Lucy looking over her shoulder from time to time, but she glanced away before their eyes could meet. She judged her—Aura could feel it. Lucy was always too sweet, too gentle, unable or *unwilling* to accept the wickedness of the world. *A lamb,* Aura used to call her in their private moments, where Aura was the wolf. *Ruthless and honest,* she might have said, but not this night. No cold words of strength came to Aura this night, and the world closed in on her fragile heart. Aura was ashamed—perhaps for the first time. Her hands were clammy, constantly clenched and white like the snows of a few months past. She choked the tears back. *The snow was beautiful the night of the Ball*, she remembered.

Lucy's icy demeanor spelled shame in her, too, Aura knew. She swallowed down her own shame as best she could, but Lucy's quiet cries echoed as they walked. She sniveled and whimpered and wiped her eyelids with her free hand as Aura could do nothing to comfort her. *There, there*, she thought, but the words never found the courage to pass her lips. *It's all my fault.*

Another hour passed, and the shivering set in. Their smocks were damp from sweat, and their holey leather shoes ensured they felt all the bumps of the road, burdens themselves, rubbing their heels raw. Lucy had pulled a blanket from her sack and wrapped it across her shoulders, but Aura had no such comfort. She abandoned the piece of bedpost. She couldn't stand to see it—*a token of my sins.* The malevolent red had turned brown, drying, hardening, solidifying the wrong she'd done. Aura hurled it off a stone bridge along the path, and Lucy said nothing. The wood splashed in the pond below, bobbing on the surface atop the ripples, lingering among the vacant silence of the ebony pool that swallowed the rest of the world in the moment. *Sink, damn you.*

When Aura turned, Lucy was standing still just beyond where the bridge met the road. She eyed a decrepit signpost with crisscrossing twin arrow planks. The wood was shaded and stained, overgrown with ivy and moss. The shade of the pine along the post was a scant darker in some places, indicating a few missing arrows, and splitting deeply down the rails to the earth—worn, neglected, and dying.

"It won't ever be the same, will it?" asked Lucy.

The words hung in the fog, and the noiseless night crept back in. Aura clenched her numbing fingers together in a tight ball, but the welling in her eyes spilt over their lids, streaming down her cheeks. *Cry when it's over*, she admonished.

Lucy turned to faced her, but Aura found a different face than that of the friend she knew. Her brow furrowed, lips trembled, and eyes filled, but her gaze held firm. *A loathing unlike any I've seen.*

"We can never go back," Lucy insisted.

"I…never.…" Aura's eyes erupted. Her words abandoned her. She tightened her chest and clenched her fists, daring not to sob the rest of them out, but the levies began to burst. Aura's heart spilled from her chest as all the pain poured from her eyes with her bawling. Lucy offered no comfort—for she deserved none—and without a sound or a gesture, nary a smile or even a blink, she turned for the path. *I deserve nothing more.*

Click. Lucy startled, backing into the marker and knocking the whole thing over. A man appeared from the wood line behind her, pistol drawn and barrel resting inches from the bridge of her nose.

"What—who?"

He wore a long black trench coat and a ruby brooch just under a maroon kerchief. The livery hung between tall buttoned collars that covered his face from the nose down. His tricorne hat was embroidered with a feather, while a ruby plume jutted from the top, and the shoulders of his jacket were feathered, too, with matching layered leather strands and ornate steel ringlets hanging it all together.

"Please, please," Lucy pleaded. She extended her hands sympathetically to the stranger, relinquishing whatever strength Aura had seen before. She'd returned to the scared girl from the priory, and Aura feared for her more than herself. The man in black steadied the pistol on Lucy's forehead, turning to see the other girl down the bridge.

The skin across Aura's knuckles stretched tighter than ever. The tears had turned to rage, boiling in her eyes. *I will not succumb to this.* "What do you want?" She gnashed her teeth with the last word.

The man gave a nod, beckoning at something behind her. Aura spun round. *Too late.* A burly brigand with a thick beard and a putrid stench curled his arm around her throat and held a pistol to her temple.

NO, NO, NO. The brute's breath poured over her neck with his hearty laugh, scorching her nose. *Gods, the stench,* she thought, *like decaying innards marinating in rotting onions.* He choked on harsh granules as he hacked and laughed at the same time. *Repulsive.* A thick musk sprang from every exposed pore, his bushy forearms uncovered and cutting along Aura's neckline like the bristles of a wool sock. He pushed the pistol deeper into her head, and she winced—an agony beyond the flesh. She could feel his rotund belly arching her back as his arms hugged her midsection.

"I'll have your fucking head!" she shrieked.

"Ooh, this one's gutsy," he said, his mouth full of marbles. "Mayhaps we sing to 'er? Dat oughtta cheer 'er righ' up." The man in black nodded again, soundless. He turned back to Lucy and grabbed her by the throat, much to her despair.

"Git," prodded the ape, thrusting Aura forward as he jammed the barrel deeper.

Warmth tickled her cheek and jaw as blood beaded from the barrel. It remained buried in her temple as the brigand marched her unto Lucy and the fiend holding her up. Underbrush on either side of the trail rustled the stillness as a troop of highwaymen appeared from the tree line—*a dozen, no less*—a parade of long coats, bandoliers, and six-guns flickering in the darkness.

Lucy's sobbing pleas echoed from the pond to the trees as chuckles and whispers permeated the night air. The men removed their kerchiefs, their faces contorted in the brooding, malignant lamplight as they guffawed. *Hyenas crowding 'round the carcass.* Aura's eyes darted from man to man and the armaments among them, seeking the weak. *Any feeble or drunk? A child, maybe? Or a woman might do....*

Her heart sank as more cutthroats spewed forth from the wood line. *They'll rape us,* she thought with horror. *They'll rape us and kill us and leave us to the wolves.* Aura panicked. The fat man wrestled her over and slid the barrel under her chin. His grin was the color of spoiled mustard, joined with a more pungent whiff of his rancid redolence. His beard tickled Aura's lips, and she reared, drooling at the urge to hurl, hacking and spitting in her desperation. She could taste the grease and gristle of his leathery hock, half jammed into her mouth and crushing her throat. The more she writhed and thrashed, the further his pistol dug into the folds of her fragile neck. Her skin enveloped the muzzle itself, as her weakening state began to cast her shame in granite for all the world to see.

"Dis one's a beaut!" he crowed. "I'll be feelin' real saw'ry fer what I'm 'bout to do to ye."

Aura reared her head as far as she could and slammed it into his sneering mouth.

He recoiled, "Oi you fuckin' *cunt!*" The brute whipped the pistol across her cheek with a crack, and darkness took her.

IV

BRYNJARI HEARTHS

Reed

Reed Mason recoiled at the smell of blood. *What a hateful stench*, he thought. The hairs on his neck stood up as the butcheries lined the stalls beyond Norsefyre's city gates. He tried to ignore them, but the cacophony of cleavers slamming one after the other onto their cutting boards clanged sharply in his ears. *I know that sound*, he thought squeamishly. *It's all I hear.* He gripped the reins and lowered his head between his shoulders.

The sun set low over the market district of Norsefyre as Reed and the prince of this strange city rode through the outer wall, en route to the blazing, sundrenched fortress atop the hill. Eydian Brynjar, his friend and confidant, shouted salutations to one of the guardsmen as they passed through the portcullis. "To the honored living," he said.

"And the glorious dead, Master Brynjar. Welcome home."

The heir-apparent of these very streets sat smugly in his saddle as their horses took to the Regal Mile. A scattered sunset streaked the buildings and steeples, cloaking some others in shadowy contrast. Thundering church bells rang atop the nearest belfry as the shops and peddlers sang the close of their businesses. Streets were lined with the same worn cobblestones of Nysa, Reed's familial home near the great Seawall, with a sea of common folk striding along. Passersby from wretched to wealthy and all in between bustled through the stuffed alleys and thoroughfares.

The path meandered through tight corridors and opened to opulent courtyards. The miles of road littered with lampposts and trifling debris were punctuated with tricorne hats bobbing up and down the way. Reed's and Eydian's horses clopped through mud and stone as the streets crowded by the block. There were carriages and stalls filled with livestock and fresh cuts of salt boar and jerked aurochs surrounded by beggars, shop keeps, bookmakers, brigands, and whores all alike.

The sun crept below the horizon, and the people hardly noticed, still sauntering in droves—loud, smelly, and abundant. Reed could hear tradesmen yelling about the end o' day prices on tanned leather, and he could smell the putrid fish market from blocks abreast. *As if the butcheries weren't enough…first blood, then the rot.* He heard the calls and whistles of the men and the harlots they wooed, lining the balconies above the street or dutifully dancing behind the swinging doors of the block's brothels, of which there were plenty. The low ceilings of the street front stood dwarfed by tall steeple spires, jutting from every other corner. The city of steeples, they called this place, and for good reason. Their tops scraped the stars like obelisks rising above blazing chimneys or great trees towering over a smoldering forest floor.

The beasts twitched and brayed at the errant touches of men and women squeezing by. Reed stopped a time or two, offering a comforting pet or a whisper, but he grew tired of consoling the frightened mare. His last mount, Sphinx, would have never scared so easily. She'd been a companion from as far back as the Seawall. *'Twas a good horse,* he thought. She was a war horse, tried and true, surviving every bit of the Forge with Reed, only to fall at the bitter end, shot out from under him. He had been tired in his bones, he remembered, as tired as he'd ever been. He'd slept not a wink in a week, with only scraps of food and water scarce like gold. He remembered what it felt like to long for those things—truly long for them—the way he could smell and taste and *yearn* for them in the most disturbing of places. *Do you know how much a man thinks about food when he's hungry?* Reed mused. There was nuance to this fantasy—all the things he'd eat and drink after. He composed it all in lists that went on for pages: roast mutton, brined burgundy beef, goulash, and all the ale he could find. His desperation worsened with the days, and he noticed the bark on the trees, the grassy moss that grew on roots and rocks. *My fingers*, he had even thought. *I don't need all of these, do I? Or perhaps, my toes? I have little use for those.* His mouth began to water at the thought.

Reed forgot the city and the ride. He thought of *Softnose*, his silly nickname for his sweet girl, and it stung a bit. The bullet had caught her chestnut brown neck on the last day of Reed's crucible—the final trial and culminating event of the Forge of the Furii—*the gateway to the gods.*

She was slender then, as was he, so weak from the rite and the starving. She'd toppled, throwing him from the saddle. The blood had all but corrupted him, but he'd managed to fight on, heaving and blinded by a new kind of rage, or perhaps, a final sort.

His withered arms rattled under the weight of his sword and pistol, but his soul survived beyond his failing body. *I killed them all—* some with a few last shots, one with a rusty blade to the eye. Reed cut through all of them only in time to collapse into a heap next to poor, poor Sphinx, the last innocent life lost in the ceremonial burial of his old way of life.

The ambush took its toll—each and every ball and all my powder. His vigor had died with the last assailant, he remembered. *I nearly fainted.* The Blood Rite had humbled Reed to pitiful ash and dust. *The final form. Transformation. Metamorphosis.* The transfusion—the rite itself—the forging of the Furii comes just before the final crucible. They called it the grueling week—*the time it takes to shed the husk.* The blood of the old gods was poison, cruel to body and mind as Furian candidates navigated their trials in terrifying sickly, starving solitude, oft underground. Reed's grueling week was the worst of his short life. The cinders burned hot as they branded him into the dirt, Reed remembered. *Reed Mason is dead; long live Ol' Stonehands.*

The blood and dirt were layered thick. *I could scarcely keep me britches up,* he remembered, fashioning his belt into suspenders. Reed relived the clangs of sabers and the cracks of gunfire. He killed enough to wish it upon himself as scarlet sins burdened his soul like his skin.

Sphinx looked so scared. The blood had squirted from her neck in a rhythmic pulse that drained like the warmth of his face. Despite himself and his surroundings, he had cried for a time before he could bring himself to do *what needed doing.* He could murder a man—brutalize one, in fact—without so much as a flinch or a doubt, but his own loyal horse was beyond his courage. With all the strength and speed of a Furii—all the power that hardened his veins—he sat next to his poor old nag, sobbing like a child as he sank the blade into her side, destroying the last piece of a self he would no longer be able to recognize.

The pain of the past is etched in unforgiving granite. No hope, there is, for poor old Sphinx. He dreamt and hoped and wished for something desperately different—a chance that he might go back, somehow, to another path, away from the bushwhackers and the brigands and the Forge altogether. Or, perhaps he wished that he might've saved one last shot for Sphinx—*perhaps, one last kindness.* She deserved that, in the least, if not so much more. Reed's past haunted and lurked in his dark imaginings, day after day, night after unrelenting night. The same cruel ghosts forced him to relive what happened next on that awful night. *I—I was just so hungry.*

"Reed," Eydian said. Reed flinched and caught a glimpse of the Brynjar a few leagues up the way. "Lost your mind already?" he asked, as a grin grew to a full smile.

Reed dropped his gaze again and let out a nervous chuckle, dragging two fingers along his chin and wrenching heels into his mount. *Perhaps too hard,* he fretted. The horse neighed and galloped up to Eydian's just ahead of the next alley, startling a few peddlers as he went. Eydian smiled once more. His horse turned for the walk as they made their way to the Regal Mile under a darkening sky.

"We're late," Reed said.

"My father's waited four years," Eydian said. "He'll last a few more hours."

"You dare keep Tytan Brynjar waiting?"

"Gods, what's become of me? How dare I betray my own father so?" Eydian pointed a finger into his mouth and faked a gag.

Reed laughed.

The sun was almost fully set, and people were heading indoors by the time the Furii and their horses came upon the Mile. Their road ramped to a great bridge bisecting the city of Norsefyre, ascending to the vibrant fortress on the hill. The bridge was lined with lampposts, fountains, statuary, and ornate stonework built into railings and floors alike. A rolling mural decorated the ground beneath the horses' feet, with depictions of animals, gods, and heroes of old that were themselves older than Reed knew. Every few paces came the face of a new statue, most with delicate mixes of marble, granite, and cast-iron—a style Reed found particularly pleasing. One caught his gaze—the goddess Ares, with a white marble face, hands, and feet, but a dark black cast iron veil that draped over her figure, shaped with folds and frays fitted perfectly in place.

"Beautiful…," Reed muttered, gazing into Ares's empty eyes.

"Our beloved lady," Eydian said. He blew a kiss as they passed, the flicker of the lamplight splashing oranges and yellows on the statue and the man alike.

The two Furii came to the inner gate—a monstrous piece of ironwork that opened to the Cathedral District and Bore's Fortress further on. The sentries, with lanterns in hand and rifles resting on their shoulders, met Eydian and Reed before the gate. The men looked peculiar to Reed's eye—no wigs or tails, nor armor of any kind, for that matter—just worn old dusters like the plebs of the market. Their jackets were frayed and worn, hanging over harsh riding boots, and they wore equally tattered tricorne hats. *Equipment more fitting for a highwayman than a guard.* Reed couldn't see the shape of the weapons in the dark, but he wondered if they matched the quality of everything else these men carried. *These are a sad sort, to be sure.*

"Gud evenin', sirs," one of the guards said. His beard fell to his mid chest, thick as a meadowlark's nest. "Lord Brynjar be expectin' ye," he said, lowering his head and spitting black goo onto the cobblestone.

Charmed.

Eydian smiled wide. "Thank you kindly, gentlemen. Is my father in his chambers? Or the war room perhaps?"

"He's in the dinin' hall, sir, makin' merry wit' da guests."

"Guests you say?" Eydian's horse clopped in place for a moment. "Do you hear that, Mr. Mason? Our guests await."

A different guard approached Reed and grabbed the bridle, petting the mare's nose as he did. "We'll take the horses to the stable, sir." Reed looked to Eydian, who'd since dismounted and began fetching contents from his own pair of faded saddlebags. Reed followed suit, swinging a sore leg over saddle and rummaging through his own, but somewhat unsure of what to bring. He was far more nervous, as no man had ever called him *sir* before.

"We'll deliver your belongings to your quarters, sir," the younger man reassured. Reed offered a crinkled lip and removed his hands from the bags.

"Mr. Mason, you would leave your arms?"

"Surely not, sir." Reed's face burned as he struggled to free one of his swords from the straps.

His fingers found the loose leather ties holding his shortsword in place. A *gladius,* the monks had called it. He hadn't found the scabbard for it—*or perhaps it was lost to begin with?* He couldn't recall, but now, standing beyond the monolithic Bore's Fortress, he felt foolish. The modest blade tied to his tack was blanketed by layered rolls of dirty canvas. *This won't do.* He looked to his other blade—his *real* sword, he called it, and Eydian agreed.

"You're leaving the messer behind?" Eydian asked, nodding to the wide broadsword cresting the other side of the saddle.

"I shan't bloody well bring it into the hall" barked Reed, "unless I plan to eat off the damned thing."

"I daresay, there isn't much in the whole world that makes my father happy, but a big fucking sword at a dinner party? That might do."

Reed rested a hand on the horse's back and chuckled a little. "That would be splendid, wouldn't it?"

Eydian faced Reed and put a hand on his shoulder, "We've come so far, brother, just for moments like these. Let us revel in them." He offered a smile. "Come, these faces won't paint themselves."

Reed relented, unseating his messer in the same manner and settling the strap over his shoulder. Since his Ascension over the Forge and natural man alike, Reed settled on the mainstays he carried here: the gladius on his hip and the two-handed messer peeking from over his shoulder. *A small sword for the small men and a big one for the gods.* He carried guns, too—an old single-action that worked only half the time and the other, the only gun worth having—his hungry boy—a sawed-off twin-barrel shotgun shoulder-holstered under his coat.

Unlike the shortsword, his messer was scabbarded in fine leather, made with wooden anchors and a bit of steel at the end to stay the blade. *A much prouder weapon,* he thought. His eye caught the faded name in the sheath as it swung over his back—*Josey.* He'd carved the letters on the scabbard and the blade, too, as never to forget.

And I never will....

A seemingly endless march up a winding stone staircase opened to another palatial courtyard dampened by the night. Their sentries led them to a humble servant's lavatory beyond the carriage entrance across the way—nothing more than a rusted well pump and adjacent outhouse. *Perfect,* Reed thought, *a quiet place to cleanse the dirt from the road is all I need.* With quick work, they did so, washing the chill streams over face and neck before the Furii refreshed a few layers of thick black vultus paint on their eyes and cheeks—a custom of their kind.

Reed's quiet moment was interrupted, noticing the coarse wool wrappings layered around his gladius, the fabric scratching under his palm. *A paltry sheath for any sword, let alone a Furii's sword.* He rolled his eyes at the thought of the steelworks he'd sighted or the tannery he'd missed on the way into town. *An easy fix, it might've been, if you weren't such a dolt.* But there was a hope in him that it wouldn't matter. *The sword is but a tool—its sheath, a symbol.*

The Forge taught Reed the way of war. An ironwork of the mind, the Forge molded its myriad types and styles into a singular vision of violence and the will to realize it. He thought of the Reed Mason who had walked into such a place—the belabored candidate, the survivor as the water's plunging cold burned over his neck and eyes. He scrubbed and scrubbed, but the dirt wouldn't lift—*couldn't.* He fought his way through those four forsaken years, through their savagery and unrelenting bloodshed, pondering every day the mounting sin building atop his shoulders. *A hammer or a quill,* he used to say, *all are tools in godly hands.*

The act of choosing a weapon, then, brought on a different sort of fear—advantages, pitfalls, and the terrifying, unknowable future that haunted his every move. *The Forge was easy,* he'd say. *I worked with what I was given.*

But now, surrounded by all that Tara held, choosing was far more difficult. Reed had favorites, it was true, but little loyalty in the way the northern families knew, and he was glad of it. The Patrian noblemen passed down their ceremonial swords for generations, but Reed had no such noble parentage. A layman bastard from small Nysa-by-the-Seawall, Reed Mason had carried no more than a few shillings into the Forge, and he'd returned with the blood of the gods. *I will be to them a noble vicar and not with no blasted curved blade, neither.* Besides, he knew no man—Furii or otherwise—who could parry his heaving Josey when he put his weight behind her.

"Mason, you finished?"

"Aye," he said, dabbing the last bit of black over his eyes and cheeks and standing.

The younger sentry nodded up the way, and the Furii followed. Beyond a simple gate and a servant's corridor, Reed Mason and Eydian Brynjar stood at the foot of a marble staircase, gazing to a pair of twin black doors with a warm glow seeping from their cracks. The noise poured through as well from the hinges and cracks and small spaces between the heavy steel and the stone that suspended it.

Eydian looked back with a smile as they closed the distance. The booming, thumping cacophony grew louder as the two men climbed. *Boom...boom...BOOM...*like chaotic heartbeats banding together, plucking at the hairs on his neck and forearms behind the cheers—*or screams?* He couldn't tell. His addled mind tore him back to the black tide of Goria and...*the Bloodmoat....*Reed began to panic.

"Peace, brother," Eydian said, slapping a hand firmly on Reed's shoulder. "Can't lose your mind yet, pretty boy, we've only just begun."

Reed remembered himself and let out a laugh. *Breathe, damn you, and remember yourself.* With a long, deliberate sigh, he nodded to his friend, and Eydian nodded back.

"Gentlemen, welcome to the great hall," said the sentry, squealing the latch key open and the double doors just after.

The light met Reed's eyes, blinding him for a moment. He held a hand to the source—a dazzling gilded chandelier shooting the radiance of a thousand suns right into his eyes. *Almost forgot where I was*, he thought. The sounds could just as easily be mistaken for a battlefield, littered with the uproarious applause and gleeful shrieks of drunks at their leisure. And music—*Gods, the music*—bouncing jovially to strings and drums and even brass horns honking away to the melody. Sounds echoed from every corner with glasses clinking together or scratchy knives carving aimlessly into their plates as the wooden floors and benches creaked and groaned under the weight of feet and arses all alike.

Two nameless footmen promptly manned the doors, heaving into the old iron as the hinges spat clouds of rust. The bustling room halted with the resounding slam, and the music slowed and ceased as revelers and footmen turned to face the doors and the Furii that walked through them. Reed's gaze moved across the crowd, the dead stares of strangers picking away at his pride. In the shadows of an instant he found no friend here, only the fear from before. *These are my enemies. They mean me harm.*

But his worries were disarmed at the crowd's first sight of Eydian Brynjar, the Prince of Norsefyre. A man quickly named him as such. "Look! Yonder stands Eydian Brynjar, the newborn Furii!"

The visibly drunken crowd erupted in applause and shouted "*RAH!*" the old Brynjari battle cry.

Men close and afar ran in, attacking their prince with claps on the back and hearty embraces. They grabbed and shouted, and with their smiles and cheers they filled the hands of the Furii with mugs of ale that Reed prayed would never empty. The music returned in a violent tempo, swelling with the new mood of the evening.

"Where is my father?" shouted Eydian to one of the guests.

"Huh?"

"MY FATHER!" he shouted again, but unto deaf ears.

"Aye, sir, you *are* a Furii indeed!" the man replied amiably, clinking his mug to Eydian's.

Reed laughed over a sip of his own, spilling it down his front a bit. He paid it no mind at all. "Eydian!" he called out, pointing to the head tables across the way. Eydian nodded.

The feast was bigger and brighter with every sticky bootstep. Men and, much to his surprise, the women, too, stood atop the long running tables and drank deep to their health as they pushed through. They even reached out, dragging dubious fingers across the Furii's faces in order to catch a few flecks of vultus paint and don it themselves. The people squeezed their shoulders and nicked at their swords and slugged their chests and arms in comradeship, and Reed admitted to himself that he didn't mind. The group was raucous, unlike any he'd yet seen at a brothel, let alone a dinner party, but then, this was *far* from a dinner party. *Tis a feast.*

Then, a booming voice pierced the noise. "BROTHERS AND SISTERS!"

The horns tooted to another halt, and stillness fell upon the hall once more. Here was a different kind—a sudden, disciplined, crypt-like silence took the air from the room as Tytan Brynjar stood from his hallowed seat. Even the drunkest among them swayed in quiet, respectful esteem. Reed's stomach plunged from its usual place, and he looked to Eydian. The prince held his hands together in front of him, eyes fixed on the floor, and Reed quickly mimicked his posture.

Tytan's high table towered over the others, and the King of Norsefyre towered still. He gripped his goblet—blazing emerald and silvers worthy of such a man—as he lifted a boot to his chair and then to the table. "Pray, hear my words, one and all," Lord Brynjar belted to a noiseless crowd.

He took wide, slow steps down the table as his courtiers giggled more loosely. Reed heard the clinks of the silverware and slops of spilling food and lifted his gaze as the other guests bravely chuckled to themselves. They watched on as the lord of Norsefyre marched his way down the fine linens of the king's head table. His own closest patrons sitting below even laughed aloud, jesting their forks and knives at his legs or mouthing, "I was going to eat that!" The hall smirked together as he paused, turning back to his only son and the man that stood beside him.

"I sent Eydian Brynjar to the Forge as my son—a mortal man— and now, he may more aptly be called my brother!"

The crowd roared again, hammering the tables with boots and fists.

"And the man who stands with him—hero of the Blacktide and the Bloodmoat, Master Reed Mason of the Dunnmoor Seawall."

More jubilation sounded across the hall.

"I, like all of you, am proud to be in the same room as these noblest of men, let alone so dearly acquainted. To Eydian, my son, my brother in arms, my blood—I salute you."

"*SALUTE!*" echoed the crowd.

"And to the newest Furii under my employ, Mr. Mason, my newfound brother, long have the wall clans pledged to my banner. You and your countrymen have honored me on the battlefield more than I rightly deserve. You are every bit my sworn sword and kin-blood—salute."

Reed raised his glass high, choking down the inklings of a tear. *Remember yourself, damn you.*

"Ladies and gentlemen, may I proudly present to you these fearsome youngbloods—forged and unbroken sons of Ares, lords of war, and vicars of the immortal gods! Drink to their health, drink to their swords and their guns both, and drink in fear, for they have none!" He raised the goblet high over his head and yelled the oldest oath, "TO THE HONORED LIVING!"

"AND THE GLORIOUS DEAD!" the host shouted.

The crowd roared louder with hails and salutations as the Brynjar lord himself upended his goblet, liberating every last drop. He threw it clumsily to the table, shattering a nearby porcelain to smithereens, as his table guests laughed and ducked for cover. Lord Brynjar wiped his black beard with a sleeve and belted over the party once more his house's famous Borean battle cry, "*RAAAHHHHHHHH!*"

Eydian sped toward the head table, thrusting revelers away, decidedly moving to his father. Reed followed with a hand on Eydian's back but lost him in the fray. *He'll stop at nothing.* Four long years shone in the vigor of his gait. Mortal men might never understand the weight of ascension. *Ah, but they might,* he thought. *The Bloodmoat taught me all that I needed—the Forge, a simple repetition.*

Reed chased after Eydian but got bogged down between the revelers, now shoulder-to-shoulder. "Pardon me," he said, looking up in time to see Eydian nearly tackle his father. The lines of his jacket deepened with his tight embrace, raising him off the ground. Eydian retracted an open hand and slapped it loudly on the back of his father's neck, pulling Tytan's forehead to meet his. Both men were wearing a similar vultus—blacks and dark blues striped and smeared thick across their eyes and mouths.

Strange, Reed thought. The vultus was a customary adornment for Furii in all settings, among any company—*friend or foe*. But, the layman in Reed survived enough to find it foreign and savage. Still, these were Brynjari colors on the faces of Brynjari lords, now both anointed Furii and warriors ascendant. Reed stopped short, politely making room, if only to watch. Eydian smiled brightly and laughed over the deafening crowd. *I have no family*, he thought, *but here, I may find one.*

A woman appeared, embracing Eydian hurriedly, desperately. *Reunion.* She was donned in fine black from the neck down, and she was kissing him relentlessly, mashing her face into his, smearing the paint, even. Envy burned in Reed's ears. *I wish but once that a lass might kiss me so.* But then, relief—Lord Brynjar wrapped his burly arm over the woman's shoulder pulling her close. He then did the same to Eydian. *Thank the fuckin' gods,* Reed smiled. *His sister.*

The woman's smile was dazzling ivory, glowing as she giggled into her father's ear. She placed a kiss on his cheek, too, this time with the tender grace of deference. Reed was as jealous as he'd ever been. *A kiss like that could fill my heart…and my cock, too, I s'pose.* He blushed at the thought, tugging at the new boyish tightness in his trousers. *Don't be such a barbarian, for Gods' sake. Remember yourself.*

With another sip, he was a boy again in the village of his birth. He might've embraced a father and sister so—or a mother, even—in small Nysa-by-the-Seawall, but that was a life he would never come to know. He had been robbed of it, like so many other innocent children orphaned by the wars of their fathers. Conscription was an escape for Reed, surely, but the end for so many others. *A tragedy that begets all others*, he thought.

"Mr. Mason!" Eydian shouted. "To me, damn you, to me!"

The words jolted Reed back again. "Moving," he replied, dodging and weaving as he did. *Think, damn you.* The head table received him in open arms, to his humble surprise. Wholesome hugs from strangers came one after the other, relenting finally to the man who'd changed Reed's life all those years ago—Tytan Brynjar, the Torchbearer.

He'd only met him the once—after the Blacktide, atop the cliffs overlooking Goria, easternmost of the Four Impregnables—*or, the Four Furies, depending where you're from.* The man hadn't aged a day. He was younger-looking, even, without the muck and mire of the battlefield. His vultus was the same black and blue of the banners that plunged from the rafters, and Reed felt the weight of his influence. A partially receding hairline met his thick black beard at the sideburns, and the twinkle of his black eyes pierced through the shadows of his face. Reed saw the hunger in his liege lord's eyes, like the lingering gaze of a wolf in the night. The hairs on his neck stood tall.

Tytan Brynjar wore a handsome wool coat and pearly white trousers—*the ol' salt and pepper*, Reed recalled from his years in the barracks. His chest gleamed, bedecked with the pins, cords, and medals of a king, as a flowing scarlet satin sash draped gracefully over a shoulder. The man's collar was informally open, and the room was stifling as it was, so Reed unclasped his own. Tytan Brynjar was a great southern lord—the greatest, no doubt—and Reed expected the grandeurs and posterity of a thankless king, but found scarcely little in the Brynjars' household.

"Brother," Tytan greeted, extending a hand.

"Lord Brynjar," Reed said, "an honor, my Lord, truly."

"You've grown since last I saw you—a boy you were, eighteen or so?"

"We've both grown, father," Eydian said, jesting a punch to Reed's gut. Reed flinched nervously.

"Aye," Tytan said, "but him a little more than you, it would seem." Tytan Brynjar grabbed Reed's shoulder and turned him 'round, eyeing the messer that slung from his back. "Is that what I think it is!" he exclaimed.

"A man after your own heart, Father," the woman in black laughed.

"Indeed—she's wide as a dinner plate! How heavy?"

"Nearly a stone," Reed blushed.

"My gods, you beautiful brute! I knew sending you to the Forge was no waste. Oh, dear me," he caught himself, wrapping a mitt around the back of his daughter's slender neck. "Where are my manners? Mr. Mason, this fair lady here is my eldest daughter, Miss Eryn Brynjar."

"His oldest, but certainly more than a mere lady," Eryn scoffed, offering her hand to Reed.

"Charmed," Reed said, lifting a hand to shake before his eyes met hers. *What a lovely pair of peepers...then, the smile. Please, smile again, for the love of the gods.*

She smiled. Reed darted his eyes to her father, as not to stare, but her portrait burned pristinely in the mind. The Brynjar spoke, and Reed heard not a word, possessed by the statuesque Eryn in her raven-black dress. He stole glances carefully, as not to let on, but beyond his neutral brow and untelling eyes, Reed secretly savored and worshipped. From ankles to the top of her neck, she was covered in slimming ebony, and Reed pined for what might be beneath.

Her father's high cheekbones poked through the gaunt of her face. She held her head high over a slender neck and narrow shoulders. Reed's glances turned to a longing stare, hypnotized by her heavenliness. *Not lust,* he lied to himself, *for she is a classic beauty.* Reed found gravity in the glimmering green of her eyes. *A love, she could be—unbroken by a thousand moments, or even one. It's her eyes,* Reed thought. *What is it about those eyes?* Hazel hemmed in a dazzling emerald, they bounded around the room at people and things that Reed Mason so desperately wished were him. *To me, damn you. Just once more.* Her eyelids and the bridge of her nose were painted a thick black and winged at the edge of her hairline, brightening the green in her eyes all the more. *Look at me, please, but for a moment.*

"Careful, brother," Eydian whispered, nodding his head toward his sister. "She bites."

Reed shook it off and turned back to the master of the house, who'd since secured another round of ales for the others. *The nectar of the gods,* Reed thought, receiving the refreshment graciously. The Brynjar smiled and laughed, uttering a few pleasantries before clinking mugs and taking a stiff sip himself. He took his daughter under the arm as he asked Eydian questions about the road and the Forge. Despite himself, Reed's mind and his gaze wandered, taking it all in: the party, the drink, and this new Eryn Brynjar, though she paid him little mind.

Congratulations to you, Reed. You're a Furii, a son of Ares—hero of the Blacktide, even—but a virgin still. He sipped on his ale and sighed his relief into the drink. The wet mug tingled his fingertips, and he smiled. *You are my greatest love, sweet brew—always by my side.* He thought of kissing the mug then, if only for a laugh. Lifting his cup and his gaze, he found none other than Eryn Brynjar staring back with a toothy grin.

Reed's ears and cheeks burned hot. *Don't panic.* He slowed his hand, chuckling at his own foolishness. He raised the mug to the Princess of Norsefyre and winked. She raised her own along with an eyebrow. With another disarming smile, she brought the glass to her lips and tilted it back, gulping down every last drop in an instant. *Holy ever-loving shite,* he thought, adjusting himself. He blushed and laughed, clapping with the others as Lord Brynjar guffawed.

"A Brynjar she is and will ever be!" Tytan roared.

"Your turn," she croaked, holding a hand to her chest, looking to Reed.

"Huh?" Reed blushed.

"You'd let my wisp of a sister drink you under?" Eydian taunted.

"Never!" Reed shouted. He took a knee, raising his tankard high, before upending it. *Too much.* He choked hard, and the beer ran over the cup and down his front. He coughed and continued, but the damage was done—the others hooted and horned, and Reed turned the color of fresh tomatoes. *That's right. Drink up, you moron.*

With the last gulp and a hiccup, Tytan helped him to his feet. "There, there, lad—we'll work on that."

Reed coughed and nodded, watching as Eryn left a last kiss on her father's cheek. "Until next time, Mr. Mason," she said over her shoulder.

Tytan patted the two for the last time. "I mean not trouble you so soon after your travels," he said, "but the hour is late, and we have much to discuss in the coming days. Drink up, lads! Enjoy your long-awaited, well-earned rest. But know that we have business in the morn."

"What business?" said Eydian.

"Later," he smirked, "Furii business. The good fight." Tytan took a sip. "We have some suns to set—some curtains to call."

Reed smiled, "Cheers." He drank.

V

THE BIRDSONG BRIGANDS

Aura—Past

"It wasn't me, Aura. You know it wasn't—"

"I know, but...."

Aura came to, confused and slow, like waking from a foggy dream. Moments of wakefulness passed in and out, segmented by missing memories or nothing at all. *Frightening nothing.* Fragile flashes of clarity were drowned by the terrifying unknown, and her heart sank. *What have they done to me?*

She concentrated on the things she could remember—the brute that carried her from the road, visions of fallen leaves, the legs and back of the burly brigand, and a dagger bouncing across a sweat-stained lumbar. The cool, wet dirt soothed the heat of her cheeks as the dry blood tugged and cracked across her forehead. The rest of her—face down in a clearing someplace well away from the road—was a much less soothing prospect. *Get up, Aura. You must get up now.*

Her hands were bound behind her. The grit of the ground scraped across her teeth like sandpaper—warm drool, or blood maybe, pooled in her mouth as the spit leaked from the corners down her chin. Her feet were bound, too, dragging across the mud and the leaves loudly with her squirming. She froze.

Voices echoed through the wood as the blurry flickers of firelight bobbed in and out of the corner of her eye, half swollen shut. Aura widened the lid, met with figments and illusions of human silhouettes and ambient firelight, all stained red. *Lu...Lucy....*She choked on the thought. Two of the silhouettes moved differently than the others, as if bouncing up and down while the others stood still. The laughs and the jeers were interrupted by another voice—a softer one made to shriek and scream, like a lamb for slaughter. *Why torture the creature?*

Her vision cleared as she blinked hard and wiped the muck away with her shoulder . Her gaze darted from man to man in fruitless hopes of counting them. *So many! Lucy...,* Aura thought. *Where's Lucy?* The emergent screeching of the wounded animal worsened. *A hound, perhaps?* The sound turned to yelping yips, as if someone were hacking at the poor devil while it was still alive. Aura's eyes shot 'round the campsite, looking for the dog or the deer, but found no animals but the ones that surrounded the fire.

And then, her world came crashing down. *No,* she insisted, shaking her head. *No, I won't believe it.* Her heart absorbed the words her mind rejected. *Not a dog...not a deer.* A pale white face shone in the distance between the silhouettes, illuminated by the campfire. *Lucy.* Her small face peeked through the shadows under a brigand's strained hand, gripping tightly between chin and neck. Her head bounced back and forth, left and right. A man stepped forward, blocking Aura's view. *He's unbuckling his trousers.*

Aura swallowed hard, as not to vomit. She couldn't look away—*wouldn't.* Her gaze was fixed, seething like a hot iron brand. The knave slapped the poor girl as he forced his loins on her face and mouth. Her twisted face contorted, and her tears streamed as one of his hands gripped her hair and yanked it back and forth. The other tightened around her slender neck, now lined and wrinkled by unnatural angles as the brigands brutalized her from both sides.

She is the animal. Aura felt a crippling guilt. *I couldn't find her,* she thought, *because they took the humanity from her.* She couldn't recognize the man behind Lucy, only her naked upper half insufferably gyrating under the predations of the monsters that maimed her. Aura wept as quietly as she could, sobbing to herself as her vision dissolved into tears. She wished it was only for her dear friend, but her tears were the selfish kind—pitying, even, knowing that she would be next. *They will take me next, and I am helpless to thwart them.*

She thought of the fight she could make for them. *Not much more than a child to them, most like.* The dreadful details began to panic her. *I must kill myself.* She looked desperately for anything sharp. There were barrels of ale and strewn boxes, nothing useful. She rolled quietly over, eyeing the area behind her. *Horses.* All she had to do was free herself from the bonds around her hands and feet and get there. She could find a weapon, a sword surely. *For fuck's sake*, she chided. *It's a horse! You could ride away, Aura!*

Aura wrenched and tugged, but to no avail. Her ties stayed, so she gave rolling a try. She eyed the path over her shoulder, rocking back and forth as soundlessly as she could. The dead leaves crunched beneath her legs, and she froze. She buried her face deep in the dirt, expecting the uproar of an audience that didn't exist. She closed her eyes and prayed harder than ever before, but no one turned her way. She scrunched her body into a ball and pushed up, inch by inch toward the nearest horse. Aura grew bolder with her noise, covered by the jeers around the fire and the punishing sounds of sacrifice pouring from her friend. She was shivering violently as she moved, closer and closer. *So close.* Her head was a thumping nightmare— eyes cloudy and rolling in the back of her head, her mouth full of copper from the earlier blow, but fazing her resolve not a smidge. *So close....*

But then, a boot. It stepped lightly atop Aura's back, pinning her in place. *No.* She rolled over hard to face her assailant. A cloaked black shadow looked down at her, but Aura didn't wait for an introduction. With all the strength of her back and belly, she produced barely a modest headbutt, one that the figure caught in one open palm. Another lightning hand clapped over her mouth, muting her wails.

A woman's voice came from the shadow. "Shh-sh-sh, make no sound, dear. I'm 'ere to 'elp."

Confused, Aura froze. The figure drew a knife, and Aura recoiled. "For the bonds, dear," the woman said, sawing at the ties of her hands and feet. The woman's gloved hand moved from her mouth as she freed her. Aura didn't make a sound, transfixed by the steely glimmer of the stranger's mask. A tattered garb tickled Aura's exposed arms and face as the woman in black freed her. With one hand and not so much as a grunt, she brought Aura to her feet. *Who are you?* she might've asked.

"Lucy...." Aura heard herself say.

"She's good as gone," the woman whispered, putting a finger up to Aura's mouth, "and we will be, too, unless you follow my instructions to the letter."

Aura was queasy and faint, but she nodded. The woman moved to the closest horse, fidgeting with a few straps before unsheathing a rifle and placing it in her hands.

"I...I've never—"

"It's loaded," the woman interrupted. "You need only pull the trigger."

Aura looked down and back up. "How do I reload?"

"Don't worry about that," she said. "On my signal, shoot once into the crowd. I'll do the rest." The woman put a hand on the rifle and dragged Aura with it to a new position behind a stack of broken boxes. "Here," she said, pointing into the heart of the crowd. "When I say, pull the trigger and get down—in a hurry, mind you."

"Where will you be?" Aura asked.

"Just here," the woman said, pointing at the far side of the group. "You should see me in the light."

Before Aura could say another word, the woman in black was flying over barrels and boxes into the darkness. She moved like a whisper—so agile and quiet, dodging the lambent firelight with every footfall. Aura found herself alone again, gripping the rifle tightly. The few minutes between felt like hours, her panic amplified by Lucy's unrelenting wails and Aura's newfound hope of escape. Aura was left alone with the sordid laughs from the fireside, waiting for the woman in black to come back and...*what, kill them all?* No less than a score surrounded that fire—large men with guns and steel, and drunk to boot. Her eyes danced frantically from tree to tree, barrel to barrel, body to body. *Gods, her screaming....*

The screaming ceased. Aura's heart sank, eyes desperate to avoid her muted friend, but searching nonetheless. *She's gone*, Aura prayed. *Please, let her be gone.* She couldn't see as much from the new spot, only the bobbing heads of the crowd and light through the cracks. Aura looked over her shoulder to the horses, munching at hay strewn across an old wagon. The reins were right there, barely tied, and loosely at that. She hungered for escape over revenge, so much so that she began to drool.

The nearest horse was no more than a stone's throw—a hop and a skip, and she'd be riding into the darkness and away from this hell. She'd gone so far as to begin putting the rifle down, inching toward them and avoiding the lamplight. Then, from the corner of her eye, the woman in black emerged from the distant tree line.

A gloved hand waved from the bushes—the signal. Aura's rifle was already resting against the box. She looked over her shoulder again to the horses, then back to the crowd. *Run, Aura! You're already there.* She turned away from the gun, crouched, and ran toward the horses, quick as she could. She was committed, abandoning each and all—Lucy, her masked liberator, and the despicable creatures gathered around the hellfire disguised as a hearth. Hope consumed her as she saw herself riding through the night air to somewhere, *anywhere*, or nowhere, even. Her heart was a new kind of pounding violence in her chest, and she longed to be free. She felt little for the people back there, only the baser need to survive.

Her body froze in place as she remembered a moment from earlier that evening—a distant memory, it seemed, but it haunted her thoughts and shackled her feet to the hallowed ground. *Sister Gertrude.* She turned about. The poor woman's face, the round spectacles, etched itself in her head. *The looking glass of unblinking eyes, dead and gone.* The lips had curled, too, like a snarl to follow the sickening crack of bedpost on skull. The blood pooled from her temple ceaselessly as Aura wrung the sweat-drenched wood in her clammy hands. She recalled the splash of the pond and the weapon's insufferable floating.

And the portrait worsened still, exaggerating the horrors of it, making monsters of Aura and Sister Gertrude both. The nun's face sagged and stretched into a haggard, bearded brute—*that cunt unbuckling his britches.* Aura's hunger turned its focus as the man in her vision yanked his unshorn, putrid loins from their enclosure and proceeded toward her. The fear pulling her away was gone—*only anger left. No, not anger,* she shook, *rage.* She was tethered to the spot. The rifle back in her hands again. *I never put it down.* She lined the sight to the biggest man among them and eased the trigger back.

BOOM. The weapon hit her shoulder like a cannonball, throwing her backward. The damned thing jumped from her hands and knocked her flat to the ground behind a box. The fireside erupted in shrieks and gunfire. Aura kept her head close to the dirt, the mind she'd lost coming back to her as her heart thundered along to the skirmish. Screaming and braying and more gunshots sliced past Aura's ears, shredding the boxes before her as splinters and debris sprayed her face and neck. Rounds cracked and zipped over her head. She buried her face in her hands. A few more shots thudded in front of her as she scooted back, lower than she'd ever been, her face sliding through mud and leaves whilst she crept. The boxes offered little more cover than the darkness itself, and the unbridled chaos unfolded all around in sickening unison. Men stood in a hamstrung circle, guns drawn, shooting aimlessly into the night in every direction.

A bullet struck the closest horse, puncturing the fold just between the beast's neck and chest. The nag let out a woeful screech, cowering low on paralyzed front legs, head and neck quaking and convulsing as the beast rolled over with a sickly wheeze. The neighboring mares startled, jerking at their ties and yanking wood and nails free from the derelict wagon and egressing from the violence in all directions, leaving Aura alone in the thick of it.

Gods be damned! She cursed them as she crawled, while more bullets peppered the leaves and the grass. Aura could hear the distant screams of men beneath a sort of ripping sound nearly as loud as the gunfire. One voice rang out in the darkness over and over, the high squeals of a girl quite in the thick of it, unsure of what it meant.

...

The shots waned, and the yelling turned to dull groans, petering out until silence fell on the night air once again. *Absolute silence*, Aura thought. She heard nary a horse or man...*or Lucy*. Aura was petrified in place, her hands glued to the back of her head, her face pressed hard into the dirt. The pressure was building behind her eyes, and a sharp tinge pierced her mouth and lips as her saliva turned to copper. Her head swirled, and she was sure to hurl if she stayed like this, but crunching footsteps broke her trance. She thought to play dead. The footsteps came right for her, louder and louder, bringing anguish and torment with every inch.

Fight, Aura! Fight! She exploded upward, lunging at the shadows with every ounce behind her. *Not enough.* An outstretched hand caught her face, its palm squashing cheeks and eyes, and Aura yelped. Her hands ripped at the stony arm, but the iron grip stayed. She wailed, "Help! Help!"

"Quiet, damn you, girl!" the voice hushed.

The hand loosened from Aura's face, and she quit her struggling. *The woman in black.* She let out a few pathetic coughs as she rubbed her neck, tears filling her eyes and streaming down her face as she collapsed to her knees. "Where's...where's Lucy?" she whispered.

"Your friend is gone, dear, and we will be, too. Come—we must fly."

The woman in black had a new hue about her, a stickiness faintly shimmering in the moonlight. *Is that…blood?* Aura caught a glimpse of twin sheathed daggers behind the woman's back as she swung her coat on and hiked toward the embers. She reached down, grabbing the strap of a bag or perhaps a box.

"Put these on," she said. "You'll perish before morn in that skin you're in."

The bag thudded at Aura's feet. "What do you mean, *gone?*"

"You know precisely what I mean."

Aura turned, but the woman snatched her shoulders.

"There are others, child," said the woman, "more Birdsongs in these hills. They'll 'ave heard."

The woman in black put her foot beneath a grounded rifle and kicked it up and into her hand. The leaves scattered from the barrel as she slung it over her shoulder.

"Where is she?" Aura asked.

The woman stopped. She didn't answer, only met Aura's wanting stare with the cold emptiness of the mask, shining resplendently in the moonlight. Aura glared for a moment, catching the smaller, finer etches carved into the worn steel. *A tear*—it dripped from the hollow eye hole, down the metallic cheek, symbolic of its patron. *The tear of Ares.*

"I want to see her," Aura insisted. The tears welled their hardest, but she choked them down. *Cry when it's over, Aura.*

The mask returned to the scavenge, and her words were cold. "If you delay me with one more word, by the gods I will leave you to them."

Aura swallowed hard and opened her mouth. "But—"

"They will rape you all night and cut your throat at sunrise, mark my words."

"I won't leave her here."

The woman shook her head, trudging away toward more strewn

armaments, her coat shimmering more clearly in the waning firelight. A sickly deep crimson sludge painted her shoulders, arms, and mask. Aura dropped to her knees and opened the bag, finding the ill-fitting breeches with the tattered boots of a smaller man and a hooded canvas cloak not dissimilar to that of a vestal's habit back at the convent. *Fitting*, she thought.

She donned them quickly enough, slinging the cloak over her shoulders and instinctively pulling the hood over her chestnut hair, now darkened by sweat and dirt. She mimicked the woman, in some sense, but dared not touch the bodies. She paced among the wagon and boxes, eyeing a rough-spun blanket, an old pistol and powder horn, and a bullet box to go with it, she hoped. *Are these bullets the right size?* A canteen caught her eye, draped from the edge of the wagon. Reaching, she found a steady stream of water trickling from a bullet hole on the far side. *Useless*, she sighed, *but what a shot it must've been.*

"I have enough water and food," the woman said. "We must take our leave."

"Please," Aura could barely say. "Please," she choked. "Let me—"

"Easy, dear." The woman moved carefully to Aura, now sputtering to herself. Reality had yet to set in, and Aura's breath overtook her tears. The small intricacies of the mask appeared more vividly as the woman approached. The metal was old, roughened by the road but with the soft elegance of fine marblework. Ares herself was etched upon her face, with the supple, silvery lips of a goddess and the blank eyes of the dead. The woman put a hand on the other side of Aura's neck, this time with a soft, tender touch, her thumb just under Aura's ear.

"There's nothing for you there, dear," she murmured. "Only pain."

"I...."

"We must go, love. The path is just here....I beg you—come now."

With her last words, the woman squeezed, and Aura's head dropped into a low nod. *Prostrating*. Aura's eyes rose to meet hers, the ones behind the odious black holes in her plated mask. She felt as though she gazed upon a skeleton—the hollow eyes of death itself staring back at her in the darkness. The tears left her. She gulped them down and nodded back.

"Good girl."

...

The two women trudged through trees and underbrush all night. Aura saw nary a road or trail, or even a lamppost in the distance. The weather stayed brisk but calm, the only noise to be heard under Aura's feet as she clumsily crunched on the forest floor. The moon shone through the branches as they moved. Her eyes caught glimpses of the woman's feathered cloak gliding behind her as she crept across the landscape. They must've walked for hours before either spoke. Aura let out a cough or cleared her throat from time to time, hoping for conciliation or even a grunt to break the cold dark silence of the eventide.

She wanted to ask the woman who she was, why she'd come, or even her name. *How did she do that?* Aura hadn't stopped to think for a moment about it—how one man, let alone one *woman* could cut through a score of burly barbarians armed to the teeth. She had, hadn't she? With her flashing twin daggers like lightning strikes zapping and ripping through a fleshy crowd. What *had* happened? Aura had pulled the trigger, and the damned thing had bucked like a branded ass, nearly knocking her senseless. The next thing she knew, she had been crawling under hails of gunfire. Her mind raced. She wanted to say it out loud, to scream it at this *stranger* who'd appeared as if from a dream—a shadow of a wish come to save her. She choked down the tears again and mustered the words but just barely, and they weren't the ones she thought.

"Thank you," Aura said.

The woman glanced over her shoulder but offered no reply, trudging on through the underbrush.

"May I...may I ask you your name, madam?"

Silence. Aura's troubled mind began to wander again, back to Lucy, but the woman's low, soothing voice interrupted her.

"Kora…Kora the Crow, if it pleases you."

"Kora," she echoed. "You're…you're a Furii, aren't you?"

The Crow walked a few more paces. "Aye, that I am."

"How did you—"

"Those beasts back there were more carrion than songbird."

"Songbird?" Aura asked. "I don't understand."

"You've ne'er heard of the Birdsong Brigands?"

Aura stumbled on an errant root and stopped in her tracks. "Those were the Birdsong Brigands?"

"That they were," Kora said. "A plague upon this wood, no doubt."

"But…the stories—they give their spoils to the poor, heroes of the downtrodden…'honor among thieves' and all that…."

"No such thing," Kora said. "Honor is a fickle thing, my dear— the first thing to go when the road gets rough. Maybe it existed once, but that's a day long past, I fear."

Aura took a few more idle steps. "Where are you taking me?"

"I'm not taking you anywhere, love. In fact, I expect you're safe enough from here, should you wish to leave. I make way for the Forge, myself."

"The Forge?" Aura asked.

"Aye, the Forge," the Crow said. "Midway between Heraclion and the Tear of Ares, there," she said, pointing at a wayward road sign. "The place of 'baptisms and reckonings' one and all. Have you never heard of it, dear?"

Aura furrowed her brow. "You don't mean the Furii's Bastion, do you?"

"Indeed, one and the same," Kora said. "I forget you Northerners call it that. I suppose there are many names for it, for a great many things do happen there."

"We're you baptized there?" she asked.

"Yes—same as every Furii, at least these days. Tis the last hearth for all things Furian—a sanctuary, immune to the petty squabbles of the trifling kingdoms and politics and the like."

Aura took a few more steps. She rarely had such an inquisitive side, but her curiosity in the moment was unusually abundant, if only to offset the tears. Her eyes were still swollen and red, and the questions kept coming. "More fortress than sanctuary, I should think?"

"More monastery to my kind—but with a hidden violence, perhaps."

Aura tried to hide her appalled look, but with little success. "How did you become a Furii?"

Another pause emptied the air before Kora answered. "Interestingly enough, I was not in a far different circumstance from yours this night. A graver tale from yours, though, I'm afraid. No Furii came to my aid."

"But, you survived," Aura observed. "They didn't kill you?"

Kora shook her head, the mask gleaming as it bathed in the moonlight, "Nay, I slew them all, if just barely. No one to save me but myself."

"We're you on the run?"

"No, dear child. Eons past, lifetimes ago, I was on a different path—no vestal virgin, that's for certain. They stole me from the brothel."

"I am *not* a vestal—wait, you were a whore?" The words stung her lips and tongue as they left her mouth. She winced, wishing so badly she could take them back, but Kora seemed to pay no mind, merely held up a hand as she chuckled.

"Ha, dear me, child, yes. In fact, I was raised in that brothel. You seem to my ears among the gentry?"

"Aye," Aura admitted, "but in a past life now."

"None of us are lucky in the end, dear, but at least some of us are born lucky. I was not among them, sadly, and life can be quite brutish for us, as I'm sure tonight has taught you."

"I'm so sorry, madam."

"Please, pay it no mind, dear. You are so young, and as I say, 'twas more than a few lifetimes gone by, at least by the mortal man's pocket watch. I barely remember that person. I killed those wretches with a dagger I found near the post I was tied to. They were drunk, you see, and sleeping, and I'd escaped my bonds. I was patient. All I seem to remember is hacking and sawing at their throats with that rusty old blade, one by one. I was surprised how long it took for the others to alert. I expected only death, to be sure. My plan was to kill as many as I could before being slain myself...."

"But you survived," Aura said.

"Aye, that I did. And I sat there in the darkness, once it was all over, with the blade at my wrists, vying for courage I did not possess."

"You were to take your own life because of them?"

Kora let out a sigh. "'Tis a funny thing. You do so much to survive, yet the pain of doing so can be quite enough to best you. 'My own worst enemy,' as it were."

"Indeed," Aura said.

"But, alas, the gods had more planned for the likes of me. I decided instead that, if I was to take my life, it wouldn't be surrounded by those devilish fiends in a dank hole smelling of blood and piss. I'd find a nice cliff to jump from or a sea to drown myself in. 'Twas my life to take, after all, not theirs. I walked out of their camp and found a small pool—washed away the blood from my face and hands. I'd found some clothes to cover my nakedness and walked along further. I ate their food as I hiked the mountain tree line, and the path I took led me to a road and, farther on, a stone tablet carved into the mountainside that spoke only the truest words:

"*No peace for the Furii, no honor, nor shame.*

"*Only peace for their enemies, in the ground, may they lay.*

"*One strike with sword, another with spear, no peace for the Furii, no pause, no fear.*

"*Let blood flow, let sons grow, no mercy, no fame.*

"*No peace for the Furii, only fire and pain.*"

Aura recognized the words. "The Auger's Memento," she said plainly.

"Top marks," the Crow said. "But, I had no such knowledge of it. The words spoke to me all the same—enticed me, and I took the exalted path without question or qualm. Soon I found myself at the mouth of the very place that would, in time, forge me anew."

"They say the Auger was the very first of the Furii, a Precursor."

"Aye, our ancient Furian progenitor—mythed to be Ares's son himself, he who set fire to the very kiln that shapes us," said the Crow.

"Will you pass by the Memento on your way to the Forge?" Aura asked, a slight crack in her voice.

"I shan't miss it, even if I wished to," Kora said. "Would you like to see it?"

"I—I mean no impertinence....I have nowhere else to go," Aura said, her gaze dropping back to the forest floor under a blanket of reddening cheeks.

"That makes two of us, my dear," she said. "Tell me, do you know much of these parts?"

Aura shook her head. "Only that we rode south from Clydae—near the Tear of Ares, maybe."

"Aye," Kora nodded, "quite close, but this is a hallowed place among the rest. Vast swamps and wetlands span for seven hundred miles yonder"—she pointed—"and three hundred, that. The men of this land sold it to foolish dolts from halfway across the world. A swindle. They came and sank and said things like, 'I'm buyin' water, not land!' It swallowed them, slowly but surely, like their crops and homes and innocent children from time to time. The Tear of Ares is an ancient place, perhaps the oldest there is. Full of power, these places are, and for the blink of time that we walk Tara's sacred earth, the Tear of Ares has lived on for a million moments and one. Whatever power we believe we have over this land, it is misplaced. These woods are the true gods—indomitable to man's crooked price. We are stewards, not masters."

"The people—the Pleb, I mean, from my country—know this place by another name."

"Ah," the Crow eased, "superstitious, are you?"

"I think not," Aura scoffed, "but you said the words yourself, didn't you? The 'power' over this land?"

"I know the name," she laughed, "and well-earned it is, though I dare not say it aloud."

"Why not?" *What harm is a word?*

"I am a humble Furii," Kora said. "I dare not tempt fate, not here, not now. Though you'd never know it, there is a storm brewing on near and far horizons." She paused, facing Aura and placing another soft hand on her shoulder. "You, dear, have one of these burdens to bear, should you accept my charge."

"What charge?" Aura asked.

"The Furii's charge."

The Furii? I couldn't. Aura shook her head, "I couldn't—"

"You could," Kora said firmly. "What left have you here? What family? Or *friends?*"

Aura shot her a heated look.

"I'm sorry," she said. "That was…unkind, given the circumstance."

"Bane," Aura whispered.

"Hmm?"

"The old name of this place—the god-fearing one. Let the gods hear, and fate even, for I shall be her temptress. BANE!" she shouted to the darkness.

"Dear me, quiet!" the Crow hushed.

"I feel as if I'm in a dream," said Aura, wiping her brow. "So real it is—and you…I cease to wake. I wish Marcus—"

"So convincing it is, no?" came the Crow. "This dream of ours? Then, why not wade a little further? It can be no worse than what came before."

"Aye, surely." She sniffed. *It can be no worse.* "We—we're through the looking glass now." *But, those words…where have I heard them?*

"It is early still," said Kora, "but you should know that the world you know will change—deepen, even, to put it lightly. A strange thing it is to describe the upending of one's world, but it is one you will inevitably come to know, should you walk the path of the Furii. But, that is just it, my dear—this burden you bear is no veil or shroud, no parlor trick or devilry. It is the labyrinth that lies beneath, seen only by the eyes of the divine."

"I don't understand," said Aura.

"You will, dear," Kora said. "You will."

VI

THE ONE-HUNDRED-TON GUN

Cyrus—Present

My Aura is quite like Ares, Cyrus thought as he eyed the statue of the goddess upon the Regal Mile. Her hands and face held a dark hue that lined the soft plump curves of the marble. The shroud was cast in iron, to Cyrus's eyes. *Terribly ugly,* he thought. *What sort of monster could cover up such beauty with something so hideous?* The Sage blew a kiss to his Furii patroness, but the Raven paid no more mind. *Besides,* he thought, *it looks nothing like Ares.*

"Do you know what they call this bridge, Raven?" Deimos asked.

"Come again?"

"The name—or, the nickname, rather?"

"No, I'm afraid I don't," said Cyrus cautiously.

"Agathe's Agony," the Sage replied.

The words alone were enough to raise the hairs on his neck. "Charming," he replied.

"Our spring goddess is gracious and kind. Agathe sows and grows, tirelessly, that the summer god may reap his bountiful harvest, and so on. But, just beyond is ol' Bore's Fortress, the seat of the Brynjars and the goddess of war herself, or so the Brynjars might have people believe. When those gates open, Agathe weeps, for what comes forth, comes for war."

"Hardly," the Raven said.

"Pardon?"

"Do you fear the Brynjars' barbarous hordes, Deimos?"

"I daresay I do, Cyrus. I daresay I do."

The ride was dull as the day before. Aside from a few hairy eyes from passersby, the two rode through the barbican in the late afternoon without issue. They were supping in the cramped quarters of the east wing of the citadel by nightfall. Like the last visit, Tytan Brynjar knocked at the steel door at half-past midnight, accompanied by a steely praetorian who, to Cyrus's eyes, looked more like a monk than a watchman. Deimos unlatched the lock and dragged the door across the stonework with a heave.

"*Woof,*" Deimos groaned, "heavy ol' bastard."

Lord Brynjar shouldered into it as he crossed the threshold, the steel screeching on the stone as it pressed Deimos out of the way. "Shite, watch it!"

"Is it done?" Tytan asked tersely.

Deimos smiled. "Aye, sir, it's settled."

"I want to hear you say it."

The Sage moved away from the door and back to a pile of jerked aurochs he'd fished from his luggage, popping a fat handful into his mouth. "'Hear it from Cyrus." He coughed, spitting and chewing as he spoke. "He put a…*ahem*—"

"Spit it out, man!" shouted Brynjar.

"Father, please," came a woman's voice behind him.

Gods in hell. A slender young woman followed the words into the room. *He brought his daughter?*

"We are all on the same side, surely," she said.

"Says you, stranger," Deimos said, mid-chew.

Shite.

"Pardon," she replied. "Father—"

"You would be careful not to speak to my kin so, Sage."

"How was I supposed to know?" He chewed on. "Been here a time or two and never seen you bring a damned woman—"

"Deimos," Cyrus hushed.

"Well, then, I s'pose I hope I shan't disappoint," she said.

A new voice came from beyond the doorway—another woman, to Cyrus's ears. This was a deeper, older voice—one that he recognized from the first syllable. *I know that voice*, he thought. *Tis the raven of my mind, cawing her delights—the mark of Ares, that is*. As the door squealed across the stone, Cyrus felt a smile. *No, not a raven…a Crow*.

"Is your mother going to walk through that door next, Brynjar?" asked the Sage.

"No, dear," the woman said, entering. "Just ol' Kora the Crow, at your service."

"Kora." Cyrus smiled.

"Salutations, Cyrus. Lovely to see you again." She outstretched a hand and rested it softly on Cyrus's shoulder.

"It's been far too long," he said.

"Just long enough, I'd say."

Cyrus nodded. "The pleasure is all mine, my lady. Did you travel—"

"Raven," Brynjar interrupted.

Fucking titles. "Aye." Cyrus nodded. "The Bishop's dead." He scraped the serpentine dagger harshly across the leather in unison with the Sage's juicy, noisy chewing. "What the hell is she doing here?" he asked, pointing the tip toward Brynjar's daughter.

"Never mind her." Brynjar waved. "Like a trusted heir."

"Your own daughter?" Deimos pointed.

"A son in the Forge is an honor for any father, but a risk, too, Master Sage. Eryn was asked to shoulder the mantle at home, and she continues to do so."

"I've seen it with my own eyes," Kora said.

Eryn smiled at the Crow.

Cyrus and Deimos both shook their heads. *Gods, Brynjar'll be the death of us, for sure.*

"Do you think it inappropriate, Master Raven?" Eryn asked. "I am just a woman, after all."

Cyrus rolled his eyes. "Your womanhood betrays you no more than your insults, Miss Brynjar. Let us be mature, shall we? You are a stranger amidst a delicate matter. I do not know you or of you, only that you have ears ready to hear and lips apt to speak of it."

Her hazel-green eyes were vexing, Cyrus admitted. Eryn's piercing gaze hung for a time before her retort. "Then, I understand your concern plainly, Furii, and seek to reassure you."

Her words were like butter scraping over warm toast, disarming him. *A succubus—I shan't be tempted.* "I am no Furii, madam. Perhaps your father might've shared more—"

"Cyrus the Raven is more than a Furii," she interrupted. "Forgive me. So gifted, I hear, with those six-guns and daggers and that engorged needle for a sword you carry there…." She pointed to the scabbarded estoc across Cyrus's hip.

Cyrus clenched his jaw, and Deimos let out a laugh.

"Mortal or Furii, it makes no difference who you are. I am Eryn Brynjar, Princess of Norsefyre and her people, too. My loyalty in this matter outshines yours like the sun does the stars."

"Then consider me reassured, Lady Brynjar." Cyrus nodded earnestly. *She has a point.*

"Such a Thornbird, you are, madam!" Deimos laughed. "I see a bright future for you yet."

"I am most concerned with the present," she replied. "Father? Father!"

A strange humor had taken over Tytan Brynjar. The lines of his face deepened, leering in boyish bemusement. *Murder his clergy opposition in cold blood, and he's a schoolboy about it.* A stranger occupied the boots of stoic Tytan Brynjar, hunched over like a wretch clutching a guinea. *Is he giggling?* Cyrus stopped his scraping and looked to Deimos, now laughing unapologetically.

"Dear me, Brynjar," he howled, "the Burden has its teeth in you like a Blackwood tick!" Deimos reached out, but Tytan swatted his hand away.

"Get that thing away from me!" he spat.

"Father, come now," Eryn gently said. "Remember yourself."

'The Furii's Burden comes for all,' Cyrus remembered. *But shite, no kings, I should think.*

The Brynjar's balled fist creaked under strain, the veins of his forehead thumping under the skin, fixing to burst. "*B-b-balance...,*" he choked through gritted teeth.

"Balance, father." The woman's soothing words seemed to cool the heat of his cheeks, returning his color. Bloodshot eyes began to whiten, as the veins sank back to calmer depths. She stroked the inside of his forearm with prickling fingertips. "And so, your balance remains."

Brynjar gulped air steadily, and the others politely sat in silence, such that he could compose himself. *Every man's dignity, I should think, if not a king's....*

"Bravo, gentlemen," Tytan croaked, recovering. "I'd heard word of a different sort."

"Oh?" Deimos swallowed. "Who from?"

"No matter." Tytan sighed. "Cyrus, you're sure the deed is done?"

"Sure as the brains that painted his carriage," Cyrus said, eyeing the blade in the firelight.

"Then, our time cometh, brothers and sisters."

"How many more times must we sully our mortal souls 'fore you tell us your masterstroke, Brynjar?"

Tytan shook his head. "No more clerics—we must ascend ourselves. Ah, so close!" he exclaimed, slapping Deimos on the back and rearing back to pat Cyrus.

I dare you. "We kill not a soul more 'til you tell us what it is you're planning," Cyrus said, eyes still fixed on the blade.

Tytan stopped pacing and faced the Raven in the corner.

"Let us remember, Master Raven, who pays *whom*. I've offered you a small fortune for your...discretion. All I require is—"

"I'll gladly slaughter thirteen *more* clerics should you wish, Ty, but words are lethal like the blade," Cyrus said.

"Speak to me that way again, sir, and I will find myself a new man for the job. And as for you," Tytan said, turning to Deimos, "I care not for your feats, old Furii. If you dishonor my daughter another time, I will unseam you from belly to brow." Brynjar's hand rested atop a kukri hilt sheathed on his waist.

Cyrus's eyes left the poniard and found the Brynjar's in the flickering lamplight. He said naught, only smirked and let out a patronizing chuckle as he labored again on the steel.

Deimos chuckled, too—an awkward, wide-eyed sort of chortle with a smidge of drool at each mouth corner, his own hand caressing a dagger. "I've been ready a long time, Brynjar. I've skinned men bigger than you...."

"So, this is it, then?" Eryn asked, rolling her eyes. "Are two great Furii lords to stick each other in a bout over my honor? And here? Don't be children."

I may have underestimated this Thornbird after all.

The Brynjar's eyes bounced to Eryn, and his shoulders loosened, his fingers uncoiling from their strained clutching. "Do you know much of this great city, gentlemen?"

Deimos took a sloppy sip of ale, washing the jerky down with a gulp. He followed with a garish belching crescendo.

Tytan winced.

"Norsefyre is not one city but four, in fact. Four ancient poleis: Goria, Finia, Fallia, and Muria—have you heard these names?"

The Sage shook his head.

"I suppose that should be encouraging. They are the forsaken names of the peoples that came before, which I have fought most of my life to erase. Their colonial names—their Patrian names—do them dishonor. I killed Gorians at the Blacktide and Murians in the Bloodmoat, for that is what they called themselves, loyal still to the knaves that abuse them. But to me, they were the sons of the house of Brynjar still, if only led astray."

Cyrus spat on his knife.

"For the Brynjar legacy lives today on the shoulders of one—"

The Raven dropped the blade noisily atop tools and enamelware. "If you wish to sing of the greatness of your house, I'd ask you save us the trouble, Brynjar."

"Peace, dear," said Kora. "Let us hear."

"Ah," Tytan sighed. "So, you know the story, don't you, Cyrus?"

"Must I tell your tale for you?" the Raven shot back.

"Bore Brynjar, the Conqueror," Tytan said, flatly. "You've heard of him, I take it—we're in Borea for gods' sake, so I assume so. But few know more about the man than that, I daresay. He was a mortal man, for instance, not a Furii. Isn't that peculiar?"

Cyrus swiped the knife hard.

"The redeemer of a dynasty—namesake to the country he founded, even, and all without the Blood Rite. Surely that's encouraging, eh, Cyrus?"

Cyrus said nothing. *Burn in hell.*

"Bore was more than a man. A thinker, he was, and a mathematician. The nights he didn't spend at war he spent in a library, learning the ways of war as best he could. The Bryndelwald was home to our kind then, surrounded by the warmongering clans of the Blackwood and the Seawall and the Wrath all at once, robbed of our ancestral home by patricians from half the world away. He was no better than a barbarian to the Patrian North, with a meager rabble of skirmishers, brutes, and criminals from across the wood. Out of the cold depths of winter, his army came. Three legions of fighting men answered the call, if not for their loyalties, tempted by the spoils of victory—"

"Loot and peasants' daughters?" asked Cyrus.

"Glory, Master Raven…what's more, retribution for centuries of Patrian cruelties. And so, Bore Brynjar marched his army of fifteen thousand strong to the outer gates, just beyond where Bore's mighty fortress now sits. He commanded no siege engines, no towers, nor catapults or even a battering ram. Instead, he commissioned a cannoneer—"

"Is a cannon not a type of siege engine?" Cyrus pointed out.

Tytan ignored him. "Nerva was his name," he said, "a young Antigonian with a penchant for metalwork. Cannons were primitive in Nerva's day, but his prodigy preceded him. He was an artist, rather, casting new makes, each more meticulous than the last as his black powder concoctions yielded explosive new heights—"

"Saltpeter," said the Sage.

"Come again?"

"Saltpeter," Deimos said. "It's the difference."

Tytan glared at him.

"It's what makes it gunpowder. Come now, Brynjar, you should know this. Your forebear was the alchemist."

"Yes, I do know. Thank you very much. I just didn't see it being pertinent. May I continue?"

"Of course," Deimos said, taking a swig. "Just tyin' up loose ends is all."

Tytan rolled his eyes. "As I was saying, word of the Antigonian's new design spread like wildfire across Tara, portending the largest cast-iron cannon the world had yet seen, and Bore found his chance. The 'One-hundred-ton Gun,' they called it. A single ball weighed thirty stone and could hit the broad side of a man at a mile."

"Not that there'd be much man left," Eryn replied.

"Bore moved the weapon by land—I can't imagine what it must've taken. I think of petty rolling logs and oxen trains, but the figures escape me. Did they travel in the heat of the day? How many rounds could they have brought with them? How many tubes? I watched scores of men try and fail to drag one measly cannon a few yards in the sand at Goria. Bore's legions labored nearly a hundred miles over the Tear of Ares—a feat like none other, I'm sure. And so, with Marius Nerva, his newfound Master o' Guns, and a horde of Waldermen behind him, Bore Brynjar stood beneath the loneliest part of the Patrian wall, looking to the sentries. Do you know what he said?"

"Give us your daughters and prettiest sons!" Cyrus aped.

Deimos howled.

Cyrus found Kora's mask shaking at him, but he smiled back. He couldn't see her eyes behind the mask, but he could feel their staring. He shrugged. "What?"

"He made his promises," said Brynjar, "generous as they were. He gave them a chance, offering peace to the legionnaires, homes to their families—he even conceded to honor the nobility of their patricians, requiring only their fealty in return."

"How noble," Deimos sniggered.

"And not unlike our dear Sage here, the Patrians laughed. They hooted and horned and bathed in their hubris. 'Let them siege,' they said, 'tis winter, and they'll break 'fore spring.' Bore was patient. The Patrians shouted their curses and insults from their high walls, but once quieted, he spoke his final piece. 'Be wary—if my army breaches these walls, we will raze your city to the ground,' Bore said."

"And how did the Patrians receive him, I wonder?" said Cyrus.

Tytan took a lingering step toward him. "'*If*,' they scoffed."

Brynjar hovered over him with a soundless stare. Cyrus raised his piercing blue gaze to meet the Furii. *Give me a reason*, he thought. *Give me a reason, and this knife will drink from your throat, damn you.*

"I think we all know what happened next," said Eryn.

"Remind me," said the Raven.

"His big bad gun blew a hole the size of Tara in the heart of the Furies," said the Crow.

"The bulwark took but one round. They say the Acolyte rode out to meet Bore on the field, only to perish at the hands of his stalwart bannermen."

Deimos shook his head. "Let his dogs do his fighting for him, did he?"

"By the look of it," Cyrus agreed.

"He burned the city, slaughtered her patricians and enslaved the legionnaires...not even the peasants' daughters were spared."

A stillness took the room. The others looked to Brynjar, but the Crow's gleaming mask stayed fixed on Cyrus, who nodded. *Yes, Kora, I'm listening.*

"And that moment, gentlemen, is the culminating event that guides this epoch. The moment that iron and steel brought crumbling down the stone walls of antiquity...the moment when kings could no longer hide behind lavish high castles or abuse the layman that works the fields for the scraps of what he sows. It opened the door for mercantile markets, science, and industry...the dawn of a new age led by one man's ambition."

"And to think, the Furii were a mere *trifle*," said Cyrus.

The Brynjar leaned down to the seated Cyrus, meeting his eyes in level intensity. "Aye, Cyrus"—he nodded—"truer words were never spoken."

"Were you trying to make a point just then?" Deimos asked dryly.

"Indeed, Master Furii, but more will follow in the coming days. A new offer."

"An offer?"

"I could call it an order," Brynjar said, "but I doubt you'll refuse...."

"He won't," said the Crow.

I can't, Cyrus thought, *however I may wish to.*

"Do you mean to 'shatter the walls of antiquity,' Brynjar?" asked Deimos.

"In a way, yes," said Brynjar, nodding. "I mean only to do what Bore Brynjar did—"

"Pick a fight?" Cyrus asked.

"Exactly," said Tytan.

Cyrus shook his head. "The Church has enough men to storm this castle without a rifle among them. A *true* horde, like those you describe. But, they aren't a horde, are they? They have more men than you have bullets, but they also have more *bullets*. You must be smarter than this."

"Careful, pleb," Brynjar spat.

"You kill these poor fools—or rather, you have *us* do it for you," Cyrus said, "that your power may be unquestioned, but so too it is unearned. How, then, do you defend the murder of your own countrymen? Have we not killed scores of the innocent on this errand?"

"Noble deaths to my kind."

"Is that a joke?" asked the Sage.

"Do you understand how sin works?" came Kora's soothing voice from the corner.

Tytan and Cyrus both paused.

"Not the way you think," hummed the Crow. "You see, it's not the act itself, as the Church might teach us. Your soul is not your own. In fact, it is something to be used—ammunition for your...well, your betters."

"Betters?" asked Deimos, raising an eyebrow.

"All these pious priests—so proud and wrong they are!" Kora laughed. "Like a mob of superstitious crones scraping fortunes into tea leaves."

"They know not what they do," said the Sage.

"And so they must die for it," spat Cyrus, gulping down some ale.

"You know not of the ruin they invite," Eryn declared.

"That is not an answer," he replied.

"'Tis," came Brynjar. "Tara teeters on a razor's edge. You think this about great kings, or gods, or power—gods, power! To think of what little there is for the small likes of us, yet we crave it so. Our clerics meddle in the darkness of the past, tempting fate all the while without a clue. We invite the ruin of the cosmos with every minute we put behind us."

"What are you getting at, Brynjar?"

"Peace, Cyrus," said Kora. "The Pontifex must live. You will secure him and bring him here. We shall do the rest."

"What's the 'rest'?"

"I need not explain myself to you, dear. And you," she said, turning to Brynjar, "you will reap your benefit—secure his seat south of the Tear of Ares for all the world to see. Swing the tide of the civil war in Antigonia, and bring about your new Brynjari Dynasty. The slow dismantling of the Patrian aristocracy will follow, gods willing. And besides…." Kora stood, motioning to the door and pulling it gracefully open. "A new orthodoxy altogether may be just the thing."

"A new what?!" shouted Deimos.

"What?" Eryn echoed.

Cyrus stood, too, making a point to yawn. "You'll start a new faith altogether, then? Is that it?"

"Silence, little bird. And to the rest of you—unseat the Pontifex from his Eryx, and there will be a paradigm shift in the order of power across Tara's lands. It will be a time of rebirth and reclamations—make no mistake, anything is possible. You will have your options, Brynjar."

VII

SYNERGY

Marcus—Past

I saw her then. I see her now, and again. The moonlight paints every curve—it dances in her hair, and her eyes all the more. They spoke to me the first time and forever after, they call on me still. She is my guide in all this, I see, a handler of sorts for my woes and my aches…and my heart. Her gentle white fingers reach out, as if to yank the beating thing from my barren chest—a gift I give willingly.

Take it, it's yours.

My lady sits with me from time to time, but she stands above. She walks and she dances and whispers her songs to the fabric of my mind, naked with her melody. We talk, and we read, and she loves me with her soul and her body both, and I feel unworthy, evermore.

I so wish to be worthy.

She meets me in the library at a quarter past midnight, our place of a few times before. My hands—clammy and rough—shake as they find hers.

I am greedy with my touches. She grips my hands tightly and moves them herself, passing over my want and concern as they glide the landscape of her figure.

She is like a spring blossom betwixt cold winter breeze. I worship with my fingertips and she caresses my lips before she lays a blessing upon them. She is my altar—my heart so faithfully kneels. I am a servant and a slave, where her heaven lives and my darkness fades away.

"I love you, Marcus," she softly whispers, her eyes ever twinkling in the moonlight.

No, not now, not here—these words are wasted. The library is perfect, as all places are—a place both old and new, where dreams breathe as the living do, and my love and I live here with the rest of space and time, as our worlds collide again and again.

I am hers, and she mine. Our oaths are shared in a language unknown to us. She speaks my name with soundless kisses and whispering touches, and so generous they are, caressing me in her kindred spirit, the missing half to my whole.

I made my promise as best I could.

Her eyes are like hazel windows to our suspended paradise, and the lonesome world feels far less alone, halted somehow on its spiraling descent.

Ours is reunion, not romance—a rejoining of the ancient and the divine. Her power over me commands the stars. I know now that I will be hers, in this life and onward, if only for this moment and my memory, and I'll be sure to remember all the more.

"Ours is a cosmic love," I say.

She smiles, slipping the straps of her dress past her shoulders. "I love you," she replies.

VIII

THE WAR ROOM

Reed

When Reed Mason heard "war room," he imagined a cold, hard place in the heart of a bunker. He thought of fine paintings and high walls, full of ironclad countrymen armed to the teeth, laboring over maps or a distant battlefield. This was not that sort of war room, not by a long shot. A bold carpet lined the floors, muddied by the inconsiderate boots of a twenty or so occupants. Reed looked to the flaps of his own cavaliers, dripping the same disrespect onto the Brynjar's fine floor. *Try not to get fired on your first day, Mum might've said.*

Incandescent iron lanterns mounted the stone and statuary, softly warming the shadows of the evening. Reed could barely keep his gaze from the three colossal mural paintings that lined their walls from corner to corner. Reed recognized the gods, but only in the one. Two more offered stranger gods—*of Progenitors and Precursors*, he recited, but without truly knowing.

"The Precursors," Eydian said.

"Pardon?" *Get out of my head.*

"Those murals there, strange, aren't they?" Eydian smirked. "They are the last of their kind—no other exists. The only living depictions of our progenitors."

"Their garb is strange," Reed admitted.

"Aye," said Eydian, "but so mysterious, they are. Only a few of their artifacts remain on the shores of Tara, if you can believe it."

"Lost?"

"That, or missing altogether. My father's sources tell me that the Precursors come from the Dark West continent—"

"The Prison?"

"Aye, the very same. My father's sources say they brought it on themselves—the darkness, I mean…swallowed them whole."

"Has no one ventured back?" The hairs on Reed's neck rose.

"And returned? None besides those in folktales, I daresay."

Reed Mason and Eydian Brynjar sat at the table with the others in the center of the room. An immense sandtable map stood in the corner, drawing Reed's eye from the murals. Made of more than parchment, too, the map fit into the carven side of a mighty oak with intricate details of mountains and rivers and cities that covered the surface of Tara from Fort Redoubtable and the Wrath all the way to Cape Corinth and Nine Foes. Stenciled etchings lined its dimensions, labeled and numbered and intersected beyond Reed's reckonings.

"Tis a wonder, truly," said Reed.

"Tis," Eydian agreed. "Crafted by the late Quintus Nerva, the Pious Cartographer."

"I—I've never heard of him," Reed admitted.

Eydian smiled wide. "The greatest mapmaker our realm has yet seen. Story goes that he murdered his wife, and as punishment, my grandfather cut out his tongue."

"Why not just execute him?"

"Quite the waste of talent, I should think…."

Reed smiled, glancing at the faces surrounding him. He recognized a few from the evenings prior, but as many strangers were seated between the few dozen spots at the table, with elbows and tankards thumping ceaselessly. His eyes danced from parchments to pewter to people, laboring over the topographic details of each—some big men, some small, and a woman, to Reed's surprise, but not Eryn Brynjar.

Disappointing. All were clad with arms and armaments, buckles and broaches, pistols and powder horns, but some much more concealed than others.

A particularly large man sat in the corner with his arms folded, puffing on a long pipe. He wore thick steel ringlets topped by bulging pauldrons—an antiquated armor with a medley of furs and plates positioned over muscle and bone. His arms were bare, coming from the shoulders like fresh hams in a butchery. *That's the biggest man I've yet seen,* he thought. He was near as tall as Reed just *sitting* there. Reed saw a horned helmet sitting on the stone floor next to him with one of the horns missing, and his mouth fell open. *Gods in Heaven.*

"You're…Einar Dagfinn…the—the Ram," he sputtered.

"The Hornskewer himself," another voice affirmed. The man snorted and looked away, taking another drag from his pipe. Reed found a shimmer in the corner of the room—a thin sword, to his eyes, unsheathed in a man's lap. *Quite strange,* he thought. The man wore all black, and Reed quickly recognized him from the feast the night before. *We were never introduced—another of Lord Brynjar's guard, most like.* The stranger's jacket looked odd in the lamplight—a black mess, almost torn or shredded, as pieces hung off in thick clumps and strands tattered all the way from the shoulders and nearing his knees. The simple light flickered over steel gauntlets and leggings that shone through the mess of hempen black draped over chest and thighs, and his boots came to sharp steel points at the toes.

Malice lives in that man, Reed felt. Plain from the garb and the gall—*an unsheathed sword in the presence of a lord? Shameful,* he thought, *even for a guardsman.* He wore a hat indoors, too—outrageous, even among commoners. *Even I know that.*

The stranger's black wide-brim hat hung low and covered the eyes, exposing only the chiseled, thin-bearded jawline. Pocked with a cheeky grin, the man's mouth dripped with malcontent. Reed's fingers tugged toward his hilt. A chill tickled Reed's neck and arms, and he clenched his jaw. Words poured from the man's mouth to a few of the others, and Reed's ears rejected them—*hated* them, and the man for it—like he might a barking dog in need of a muzzle. *I should quite like to muzzle that one.*

He spoke with an eloquence that most men—most *Furii*—didn't possess. His voice was like a low boil, with each word smoothly rumbling past his vocal chords. *The lasses must swoon over this one,* he thought. *What defense does a lady have against a charming Furii?*

"Let the new blood introduce themselves, that we may know their triumphs," said the stranger.

Reed scoffed. *Nothing but a hissing snake, to my ears.*

Eydian stood and delivered a deep bow, his dark gold coattails dragging on the stone floor. "Eydian Brynjar, son of Tytan," he said.

"No title?" the Ram heckled.

Eydian smiled, but not with his eyes.

"Nary a Furii survives the Forge without at least one, brother," Einar pressed.

Eydian's smile waned, and he cast a doubtful look. "Golden Sun," Eydian replied. A subdued mirth bounced from wall to wall and between them, and Eydian's nostrils flared as his cheeks turned red as radishes, striking through the harsh lamplight. He sat down.

"Pray tell, sir—why 'Golden Sun'?" asked Einar. "Your warm personality, perhaps?"

Eydian sat upright in his chair, motioning to speak, but the words remained stubbornly inside his mouth. He parted his lips just in time for another interruption from the Ram.

"And you, with the gaudy sword, wide as a dinner plate—pray, what is *your* title, that we may know *your* feats?"

Reed's blood began to boil. *Splendid—I've never killed a man this big before, nor one of my heroes, for that matter.* "Stonehands," he replied.

"*Stonehands?* They look quite like flesh to my eyes," said the Ram, nodding toward Reed's trembling fingers. The others snickered.

"Why not come closer, sir, that you may get a better look?"

With awe all around, a single voice rang through, "All balls but no brains, this one! He should do nicely."

That bastard in black.

"You offer me insult, boy?" the Ram asked Reed, slamming his cup on the table.

"Only in return for yours, sir."

A stillness took the chamber with Reed's last word. *I don't know that I could kill this man, if he is a man at all.* The legs of the Ram's chair squealed on the stone as he slid it from the table and lifted himself out of it. It creaked as he stood up, rising a full seven feet, by Reed's measures. *That is no man at all, but a mountain.* His leathery hands rested across a strand of belt webbing, a spot so menacingly close to his pistol that Reed's finger twitched at his own. The giant's brow furrowed, hanging low over his eyes.

Reed's fingernails cut into the palms of his hands, *craving* the leathery hilt of his messer. He saw the gun so near to Dagfinn's hand, but his insides writhed with instinct, jerking his uncontrollable nerves beneath the skin, as his mind looked for a solution. *How do I fell this tree?* The rage reddened his face and plucked at his urge to unleash it. *Do it*, he thought. *Draw, you coward. You're faster; you know you are.*

The Ram's hands flew into the air outstretched. Reed nearly jumped from his skin—his panicked hand jolting for the sword. The Ram's fur-draped shoulders loosened as the crow's feet on his face surged with a warm, hospitable smile. "Ha! Keep safe those balls, brother! And you, dear Princeling, I jest, nothing more. Please, take no insult. You're a young Furii yet—it's only tradition to prod."

The Ram drank deep and let out another uncharacteristic chortle. "Must've killed quite a few to earn a title like that, eh?"

Reed removed his hand from the leather grip and joined it with the other in his lap. "Just one."

"Your very first, if I remember," said Eydian.

"Eydian," he warned, the sharpness in his voice matching his gaze.

"My boy, tis nothin' to be 'shamed of," the Ram said, taking another monstrous swig of ale. "Every Furii remembers their first—most in the Forge, to be sure, but some not."

Reed did his best not to indulge, but couldn't resist. "Honor is a fickle thing, my lord."

A few drips of beer beaded down the Ram's silvery red beard. "I know all too well, Master Mason, about the nature of honor." He took a sip. "Killing is another matter. Honor is for the man right up until his blade finds the open air. But, unleash the beast…"—he leaned forward—"and suddenly, killing is all there is."

The room quieted as the Ram sat back into an aching chair.

"Do you remember your first kill, Einar Dagfinn?" Reed asked.

"Aye." The Ram smiled wryly.

"The first man?" asked Eydian.

"As opposed to what? The first dog?" the man in black chimed in.

The Ram shook his head. "Not so much a man, I daresay."

Eydian's mouth fell open. "You killed a woman?"

The Ram looked up sharply. "Gods in hell, of course not!"

Of course not.

"Not a woman—a boy…."

"How old?" Reed asked.

"No older than thirteen, I expect," the Ram said. "Perhaps younger…they never tell you how young they are—the old songs, I mean—they sing of warriors and heroes, but never boys."

Reed's ears and eyes piqued, fixed intently on Dagfinn's words and the lips that spoke them. "How did it happen?"

"A drummer," he said, "he must've been—"

"You killed a fuckin' drummer boy?" snorted the man in black.

"Aye, a fuckin' drummer boy. 'Twas an ambush," the Ram said. "The Peninsular War, all them years back—the boy picked up a bayonet and tried to stick me with it."

"Did you let him?" The stranger smirked.

"What?"

Is he having a go?

"Does the Ram not welcome a good sticking?"

He's—he's a madman. A few laughs came and went before quiet gripped the room. *There are a great many men a man might jest those words to, but certainly not this one.* Reed shot glances between the man in black and the Ram and back again. He couldn't find the stranger's eyes, but the Ram's gaze smoldered, nonetheless.

"Take heed, Cyrus," the Ram said with a curt grin. I've been a patient man for quite 'while, but speak like this again, and I shall drink to your bones 'fore sunrise."

So, Cyrus is his name. The man said nothing.

Another stranger spoke in his place—the man sitting beside him. *"Happy shall he evil be,"* quoth the other, *"that taketh and dasheth thy little ones against the stones, for Hades he shall surely find...."*

Is that Canon? Reed scratched his chin.

"From *The Decretum,*" the man affirmed, "Chapter XIII, verse IX."

Who is he, then? Reed thought, nudging Eydian, pointing. "Who is—"

"You come to defend him then, Sage? That is you, is it not, Deimos?"

Not much a sage, by the looks.

"Peace, brother," said Deimos. "I defend truth, only."

"I s'pose I should've sent the boy home to his mother, then?" asked the Ram, meeting with a few more laughs. "Is that it, Cyrus? Alas, not what ol' Dagfinn was there to do."

"Then, why?" Reed slipped.

All the room turned to face him. A score of strangers glared him down, and he blushed, plunging his gaze to his lap in silent surrender. *Now you've done it.*

"Why?" echoed the Ram. "Why not?"

Reed shook his head. *Tis not your place,* he thought, but the Ram reacted in the negative.

"You disapprove, youngblood?"

"I disapprove, for what it's worth," said the man in black.

"What?" The Ram swung around. "You dare speak to me—"

"LISTEN HERE, YOU OVER-SIZED, SILTED SWINE!" Cyrus shouted over him, finger needled toward Einar. "I've heard enough of your bragging gob, downplaying cruelties as if they were sport. Am I alone? Or do—"

"WHAT?!" roared the Ram, jilting his chair over as he stood. "OUTSIDE, YOU—"

"Why? That I may bend you over my mortal knee and spank the quim from you?"

Gods in fucking hell.

"To anyone here," sang Cyrus to the room, "shall we bend our knees to the Ram's merits? Tell me, Dagfinn, you giant cunt, could the boy even shave before you rent him limb from limb?"

"Cyrus," hushed Deimos.

Two others were standing too, holding Einar back from upending the table and wrapping his hulking hands around the Raven's lean neck. *The man wants to die,* Reed thought, but the red of Dagfinn's face dissipated more quickly than it came, and he ceased his struggling. "No, Master Raven," eased the Ram. "I'd give you naught, nor the time."

"No? Pity."

"Youngblood," said the Ram, pointing to Reed, "do you know what 'Furii' means in the old tongue?"

Silence.

The voice of the man in black rang out once more in the place of Dagfinn's. "It means 'demon.'"

"You see, young Furii," the Ram said, turning back to Reed. "The Forge is enough to make a man a god, but little they say of the man we leave behind. Men like him'll sing songs of you before the end—drink to your health and your might, even, but your accomplishments… they will be sins, and so it must be. The will you inherit from your Furian fathers is eternally ill. You will do far more evil unto others than good. We should not expect men like *him* to understand."

Reed nodded. "Agreed," he said.

"Hear, fucking, hear," chided the Raven.

The door burst open behind Reed, startling him upright.

"RISE FOR HIS LORDSHIP, TYTAN BRYNJAR, THE TORCHBEARER," shouted a guardsman.

Reed stood, clumsily.

The lord of Norsefyre entered hurriedly with an entourage of men at arms in tow. The Furii stood at rigid attention, as if the whole of the room forgot to breathe. Tytan's gliding steps echoed across the stone as he headed toward his place at the head of the long table. The heels of his boots clapped on the stonework as he moved, the pangs bouncing from wall to wall and through Reed's ears. With a final stride, Lord Brynjar shouted an order in a disciplined, military bark. "TAKE—SEATS."

A pall hung over Einar Dagfinn as his seat dragged and the war room's occupants noisily sat. *If only Brynjar had heard those words*, Reed thought, *might there be a duel after?* Tytan sat in silence for a time, leaning to one side of a polished chair, hand resting on his chin. An index finger rose to his temple, softly scratching.

"How does one beat the unbeatable?" asked Tytan.

Arses shifted in their cushions as silent onlookers sipped from goblets, but none spoke.

"Beg pardon?" Eydian replied.

Gods, Reed thought, hushing his friend with his eyes.

"I've summoned every Furii in this room with detailed and individual purpose—one and all," Tytan said, raising a vast hand across the table. "Here sits Iron Blake Bowman, with emissary...."

Two men at the end in dingy coats hammered the table proudly.

"There sits Faustus Fabrica," he said, "and my most loyal stewards of the Four Impregnable Cities. Here are the sons of Waller and Dunn clans of the Seawall—representatives from Nine Foes, the Laurentine Isles and the Tear of Ares, and my own son and kinblood fresh from the 'noblest of meat grinders' with the hero of the Blacktide himself!"

The table laughed and cheered and slammed their fists while a few of the overzealous upended their tankards. A lonesome eyebrow raised on the Ram's face as he mouthed, *Hero of the Blacktide?* in confusion. Reed smiled.

"And look," Brynjar continued, "here sits Deimos Helicon, the wisest ass I've ever met! And there, *there* is the sharpest shot in the whole of Tara, the Furii's Bane herself, the Swansong of Splintwater!"

More cheers came with a flush of Reed's cheeks. *Is that the Swansong just there?* he thought, sobered by the celebrity surrounding him. *I'm a nobody, standing atop the shoulders of giants.*

"AND YONDER SITS DAGFINN THE RAM, THE HORNSKEWER HIMSELF!"

The table nearly gave out under the pounding that followed the Ram's introduction.

The man in black is sorely outnumbered, thought Reed.

Tytan raised a hand, quieting the others. "Alas," he said softly, "amidst the talent housed here—the feats of these Furii, and at my table! My loyal knights, you give me such faith and hope. But, practice keeps the steel and the mind sharp, and first, we must practice before we can play."

"Play?" Eydian said, almost carelessly. His smooth and hairless face was all the more striking compared to the hardened men at the table. Furii Eydian may be, but he was far younger than most Furii, and Reed recoiled at the thought of his brashness.

"Yes, *play*," Lord Brynjar said, lifting his head from his hand and offering his son a stern stare. "The only game worth playing, in fact." Brynjar kicked out of his chair and stood, resting a hand on his hip.

A gentlemanly pose, Reed thought.

Lord Brynjar took a few steps toward the stained-glass window at the head of the war room. "It all starts with a question, my dear brothers and sisters, and the question I posit is: how does one beat the unbeatable?"

His words were met with more extraneous coughs and sips and squeaking seat cushions—a far cry from the uproar of the moments past. Reed's eyes bounced among the audience as tension grew in the air. Before he knew it, he was speaking. "Exploitation, and, um, adaptation?" He shook his head and mumbled under his breath. *Fucking schoolboy.*

Tytan Brynjar spun around. "Indeed, young Furii, but vague. Tell me, what do I mean by 'unbeatable'...or, rather, *whom?*"

Reed's mind raced with answers, but nothing came to him.

The man in black piped up, "The Patrian League, of course."

"Aye, the blasted Patrian League," the Ram spat at the Raven.

"Pray tell, how many winters have we bent the knee to the Patrian Peninsula? I doubt any soul in this room knows, though some of you are elder Furii, indeed."

"Four score, and four," grumbled the Ram. "Come now, Brynjar—the Sage and I were there—"

"Of course," he nodded, "my mistake, gentlemen. That number embarrasses me, as it should every patriot south of the Tear."

"You mean to go to war then? With the Church and the Empire and all that?" asked the Ram.

"Perhaps," Tytan replied.

Another man—Faustus Fabrica, by Brynjar's introduction—rang out, "Where would this war be fought, my lord?"

"Hold your tongue," Tytan said, halting him. "To Dagfinn and Faustus, and all the rest...do not misunderstand me. Though my courtesy is both gracious and bountiful, do not treat with it as weakness. I am Tytan Brynjar, Lord of Norsefyre and the Four Furies, and every man, woman, and Furii in this room swore an oath to my banner. This meeting is not a discussion, nor is it a forum for you to voice your dissent—*that*, brothers and sisters, is *disloyalty*. Show its face again, and I shall hang you in this very room."

The man waved his arms frantically. "Sir, I never meant to—"

"*Silence*, Faustus."

Faustus Fabrica dropped his hands and resigned himself further into his seat.

"The answer to my question," Tytan said, his voice returning to its normal octave, "is open-ended, surely, but I shan't skirt corners or dance around my objective. I mean to bring about the fall of the Patrian regime, and all of you will help me do it."

The room was quieter than the crypt, as most eyes narrowly moved from the floor. A room of lions was replaced by one of sheep. Tytan's gaze danced between them with the same power, as none other than the man in black opened his mouth again.

"Tis a tall order," said the man in black.

No 'sir'? And why did Brynjar not introduce him? Who is this Cyrus?

"Tis"—Tytan nodded—"but an opportunity has presented itself that will never come again. The time to strike has come."

"How do you mean, sir?" asked Eydian.

"Antigonia," said a woman's voice.

Reed's eyes found her—Swansong. Her bright red hair glowed behind an olive hood, like the flaming shades of Seawall coral, reminding Reed of home. *She was at the Blacktide*, he remembered, *the angel on my shoulders.* He regretted missing her then, wishing only to thank her or simply speak. *She was there*, he thought again. *She saw the Bloodmoat, same as me.*

Tytan nodded. "Aye, the civil war in Antigonia is just the beginning."

"How do you mean?" Eydian asked again.

"You're a peppy one, aren't you?" prodded the Raven.

"Pray tell, sir—who are you, and why offer me insult?" Eydian's brow took a sour turn, as did his father's. "And the Ram, for that matter?"

The man's messy black shoulders shrugged. "Me? Nobody— just a fly on the wall." He leaned forward with a wink, and Eydian rolled his eyes.

"A carrion crow, more like," spat the Ram.

Tytan simply responded, "In case this news has eluded you, Antigonia now stands in the thralls of open rebellion against Church and State. My sources say that word of revolution has spread as far the Heraclion Hill and the very heart of Patria herself."

"You've quelled many a rebellion, father. How is Antigonia any different?"

"Heresy and hedonism," offered one of the Wallers.

"Hear, hear," answered another.

"What about the Church, my lord?" asked Reed.

"*That*, brother, is the fuse to this powder keg."

"What's that s'posed to mean?" asked the Ram, gulping another half-tankard.

Tytan's eyes were glowing bright blue. "I mean, of course, the Pontifex."

"A weak sister, I hear," said the Raven.

"Aye, leaving our Holy Church in disrepair," came Faustus, "all orgies and opium."

The Sage leaned forward. "You—you mean to *kill* the Pontifex?!"

"*No*," Tytan said flatly.

"Then, to what end?" he asked. "'Tis not a matter of cutting the head from the snake—another will take his place—and what villainy! You'd be burned if—"

"If?" growled Tytan.

Reed felt a burning heat behind his eyes. He shot looks among the crowd but rarely wavered from the stoic Brynjar. The man wrenched his hand over chin and beard, facing the stained-glass, and Reed feared for his rage. *Remember yourself, sir.*

"As a godly man myself," Tytan continued, "I see how heaven's mandate has long abandoned this Pontifex. He is no more the vicar of gods than he is a Furii."

"But who shall replace him?" asked Faustus.

"They've kidnapped Pontiffs past, I grant you," said the Sage.

"It has…been arranged," Tytan said, ignoring him.

"It's never gone well, I daresay," smirked Deimos.

After another heaving gulp, the Ram pushed out his chair and let out a sigh. "Forgive me, sir, but what about the flying rock in this here glass house—the Acolyte and his Furian zealots, the Tattered Banner?"

"Why do they call them the Tattered Banner, anyway?" Eydian asked.

"Quiet, *boy*," Tytan spat. "Another arrangement, I daresay."

"The Tattered Banner is no mere rabble of fanatics and dogmatists," said the Sage, "for a Fist surely has fingers. The Acolyte himself is the eldest Cornicen—Elatreus is his name. They say he's the best swordsman living."

The Raven snorted.

"And what about his faithful lieutenants? Searix Uro-Genos—the Iron Bull is a full head taller than our dear Dagfinn here and wielding a claymore near as heavy."

"Oi," the Ram huffed. "It ain't about size. It's how you *use* it." He winked.

The Sage spoke through a smirk of his own, "Aye, and how about his cousin, Devorix Dumno-Genos? They call him the Apocalypse—how do you suppose he earned that moniker? Or old Horace Wijnberg with that axe of his?"

"I saw him," Faustus piped in, "in tournament. 'The Herald with a Halberd,' they called him. Could cut the wings from a butterfly whilst carrying a tune."

"As I live and breathe," said Cyrus, sipping a flask produced from under his coat.

The room returned to momentary stillness, where most eyes found only distant focus and more fingers found lonely chins as the candles burned low.

Amidst a few errant sips and coughs, Tytan spoke. "You're missing one, old friend," he croaked.

"Aye," said the Sage, "Hecate herself."

"That bitch is still alive?" Dagfinn groaned.

Tytan's eyes cut through the Ram's gaze. "Dear Einar—would you not know if she'd been slain?"

"Aye." He shrugged. "I suppose I'd be the first to know, as it should be *me* who rips the life from her...like I did the drummer, eh, Cyrus?"

The Raven said nothing.

"Pray tell, who is she?" Eydian garbled over ale.

The Ram's eyes rolled white, followed by a growling sigh. The Sage leaned in. "Come, young Furii," he said, "you've heard tales, haven't you? Isarna Iomara of the Blackwood?"

Eydian shook his head honestly.

The words shuddered Reed's insides. *I know all too well of the Blackwood and the witch that lurks there.* "Hecate is an old word, Lord Einar," he said. "It means 'necromancer.'"

"But that's not what they call her...."

Eydian shrugged.

"You know not of the Iron Witch?" growled the Ram.

The light in Eydian's eyes clicked. "The Iron Witch is still alive?!"

Why each Furii must have so many godforsaken titles, I'm sure I'll never know.

The Raven let out a laugh. "Careful, youngblood, she might turn you into a newt."

"Shall I turn *you* into smithereens, sir?" he shot back.

"What does one get when Searix Uro-Genos and Isarna Iomara fight on the same side?" asked the Sage.

"Gods," sighed the Ram.

"The Iron Bitch." He laughed.

"Enough," said Tytan, "this counsel has taken a turn—one confusing, I believe, to the spirit of our endeavors. You are *my* countrymen, and *my* sworn swords. In the simplest of terms, you are indebted to me, one and all, and you *will* execute this vision of mine with care, precision, and the utmost loyalty. Elsewise, I shall remove your sorry heads from their sorriest of shoulders. This is no discussion—tis an order, and many more nights like this are still to come."

Nods and *Rahs* pervaded the room, and Eydian's gentle voice pierced the dimness once more. "Noble father," he hummed, "what is the *sum* of that vision? What is our aim in all of this, that we may do your bidding?"

Tytan unfurled his fist and leaned back from his hunch. The crow's feet at the corners of his eyes deepened with the congenial and sensible demeanor from evenings prior. "Friends," he professed, lips curling, "Furii, and my most loyal countrymen...." He leaned in with the same glowing stare, a haunting white-blue overpowering the waning lamplight. "You shall cast down the fiend in white robes from his ivory tower. Bring me the Pontifex of the Ashen Eryx, and I shall bring you the whole of Tara."

The hairs of Reeds neck stood up.

"Who will go?" asked the Raven tersely.

The Brynjar turned. "A small team should do. Take no chances."

"Take some chances," Swansong replied, tersely.

"Hear, hear," the Raven agreed.

Is Swansong not a Furii?

"The Sage and I, surely," came the Ram. "I trust him, if not the pigfucker beside 'im...oh, and I dare not leave Borea without dear Swansong's curtain calls."

"Aye," Reed murmured.

"And how shall we get there?" asked the Raven.

"By sea, of course," answered one of the Wallers.

"Not if I've anything to say about it," the Ram replied.

"YOU IMBECILE!" roared Brynjar.

Muffled voices stumbled to stillness as the room found Tytan Brynjar, King of Norsefyre, clawing angrily at the corner of the table. Reed found the stumpy red of his fingertips painted in lines on the white linen, boring through to the wood, in some places.

"Forgive my outburst," he choked. "I...."

His face turned away from the rest of them, leaving only a creaking fist, swollen and red. A terrible shame gripped Reed then, snatching his gaze from the poor man, rending under the weight of his own Burden. The Burden comes for us all, he remembered, offering only his quietest condolences.

"The Furii's Burden falls especially hard on my shoulders...." The tension of Tytan's clawing hand hardened, steadying on the edge of the table. "Balance," he whispered through gritted teeth.

They sat in silence for a moment, one that each of the guests accepted—even the Raven, to Reed's surprise. A crunching came from Tytan's hand, chipping and cracking at the table's edge, and Eydian moved toward him.

He was a good son, bringing a hand to his father's shoulder in calm comfort. "Balance, father," Eydian said. "You are a balanced man."

The Sage continued over Eydian's whispers, "How will we get them to the Eryx?"

Reed shot a look but caught himself. *The Sage offers a kind of privacy, I should think.*

"The Wallerman says sea," came a new voice, "but he is mistaken, as the Brynjar said."

Reed's eye found the man—smaller, with a shining dome and a long beard, plunging to his lap.

"Could we not smuggle ourselves in?" asked Reed. "Surely the fastest and the safest route?"

"I am but an 'umble privateer," said the man. "Blake Bowman is my name, earnin' my keep in service of our lord, same as you all. But, I tell ye, it surely ain't the safest."

"How so?"

"I won't shy away from it, Master Mason," interjected the Ram. "There's but one weakness a Furii has—and only one, if he's good enough—and that weakness is the sea. We here are a noble caste, but we drown like dogs, and I daresay I fear a pool of water over a pool of blood, eh?"

Reed laughed.

"Aye, you look like a sinker!" laughed Bowman.

The Ram merely stared back.

"Ahem, beg pardon, sirs, but I speak o' the route, not the sea. The Clearwater Whip and Breezeblock mark the path—rough sailin' this time o' year. And the pirates—"

"And the imperial navy," said Cyrus.

"I do not fear pirates or Patrians," croaked Tytan, returning. "What I truly fear is betrayal."

The room quieted.

Tytan coughed again, tugging at his collar. "I am no fool," he said.

"Do you know how many types of shot there are, Master Brynjar?" asked Bowman.

"I do not, Mister Bowman," he choked through his hands. "Pray tell."

"The fleet has every kind o' gun the blacksmith can bless us with—thirty-six pounders, twenty-four pounders, eighteen-, twelve-, eight-, and six-pounders, all fightin' the good fight. We got long nines and carronades, swivel guns and smashers, even. We got round shot and grape shot and canister shot and chain shot and molten iron shell—"

"Do you have a point, Captain Bowman?"

"My point, sir, is not a single one o' them fuckers so named could do a lick to the likes of the Ashen Eryx. Tall walls jutting from the rocks, twenty feet thick—"

"You mean your molten rounds couldn't penetrate?" Eydian asked innocently.

"I mean, sir, that we'd be outranged from the start—fish in a barrel. You know your own keep, do you not?"

"Careful, sailor," came the Ram.

"I mean the guns, o' course. The guns atop these towers are new and lethal—'howitzers,' they call them. You might have some yourself here in Norsefyre. Rifled barrels, they have, and explosive shells. And the mines—"

"Enough, Bowman," Tytan said, extending a hand. "Enough. It appears I have deceived you, in the place of our beloved Pontifex. I mean for your fish to avoid that barrel. A snare we must set for this plan to succeed, and you will be the lure."

"Ah, like an ambush?" he asked earnestly.

"As you say, Mr. Bowman, they rely on their high walls and big coastal guns, but not on their navy. At least, they won't here. They'll muster only what comes from the wharf, and it won't be much for your vast arsenal, as you said yourself. Sink a few Patrian ships, and stir the pot."

"Aye," Bowman agreed cheerily, "I'm an honest sailor, always 'ave been, lookin' for honest work and a fair price for the lads. But, I think we can all agree, I was born to stir the ol' pot!"

The group laughed together, Brynjar included, and Reed felt the tension between his shoulders subside for a moment. He looked to Eydian and raised a brow sympathetically. He smiled and mirrored Reed with his own exaggerated astonishment, sipping an ale as he leaned back in the unrelenting creak of the old chair.

"Adorable," spat Cyrus.

What an insufferable swine, Reed thought, laughing all the same. *Here to ruin everyone's good time.*

"I know of coin and cutthroats," Tytan bellowed, "and I'm likely to trust you all more than you deserve as it is. But risk, brothers and sisters—risk will be our business, as risk will be our undoing. Risk of capture is a great deal higher on the wharf. Same for pirates combing the shipping lanes and the squalls of the Breeze Block. The Pontifex is only one kind of man, but his servants will be another. The Acolyte is another still."

"A thousand miles stands between us and them, and no closer by sea. We must march through the Tear of Ares," said the Sage.

The Raven turned to the man next to him. "To the bite and the bane, then? Do you hear yourself? That is no small errand."

"'Tis no errand at all," said Tytan, "but a pilgrimage."

"A pilgrimage?"

"Aye. Like those of so many who've come before—Boreans and

Antigonians and Patrians all alike—all make pilgrimage to the Ashen Cathedral to pay their dues, and we shall be among them, humble servants of the gods that we are. Furii and laymen—men, women, children—all are worthy in the eyes of the gods."

"Will that not dishonor them?" asked Eydian.

"Dishonor? Lad, it is the highest honor—one that transcends country and creed. We seek to depose a fraud and convert him. We do the gods' work!"

"Hear, hear!" shouted a few of the guests, slamming their fists on the table.

"That'll be the day," the Raven murmured.

"Pardon?"

"Nothing."

IX

THE PRISON WITHOUT WALLS

Marcus—Past

My eyes are heavy as lead. Their lids flutter and twitch, but fail to rise. The relentless cramps remind me that my arms are still attached—numb, useless vestiges distending from the chains above, like they are chains themselves. My good eye finds the strength, standing tall and letting the scarce light in. A haze of tears and blood cloud my sight, but I am alive, despite the jailor's relentless predations. A cruel buffoon he is, and one I'll gladly repay, once I have the strength. My knees sear with pain—I shift my weight, fruitlessly, as the cold and the emptiness set in, bloodless and painful, but absent depth. I breathe, but barely—my diaphragm falters under the full weight of my body and the ceaselessness of time.

This place is as vacuous as my comprehension of it. Green moss paints every stone, slimy and cold, where flora cling to a blighted but desperate existence. The moss chills my feet and legs with a cold and comforting softness. It tickles my nose with fragrant wildness, cutting between the putrid stinks of the ancient cell.

"I'm to die, then?" I say.

"Aye!" the jailor delights, "but not yet."

"Please, sir, I beg you."

He won't oblige. I hang my swinging head between tired shoulders and feel sleep rapping at my wakeful mind's door. I cough and wheeze as my breath gives out again. No need for an executioner, *I think.* I'll surely die here all on my own. *My ears find more of the room than my weakening eye, as noises bounce from her cracks and corners. Trickling dew dribbles down the walls and drips from the skylight, clopping in shallow pools. The air thickens, where sounds resound all the more, through the deeps and darks with fluid clarity. I hear far-off church bells and imagine home. They ring soft, like winter chimes, and I take small comfort.*

I hear a cawing above. A raven dances between the rusted grates of my modest window. There's a hole just large enough, and she slips through, flapping to a hopping halt in the sundrenched spotlight.

"There she is!" The jailor laughs, jingling his keys. "The carrion crow marks the dead, boy—tis the mark of Ares, that is."

My heart sinks at the words. The crows will devour me here, live or dead. I know it to be true, but as my ruined eye finds the scant black creature before me, I see no malice in her eyes. She cocks her head and squawks again, lending one hollow eye to the intimacy of my features. She hops and hops, exploring and cawing with flighty spirit and that avian sleekness I admire. She's a beauty, she is—elegant and ever graceful. She has a soul, *I think. I sit here, broken in both body and mind—at the end of my coil, no doubt. She is here to guide my spirit, I believe, to consume my remains and ferry me to the afterlife with the autumn goddess's blessing in hand.*

"Marcus," comes a familiar voice. The jailor unbolts the iron bars under a cacophony of clanking keys and screeching hinges. There's another man, taller and lean. He looks out of place here, where vibrant colors clash with the drab backdrop. I can't make out the face, and my neck fails to support my head for the moment.

"Who are you?" I ask.

"Acheron Pontius Petronax," the voice says, "and I am your father."

Relief. Tears pour out as I heave and hack through a smile, of all things. "Father," I plead, "thank you, by the gods, thank you."

"Easy," he says. "Be still, Marcus."

I find his eyes near to mine, but I feel shame in my fragility. His gaze is focused and strong, and I am afraid.

"Release me, father."

"I'm afraid I can't," he says, unwavering.

My heart sinks all the more. "Wh—What?" I cough and choke as my lungs labor over the word. I don't understand.

"I don't presume to know what words might suit this moment," he says, lifting a hand to my chin, "fruitless as words can be."

"Father, help me—"

"You won't understand here, Marcus, but one day, I believe you will."

"What—what don't I—"

"Your fate is written in the stars, my boy. A man you shall die, and a god you shall be reborn. Trust in this." He stands tall and backs away as a crowd of other consuls enter the room.

The blood pools in my face as it swells and tightens. A warm pain tickles my cheeks and chin. I wonder if I might finally be allowed to die. The sweat drips thick in my face and sears the gashes there. I know now that they have maimed me—irreparably so—and I succumb to the despair in my brittle heart. I pray for death over deliverance.

"Marcus Furius Petronax."

My broken ribs ache between metered breaths. A few fingers are broken, too, and perhaps my nose and maybe a wrist. The cold defeats me more than anything, and the shallow breath that emanates from my mouth spews forth as wet fog, and I shiver all the more. I see my bare chest and belly through the grit of my vision—stained black and blue with enough red to turn my stomach. The jailor sang of my guilt, and I am starting to believe him.

"In the presence of the gods, the honored living, and the glorious dead, you are charged with the rape of a vestal virgin. How do you plea?"

I cringe at the question. Robbed of my senses, I wheeze in place of a shout—screams in my mind turn to writhing coughs as they fall from my mouth on the consuls' deaf ears. "Guilty," I wish to say, if only to end it, I think—a swift execution that could liberate my soul from this broken body. Something mutes my speech.

"Marcus…how do you plea?" my father asks.

"BETRAYER AND BRUTE," I cry. "FIEND AND SCOUN-DREL," I call him. I gnash my teeth as rage boils my blood. "And to the rest of you," I hiss, "I am the heir of Clydae, a nobleman and son—"

"Order!" cried one consul over the others.

"Disloyal swine, I say!" I choke down another cough and heave another breath. I rattle my chains. "I've done nothing. I am not guilty, you corrupt ingrates—"

"ORDER, I SAY," my father roars.

A pall hangs in the air. Echoing drips dance and ring across the chamber like pattering fusillades on a distant battlefield. I feel their judgmental stares tickling my insides and prickling the hairs on the back of my neck. Contented, they are. They will ruin me, and my father is going to let them.

"In the presence of the gods, the honored living and the glorious dead, I invoke the rite of Patria Potestas," my father says.

Mutterings and whispers dart from their mouths to the rest of my cramped chamber as the other consuls murmur to one another. "Heretic," I hear, and "demon," too. I lift my gaze to meet his, but a glimpse is all I manage. Confusion plagues my exhaustion, disbelief and more building anger as the words sting with time. Only my father, *I think.* Hope *again—real hope, I have, that he might reverse this certain doom.*

"Father...."

"I am Acheron Pontius Petronax, son of Phobos Arrius and pater familias of all Petronax patricians, living and dead. I hereby sentence you, Marcus Furius Petronax, to wander the Prison Without Walls for the rest of your days—"

"Father, please—" I choke.

"You are hereby stripped of land and title, and are no longer a member of my household. You will die in the darkness worthy of your malcontent, as you are no longer a patrician, no longer an Illyrian, and no longer my son. May the gods have mercy on you. Go now, and die with what little honor you have left."

My insides burn. My mouth hangs open like that of a confused child, and I shut my eyes tight. Tis all I can bear. More words come, but I fail to hear them.

Knock, knock, knock.

No, not the gavel....My breath overtakes me, but despair curls its fingers around my throat, suppressing the words and the breath and the life that linger inside me. My weakening vision fades with the stars as the world shrinks through a keyhole. The muscles in my arms and back spasm and loosen, despite my fruitless attempts to tighten them. I'm desperate—my mind pleads with my body to hold itself up but a little longer, to persevere, but each attempt is met with convulsive resistance. The muffled murmurs of the other consuls sound miles away as the blood itches beneath my skin. A storm builds there, one of raw heat. The rage battles my body for control over my soul, and I embrace the chaos. The essence of my spirit lingers in the fray someplace, I think, an engine burning with the heat of my life, what little there is left.

I gnash my teeth like a wild dog and writhe through the roar that yearns to escape the bonds of my crippled lungs. My head finds strength atop my neck, and I look unto the pedestal—the site of my father's infamous rite—and I scold him with my eyes. I know he sees fury there—a window to the enmity that spills out in generous portions for the swine across the room. I am an animal now, far above man, one with fangs and claws and a thirst that must be quenched. Red stains my vision, my hatred for Acheron transcends space and time, and my heart fills with thick lifeblood to accompany the mounting hate. It pumps to a quickening heartbeat. I feel veins thumping under skin and fueling my rage all the more. My jaw tightens, and I fear that my teeth will crack under the pressure.

Something cools me. Consuls shuffle out of the chamber as my breathing calms. A noiseless tomb it becomes again, naked of human corruption, bathing in renewed sounds of a natural world. The drips return to my ears with a flourish, and the wind sings over the barred window. The color softens, where blinding white turns to warm orange and cool blue...the color I remember....These perfect colors.

Men approach with keys and buckets, unlatching my shackles. They *let my battered body fall limply to the ground, and so do I. My face slams down on freezing stone, but the damp relief of thick moss pillows the fall. My good eye stays closed, resting with my cheek in cold solace. I resign myself to the darkness that is soon to be mine. The raven caws in the distance, but I offer no reply. She caws again, this time in my mind—it's a voice. She comes to me in this abyssal place, with words like honey that dance past shapeless lips. "Cry when it's over, darling," she says to me, "but it's not over...."*

I feel a smile tug at my swollen cheeks. The cuts of my face sear in contortion, but the life inside shines through. I think of her, of Aura. I feel her fingers between mine. I taste her lips and the tongue beyond. Her eyes are the focal point of my imagination, the backdrop to my wakeful dreaming. "Aura," I say, "Aura." Aura...she is mine, after all, my moonlight, and I need her now, and forever.

"For Aura," I say, "forever...."

X

AURA'S ANTHEM

Aura—Present

"I know he is innocent, father! Listen to me, please—"
"I'll hear no more of it, damn ye! What lunacy to think you a daughter of mine!"

"Father, please! Mother—"
"You're to go away, darling," she says, tears running the length of her face.

"Where?"
"To the priory, child," my mother chokes back.

"To the priory, to the brothel, to the bloody street! I care not where," my father roars, "but only when, and when is certainly at once."

"To hell with you then."

A year removed from the Forge, and Aura was a working Furii—with a riding partner, even. Elya Dair was her name, and she was a whore. *Or, a prostitute, rather?* Aura wasn't quite sure which was more polite. She'd done her best to get used to the idea. Aura meant no disrespect, for Elya had grown into a fond friend, but her roots in the brothel persisted through the Forge and well into her Furii career, much to Aura's surprise. *An admittedly strange fact to square, no? Why keep up? To what end?* But Aura minded not to judge as she might have before all the unpleasantness of recent winters. *A whore saved me from a certain death, and I…well, I shan't tempt the gods. Freeing somehow,* Elya always used to say, and in the year of Aura's short Furii patronage, Elya's old ways brought astonishing results to their modest business. *For Furii are in the business of killing, and killing's what we do best.*

For Aura Westfall and Elya Dair, business was booming. Aura felt a bit a whore herself, if only in association, unceremoniously *whoring* themselves to the Heraclian aristocracy, if not in the 'services rendered' sense. *Tis the fashion of the day,* Aura might protest, *that wealthy noblemen should rightly pay attractive young Furii ladies to guard them during their fulsome social endeavors*—a quest very much unlike that of a traditional Furii. Alas, Aura found no tradition in her—of any kind, let alone that of the Furii. *I do not bow,* she thought. *That is my only stipulation.*

She found her newest mark agreeable, to say the least. Rufus Pompey was his name—a self-made man swimming among the old monies of the renowned aristocracy of the Heraclion Hill. *A pleb like me,* Aura thought, quite unlike the classical Patrician families that dominated the Patrian Peninsula's swaggering social circles. He had a broad chest and was quite fit for a mortal man, with a thickness to him that spelled strength and warmth beyond his middling peers.

This was the sixth outing with Rufus, by Aura's count, and she was comfortable in calling it a date. Her role as bodyguard felt absurd given the state of things. She rode in his stagecoach, sat at his table, and slept in his bed from time to time—*not that I was made to,* she always told herself. He was a kind man, and clever, with all the propriety a young gentleman of his standing ought to possess, however forced it felt to the unrefined pleb that she knew he carried with him. Like Aura, Rufus played his hand quite on the defense for the better part of his adult life. He was at a disadvantage, after all—younger than his peers, and foreign, hailing from pauper parentage from some Seawall clan down south.

New money was an unsettling prospect for the monarchists and the old-fashioned, and Aura reveled in the thought. *Beat those tophs at their own game,* she'd say. *Let their world burn with ours.* But, despite their wretchedness and smarmy swindles, Rufus's cup runneth over still. This was a new world, after all, one of industry and opportunity, with rich good earth ripe for the taking, and Rufus took far more than he gave in that respect.

This night, Aura and Elya rode like queens through the city streets, bouncing their way to the symphony atop quite possibly the most expensive coach in all of Tara. Elya's date was Brandon Senn, one of the unexceptional chaff to Rufus's wheat, and the man's inseparable confidant. He was a taller fellow, and portlier by a mile, but Elya never bothered about looks. His quick wit and hearty laugh did all but melt the heart of the fun-loving Elya Dair. *I wonder if he knows?* Aura mused as the stagecoach bumped its way to a halt. The driver announced their arrival. The door swung open, and a golden man wearing a white powdered wig bowed deeply.

"My lords and ladies," he said, "welcome to the Heraclion Royal Theater. May I—"

"Now, now, my good man, does this look like our first visit?" Brandon said.

"I beg pardon, my lord, right this way."

The men disembarked first, turning about with arms outstretched, as to guide the gentle hands of their lavish ladies. Aura felt Rufus's hungry eyes bounce along her topography, laboring from the top of her head to the tips of her toes the way a dog might do a roast, his hand steadily guiding hers down the gilded carriage steps. She caught Elya's eye, winking. *Let them gawk, I say.*

"My dear," he said, twirling her hand over her head, "it would seem that I have yet to fawn over you, as you so ceaselessly deserve. You are…a marvel."

Aura blushed and offered a smile. "I might say the same, sir."

"If I didn't know better, I'd kiss you here and now, in front of everyone," he said.

"You'd just as soon catch Mercy in your mouth!" Elya enthused, laughing as she clinked a finger on the curved sword hanging from Aura's hip.

"Elya!" Aura laughed, pinching her.

"Darling, why do you wear such a harsh vultus in a place like this?" Elya teased, smearing the paint under Aura's eyes. "Tis a symphony, not the bloody Blacktide."

"Good heavens, you'll be the death of me, woman," Brandon said, shushing her.

"Ha! My good man knows better than to stifle my passion," said Elya. "Besides, my Aura's vultus is as much a part of her as the very shape of her nose, or the *perfection* of her eyes…like…bright enough to match the moonlight itself."

Aura winced at the word. *Marcus haunts me, even here.* "Please, sir," she said, swatting Elya's hand away from her painted face. "It—it matches my dress."

"To be sure," he said, "and all the more striking." He offered a sympathetic arm, and Aura took it with vigor.

The four marched the carpeted trail to the glistening archway, following a crowd full of sequins and corsets and powdered wigs as far as the eye could see. Aura found Rufus's look welcoming among them. He wore no such wig this night or any other, no matter his wealth. *Thank the gods.* His neat, dark hair was gathered in a tidy tail that bounced on his shoulders and bound in a sleek navy ribbon matching Aura's dress.

Aura did her best to guard her fondness, but Rufus loosened more than a few scales in her hide. She saw through the parties, the refinement, and the spectacle of it all to find the enduring darkness looming, which she feared may ruin them. Alas, a savage soul stayed hidden behind the gentle façade of blue bell sleeves and layered trim that quite complemented her curves under the decorative brocade wrapped over her shoulders.

She wore a dress fit for a queen. *My own mother never wore a dress such as this.* But it was all hers, courtesy of a man she barely knew.

Perhaps I should see the world as Elya does, and view Rufus as pet more than partner. The shame had come a time or two. *The man pays for a service,* she'd say, *showers one with gifts and gold. He expects nothing in return, does he?*

But Aura was tired of it, all of it, for her real partner died all those years ago, and she missed him like yesterday. She sought not to bury or ignore, but Aura felt something for this new man more than any other since. Aura's fingers prickled in his. His aroma greeted her in a living way, breathing a heartbeat she'd recognized in Marcus. *Marcus....*

"Darling?" Rufus said.

"Hmm?"

"Darling, I asked if you should wish to sit in the usual box, or perhaps with the Denicen gentlemen, remember?"

"Oh, dear Mr. Pompey, surely you don't mean it?" Elya interjected.

"Beg pardon?"

"Those cretins? Bumptious hounds, in search of a *bone*," she said, winking at Aura.

"My dear lady, I shall have to give you a spanking, should you keep misbehaving," Brandon said.

"My lord, I merely speak the truth. Please don't punish me so. I'll be a *good* girl, just for you."

Brandon Senn took a finger to his collar and yanked sympathetically, letting out a muted laugh. "My, my, what am I to do with you...?"

"I agree with this wretched lady—how could we sit with them darling? They'd be *awfully* jealous," Aura said in her most convincing impression of Elya.

"Ah, of course," he said, "where are my manners?"

"Surely," she said, squeezing his arm tighter.

The group moved through the atrium amongst a thickening crowd of more lavish patriciate. Aura found it stifling. *Ornate livery, jewels, and dress that could sink a galleon should enough of these tophs come aboard.* There wasn't a man or woman in all the place without rouge-caked cheeks and a thick coat of powder staining their faces like their wigs, Elya included. Elya Dair would confide in Aura from time to time, describing her haughty makeup as her true *vultus*, still. *A form of camouflage—hiding in plain sight. She is the Viper, indeed.* But Aura's *vultus* was borne of thick ebony ash, striped across her veiled eyes. *The lion shan't hide, lest the sheep forget their betters.*

Once through the vestibule, the theater opened to an entrancing dome ceiling with unmatched ornamentation—a sight to behold, lined with ogival arches trimmed in delicate acanthus leaves, volutes, and garnished rosettes of equal mastery. The stage stood atop a line of identical fluted columns, each glowing an eerie white among the lamps that littered the arena. The dome itself was painted in the Heraclion style—segmented frescoes, picturing the four gods and their armies of children, heroes of old, grappling with the titans of Tartarus and the devil himself, all entrenched in everlasting battle. Aura gazed up for a while as she had each time. She saw Ariston—the gallows god and patron of the summer harvest—with the iconic three spears jutting from his back as he clashed with the great bearded Antigonus and his hulking hammer, his mighty Wolves of Winter in tow. *There's Lady Agathe*, she noticed, the spring goddess of motherhood and fertility portrayed riding a clam and looking sultry as ever. *Where is Ares?*

"Careful my dear," Rufus cautioned. "You'll strain your fair neck."

She snapped from her trance. "You mind yours, and I'll mind mine, sir."

"Of course." He laughed. "Perhaps you could mind mine, as well?"

"I s'pose it is my job." Aura smiled. Her fingers reached out to find his, forgetting herself. "Public, right," she blushed.

"No," he said. Rufus's eyes seemed full, glistening. He caught one of Aura's hands before she could take it back. He curled his fingers tightly under hers, refusing her soft tugs to free it. "Shall we?"

Aura's smile widened. She felt warmth flood her cheeks and she relented to his soothing touch. "Let's."

Brandon Senn beckoned from up the way, motioning at a footman inspecting his tickets. The man turned for the stairs as Brandon waved to the rest. Aura and Rufus followed, but slowly, guided by perhaps the oldest usher in living memory—an ancient fellow leading them to their seats no brisker than a tortoise, and perhaps a particularly *slow* tortoise at that. Aura was convinced he'd gotten lost, motioning to Pompey's pocket watch from time to time. *Time?* she mouthed. At last, the poor old man arrived at their box and offered a humble bow despite his wheezing huff.

Elya put a hand on his shoulder. "Thank you *kindly,* sir," she said, steadying him as he shakily stood.

Pompey and Senn held their chairs as the ladies plumped their dresses and sat. Rufus took his place beside Aura, reaching for the small wooden cupboard and producing a monocular and offering it to her.

"No, thank you," she said. "I…I'd prefer to close my eyes."

"Of course," he said.

"Is that strange?"

"Gods, no, my lady—I might try the same." He stuffed the piece back in the drawer.

Aura reached for his hand resting in a warm lap. "Do you see a program? What symphony is this?"

"I believe it's called *Seasons,*" Brandon piped in, "from some Southern fellow, I daresay."

"Indeed, *some fellow* who also happens to be the marvel of our time—Faustus Fabrica—and he's Borean."

"Oh, big difference that," he said, "traitors all the same, if you ask me."

"Traitor? The man's a composer, for gods' sake!"

"Yes, a composer from a cesspool country that can't stop eating itself. I've quite lost my appetite," Brandon said, shaking his head.

"My apologies, ladies. Politics is where my friend and I don't quite see eye to eye," Rufus said, nodding to Aura, "but not a subject worthy of such loveliness this fine evening."

Aura snorted. "We shan't speak of politics for our sake? Our tender ears can't be disturbed with such trifles?"

"I meant nothing of the sort, only—"

Aura cut him off, "Do you forget, sir, that we here are Furii, *daughters of the autumn goddess*, and—"

"*And* we've killed people," Elya interjected, waving her feathered fan in a flurry.

"Yes, indeed, so whatever politics you think so above us, you can be sure—"

"Wait, have you?" asked Rufus.

"Have I what?"

"Have you—have you…you know…," Rufus said, bouncing his finger but choking on the words, "*killed* people?"

Aura felt a terrible guilt all of a sudden. She'd been careful not to tread so casually to this point, forgetting how the laymen respond to such things. "I—well, I mean—"

"Of course she has. She's a Furii, isn't she, love?"

Shout it, Elya, why don't you?

Rufus looked away, letting out a nervous chuckle as he did. Brandon cackled, as if in on the joke somehow, despite the harsh truth in it. Aura's cheeks burned bright red. She wanted to offer some conciliation, but there was none to be had. She had killed, scores even, and not just since her ascension as a damnable daughter of Ares. Elya and Brandon laughed on, pinching each other playfully as Aura and Rufus sat with gentle smirks, hiding what lay beneath.

"Does that—does it bother you, sir?" she asked, a trill in her voice.

"No, I…." He paused before stammering, "I—you ladies look so wonderful—*the fairer sex*, as they say, but so wrong they are…."

Aura looked away, but he put a hand to her chin and brought her back. "I must say," he continued, "'tis all new to me, every bit of it. I don't know much about the Furii, but perhaps I ought to. I've gone and put my miserable little life in your hands, after all."

She squeezed his hand and brought her eyes to his. "Anything you wish to know, I will tell you. You have my word," she said, "but know that my life—and the life of every Furii—is a wretched affair. No fondness to those memories, I assure you."

"I mean no impertinence, madam. I just—"

The strings of the orchestra interrupted him with a deep and resonating swell, reverberating across the hall and plucking gently at the heart strings of every patron in the place—and Aura's doubly so. The room darkened as an army of valets shaded candles across the theater in a swift coordinated attack, where the barrage of claps welled from a delighted audience. The note itself surged through Aura like the gentlest of lightning strikes, fluttering her nerves and removing what little breath was left in her chest. Her eyes welled when she looked to Rufus, finding his suspended, glistening, and she closed hers in comfort. And so, the music took her—her hand, contently in his.

I hear a theme amidst the notes, she thought. *So plain it is—spring. It's here for all to hear....The birds sing of Agathe's return as the breeze caresses her murmuring streams. Thunder crashes; roars, even—and the rain shatters as it pours—each, heralds to their beloved lady. They darken the heavens and deafen the rest, but so soon comes the silence of the blossom, and the chirping want of the new life, aching to breathe....*

Then came a soft key tone, breaking Aura from her trance. A sad song that seeped in, somehow, beyond the blood and the bone. *Is this my song?* she wondered. The minor key starkened her allegro—a dour aria from the loneliest violin, pointing its haunting gaze to the moonlit night of Aura's past, so safe in her clutches. *The Crow comes to me,* she thought, finding the same gloved hand.

Another movement, she heard. *A hard season begins beneath the fiery summer sun. Ripping scythes tear across the fields as the heat of Ariston beats down. So too come the winds of the North, sweeping all to her tattered side, as the heavens roar with the rain and the hail....And with the violent crescendo comes that song—my song—so loud and true and darker still, as the summer battle thickens....*

She opened her eyes, gazing upon the man whose music won her heart—this 'Borean Sensation.' His slender arms swung wildly as the baton flicked in delicate time. The sweat of his brow shone from the gallery's distance—*his very own vultus*, she thought. The man's eyes were glued shut, and a look of pain contorted the lines of his boyish face. He flailed and danced—unnaturally, and out of tempo—save for the unyielding count of his baton, never wavering from the notes. *The rhythm lives in his very heart.* Tears ran down her face, and she let them, closing her eyes in time for the music to blanket her in another warm embrace. She squeezed Rufus's hand.

The pleasures of bountiful harvest pluck at the strings, firing the drink of a well-earned autumn. But Ares emerges with her hunters in tow, and the guns and the dogs horn the beast from his lair. The murmuring streams do not murmur at all, for the blood of this world is drying. When the beast finally dies, after fleeing its last, the revelry returns to the melancholy tones of my anthem....

Aura trembled. *I know what comes after autumn*, she thought, wading through the winter of her mind. *Antigonus's icy breath cuts through to the bone. I tread the icy path, fearing the ground beneath me as I do the hardness of this place, so peaceably dead. Deeper than the depths of horrid winter, I descend, reclaimed by the old dark that came before. "Marcus?" I call, but feel no answer. A final sonata, bathing in shadows and resplendent moonlight, as I walk the lonely path to Marcus's door. The moon and her stars welcome me*, she thought, *as I will welcome him, evermore....*

But the myth of hope stung painfully true as the last of the notes plucked the softest version of Aura's lonely lullaby, twinkling like the fresh snowfall, both beautiful and cold. *Marcus is gone*, she woefully remembered. *Do not chase his memory.*

Faustus Fabrica faced the audience on the verge of collapse, bowing deeply at the patrons and slicking his dampened curls back as he modestly raised himself, nodding his delights. He turned about, poising his baton high—suspended in complete, finger-biting tranquility. He looked out to the crowd, gliding his gaze across the flickering scopes and spectacles and the shadowy faces. His eyes found Aura's, she swore it. *He knows this song is for me.* His gentle hand dropped like the guillotine—*with the cutting swell of every string*—and tears poured past her futile objections.

The walls rattled under rapturous applause. *Is it over?* The symphony was ended sooner than it had begun, much to Aura's disappointment. Rufus smiled at Aura as he rose, offering a hand, and they followed the sea of patricians flooding into the corridors, herding back toward the entrance. Elya and Brandon's chortling overtook the conversations around them—their incessant inuendo causing her stomach to turn. *I'm suffocating.*

Brandon shouted to a man—*a colleague, maybe? From the banks?* Aura noticed the slur in his voice as he pulled his prize Elya with him. A drunkard's pantomime seemed to be Brandon's introduction, motioning at Elya with a shaky sausage for a finger. *Gods, what an oaf.* The stranger feigned a few jovial shadow punches to Brandon's abdomen as he mimed an overreaction. They laughed heartily. *Far too hard, the cunts.* Aura rolled her eyes. *Two prize hogs, but no apples to gag them.*

Rufus crinkled his brow, catching the attention of Aura's rolling eyes. "Would you walk with me?"

"Yes," she said eagerly. *Anywhere but here.*

Rufus pardoned his way to Brandon, tugging at the elbow of his jacket. With a few words and a pointed finger, they made their escape. Aura was soon breathing in the cool night air, holding Rufus's arm under hers. The wind tickled her skin, rustling the trees and flickering the lamplight of the netherfield path as the Royal Gardens routed to Uptown—Pompey's posh neighborhood district. The trees darkened under the lonely torches that glowed into the distance. Radiant moon dripped through the branches in rays of ethereal white. *I hear her lovely tune, her music, of the moon....*

They turned for another gravel path leading to the park, and Rufus squeezed her hand. "I—I wish to know," he said.

"Know what?"

"All of it," he said. "No lies—no omissions for my gentle sake—the truth of you is all that I desire."

Your words cut, sir. She nodded. "I suppose I promised, didn't I?"

"Thank you, Aura—may I call you that?"

"Naturally," she said, grinning. "'Tis my name, after all."

"Yes, 'Aura' it is. 'Miss Westfall' was becoming quite tiresome."

We've slept together for gods' sake, but my name is a bridge too far? Aura frowned at that. "Agreed," she said, "but you must make a promise, too, sir."

"Anything," he said.

"There are things you will not understand, should you explore them. I cannot deny it—what Elya said—"

"What Elya said is exactly the truth I seek," he interrupted. "I do not fear what I might find."

"Dear me," she laughed, "careful what you wish for."

The cobbles tore at Aura's heel, and she slipped. "Oops," she laughed, caught by Rufus's firm hand. She blushed, but the smile waned as her eyes caught the archway of a small stone bridge up the way, overlooking a moonlit pond rippling black and white, and she remembered herself. Her giggles died as the darkness laughed back. *Sink, damn you.*

"Careful." He smiled. "Shall we start with where you come from, perhaps? Clydae, no?"

"Aye, indeed I do," she replied thoughtlessly. *Jitters.* "Did I tell you already?"

"I thought so," he said, "but then it could be your accent—I'd know it from a mile. How do you find it?"

"Find what?"

"Aura." Again, he smiled, lifting a finger to her chin. "I am here—speak with me, not the shadows...."

"I...*aye*." She nodded. "Forgive my foolishness—"

"I won't hear of it," he interrupted. "Who were your parents? Why did you leave?"

The words didn't come to her as she wished they would. *I think so little of them,* she admitted, *so weak and mortal.* "My parents were… servants," she said, "to the House of Petronax. My father the head butler, and mother, the Lady Lucretia's lady-in-waiting." Each word seemed a needle for Aura to cough up. *I owe little loyalty to their feeble old blood.*

"You don't say?"

"Does that surprise you?"

"In fact, it does," he said. "You're every bit the look and sound of the gentry."

"Aye," she agreed, nodding cheekily, "but then, I played with their children—parroted them from across the room. My father was so close to Lord Petronax, the man offered to pay for my brother's schooling—a Patrician education…at least, before that was no longer an option."

"Why not?" he asked.

"I…well, that's just it, isn't it? The beginning of the end, I should say. The *hard part*…."

"Please, take your time, my dear. I'm here only to listen. You'll hear no judgment from me, I swear it."

"Is this to be my soliloquy?" she joked. "My songbird voice to sing sonnets like laments?"

"This is to be anything you need it to be," he said firmly.

Aura smiled. "I know you mean well, sir, but this is for your sake far more than for mine."

"For my sake, then," Rufus said, irreverently.

"What do you know of the Prison Without Walls?" she asked.

A harsh gust suddenly swept across the pond, shattering the moon's glowing rays on the glassy surface. *Ares hears me, does she?*

Rufus shrugged. "*Far to the west, through storm and squall*—that sort of thing, ye mean?"

"*The Prison calls to one and all,*" she rhymed along. "*Sirens of mind, so oft left behind, and fear, ye mighty, thy fall.*"

"Top marks. You know the rest?"

"Nay." She smiled, shaking her head.

"Why do you mention the Prison, then?"

"Have you known anyone to be banished there?"

"That would be quite a severe crime," he said.

"Funny, you didn't say *no*...."

"Didn't I?" He smirked.

She glared for a moment. "Apostacy."

"Come again?" he said.

His eyebrows look like wriggly caterpillars dancing around on his face—absurd and adorable. "The usual fare," she said, "the books say apostacy—refutation of the faith, and so on...that's the punishment."

"Are..."—he paused—"are apostates not sinners like the rest?"

"Who cares?" she replied. "I speak of someone who sinned not at all, or far beneath his charge, anyway."

"A boy, then," he said.

He has a name. Aura's jaw tightened. "Aye. You see, in good ol' Patria," she said, motioning to the woods around, "the father's hold their bullocks atop high pedestals, wielding their power of pater familias over their sons and daughters and grandsons and grand-daughters like a plague—"

"I understand, madam—"

"Yes, I'm sure you do," she said, halting him with a hand. "Northern families know the wrath of their fathers. But these sins I speak of, they were committed by man, and those debts ought still be repaid...."

"Aura, my dear," he hushed, resting his palms on her shoulders. "Be with me and loosen your grip. Tell me what happened, that I might help in repaying those debts."

A crooked smile took her face. *Those are the right words, I admit.* "Aye." She laughed. "I was intemperate in my youth—I won't deny it...as I have been with you, I might remind."

"I shan't judge," he said. "I am a bastard, after all."

She winced at the word's harshness. *I forget sometimes,* she thought, *that he is still lower born than I.* Aura felt the wind rush through the trees again, loosening the strain of her jaw and wrist. "I'm sorry," she said, laying one hand gently over the buttons of his waistcoat, comfortable in the privacy of the dim glow of lampposts and the creeping dark. "I promised truth, and I mean to give it to you."

"Yes, my dear, please *give it to me,*" he said.

He's gambling, she thought, but Aura laughed, nonetheless. "You are by far the *worst* gentleman I've ever seen."

"No, I won't stand for it," he said, swinging her around by the waist. "Surely, Brandon Senn is far worse."

"Oh, indeed, I nearly forgot," she admitted, "a walking waste of skin, that one."

"Aura, he's a friend, for pity's sake!"

"I'm sorry, dear, but I won't abide it, earnestly. He's a fool and a drunk, and I'd have his blubbery pelt over our mantlepiece if we were to be together—"

"Be together?" he interrupted.

Shite. "I...I was just—"

"No," he said, "whatever kind of backstepping jig you appear to be doing, let it stop. Tell me of the boy back in Clydae and the Prison Without Walls. Then we will discuss *us.*"

What am I to do with you? "What, then, do you know of the Petronaxes?"

"Ancestral seat of Clydae—'Acheron the Altar Boy,' right?"

Aura slapped a hand over his mouth. "*Shh...*where do you think you are?!"

"What?"

"I may not know much, but at least I know you can't call Acheron Pontius Petronax 'the Altar Boy' in these parts and keep your tongue in the process," she whispered.

"Once, that may have been true," he agreed with a nod, "but the influence of the Petronax name dwindles like their accounts."

"Come again?"

He smiled. "I'm a banker, madam. I may not know much, but I know money—the kind of money these people have, and where it changes hands. The Patrian League is far from the iron triangle it still supposes itself to be, and there are few Petronaxes, Denicens, and Blackwoods left to keep safe the mantle."

"Aye," she said, "that, I won't deny."

"The boy was a Petronax, then?" he asked.

"Aye," she said again, nodding. "Marcus was his name."

The wind shot through the clearing and across the pond, whipping Aura's wrap from her shoulders and howling with the ghosts and the wolves. *Ah*, she thought, *so you are here, oh Ares....*

"What was he like?" Rufus asked.

The question surprised her. "Hmm? Oh, I need not—"

"You must," he said. "As if I don't know that you loved him? I may look a fool in these fancy clothes, but once, I was one of you. I know of unrequited love and the old crones that seek to stifle it."

"I suppose I did," she admitted. "He was to be a Furii like his father—headed to the Forge at the end of summer."

"Ah, I see," he said. "A young summer romance—"

"No," she said flatly. "A crime—an unforgivable crime—well, it ruined any chance of that...."

"Gods above," said Rufus. "What crime?"

"Rape."

Rufus said nothing.

"It wasn't me, if it's that you're worried about—"

"*No.*" His tone turned raw and strong. "Do not think me one of them, Aura." The first words came out in a muted shout, but he shored them back to a gentleman's refrain. "What I may lack in sentiment, I do not lack in sympathy. I know what I was asking for back there. Please, let me in, and fear not that I will leave."

"His name was Marcus," she repeated after a while. "He was the one with suspicions, but no one came to hear them. He was unaccounted for at the time of the attack."

"But, he was—"

"With me." Her eyes found the pond and didn't drift. "A witness came forward—none other than the Disgraced Acolyte himself, Horace Wijnberg. He said—falsely, mind you—that he eyed Marcus following the girl into the drawing room."

"The old Acolyte? He was relieved—"

"For being a drunk," Aura said. "The vicar of the gods on earth, fired for fancying the drink….That was much later, though. They took the Fist of the Church at his word that day, to Marcus's detriment."

"What, then?"

"I heard his speech and saw him oft on his stay at Clydae. There was another I saw cavorting with Josey that night…."

"Josey?" he asked.

"The girl—thirteen or so," she said coldly. "Aye, the old Acolyte—full-cocked on the wine after a feast saw a man walk through those doors all those years ago, but it was Elatreus, the eldest Cornicen, who followed her."

"Do you have proof?" he asked.

"No," said Aura.

But the memories remain. I see it now in the ripples of this pond, like I heard it in the notes of Fabrica's melody and felt it in the crack of a bedpost over the first skull I'd come to crush. I saw the boyish hue of Elatreus's jaw as he kissed Josefka in the shadows, but I saw it, I did. I watched him grip her with rough hands, hers surrendered overhead. They couldn't know, but I saw them. I thought not of Josey, my friend, but only of Marcus, and how I wished to be under strong hands like his, relenting to his kisses in the open like I did in secret.

"And it doesn't matter now," she said. "Marcus was stripped of whatever lands and titles and sent to the Prison, most assured to die there. No one returns from the dark continent…and Elatreus Fabius Cornicen was named the new Acolyte. *Full circle*, I suppose."

"What of this Josey? What did she have to say?"

"We didn't speak before our parting," Aura said. "Robbed of the chance."

"What of her now? Where is she?"

"Dead, I'm afraid," Aura sighed. "She ran from her priory to become a Furii, same as I did mine. We spoke of it once in the servant's hall. I envied her courage—she knew she'd run and fight, and her parents knew it, too, I think. A strong Furii she would've made."

"How then?" asked Rufus.

"The Forge took her," she said, "like it does so many others. Before it all, I thought I'd stay in service. I saw nobility in the work of my parents. I thought of the Furii only in grandeur, too scared to forsake the life before me. But, the walls of my life crashed down, and I yearned so deeply for escape that I was willing to kill to do so."

Rufus said nothing.

"I have killed, sir—and the first came before the blood of the gods ever touched my veins. With the Forge and the Furii I sought answers—ol' Josey waiting for me on the other side, ready for the road and revenge…but once the Forge spat me out, I saw the depths of my loneliness all too well. Whatever survived of ten years gone is now a smoking ruin, as I inevitably hold the match."

"What happened to Marcus, then?"

"I wish they'd have hanged him," she said, smearing her vultus. "No, they moved for the harsher punishment—"

"Banished to the Prison, I remember."

She nodded. "Well, sir—if you know your common law like you know your Patrian houses, you'll know too that the Prison Without Walls is reserved only for high crimes against the Church."

"Like apostacy," he said.

"*Like apostacy.* Josey was already damned to the life of a vestal virgin in the eyes of the Faith, even if she never donned the veil."

"You knew the truth," he insisted. "Why didn't you testify?"

Her lip curled. "When a father invokes Patria Potestas, there is no trial...but I did tell someone—my parents."

"Did they believe you?"

"Oh, they believed all right. I was shipped off to a convent, too...to live out my days as a celibate in Antigonia. Thankfully, I never made it that far....So, you see, fate took my wills and broke them just the same."

"Do you regret anything?" he asked.

"Yes, I suppose." She nodded. "I cut Marcus's life short, didn't I?"

"You?! I mean no impertinence," Rufus said, "but if Marcus is innocent, surely, so are you—"

"No," Aura said. "Marcus's sentence was a tragedy, but I am far from innocent."

"Well, I've met Eli Cornicen—"

"Careful," she said firmly.

"I only mean that it's quite hard to believe him capable of such knavery—without implicating Marcus, surely. I only mean I've met the man—a charming fellow, or so I thought."

"He was, I admit," Aura said, returning her gaze to the pond. "And formerly a close friend, if you'd believe it...to both Marcus and me."

"Do you think it was him?"

"Yes." *They wore the same colors that night*, she remembered, *that royal blue that matched his eyes.* "I've made peace with the idea that, whether he raped that girl or covered for the one who did, he—that *fucking* man, a betrayer and a scoundrel—is the architect of all my woes. After all of it, I won't ever be the same. I'll never come back....I'll never forgive nor forget, and one day, whenever fate decides, I will ride for the Eryx with every bullet and blade this side of the Tear, and I will sup at the Acolyte's' hearth, sitting in an ivory throne made of his bones...."

"Shite." He smiled.

The pleb lives in him still. "His insides will be his outsides before that day is done," she said. "Mark...my...words."

He snickered like a schoolboy, raising a hand to cover his mouth. "My dear! I quite enjoy this vengeful side."

"Careful, sir," she said, "do not find yourself in its way."

XI

WHERE...

Marcus—Past

Where am I? Cold—colder than before, and darker...so dark—crippling. A true emptiness, one that hangs in the air and lingers long between the crashing tides of life. I'm breathing it in. It sticks to my insides like abyssal resin, clouding me in the shadows of my surroundings. Who...who? What? What am—

"You are home," whispers the darkness.

"No," I say back, "not here."

"Welcome," it murmurs. "Welcome home."

The breaths I take sting my lungs as the cold pervades. I feel it crystalize in my deepest recesses as it does in the corners of my eyes. It yanks at my skin and cracks the frosted hairs of brow and body. I cringe and weep and agonize, and I breathe it in all the more. It freezes my heart and encases my soul in stone. A smile streaks across my face through the sea of pain. I contort and struggle here, at the bottom of the sunless sea, where darkness lurks and nothing else—

"Not nothing," the voice rings out.

I see naught, but I feel—a pointing arrow, guiding me through the abyss. "I beg you, spirit," I cry out, "what is to become of me?"

My gut warms, and the arrow tugs harder. Something—far off and faint, but something. A flicker dancing in the distance, a lonesome light twinkling alone in the black, beckoning.

"Reach out," it says. "Take it."
"What—what is it?" I choke.

"The cosmos."

XII

SEASONS

Aura

"Might we walk?" asked Aura. *"I couldn't care for a carriage on an evening like this."*

"Of course, madam," said Rufus, bowing. "'Tis a long walk, though."

"Perfect," she replied. "Perfect in warm company, I should say."

"Indeed." He smiled.

What Rufus failed to say was just how tall the Heraclion Hill could be. The walk proved to be steeper than it was long. *Poor Rufus Pompey,* she sighed. *I can hear how hard his heart is beating.* The moon disappeared behind a blanket of silvery wisp, shadowing the buildings from her cold rays. Lamplight dotted the incline, glowing in the mist that crept across the cobbles and cracks. The sleepy city streets were shuttered, leaving Aura's worries behind her as she walked the lonely hill with her beau, arm in arm.

Their conversation waned as the hill took Rufus's breath away. She laughed at him a bit. *What a wind bag!* The dampness came through his shirt. *Leave the poor man be,* she thought. *A man should surely sweat for what he sows.* His company was a far cry from Elya Dair's, for which she would always afford him great credit. *Elya could be dining with a prince and chasing chickens in the same afternoon.* Rufus was still modest to her eyes. *It takes a brave one to hike the Hill with a Furii.*

Aura's eye wandered out across the crowded hillsides. They were close to his estate, with full view of the seven glittering steeples dotting the Heraclion Hill. The seven smaller hills clustered on top of one another, each with a sharp glowing spear rising through the mist from their cathedrals below. *The gods' needlework*, Rufus used to say.

"Dear me, how much farther?" He panted.

"You look tired, my dear. Shall I carry you?" Aura winked.

"Oh, sod off, madam!" He laughed. "My poor lungs...*woof.*"

Aura smiled wide. *How unusually coy.* "We're nearly there," she said, pointing. *At least the man still can sweat—he must think me a corpse.* "I...I just wanted to say, sir, that I had a splendid evening...."

"Likewise," he huffed.

"Please, darling, don't strain yourself. I've—you see, I've never spoken of this...to anyone. I'll have you know that I...well, I find you to be a fine man—"

"A fine man?"

Shite. "I, well—"

"Aura," he said, stopping short and catching a breath. He whipped a handkerchief from his breast pocket and dabbed at his glistening forehead. "I've known many women in my time—"

"*Many*, you say?"

"Please," he said, gripping her hands in his. "I've never met one like you, I swear it."

Aura didn't think she could blush again this evening, but here it was. "I should say the same...."

"I wish to tell you—perhaps you already know, but I'll say it nonetheless—you deserve every happiness and every comfort, all those that you've been robbed of...."

"Rufus," she chided.

"No, Aura, listen—I...I love you."

"Rufus, please—"

"I don't expect you to say it back, madam, but I won't hide my feelings from you—*you....*" His eyes met hers in earnest. "You...the loveliest of creatures—a mystery to me, but one that I so—*so* desperately yearn to know…to *truly* know."

Aura gulped hard. "I…," she began, but the words froze in her throat, lost.

"In any case," he said, "I hope I haven't ruined—"

She kissed him deeply, her cheeks sliding slimily over his. *A vultus is to be shared.* The black of the paint stained his cheeks, and the salt tickled Aura's tongue. *If there's a heaven, it is here, and mine alone.* She loved him—*I do*—even if saying the words was too much for her fragile pride. She pulled away after a while, a strand of dribble bridging their lips in apt absurdity. He was quite obviously embarrassed—a *salty sea dog* after the steep leagues they put behind them. Aura chuckled, laying another kiss, gentler this time, brushing just under his lower lip as her eyes cozied into his.

"I…it's not easy with me," she whispered, "and I don't want to waste words. All I know is that I will be back tomorrow, should you have me."

His warm, wide, toothy grin twinkled with the stars. "I'll hold you to it."

She squeezed his hands. "We're nearly there," she said, letting go only to wipe a stray tear from the corner of her eye. "Let's get you home, you sweaty ape."

"Ugh, look at me," he said, shaking his head.

"Oh, sir, make no mistake, I find it…*undeniable.*" She dragged her face across his moist cheeks, painting them black in the process.

"Ugh!" he groaned, rearing.

"See?" Aura smirked, clawing at her cheeks. "*Fear no darkness.*"

He smiled back. "*Fear no darkness.*"

With a few blocks, they arrived. The brass lion knockers gleamed in lamplight, reminding Aura of his station. *I forget sometimes—is it wealth I want?* A few stray words and another kiss, and Aura found herself alone in the night, marching back down the way to the shabby room she shared with Elya above one of countless vagrant saloons in the old town. *He'd surely disapprove*, she knew, but perhaps that was part of the allure—a steady reminder of her true place in Tara. The place was good for food and drink at all hours, and the price of sleep was far lesser to Aura's kind. *And yet, I still get mistaken for a working girl.*

Elya didn't mind a bit. *Brothels are safer than barracks*, she'd say. Aura spotted more than a few customers tailing Elya's skirt into their room and others, much to Aura's dismay. She'd since asked Elya not to bring them to their shared room—her only stipulation.

Aura and Elya needed minimal sleep compared to their mortal peers, another Furian gift. The sleeping city was a comfort through the wakeful nights. She went weeks without so much as a wink, finding her solace in a book or the simple stillness of the street. Rufus hated to sleep while Aura was awake, insisting he needed "less than most." She smiled at the thought of his droopy eyes, dutifully open, but aching to close.

It's better this way, Aura thought. She'd left the evening as it was—the words said and unsaid. *I should've stayed the night.* But then, tonight meant more that she hadn't slept with him. *It means more to me, at least.*

She wanted to tell him—*the truth*—that she *did* love him and that she was happy, that she felt like a living, breathing soul again, not some Furian animal or locomotive. There was a stabbing, aching vulnerability to it all. She'd never said those words to anyone else, and a subtle sigh of regret escaped her. *It's time I uncage the scorpions of my mind....*

But...no—no, I can't. His blue eyes bore into her thoughts— *Marcus*, she mouthed. A plunging sadness returned. *He's gone.* The thought stung for the thousandth time.

For a decade, Aura walked Tara's good earth in solitude and loneliness, reaching out for a hand that would never reach back. *A mirage*, she thought, *a façade*—or merely the dishonest pedestal that overbears the real, but it was clear in her mind, plain as day. The only thing preventing her from telling Rufus how she felt was the thought of Marcus's big blue eyes looking back at her...the very moonlight guiding her home. *I—I cannot part with his memory...not yet.*

Aura could hear the creaky swinging doors from a block above the Boarding House Anaconda, and her sigh grew deeper. It was nearing dawn, but the street outside the saloon was still heavily trafficked. Men and women stumbled together, soaking in their beer blankets from days gone, blotched by browning broken teeth, grizzled hair, and shaggy beards with patchwork petticoats and tricorne hats that'd seen far too many winters. *The stink of this place rivals a week-old battlefield...like a marinating latrine on a hot summer day.* The stew blighted the once-clean air, singeing the nostrils and turning her stomach. Aura held out her arm, pressing firmly into swaying shoulders and pushing past the crowd. *Leave the sheep to their pastures.* She found the doors, thankfully, this time without having to knock a few teeth loose.

Inside was no better. The soggy wooden floor stuck to her boots, suffused with layers and years of drink and derelictions. She walked past the bar and met the eyes of Saul, the barkeep. *Sweetest man I ever met.* She offered a wink over the commotion. He smiled back. *He looks tired*, she thought. He shrugged wiping a mug clean and swatted at the frothy tap.

You want one? he said with his eyes.

Not this time, hers replied.

Aura side-stepped toward the card tables, taking her normal detour to the stairs, keeping her distance from the far end of the bar. *The hound's holding pen*, Elya called it, reserved for the freshest concubines and the richest drunks, and the last stop before the opium den in the basement. *Those apes are always looking to touch and taste—and I'm in no mood for violence.* Aura found the back entrance to the stairwell that skirted the outside of the building, away from the balcony and the noise and the hookers, a not-so-quiet reprieve.

Aura slid the wrap from her shoulders and let out a longer, deeper sigh as she trudged up the shoddy stairs. She found the brass key that had been poking her all evening through her waistcoat and slid it into the door marked '3,' turning the knob and putting her weight into the door as it ground open on creaky floorboards. *Tonight is full of surprises,* she thought upon finding Elya peeking over a tattered book and a wine glass.

"Elya? Didn't expect you to be home this evening," she said.

"'Ello, love!" Elya exclaimed, slurring a bit.

"Are you drunk, dear?" Aura asked, walking toward the meager wooden table in the corner and draping the wrap on top as she unbuckled Mercy from her hip.

"Heavens no, darling"—*hiccup*—"although the night is young."

"It's nearly sunup. What happened with—"

"Say," she interrupted, "I found this here book on your nightstand. You don't mind, do you?"

Aura squinted. *First Impressions.* "Oh…no, please—I've read it a hundred times. You—"

"What?" she asked, her lips a deep purple.

"I just—I don't know that I've ever seen you read for pleasure." *The words didn't sound so harsh in my head.*

"Darling, I am capable of broadening my humble horizons," she said, giggling. "Besides, it's *quite* good—such a romantic you are."

"Ha, indeed." Aura chuckled, lifting a foot to one of the wooden chairs and unlacing her knee-highs. "What of your evening? Where is Brandon—"

"I could ask you the same, love. I expected you to be wrapping those gams 'round Rufus shoulders uptown as we speak."

Aura blushed a bit. "Elya, please…," she said. "As if I haven't fucked him already." She let out a laugh.

"Thatta girl." Elya slammed the book down and poured herself another glass. "My young apprentice may soon be the master."

"I shan't be taking customers, if that's what you mean."

"Nay, darling, I'm far too selfish.…My methods are for me and mine." Elya winked. "But, no shame in it, darling, surely—*all* of it, the love making, the *fucking*, or some fun place in between."

"Elya—wait, what about Brandon? Where did you go after the symphony?" Aura threw her boots in the corner and began working at her waistcoat. Elya merely shook her head and waved a hand in deliberate nonchalance, reaching for the book once more.

"Elya…," Aura said, "what about Brandon?" Her heart sank. *No, it couldn't be.…* She noticed something just under Elya's eye—a stain of some kind. *Red.…* Aura lunged at her, gripping her jaw with one hand, eyeing the unmistakable bloodstain strewn across her cheek. "ELYA, WHAT THE HELL DID YOU DO?!"

"Ahem," she murmured through pursed lips, holding up an envelope. The wax seal was broken.

"What tha' *fuck* is that?" Aura snatched it.

"A letter," Elya said, rubbing her fingers across the bloodstain, "from—from the Tattered Banner."

"*What?*" Aura's eyes darted over the parchment but couldn't make sense of it—the signature was from the Acolyte himself. *A bounty. A fucking kill order from the fucking Church? No…no, no, no.* The target was Brandon Senn. *Why? Why him?*

"He's an arms dealer," Elya answered presciently.

"But—"

"Selling weapons and powder by the payload to the Antigonian militias. Seems the Church found out.…"

Aura's eyes began to fill. "Pompey," she said flatly. "What about *Pompey?*"

"I couldn't say," Elya said, eyeing her fingernails. "There was only the one. Didn't say anything about Rufus. Aura, I wanted to—"

"You did it without me?" Aura's voice trilled.

"Darling, I didn't want to risk you giving it away—you understand. Rufus loves you, most ardently…and I believe you feel the same."

Aura's head spun as she threw the paper down. "I…you—"

"It's done," Elya said, picking up a nail file and sawing away.

"Elya, it'll be a witch hunt. They'll be after us. WE NEED TO RUN."

"Pipe down," she hushed. "They won't find him for days, I promise you."

"But, what if—"

"We'll leave at first light, if it pleases you," she said, "but I shan't be rushed."

"Where?" Aura asked in a huff. "*Where* will we go? Are we to be *fucking* outlaws now? You've *ruined*—"

"AURA," she said sternly. "We have instructions. We make for the Eryx. We've been summoned."

Aura shook her head and balled her fists, every knuckle in her hand cracking as she squeezed, nails digging deep into flesh as the rage came over her. She swallowed it back down. *Remember yourself, damn you.*

"You *fucking* fool," she whispered.

Elya's eyes found hers. "Excuse me?"

"We owe the Church nothing, and you just signed us to them as slaves. You do realize that, don't you? You've done their fucking bidding, and now—"

"What should I have done, Aura?! We were *summoned*. The Acolyte's name signs the bottom of that paper there—the Fist of the fuckin' Church! What was I to fucking do?"

"I don't know," Aura spat. "Anything! Spoken to me—or we could run, or—"

"Run?!" she said, slamming the file on the table. "Gods be damned! How long could we keep that up? Every hunter north of the Tear would chase that bounty—every single one. What power do we have over them? The Banner answers to the Pontifex himself! 'Tis a battle we would lose, Aura, even if you're too blind to see it."

"*RAH!*" roared Aura, turning to kick the chair. It slammed against the wall and shattered. Elya didn't move. Aura's breathing was heavy and deep, huffing through her nose as she tried to loosen the grip in her hands. *I—I can't.* She turned back to Elya, her glowing green eyes piercing Aura's with an unapologetic honesty. *That insufferable bloodstain still paints her cheek. This is why they call her the fucking Viper,* Aura thought.

"I...I don't know the answer," Aura said, unfurling the strain in her fingers. "But I do know that I will never bend the knee to those fiends in white robes."

"I know," Elya whispered. "I'm—I'm sorry....I should have told you. Before we met, I was alone for quite some time, and trust does not come easily to me...but I think you'll come to see that this was our only option."

"I...." Aura sighed. "I hate surprises."

"Aye!" Elya laughed. "What about Rufus?"

"What *about* Rufus...?"

"I know that you don't share my view on things—and I know, too, that you dislike my way with men, but you see, it's easier that way, isn't it?"

"How?"

Elya looked out the window, the first rays of dawn streaking across her cheek with its insufferable stain, but dazzling in her cat-like eyes. "As the city sleeps, so must he...but you—you must linger. Your beau will rot and wither with the seasons—"

"Yes, I'm aware—"

"But, you rot, too, dear. The slow burn that steals you from yourself—a self shattered, much like that chair, there," Elya pointed.

"Are we to die alone, then?" Aura asked. "Should we just accept our fate?"

The Viper stood from the sofa and moved toward Aura, her hands outstretched to find hers as their eyes did the same. "Aura," she whispered, "you swore the oldest oath. The blood of the old gods courses through your veins—in a sense, you're already dead."

"A—*Ahem*...a lonely life indeed."

"No need for gloom, dear—there's hope yet. Forget about love and tragedy. There's more to this …so much more…."

"How so?"

"Darling, I had a feeling you'd recognize the name on that page—"

"The Acolyte," she said, her hazel eyes blazing in the moonlight.

"Last I checked, it's still this Elatreus fellow, and methinks you have a bone to pick."

Aura dropped her gaze. *This is…too much.* "I—how could we? *Could* we?"

"We'll have some time to plan, love, but yes…my gift to you, my dear…." Elya slid her palms from Aura's and folded them together, raising them to her chin.

"A gift," Aura echoed.

"I suppose more opportunity—a choice I had to make for the both of us. I couldn't risk your refusal."

Aura shook her head. "What choice?"

"The best choice there is!" Elya chuckled, raising one hand. "Here lies happiness—*true* happiness—the layman who loves you more than you could ever hope for or deserve—not a soldier, nor a king, only a rich man whose cup runneth over, much like his heart…."

Aura's lip curled.

"But here," Elya said, raising her other hand. "Here—*here,* this here is something special…the real truth…pure and whole…savory sweet…."

"Hmm?"

"This here is *vengeance.*"

XIII

HEAT

Cyrus

Do you feel it Cyrus?

"Shut up."

Ah, you do…the shadows call to you, do they not? So gentle and cold….

"Out, damn you! Leave me be."

Look at me, dear, dear, dear…dear Cyrus. Please, but for a moment. I wish to feast on the soul of your eyes….

"Gods, save me from this wretched place…."

No gods here, sweet, sweet Cyrus. Only me! And so much do I love your perfect company—always here to touch and taste, so deeply as you deserve….

"Please, no…."

Fear not, my sweet....To friends and foes all alike, this is a place full of visions and might....Forsake your house and its hallowed halls, and always remember, sweet, sweet Cyrus...

The Prison knows no walls...

"The Ram hasn't bathed in a fortnight," Cyrus whispered, nudging Deimos. "The Eryx will smell us coming."

The Sage snorted. "I'd guess they smell us already. Subtlety is not the Brynjar's finest suit."

Cyrus hoisted himself over a rotten branch. It creaked and splintered, dotting the flaky hillside as his boots slipped in the slush. A fresh snow from yesterday was all but gone, bleeding its last on the branches and the roots and the earthen moss. With two weeks of marching, the Bryndelwald gave way to parched soil and dry scrub, the last thin flora before the vast desert Wrath. *A desert divides us,* Cyrus smiled, thinking of Clydae and the north. *Home.*

The woods reclaimed the road through the Tear, but they were much thinner than Borea's jungled underbrush as Corinth and Antigonia came and went. Cyrus spotted white birch and pole pine, red cedar and wide oak nearing the hills—all with the gentle hue of sugary snow dusting the blood-red maple leaves.

They let their horses go at Deimos's behest. *They won't survive the Great Mothers,* he'd said, *and the Bite would make quicker work of them.* Still, Cyrus remembered the tear that trickled from the Sage's cheek as he unbridled sweet Shadow and fed her one last carrot. *It's better this way,* Cyrus thought. *At least she'll have a chance.* With six pairs of footprints to replace the hooves seeping into the mud, the path ramped further up—*a small peak just beyond with hopeful vantage,* Swansong had told him.

"Eyes forward," the Ram kept saying, step after slogging step.

Quiet, you fool. Cyrus could only spare the Ram for a time—*this knife is such a joy to twist.* The Ram's clinking armor plates betrayed him, too, picking at the natural guile of Cyrus and Swansong, who were desperate to distance themselves. *Loud, blundering buffoons, all of them.* He looked to Eydian, whose wincing belied an injury with every footfall. *The road makes men of them, yet—blisters, I'd wager....I wonder if the Forge taught 'em about blisters.* Cyrus tempered himself— more confrontations with the Ram proved trying and doubly so with the stone-handed hillbilly, Reed Mason. *He's a young pup, barking his nothings to the world,* Cyrus thought, shaking his head.

"Where's the songbird?" the Ram heaved, pulling himself up from a wayward branch.

"Up the ridge," Cyrus whispered, holding a finger to his mouth, then pointing.

"An angel on our shoulders, then," said the Sage.

Cyrus cringed. *Belt it, why don't you?*

Dagfinn grumbled, "More like a rat. Tis no way to fight one's battles—skirting trees and creeping in the dark. A Furii meets his enemies in the field."

"And Swansong meets hers in hell," Cyrus said. *I can't resist....* Cyrus leapt to a moss-covered boulder, noiseless but for the wind whipping the tendrils of his feathered black cape. *And now, we twist.* "You know as well as I, Hornskewer, that Swansong is no Furii."

"And why might that be, Mister Carrion Crow? Can't fight her way through the Forge the honest way?"

"Honest?" Cyrus sniggered. "You say bludgeoning a boy to death is somehow more dignified? How honest was your bout with the Nighthawk all those years ago?"

The Ram stopped in his tracks. "Careful, Master Raven."

"Your namesake, as I understand it," Cyrus said. "Cnaeus Decima cut off your horn, is that right? Disarmed you? He might've killed you...." A crooked smile crept across his face.

The Ram's icy gaze grew colder. "I did what needed doing," he said. "Ain't no honor once a blade breathes the open air."

Cyrus lowered his gaze. "Hornskewer, I mean no insult, only to play the devil a bit. You are but an artist, painting your truth upon the world—your medium: *scarlet*. I blame you not in the least for your errs. Some men are most in need of killing, and you willed it so…."

"So?"

"*So,*" whispered the Raven, "what of Swansong, then? What of her will?"

"I suppose I wouldn't expect mangy carrion to know the difference," said the Ram, scoffing. "I forget that ye ain't a Furii, neither— holding yourself to no such code."

"Perhaps not"—Cyrus glared—"but no one may accuse Swansong nor I of being a coward *and* a cunt."

Perhaps that was an overstep, Cyrus thought. It was too late—a fist came hurtling through the mists, with Cyrus balancing calmly on the balls of his feet. *Now, then.* He lunged forward, glancing the Ram's gauntleted hand away. Dagfinn swung wildly, missing Cyrus's chest as he stepped in, pulling the Ram close.

"Darling, I was just going to ask you to dance, I swear—"

"*RAHHHH!*" roared the Ram.

*One click, two clicks, three clicks, four….*Cyrus's thumb lifted from the hammer of his revolver, the barrel buried between the plates of the Ram's chest piece. "Indeed," he growled, lips verily close to Dagfinn's. *My soul peeks through my eyes,* he thought, gazing pointedly into the tired old ones hiding behind the Ram's one-horned helm. "Your sins do damn you, brother—I fear no sea, nor stars nor sky, only you, dear brother, and your *wandering eye*…."

The Ram stood motionless.

"Your blades breathe plenty—so much so, they must drink." Cyrus pushed the giant away and turned to the others. "Spare me the pillar of sand you suppose is grace…and if the rest of you don't silence your noisy gobs, I'll fill them with a barrel."

"The Furii's curse seems to 'ave mistaken you for one of its own." The Sage laughed.

Damn you, Deimos.

"'Tis the curse of man, we can see." Deimos nodded. "All men—nothing more than a tainted soul here, with the same sickly corruption that dooms all of us, I say."

"Oh, is *that* it, Deimos?" the Raven squawked.

"How would you know?" piped Reed from a stretch down the hill. "You've never been to the Forge. You have no idea what it does or what becomes of us. You're just a man—we're ascendant."

The last word stung Cyrus's ears. *Idiot.* He laughed and shook his head. "The stone-handed speaks," he said, "but the runt of the litter troubles not the pack."

"Shall I force you to listen, then?" Reed said, curling his fingers around his short sword's handle.

"Mr. Mason, use your words. No need for threats—we're all friends here."

Eydian put a hand on Mason's shoulder. "Reed, please," he said.

Reed shrugged him off. "I'm beginning to think you're quite far from a friend."

The Ram faced the Raven. "Agreed."

"How strange," Cyrus said, turning his back to them. "Such slavish devotions to *lunacy*...."

"Do not turn your back, sir—"

"Do I boil that pig's blood of yours, youngblood?" spat the Raven. "Or do I drink it straight?"

"That's it. Fill your hands!"

"I don't think I will," Cyrus said. "Come now, cricket—all you do is sing, but one day, you must jump—"

"FILL YOUR HANDS, COWARD!" Reed shouted.

"I would, brother, but you see, I'm tired." The Raven grinned. "Your mother's talents last night were far beyond anything I could have—"

"If one more syllable," Reed growled, "finds its way out of your cunt mouth, I will cleave you where you stand—armed or otherwise...."

"If."

For a moment, the eyes that stared back at Cyrus spoke violence. He could feel the tugging inside Reed's itchy trigger finger—an urge to make good on his word. *Do it,* the Raven prayed. *Make it easy.* But a young soul stared back at Cyrus, his bluff toppling for all to see. *Runt.*

Cyrus caught the red of Reed's knuckles from the corner of his eye, straining so hard on the hilt that the bones of his hands began to groan. *A young Furii,* Cyrus sighed. *Does the Burden have its teeth in one so young?* Reed played a convincing man, but a boy stared blankly back in the Furii's stead. Cyrus felt a deepening pity—the great tragedy paralyzed the poor boy in his hate, like stone shackles. *I too know of shackles, brother.*

"Do you know how old I am, Mr. Mason?" asked Deimos.

Reed looked up. "Sage, we are quite in the middle of something—"

"Dagfinn, how old are you?" Deimos interrupted, smirking. "One-fifty?"

"One-hundred-and-sixty-eight this year," the Ram answered proudly, eyes still fixed on Cyrus.

Would you like a second spanking? Cyrus mouthed.

The Sage smiled wide. "My, my…perhaps we will call you 'Pappy' from now on. Do you know how old I am, Dagfinn?"

The Ram said nothing.

"You're older than Einar Dagfinn the Ram?" Eydian's voice cracked.

"Surely not," the Ram grumbled.

Aye. "By a century and nearly a score," nodded Cyrus.

"I don't see what this matters," Reed said. "The Raven offers offense to us all, and we'd accept it from no one, least of all, a *pleb.*"

"You debase yourself for a primitive, plebian sellsword."

"Hey," objected Cyrus. "No need for name callin', Deimos—"

"Quiet, damn ye. Can't you see I'm tryin' to undig this ditch of yours?" Deimos shot Cyrus a heated look. "I've been 'round for more winters than near any man alive, I'd wager—a Furii among Furii for nearly three centuries, and I must say, what pity I have for the sad sort before me...."

The Furii stood idly, looking between Sage, Raven, and each other for a strange pause between their tightening strings. A touch of shame seemed to scold them, each Furii bowing their head.

"How could you say such a thing?" asked Eydian.

Deimos the Sage's tone turned on a shilling, once light and carefree, now terse, deep, and angry. "*You*, dear brother," he spat, "you are a living god among mortal men. You have transcended the plane of age and time. You will likely out-live your parents and your children both. You operate outside the laws of gods, nature, and man, and you are obliged to uphold *none* of them. And yet, you let pithy words and hubris guide you into anger and disarray."

"Sage, I—"

"At ease, Hornskewer. You are an aged legend, yet I remember your great-great-grandfather—the day he was *born*. Pipe down, youngbloods, one and all. *I* will speak, and *you* will listen."

The Ram retreated.

"You think this one here is a mortal man?" said the Sage, nodding to Cyrus.

"*Deimos,*" Cyrus warned.

"Quiet, sir," he snarled. "Some black-feathered stranger? The burglar perhaps. You supposed demi-gods know so little of man—"

"So you're on his side?" asked the Ram.

"Sides? *Sides,* you fool? We're on the same side—that goes for the *both* of you," he said, rounding on Cyrus. "The Brynjar trusts this man, and so must you. Raven—you miserable troll, if you bring about a blood-fueled frenzy in your chiding, I'll hang you from your entrails. I don't care how funny ye are."

"Fair." Cyrus nodded. *He—he thinks I'm funny.*

"What if, gentlemen, you were to quarrel, what then? I'll tell you, you'd 'ave abandoned your oaths, forfeited the mission we all owe to the Brynjar, and likely ruined yourselves in the process. Confidence—*arrogance*. Pride—*hubris*. These will be your undoing. He may only be a man, but one with steady hands full of six-guns and a crack-shot beau marching up the ridge who could fill you with lead before your boots left the dirt, and then you'd be the same pile of bones as every other prideful waste of a Furii rotting in an untended grave."

"Well said," the Raven murmured.

Deimos's glare was palpable. "*Careful,* Cyrus." He turned back to the Ram, Stonehands, and the Golden Sun as he continued, "You give yourselves too much credit—*you don't know this man*. You have no idea who he is, what he's planning, or what he's inevitably capable of, but you should assume the *worst*—as you should for the rest of us. We have a common enemy only so long as the coffers stay full. Be vigilant, be humble, and be a god-damned Furii, for gods' sake."

"I was just going to say that—"

CRACK.

Echoes of a booming gunshot panged across the trees, moss, and rocks, hiding the origin altogether. *Panic.* A murder of crows emerged between the pine needles as their flaps and rustles muted the rest. Reed pulled his gladius from its sheath and lunged at Cyrus—raw instinct seemingly overpowering reason. *Ah, a jumping cricket, at last.*

Cyrus stood ready. The revolver lifted smoothly from its leather, the barrel fixed between Reed's eyes long before the young Furii could reach him, one eyelid lowering as the other lined the sight. The Sage's hand waved from the corner of Cyrus's eye. *Perhaps not here, youngblood.* Deimos's hand caught Reed, fingers deepening into the lines of his coat and halting him in his tracks. *The makings of a good scolding.*

"Put that away, you imbecile," he hushed, spitting on Reed's face a bit. "The shot came from up the ridge—the Bird sees something."

Cyrus winked, spinning the revolver around his trigger finger before sliding it back into the holster.

The Sage eased from Reed's arm, offering a slight nod. "Remember yourself." He turned back to the others. "Hurry," the Sage whispered. "She might be in trouble. Einar Dagfinn, my friend, please take point, as before."

The Ram nodded and moved to the front of the formation, pulling himself over a boulder and onto a perch. Dagfinn's concentration shone in his posture, measuring the space between shots as a small wind distorted the booms. He quit his words—only hand gestures followed as the rest continued to move. The Ram's pace quickened, where a swift crouch turned to scrappy clamoring as the steepening path approached the peak.

Crack....Crack....

The gunfire fades—three shots.

Deimos held up three fingers.

Cyrus smirked, tipping his hat. The Sage smiled, rolling his eyes generally at the others.

Cyrus returned the gesture with a nod of his own. *A smile,* he thought. *Each shot brings us closer to danger, and so too widens the grin upon my face.*

The fog's thick hold loosened at the top of the hill, where the dull gray sky turned to the soft blue. *Yes, the darkness comes, too,* Cyrus smiled on, *that I may share these scorpions of my mind with the rest of you.*

"Where is she?" Eydian huffed, bursting forth into the clearing.

"*Shh.* No tracks," the Ram whispered, pointing. "No more shooting."

Reed nodded.

"Gentlemen," whispered Cyrus, "look here."

A wooden sign jutted from the undergrowth, covered in ivy and a thin layer of leafy morass. He scraped it off with an open palm.

"Says here, 'To the Silver Church…Wonder of the Seven Summits.'"

Beyond Cyrus was an overgrown stretch of partially-covered cobblestone, weathered and derelict like the sign. A sinking came to Cyrus's stomach. His eyes meandered with the path down a scant hill and through blackened stone columns. *Gods, no.* Cyrus turned to the group, but before he could open his mouth, a church bell rang in the distance.

"She's there," he groaned.

The rings struck bone deep. *The Prison calls to one and all….*"I don't feel well," Cyrus said.

"Why would she ring the bell?" asked Eydian.

"Heat," said the Sage.

Oh, Cyrus…

No, please—

Can't you hear my beckoning bell?

Please, not here—

If you can't hear me, then perhaps I should show myself….

Cyrus shuddered. A vision appeared before his eyes: *a horse—a plain, riderless horse standing between the arches, smoldering….*

"We don't know what's down there. We can't see it," Reed said. "We should wait, at least 'til nightfall."

"Nightfall will be too late. We won't be the only ones who heard the call."

"Who else would've heard? We're deep in the Bite—"

"Deep in the Bane," said Cyrus.

"Brigands, then? Highwaymen?" Eydian's voice cracked as the words spilt out.

"Or something worse," said Cyrus. *I see him right there—don't you?! The horse with…with no rider, and…red.*

Come now, Cyrus, and bring your friends.

Heaven help us.

"Ghosts, then? Or is it just the deer?" Reed rolled his eyes.

"*Wolves,*" said Cyrus.

"Likely not," said the Ram, "but Furii hunters, looking for a score? That there's a fightin' chance."

"I'd sooner believe in ghosts," said Reed.

The Night Mare approaches—the bloodied horse of revelation, and the mark of the end of the world. "No," said Cyrus. *The bell tolls on, and on, and so it tolls for me….*

"You know not what you speak of, boy," echoed the Ram.

"*ENOUGH!*" Deimos insisted in a whispered shout. "Dagfinn—take point."

The Ram nodded, slapping his palm on his scattergun's handguard. He moved to the front, leading the others down the overgrown cobbles now one with the aged earth. The roots from the near trees grew between the stones, etching through and splitting them apart—a labyrinth of strangely squared flora growing alongside the decaying symmetries of bygone man.

A strange beauty, Cyrus thought. He looked up to find no more bloodied horse to mark his apocalypse, but the fear stayed with him, deep down. *Go back,* his guts screamed like the shadows. *The bloodied horse of the Epitaph's prophecies fortell the path…and so does the one in white.*

*A horse very well needs a rider….Will **you** take her reins?*

I dare not.

The mist thinned to a soft snow, the small flakes descending upon Cyrus. Smells of rain turned rank as the cold, haunting poison enshrouded the township below. *This is the place where the devil sleeps.* The noxious air churned Cyrus's insides. *You are not safe,* the dark called to him, *not here, sweet Cyrus.* The hairs stood tall on his recoiling neck as the steeple punched through the fog wall.

"Was this road built by the Precursors?" Eydian asked.

"Nay, I'd say not," Deimos said. "Their roads were steel—"

"*Quiet,*" Reed and Cyrus hissed together.

The Raven knelt. *I feel the souls that left this world. They show themselves—tis no sanctuary here nor there, but a tomb....*

The astral clock strikes twelve....

What do you mean, Spirit?

"Come," the Ram said. "We're close."

Dagfinn clicked the hammer of his blunderbuss back. The rust squealed in Cyrus's ears. He clutched his repeater in one hand and his crimson revolver firmly in the other, while Reed's Josey rested at the low-ready under his whitening knuckles.

I feel your deep cold, Spirit....I see it.

Would you like to feel more?

Cyrus shuddered, turning to Reed. "Remember yourself, Mr. Mason."

"Sod off," he replied.

Deimos tapped Cyrus's shoulder, and he followed. The two moved to the broken rock barriers abutting the gate, taking up cover with rifles poking down the street. Old townhomes and farm houses lined the sides, sinking on shoddy foundation and falling apart. The shadows of the brick, thatch, and plaster rotted beneath the ivy that swallowed them whole in a frosty autumn red.

The snow piled on Cyrus's shoulders and hat and hued the strands of his cape in ivory white. It melded into the fabrics and the furs, biting past the skin. The flakes collected in the Ram's beard as he sprinted to the nearest building and slid into cover, the horn of his blunderbuss bouncing all around. *Watch the business end of that, mind you.* There wasn't a sound besides them—not a bird, nor the whistling wind—only the swelling booms of the bell, eating Cyrus's insides with every haunting ring.

Your friends will love what I have in store. We must make peace with all the gods' creations, after all....

I will not barter with you, Spirit, if you are a spirit at all.

The Raven picked up next, skirting the gate and tapping Deimos's shoulder as he hustled past the next row of houses. He posted beside a hanging sign, catching a glimpse of the words written in rotting wood: 'Argentum Grata Cathedrali.'

"Welcome to the Silver Cathedral," the Sage whispered.

My heart jumps from my chest.

Eydian and Reed pulled up from the rear, heads swiveling from side to side as they scoured the postern. They pushed toward the Ram. Reed tapped his shoulder, and Dagfinn obliged, heading across the road and slamming the wall next to Cyrus.

"Smells like death," Dagfinn whispered.

"Aye," said Cyrus, "where the fuck is Swansong?"

The Ram shrugged.

Deimos caught Cyrus's eye, pointing down the way. *The well.* He nodded, picking himself up. It centered the circular courtyard at the end of the alley, surrounded by strewn wagons and debris from an age gone by. *The arena.* His gut sang, plucking at the hairs on his neck. A sapling grew through the stonework near the center, mangled and distorted, dying of a recent winter.

Mother Agathe reclaims the corruptions made by man, Cyrus thought before something caught his eye at the tree's base—plunging gashes torn into the bark. *What sort of beast is that?*

Look. He pointed, and the others saw them, too. *Why—why are they so big? Man-made, must be....*Cyrus could hear Deimos's thoughts as loud as his own, parroting the same. The stillness seeped in, casting this place in a striking scale. *That wagon there is split in two, and the holes in the wall from before, and...bodies.* Lumpy patches of flowery dirt became the remains of the long dead before his very eyes, their bones mixed to meal. *No, we must—*

CLANG.

Do you hear its ghostly call? Can you taste its ring? Dear me....

An omen, Cyrus thought, *or a curse—must be. This place is cursed, if nothing else.*

Cursed?! Blessed are those who answer the call, sweet Cyrus...and so I call for thee....

"Deimos," Cyrus said, "we *must—*"

...rrrooooooooooo OOOOOOOOOOOOAAAAAAAAAAAAA AARRRRRRRRR.

An aching groan boomed beneath the bell. It echoed from wall to wall as the wind howled along with something—*something... else.* Wooden shutters snapped loudly closed as the whistling winter hummed in their ears. The snowflakes grew thick, the tufts piling taller on their heads and shoulders and clouding the path. Cyrus shielded his face with one arm, rifle still fixed with the other.

"Deimos, *please*—"

"Look!" Eydian shouted, clumsily running forward.

Reed hollered, too, pointing to a warm red spot in the distance. "Is that a lantern in the steeple?"

"*Shh*," Dagfinn hushed. "Aye—the Silver Church, must be."

"Swansong?"

"We don't know that," Cyrus said, standing tall.

"Enough," said Deimos. "Mr. Mason, *Golden Boy*—we'll head 'round yonder to the church. Cyrus, Dagfinn—take the front. Quickly, before they get the jump on us."

"Who's *they*?"

"The figurative *they*, brother—you heard it, no? If there's a snare, boy, this is the moment. Peel them eyes."

Cyrus's protests never escaped him. *They'd call you a coward*, he thought. *I'm trapped.* He thought of the bloodied horse—*no, we must run*—but the Ram dragged him from his trance.

"Follow me, pleb," the Ram whispered, thumbing a sausage into his chest, "and stay on my arse."

Faint glimmers of the moon began to glow through the clouds but did little to illuminate their surroundings. The night was dark and thick, metered by the stifling, dank air of the derelict and the dead.

"How do you see, Master Raven?"

"Not well enough," Cyrus said.

"Aye? Is there something you won't tell us, then?"

"What?"

"I saw the way ye made that pistol spin—quickest hands of any man…could've put that youngblood pup down back there, dead before he hit the floor if the Sage hadn't stopped ye. You *must* be a Furii." The Ram snorted. "Why lie? What is there to gain?"

"I am *no…such…thing*," Cyrus spat.

Their gods are so small....

Shut up.

They know not of your power....

Out, damn you!

They know nothing of **Mine.**

Then, he saw her. *The Night Mare cometh.* The bloodied horse was there, stamping on the stones. *She shimmers beneath a blanket of blood, breathing sickness into stillness.* Cyrus froze.

"Raven?"

I see myself in those black, dead eyes. The...the Prison calls....

XIV

THE ROAD AND REVENGE

Aura

Aura Westfall and Elya Dair were riding the road out by mid-morn, the scarce possessions of their homey room above the saloon packed tightly into satchels and saddlebags now strapped to their horses. *Just like that*, Aura sighed. *All gone.*

Elya's bags were annoyingly full of perfumes and powders over weapons and ammunition. *Silliness.* Aura couldn't keep her mind from the man, Rufus Pompey. She made her lips form his name, over and over, but never gave it a voice. *A loved one left behind*, she thought, *just like all the rest.*

Aura shook her head. *I made a promise—one I'll never be able to keep.* Rufus now joined the annals of her parents and friends and Marcus—*all ghosts.* Their memories were burdens—weighted like the bags, carrying her shame and want and despair out into the world. She missed him. Aura felt the guilt of her friend—resented her for it, even—but she knew, deep down....*It likely saved his life. Death must be jealous—he loves to steal the souls away of those that come too close to Aura Westfall.*

The road out of Heraclion was winding and treacherous—a dirt twin track carved into shallow hillside and rolling green at the foot of the Great Mothers, the rocky jutting mountain range that bridged Heraclion and Clydae. The Great Mothers spanned the

Patrian Peninsula from the northern wastes all the way to the Eryxian archipelago. The quiet ride let Aura's addled mind torture her with noise and chaos. She reminisced of Clydae, inescapably. *Blazing blue eyes.…* They were so blue—struck in granite before Marcus kissed her for the first time. *I remember the taste of his lips,* she delighted, *from the first time, and not enough times after/ I feel them—biting at my neck and working down.…*

He was transfixing, she remembered—a powerful and confident love, so unapologetic and young…*so young.* Rufus was never that way. He was assured and adult, but scared—squirming and uncomfortable under the scrutiny of high society. *A corral for prize hogs, he penned himself in,* she thought. *Would you submit to them, Aura? Those sheep and swine?* Perhaps this was her way of dealing, after all—only the night before had she decided her love for him, and now he was gone, tidied up with all the rest in one of her saddlebags, already far too full. *I didn't bring enough gunpowder,* she thought. *Rufus might as well be dead, same as Marcus. Let the road carry my woes a while, that I may bask in the spring.*

She had found her next prey—*the fucking Acolyte.* It felt strange to call him that—him, the pompous posh toph that was always 'Tricky Eli' to her. *Elatreus Fabius Cornicen,* she mouthed. *How am I to kill that miserable bastard?* Perhaps he was the hope she needed. He was Elya's gift, after all—*the dish best served cold,* she'd said. They hadn't spoken of it since, but Aura's mind raced with the possibilities. Instead, her imagination shot her back to that fateful day all those years ago, and Tricky Eli's convenient amnesia about the whole ordeal, his unblinking betrayal of a friend—*too proud to testify.* Marcus's fate was sealed long before any crime was ever committed, to be sure. She labored on the hate, the one thing that shaped every misery that would follow. Marcus—*Elatreus*—the Coven—*Elatreus*—The Birdsongs—*Elatreus*—Lucy—*Elatreus*—the Forge—*Elatreus…he will pay for her suffering,* she promised. She had made the same promise on the bridge the night she bludgeoned Gertrude, fist balled here as it ever was.

Aura's horse whinnied, and she woke from her trance. A signpost up the way read, 'Ale, Wine and Everything Fine,' pointing to a cobbled path off the carriage tracks. Aura eyed the arrow and nodded to Elya. "Look here," she said. "They won't find him for days, you say?"

"Come again?" Elya said, jolting from her own wakeful dream.

"Brandon Senn," she whispered, "you told me they won't find him—that you buried him deep, or something of the like. Can I count on that as your word?"

"Ah, yes! Of course, my dear—you can count on lil' ol' Elya to bury them *quite* deep."

Aura shook her head, spitting a mouthful of saliva onto the grass, abandoning her *fair lady façade* right then and there. "Fancy an ale?" she asked. "I…I don't wish to be sober any longer…."

"Ha! Dear me, love, you're taking this harder than expected."

"Something like that," Aura said. "Come, let's get pissed."

"Yes! The road suits you, Aura."

Their horses made way up to the inn at the top of the butte overlooking the smoking chimneys and thrusting steeples that dotted the Heraclion Hill. The inn was in better shape than Aura might've guessed. A warm glow smoldered through the warped windows as shadowy figures shuttered between the lights and tufts of cotton smoke hovered over the chimney stack. There were a score of horses tied outside, chomping delightedly on fresh hay in a trough lining the shingled wall. A homey thatch roof peaked above the place, half built into the hillside with greenery and vine growing all round and above. *Perfect.*

"Oh, lovely," Elya said, in a sort of whine.

"Indeed," Aura said, swinging a leg hard over the saddle. "I'll kiss the first lad or lass who brings me an ale and a mutton."

"Not before I do," Elya said, laughing.

The ladies tied their horses with the others. Aura unfastened her bridle and reached down, clutching a handful of fresh straw and bringing it to Widow's mouth. The mare accepted with a whinny and a stamp. She had fresh carrots in her saddlebags, but decided to save them for their departure. *No need to make the other nags jealous.*

Elya had always teased Aura about the name—Widow was such a good-spirited horse, sweet and gentle, more like a family dog than a beast of burden. She found the name far too *harsh* for such a creature, but Aura paid her no mind. The name was apt as any other—more so, in fact, that she may serve a mistress as deadly as Aura. Elya's horse's name—unsurprisingly—was Chestnut. *A terrible name*, Aura thought. The horse wasn't even brown, mind you, and Aura never let Elya forget it. *I'd sooner call her 'Acorn' or 'Coconut,'* she always said.

Aura ritually tapped the coin purse hanging from under her coat and Mercy at the same time as she walked to the entrance, accounting for the most sensitive possessions. She thought to grab the pistol holstered under one of the bags, but decided against it. *No need to antagonize if that's what it comes to. Besides,* she thought, *Elya keeps those blasted derringers up her sleeve. Hell, even her rapier has a secret gun inside.* She turned for the entrance and rested a hand gingerly on Elya's shoulder.

They found a small table with backs facing the corner, and Elya claimed it with her feathered hat, beckoning the barkeep as she did with an affable hand. "Pardon, love," she said, "ales, for two, if you please."

"Righ' away, miss," the man replied, turning his wide belly to the tap.

"Sir—excuse me, sir, pardon my manners. What is your name?"

The man turned back. "Um, Roy is my name," he said.

"Ahh, *Roy*," her sultry voice echoed. "Now *that* is a name. Dearest Roy, my name is Elya, and this here is Aura, and we are to be your very best friends, just so long as our mugs never empty." With the last word, she winked, and Roy nearly turned into a radish.

"But, of course, madam," he said, clinking the perspiring steins on the table.

Elya winked at Roy, letting her smile linger as he turned back to the tap.

"This is a damned good ale," Aura sputtered, mid-gulp.

"Aye, exquisite," Elya said, licking the foam from her upper lip. "That Roy—beautiful eyes that one…so green."

"Please, leave poor Roy be."

"A man like Roy can take care of himself, I daresay," she laughed, taking a drink.

His eyes indeed, Aura noticed, catching shades of emerald passing over the bar and the room. The two paused, sipping in silence for a moment, metered only by the casual rustling of Roy's beer handlings and the everyman tapping boots on stools as laughing and pouring noises danced around the room. Aura had nearly drunk the pint before she spoke again, the words spilling from her mouth before she had time to repress them. "He was so nice," she muttered, "more than I deserve."

"*Far* more, I daresay," Elya grinned.

Aura's eyes cut to the Viper's as she took another sip. "Is there any hope of a normal life after all this?"

Elya's brows drooped, and her laugh was more pitying than encouraging. "Aura, come now," she said, "he's just a man—a special man, surely, but a nobody." Aura frowned. "Darling, I mean no ill will, but you're a young Furii yet—you haven't grasped the meaning."

"What meaning?" she asked.

"Even if," she said, heaving another gulp, followed by a hiccup, "even *if* you walked away right here and now—caught a frigate to the Wrath and lived out your days in exile—you'd never find the peace you seek. He's a mortal—he will always be mortal, but you, *you*, my beautiful huntress, are far more than he could ever be. Whether it be Furii hunters looking for a bounty, a brutish band of highwaymen, or a head cold or age itself, Tara would take him from you, as she's taken everything else."

"But we could be happy," she said, eyeing the last swigs of her ale, "if only for a moment."

Elya elbowed her then. "You're thinking of that Petronax boy, aren't you?"

"What?" She looked up. "Of course not."

"He's exactly who you should be thinking of, my dear—the same lesson we've all had to learn."

"Enough," said Aura, raising her hand and waving at Roy. *Two more, please*, she mouthed. "What's the plan for the Acolyte?"

"Beg pardon?"

"The plan," Aura repeated, "the Acolyte summoned us—how are we to navigate this?"

"Navigate what?"

Aura clenched her hands. "*You* told me that we go to the Eryx now that I may *destroy* that man. I mean for you to honor that, but much more importantly, how in the hell are we to do it without losing our heads in the process?"

"Surely they'd send us to the Prison Without Walls." Elya chuckled. Aura's gaze was palpable. "Alright," she said, "I don't have a detailed plan at the moment. It depends on so many things, dear, you understand. I thought we could arrive, take a few notes, and plan as we play, as they say."

"What?!"

"Keep your voice down!" Elya hushed.

"You mean to walk us into the lion's den without even the inklings of a plan?" Aura's temper surged, but two fresh ales arrived, and she forced a vapid smile in Roy's direction. "Thank you."

"Aura, listen to me. It is true, I don't have a plan in the conventional sense, but I've heard things…."

"Heard things?" Aura rolled her eyes and drank deep again.

"Aye, at the brothel—"

"Here we go."

"Yes, the *brothel*, and as you know, word travels fast that way. I heard that there may be a plot of sorts." She took a deep drink herself as Aura's puzzlement shone shameless across her face.

Aura let out a sigh. "Continue," she mumbled.

"I have a friend from the old place who writes to me from time to time from the Laurentines—they get a lot of pirates there, banner lords of Blake Bowman and the like."

"Who?"

"You've never heard of Iron Blake Bowman, the pirate? Well, I hear he prefers the term 'privateer.'"

"No, never," Aura said, her eyes fixed on Elya's.

"Well, needless to say, he's amassed quite the armada by the sound of it. One 'undred ships at least, all under his command, but—much more curious—they're *moving*."

"Moving where?"

"They aren't s'posed to say, or so my friend says, but she has it on good authority that the fleet sails for Illyria, and—"

"The Eryx," she finished.

Elya tilted back and sipped again. "Indeed," she capitulated.

"What about the royal navy?"

"Antigonia," she said, lingering on the word for a moment, "still blockading on the western coast."

Aura sat upright, the hairs on arms and neck standing tall. "It'd be a half-year before they could make it back in time. You're sure this is true?"

"As sure as I can be. She has no reason to lie, and the pieces fit. 'Tis far more than coincidence."

"Aye, I daresay it is," Aura replied, her eyes on a distant horizon.

XV

MALICE

The Raven

Cacophony.
A wall of gun smoke ignited behind a line of fire, and chaos followed. The noise came last. Cyrus's panicked nerves jumped his body forward and away—*anywhere but here.* The inky black of the windows on the far side of the alley popped and flared as the bullets cut through the falling snow. *Get low,* his stomach urged. *Get low and stay there.* The cobbles chipped and cracked at his heels—the house behind him, splintering. Cyrus dashed aside in aimless evasion, covering his face with a free hand.

SHITE. Something tugged hard at his ribs and back, followed by two distinctive thuds. *Gods in hell, I'm hit.* Red poured from his shoulder onto the wall as he dragged it toward the front door.

"*FUCK!*" he shouted. A ball peppered the wall just over his head.

The doorway. He lunged, throwing his full weight through the rotten wood and crashing onto the floor. *Where's my repeater?* He didn't know. *Re-revolver....* His hand fell to the pistol. It slipped between his bloodied fingers. *Too—too much blood....*

Never...

A shadow marched through the door. *Shite—shite—SHITE!* Cyrus drew, fanning two shots that punched through the door. The shadow keeled over. *One down.* He spotted another in the corner of his eye, kneeling next to the window. Cyrus rolled, narrowing the barrel on his new target as he smashed his offhand onto the hammer. *One shot. Two. Three.* The last flare of the muzzle brightened the room, revealing the viscous scarlet on the wall behind. *Two down.* Groans came from the door. *The first is still alive.* Cyrus crawled back, ignoring the plaster and debris that rained from above as bullets tore through the shoddy walls.

Silence, pig. The Raven raised his good arm high and swung down with the butt of his pistol. *One....* The first strike thudded on something fleshy—*thigh, maybe?* But the next landed with an unsettling crack and a lurch of the body. *Two....* The shadow's wailing ceased. *Where the fuck is Dagfinn?* He reached for his wounds. *Ugh.* The smell of powder scorched his nose and eyes, but the blood smelled stronger still. *The blood...*

Oh, the blood...

"*DAGFINN!*" shouted Cyrus. The gunfire thickened. *Fuckin' hell.* Cyrus crawled to cover, posting himself up with his good arm whilst holding a shaky pistol to the door. "DAGFINN, YOU ALIVE?"

"Aye, brother!" he shouted from someplace outside. "Start shooting, brother—SHOOT!"

Cyrus dragged his legs toward him and managed to stand, but his shoulder stayed glued to the wall. His back was numb, warming in wet blood, but cooling quickly in the cold. *It burns, and it freezes....* *It tore right through.* Cyrus's legs began to rattle, and his head sunk low between his shoulders. *Stay awake, damn you.* He leaned from the wall, feeling the weight of his garb, soaking wet—*too much...too much blood.* "I...can't...."

I—I can't breathe. His chest was tight—*so tight.* He ached to inhale, but the lungs couldn't take any more. *What's happening?* The left side of Cyrus's chest tugged painfully with each shallow breath, the tension building. *I'm—I'm suffocating.* The darkness came closing in. *No, not again.* His eyes ached to close. *Stay awake. Stay awake— breathe, breathe.* The world was swirling around him like a storm, the sounds faint and distant as the black swallowed him. *If I faint, I die,* he told himself. *If I faint, I die....*

What of death, then, in these strange eons?

The tattered remnants of the door fixed on hinges burst open— *more of them.* Cyrus raised his revolver up and fired, illuminating the room. *Last...ball.* The figure collapsed, smashing its head severely onto the floorboards with a clunk. *Music to my ears.* The recoil nearly threw the pistol from his hand. *I...I don't know if I can....*Smoke snaked from the barrel as it fell into his lap.

Breathe...damn you...breathe.

"Dagfinn," he groaned, little more than a whisper.

Another silhouette marched through the door, and Cyrus reared his revolver one last time, dropping an eyelid and then the hammer. *Click.*

"IT'S ME, YOU FOOL!" the Ram roared.

"I...*I can't*...," Cyrus said.

"Here—here, take a sprig—come now."

Dagfinn laid his smoking scattergun next to Cyrus. He yanked the straps of his gauntlet, baring his burly hand. With the other, he sliced a small cross in his center palm and closed his fist, easing the blood through his fingers.

"No, Don't—"

"Give me those holes, or it'll be the crows for you!" Dagfinn shouted, tearing through his shirt to the skin.

"No—*NOT THE BLOOD—DON'T GIVE ME THE BLOOD!*"

Take…my…gifts….

It's too late. Dagfinn's knuckles creaked with each squeeze, squirting hot sap into the Raven's wounds, one, then the other. *Gods in hell!* Cyrus squirmed as the blood of the old gods seared his flesh. *It's boiling—no, no, NO!*

Yes….

The skin of his back was bubbling through his coat, the blood like acid, melting the flesh as it bored deeper into his chest. *Poison—or corrosion, or curse.…*Cyrus hadn't the strength to resist, limply curled and quivering under the Ram's weight.

"Leave me…."

"You'll 'ate this part," he growled, jamming gunpowder into one of the holes, then the other.

Cyrus froze. "No, please—"

"'Ere goes," said Dagfinn, scraping the knife along his gauntlet.

Sparks. Cyrus recoiled, but the powder caught. He clenched down hard, burying his face in rotting floorboards as the powder melted his wounds shut.

"Ah, *that*, too." The Ram nodded as he plunged the tip of his knife suddenly between Cyrus's ribs.

"Ugh," Cyrus gasped.

"Don't panic, Crow," he grumbled. "You've a chest full o' breath and blood—it ain't pretty, but it'll help!" He laughed, reaching for his blunderbuss.

Cyrus heard a hissing noise coming from the puncture, bubbling past the blood. The clicking waned. "I'm…*I'm*—"

Dagfinn stood up. "You'll be fine, brother!" he shouted, firing the blunderbuss outside. "One more moment, now—the blood'll bring ye back."

The Blood will set you free....

I taste the sweet brandy of my father's hallowed halls, metallic and warm. What is the pain I was feeling before? Not that warmth, surely no? Another that lies deep....The blue of my eyes delights in the simple dark, as I slave over her secrets. Is this the world seen anew? I fear no death nor the Prison from before. The world shall know my sins, but I won't deny this sweet nectar—its aroma so savory and serene. I would open my throat but to have one drink. I daresay...I would open others....

You could be a god to them.

I will be a god to you, Spirit. Of that, you can be sure.

No gods here, sweet Cyrus...only Me.

"Wake up, there's a good lad!" shouted the Ram, handing Cyrus his revolver with a fresh cylinder. "Let us do what we do best!"

A saint must take communion—but, be careful of the drink.

"Aye, let's." Cyrus grabbed a rejuvenated handful of the Ram's hulking arm and pulled himself up with ease. *The power.* He snatched up the revolver, cocking it—*one click, two, three, and four.* He reached to the holes in his back, finding only mended meat, where the pain had all but gone. *I suppose I should have a few new tricks.* He took a deep, full breath as he peeked from the window sill, eyeing the far side of the alley, clear as day. *Let us give these scorpions a voice.*

Cyrus rested his revolver on top of his arm, firing rhythms as the glints in the distance went out. A rifle even fell from an upstairs window, clanking hard on the cobblestone below. *Music to my ears.* He could see clearly through the smoke and the fog. *Damn if I can't feel them across the wall....* Something strange tickled at his neck.

What men are we, Cyrus?

What?

"What—what men are *we*?"

"What?" the Ram shouted over the gunfire.

"Not—not men!"

"Oh." The Ram nodded. "No—*not men*," he laughed, "but Wolves...."

Wolves?

Wolves...

"Aye," said the Ram, firing his last shot. "No more ghost stories—we must move."

Cyrus nodded. A few stray bullets landed behind him, but he stood tall. *I can feel them somehow, so far away.* They thumped in the rafters and the dirt outside, tearing holes through his perceptions. A smile broke. *I won't deny it; it feels good to be a god again.* He sensed his repeater just outside. *I'll retrieve it—*

"Not that way, youngblood!" shouted Dagfinn.

I'm no youngblood. "Right," he said. *Remember yourself.*

Cyrus knelt, retreating toward the room. *Wolves,* he remembered. There lay the body of his first victim, and his new eyes found the detail of the man. *Not a man,* he remembered. *As I live and breathe, a Wolf of the Wood.* The creature was inelegant and lame, with a thick scraggy pelt lining its limbs. *More like an ape,* he thought, *but we haven't the time—I hear them.*

I brought a choir....

We have a few more to our flanks," the Ram said. "Push your own way—I go left; you go right."

"Mind the others," Cyrus said.

"Huh?"

"Mind the others!" he shouted. "If they weren't hit, they'll be pushing."

"Aye—*you* telllin' *me* how it goes, then?!"

"Ha! My apologies."

The Ram scooted closer to the door. "On my mark."

Dagfinn swatted him on the leg as he pushed outside, shotgun raised and tracking left. Cyrus dashed right, sprinting through the gun smoke to the next building. He shouldered through another rotting door and swept the room. *Empty.*

An adjacent room echoed with footsteps moving toward him, and he ducked behind the door as it opened. He fired through it, hearing the body on the other side fall forward. Cyrus pushed through, confronting the kneeling beast clutching its belly. *No quarter,* he thought, slashing his serpentine poniard out of its sheath with a ring. The wretch hacked and choked as a bucket's worth of blood spilled onto the floor. The Raven sped on.

The window. Cyrus moved closer, peeking from the corner. *The church is just there,* he noticed, the lamp glowing in the bell tower still, but dimmer this time. Doubt took him. *And yonder,* he thought, seeing the warm orange clouds of smoke behind the steeple. *Fire.* He saw the steeple's shadow among the flames, and the bell tolled—*CLANG.*

Blessed are those who answer her call....

Out, Spirit! Haunt me no more!

Even here, you dare not say my name.

I do not know it....

Yes...you... **do.**

CLANG. The bell slammed the insides of his ears. *It—it calls to me....* He covered them with his hands, even, but the bell rang all the louder. *CLANG—each like an earthquake in my mind.*

Speak my name....

Never. TOLL. The Night Mare slips between my eyelids, braying with the sounds.

Say...it....

No. His eyes shook and teeth chattered under the weight of the bell, crashing down upon him with each unbearable toll.

TOLL.

The rings swallowed him down—a purling spiral of incomprehensible reality shattered by fracture...*and that cursed fucking horse.*

SPEAK MY NAME!

Shooting pain seared his nerves as Cyrus writhed in unmatched agony. *It boils, and it freezes—not the bell!*

TOLL.

Don't you see?! That Blood makes you Mine!

No...

TOLL.

SAY IT...

Ugh...

TOLL.

SAY...IT....

...TOLL.

SAY—

"*Malus....*" Cyrus whimpered. "I...I named you *Malus.*"

XVI

CRESCENDO

The Raven

Now then, Cyrus—shall we begin?

*Sweat and tears rain down my face. Awoken, but I—I thought...
there are lumps in my arms—knotty muscle, I find—sinewy reeds layered
tightly beneath the skin, and heavy as lead....*

Metamorphosis...

A gift indeed, Spirit...

Cyrus...

...

CYRUS...

Who?

...rrrroooooooooooOOOOOOOOOOOOAAAAAAAAAAAAAAAARR-RRRRRRR...

The bellowing call roused him from his trance. *Gods in hell, the others.* He hoisted himself up from the floor. *I shall not fall again tonight.* Cyrus took a moment, loading a few extra cylinders and stashing them back in his belt box. *Remember yourself, damn you.*

The calling rang in his ears like the noiseless bell. *Did—did it ring at all?* He had to move—*anywhere but here.* He stood, kicking through the nearest door and barreling outside into the thick of the weather and wind. *The church calls to me—the others....*He moved with the shadows—faster and stronger than ever before. *I have become danger here.* He smiled again. *Is this truly what the bounty hunters covet?* He felt dread. *The beastmen of the wood crave the divine blood, too.*

The Raven collided headlong into a body—*another Wolf.* He swung his revolver high, nearly dropping the hammer when Eydian Brynjar's blood-stained face scowled back at him. "*GODS IN HELL—*"

The Brynjari prince bounced backward. "It's me!" he cried.

Cyrus sighed relief. "Gods be *damned...*what—what happened to you?"

"We heard shooting," he heaved, "ran back, but caught some mischief along the way. I...."

That gold jacket's soaked through. Cyrus's heart sank a bit. "*Easy.* Where's Mason? And the Sage?"

"Aye, I'd ask you the same," he sputtered. "We were—we... separated. They moved to the church, and I covered them. I thought the fire, but—"

"It wasn't us. Did you see Swansong?"

"Nay, but I've been shooting and pushing ever since. Need—need a...breather."

The blood painted Eydian by the bucketful. Cyrus thought it better not to ask. *Steady, brother.* He was a sickly white color under all the red, with a far-off gaze. His eyes darted back and forth, but never quite fixed on Cyrus, and his voice trailed with his thoughts.

"Eydian—oi, *Eydian*," Cyrus snapped. "Come with me."

The Ram barreled through a door on the far side. "Hurry, lads!" he yelled. "Make for the church!"

"Aye." Cyrus put a hand on the Golden Sun's shoulder. "Come now, lad—stay awake."

The shooting died off, replaced by ripping, billowing flames. *How many Wolves left?* He couldn't be sure.

"Hunters?" asked Eydian.

"Huh?"

"No, brother," said the Ram, "not Hunters."

"Aye, certainly not," Cyrus agreed.

"Wolves, then?"

The Raven nodded gravely.

"Oh, *piss off*," came Eydian.

"Earnest," said the Ram.

"I'll kill him," Eydian muttered under his breath.

"Huh?"

"Reed, I mean."

"Reed? Why him?"

Eydian smiled a bit. "He had to do it, didn't he? Go and tempt fate back there...."

"Aye," laughed the Ram, "*ghosts and deer*—is that what he said? Haven't seen any deer."

"Plenty of ghosts, though," said Cyrus. "How did they know we'd be here?"

"The question of the day, that is, Master Raven."

Cyrus eyed a few dripping wounds from the Ram's back, painting the cobbles behind him. "Einar, you've been hit?"

"Aye!" He laughed. "But, they might as well be throwin' pennies."

"I'm hit, too, I'm afraid," Eydian chirped, his face paler than before.

"Stay awake, damn you...."

The three moved slowly and quietly across the alley and winding street, arriving at the side gate with rifles raised. It stood just outside an open courtyard, leading to the ancient stone steps of the cathedral's entrance. *My word.* Columns and buttresses towered above, stabbing through the pluming ash and smoke to meet the collapsed roof. There were broken openings and coarse holes in the stone, but a large circular stained-glass mural remained intact just under the steeple, shining its color and light upon them. *Oh, the color....*

"Sing to me, goddess."

"What?" growled the Ram.

"Never mind—can't I be alone with my thoughts for but a moment?" spat Cyrus. The final word brought the cold in. *No, not again.*

"Come," the Ram said, pushing through an opening in the iron.

Remember yourself, damn you. They crossed the atrium with guns high, itching to fire. Cyrus's gaze was drawn to the hulking metal dome, shimmering through the snowfall and burning dark in pure moonlight silver. The steeple was full of holes and cracks and looming crevices—*the usual hiding spots for any decent sharpshooter.*

Eydian's pistol dangled loosely from his good hand.

"Oi, don't drop that," the Ram barked, pointing. "And stay awake."

Stay awake.... Cyrus cringed. *Ugh*—the stink was foul, spilling past his nose, inviting the plague of the land into his lungs with each breath. The overgrown flora of the path and the township before peeled away—neither flowers, ferns, nor leaves of grass grew between the iron gate outside the atrium and the entryway. The earth was a dense black, scorched and breathing its rot into the air alongside the conflagration that burned the blocks beyond. The air was heavy and hot—*full of wrath and pestilence*, Cyrus thought. Thick tufts of falling snow had turned to rain, and Cyrus shuddered in his boots.

Run, his guts pleaded. *Run or die.* But, the muscles in his back began to tighten, and a smile stretched the lines of his cheeks. *Die?* he thought. *How?*

"Where are the others?" he asked.

"I lost them just after we separated," Eydian said. "I heard shooting, but doubt they moved." He hiccoughed, covering his mouth with a dry part of his sleeve. *Blood.*

"Cyrus, help with this," the Ram said, leaning into the door.

The wood creaked, and the hinges squealed, grinding inward. The other side was dank and humid with a stronger, fouler stench springing forth like hellfire on the nostrils. *Gods in hell.* The sky ablaze beamed through holes in the patchy roof and walls, some through remnant stained glass as the inside illuminated a bit. *No sign of them.* The Ram and the Raven pushed the doors closed behind them, and Cyrus barred them with a rusted iron latch that screeched as he dragged it across its holdings.

"Look yonder," said the Ram, "the rafters—we find the lantern, we find the bird."

Eydian found the nearest pew and collapsed. "I...I don't think I can—"

"*Shh*, there's a lad," Cyrus said. "You guard the door, brother." He smacked Eydian's cheek gently. "*Stay awake.* Einar, could you—"

"I know what you're thinking, Master Raven, but nay, I can't." The Ram's gaze was firm. "Our bloods don't mix, I'm afraid, and I've lost enough as it is. I'm surprised, though—"

"Huh?" the Raven barked.

"He'll be fine—just needs a moment of recuperation. His body will mend itself, but you—well, I wasn't sure you'd survive my gift back there. Figured you were a Furii and a liar all along. Glad to see my fears proved false."

"Indeed." Cyrus nodded. "The rafters"—he pointed—"how do we—"

"Ladder," the Ram said, pointing to an old library ladder shoddily attached to a wall of ancient books on the far side, rising to the open ceiling.

Kindling, thought Cyrus. "After you. I'll keep an eye out—we can't stay long."

The old wood squealed under the Ram's weight as he climbed, worsening with the height. Cyrus laughed. *Big man, small ladder... absurd.* It creaked and swayed, rising to the naked upper floor. The Raven kept a watchful eye on the shadows of the rafters above Dagfinn, his rifle shouldered and steady.

"I'm here!" the Ram hollered down.

"What do you see?"

"No one—begin your ascent. The bell is farther on."

The hairs of Cyrus's neck suddenly stood up, all at once. *Others.* He looked to the rear door, lining the sight of his revolver as a bang shot across the hall, then another. *Bang. Bang. BANG!* The doors burst open.

"WAIT!" shouted a voice. "Don't shoot!"

Deimos. "Gods in hell!" Cyrus cried.

Deimos and Reed poured through the door, heaving. Reed dropped his messer to the floor, clanking on the stone.

"What in the fuckin' hell happened to you two?!" shouted the Ram from up top.

"Where's Eydian?" Reed asked over him.

"Just there. What happened? where were you? Why did you leave him?"

"We got separated," Deimos said.

"No shite," came the Ram.

Reed knelt next to Eydian. "Brother, what—you hit?"

"Aye, a bit," he croaked.

"He's in bad shape," said Cyrus.

"We *all* are—"

"The Crow nearly perished!" The Ram snorted. "Had to take a few sips of my secret sauce!"

Cyrus rolled his eyes and let out a long sigh, "Please—*please* don't call it that."

"You—you what?" Reed asked, looking angrily at Cyrus.

"Afraid so." Cyrus nodded, his crooked smile stretching. *I...*

can't help myself. "I'm a Furii now."

"You most certainly are not," Reed spat.

Eydian piped in, loud as he could, but wheezing, "Peace, Reed… burgundy *sauce* is better than *gravy*."

Reed laughed, despite himself.

"At least your sense of humor survives, brother," said Cyrus.

Deimos laughed, too, resting a hand on Cyrus's shoulder. "Clumsy bugger."

He shook his head. "Worrisome, to be sure, brother."

"You are no brother of his," Reed said coldly.

"Give it a rest, Mason," Deimos said. He turned to Cyrus. "You really saved our skin. The beasts ran as soon as you lit the blaze. How'd ye do it?"

"That wasn't you?" Cyrus's heart sank. "We—we didn't…." *Oh, no.*

*A noise…*low—lower than mortal ears could hear. A deep howl, rising through the bellows of the outside, poured through the walls. *So deep…*like the groaning trees and roaring flames were speaking back, and the Furii stood motionless together as the deep, deep cold set in.

No. More howls echoed the first—*thousands…*screeching, gnawing cries…roaring with the wind and the rain. *They're right outside.* Panic found him. *Not a church,* Cyrus thought, *but a tomb.*

Reed's desperate eyes found Deimos and then bounced to Cyrus. The Raven instinctively nodded to the ladder. "*Climb,*" he said, just as a booming hit shook the barred front doors.

BOOM.

Cyrus sprinted to the rear entrance, gripping the doors and nearly ripping them from their hinges as he wrenched them closed. He ran to the aisle and put hands on two benches, dragging them to the opening.

"Mason—get Eydian up the ladder!" cried Deimos, running to aid Cyrus.

"I'm fine," he said, standing up. "You first."

The front doors trembled again as another slam reverberated down the aisles. *BOOM.*

"One of you get up this *fucking* ladder!" the Ram barked.

"Reed, go first. We'll help him after—*OOF!*" Deimos grunted, hefting the last bench atop the others. *"Move, you fool!"*

"Come on, Brynjar, follow me," Reed said, swiping up his messer and sheathing it over his back as he mounted the ladder.

"I'm coming. I'm coming...."

BOOM.

Another pulverizing hit to the far door, this time spewing splinters and dust from the heights of the rafters and the door itself. Eydian mounted the ladder with shaky and sluggish limbs.

"Hurry, you Golden Shite!"

"Cyrus, push him—"

BOOM!

Heavens, help us....

BOOM!

Can you hear it, Cyrus?

No, please, not now—

BOOM!

...my beckoning bell?

BOOM!

Will you answer the call?

BOOM!!!

The final hit smashed through, clouding the opening in dust and debris. *No!* Cyrus ducked down, lunging to the nearest cover. He drew his estoc. *Take a drink, my love.* The Raven found a hole in the bench to peep through. *Where—where are they?* He dared not blink, eyeing the doorway. *The horde comes.* But, only silence followed behind the fire and rain.

Get up! his gut cried. *Move!*

Cyrus hadn't the chance. *Blinding flashes—deafening sound.* A wall of gunfire ignited the cloud—*the loudest boom yet.* The lead cracked through the pews and thumped on the floor and walls behind him. He hunkered down, but the rounds zipped narrowly over his head, pinning him to the floor. *Since when can the bloody Wolves of the Wood gather a fuckin' firing line?!* The shooting lulled, and Cyrus stole another peek. Rifle barrels poked through the new wall of gun smoke, but slowly disappeared.

The howling came back. *So—so deep…and so many.…*

RooooooooooooooooooooooooooooooooooooooooaaaaaaaaaaaAAAAAAAAAA AAAAAAAAAARRRRRRRRRR!

"*RAAAAAAHHHHHHH!*" they each cried back. *To battle, then.* Cyrus stood, marching toward the door as the Wolves barreled through. They congested in the opening, crawling over and past each other like a heap of rats. *Like fish in a barrel,* he thought, *squirming slimily.* He shot into the fray. *So…many…fish.*

Deimos followed, blasting his pistol into the first of his prey.

"Keep climbing!" he shouted.

"Hurry!" hollered Reed. He reached down with one arm. "Grab my hand, brother!"

Eydian's head bobbed uneasily between his shoulders. "I...I *can't....*"

"Don't you fucking do it!"

The ladder slipped from Eydian's clutches. His body plummeted to the floor like a straw doll, crashing through one of the pews. The Golden Sun lay motionless, unconscious—*or worse*—to Cyrus's eyes.

"No!" cried Reed.

Dagfinn grabbed a handful of his shoulder before Reed could climb back down. "Stay here, and keep shooting, damn ye! We'll tend t'him later."

"Eydian!" Reed resisted. "EYDIAN!"

The Ram released him. "AGH! *Fuck*—Mason, the windows!" he roared as two twisted bodies leapt through the opening behind them. He spun around, blasting his blunderbuss from the hip and hurling the beast back through the hole in a mist of vibrant red. The other had a weapon, too, swinging it wildly at the Ram as he wheeled back with his blunderbuss, using the butt to bludgeon the shrieking creature. "Help me, bastard! They're crawling up the outside!"

Cyrus looked to Eydian, still motionless on the floor of the cathedral, and then to Reed and the Ram. Reed drew his gladius just in time for more of them to erupt from a skylight farther on. *They're... everywhere.* Cyrus turned and ran head on, roaring and swinging. He cut clean through an exposed limb as the first beast reared back. The Raven followed with a clean stab to the chest.

"RAH!" he roared, ripping the blade past the meat and viscera, spilling it onto the floor. A crooked smile came to his face.

Drink up, Cyrus.

He holstered the revolver, drawing the poniard in its place. The dagger slashed across the next beast's neck, eagerly muting the shrieks and snarls. *Oh, how I hunger for such things.* He kicked another, burying his boot in the monster's chest, launching the beast across the hall. *So much power....*

Cyrus caught glimpses of their detail as he slew them, one by one. *So peculiar—is it...a man?* It had legs and arms—and donned clothes, though tattered and scarce. There was a thick mane of dark hair growing strangely across face and palms, or not at all. Bones poked nightmarishly through the fingertips of some, coming to bloodied, ivory points, while others carried rusty cutlasses or jagged cleavers. The foam gathered and dripped from the corners of their mouths, their lips and eyelids swollen or missing, brandishing jagged teeth.

The Raven fought on. The next victim was hairless, covered in cystic growths that poked through the skin of the neck and head. *Gods in hell, he looks so...so human.* Cyrus cut him down, but the sinking feeling remained. *Just like us....* A strange sort, to be sure, and hardly a Wolf, to Cyrus's eyes. He chopped through the fingers that held a rusted hand-axe and kicked the creature through the banister. Deimos finished him.

A screeching beast fell from the rafters, crunching on the stone next to Cyrus, the spatter getting in his eyes. "*Oi!*" he yelled. "Watch your kill!"

Deimos's free hand scrambled in his belt box. "Empty," he said.

"Aye, I'm nearly there," said Cyrus.

Deimos dropped his breechloader and unclasped Moonlight from his hip, ripping her from the scabbard. *She sings, she does, even here.* The two moved toward the door in time for it to rupture forth completely, with beasts and bodies pouring over one another and flooding into the hall by the dozen.

The Sage hacked and swung, "*HIYAH—ARGH—RAH!*"

Cyrus watched as Deimos tackled one to the floor, burying his saber deep in the belly and dragging it free. Cyrus sliced through limbs and throats and exposed flesh as the Wolves swarmed in. *They can fight.* Cyrus hadn't come to terms with it. *They can fight, they can talk, and they can set a fuckin' trap.*

The Raven slipped on the floor as the blood and bodies piled. He tripped on cleavers and clubs—torches, pitchforks, and the oldest guns he'd ever seen. *Flintlock, by the look…they use fire? They use guns?*

Reed cut through another beast and kicked him out the window. "RAVEN," he yelled, "look out!"

The last door burst open, and more of the scourge flowed through. *Shrieking and roaring and writhing*—Cyrus turned to meet them, but the crowd was too much. A thick heap smothered him where he stood, surrounded by shoulder-to-shoulder beasts as he pushed and stabbed and struggled.

The Sage's saber came into view, pushing closer to Cyrus. The Raven pushed, too, meeting his dyad back-to-back as they hacked at the fodder, in hopes of making a clearing. The Ram retreated toward the ladder; the Wolves up top were all but on top of them.

Surrounded, Cyrus thought. He caught a pistol gleaming in the corner of his eye, raising to him—the black hole of the barrel stared back, hammer itching to fall. He panicked.

SCHING—a clean cutlass sliced through the arm. The severed hand and pistol fell to the floor and discharged wildly into one of the walls.

"By the *fucking* gods…."

The Golden Sun's cutlass reared for another strike, shining in the firelight.

"*GOLDEN SUN!*" Dagfinn bellowed. "*YOU BEAUTIFUL BASTARD!*"

"*Fear no darkness!*" cried Eydian, clubbing a beast with the butt of his pistol.

The blood of the dying soaked Cyrus's coat. *It's in my mouth and my eyes.* He spat. Deimos was painted in rusted scarlet, wiping the blood from his face between his slashes and hacks. The copper singed the Raven's tongue. *Is the blood so sweet, even here?* He buried his estoc hilt deep in one of them. *Stuck.* The poniard was trapped in the throat of another as a third approached. Cyrus let go of his sword, drawing his revolver again and punching a clean hole through the monster's eye—*no bigger than a shilling.*

"*Agh!*" He recoiled, wiping the spatter from his eyes. He holstered the pistol in a flash, grabbing the estoc's handle and tearing it free with the poniard. *The blood spills over me....* They were running—*the bodies stacking.* Stragglers slipped through cracks in the walls and danced at a distance, deserting the violence altogether. Deimos freed his saber from another fallen foe as Reed and the Ram cut down the last of the Wolves up top. They made their way to the ladder, dodging the corpses or trampling them.

A corpse shifted under the Ram's boot. It slipped loose, plummeting to the floor and splattering next to Deimos. "Oi, watch it!"

The fire roared outside, louder and nearer, pushing out the rain. Cyrus reached for his wide-brim hat, but found an empty hand. *Lost,* he sighed, *but when?*

"And stay out!" Eydian said. He clutched at his abdomen, sinking to the chancel stairs.

Reed and the Ram slid down the ladder, their legs buckling and shaking as they rode to the floor.

Reed ran to Eydian. "That was quite a fall, brother," he said, running his hands over his forehead and under his chin.

"Should take more than that," he said with a smirk.

The Ram marched over to the break in the wall, fire flickering in his eyes and illuminating a sullen face. "The flames grow tall, brothers. Where is Swansong?"

"Ran, I expect," said Reed.

"Doubtful," scoffed Cyrus.

"What of the Wolves?" the Sage asked. "Do you see any of them?"

"Nay, but I can hear them...breathing," said the Ram, "*lots* of it...."

"Aye, I hear it....I...I just don't know...." Cyrus was drawn to the black beyond the broken doors. *Perhaps I am the Night Mare,* he thought, eyeing the blood that dripped from his feathers. The other side of the chapel away from the flaming squalls and the collapsed vault was shrouded in shadow, but the sounds cut through. *What lingers in the deep?*

"I—I hear it…," said the Raven.

"Cyrus," said Deimos, "where are you going?"

"It…*calls….*"

"Cyrus—"

Breathe it in….

Reed backed away from the doors. "If the rest knew any better, they'll be long gone."

Cyrus returned from his trance. "I'm sure that's what the deer say, right before the bullet."

"Pardon?"

"I don't hear *long gone,* brother—I hear scores, and I hear them close—"

"The fuck would you know, Raven?"

Breathe Me in….

"Peace," Deimos hissed. "Cyrus may be right. An ambush."

Reed scoffed, "You really think *they* planned this?"

"Aye, and if you had any sense, you'd feel the same—"

"What guns they've left will line the trees, I'd wager," the Ram said. "We took the bait. We cut through the chaff, exhausted ourselves and our supplies." He nodded to Eydian. "We'll die tired at the mouth of the trail." He uncorked his canteen with his teeth and took a deep pull.

"Those creatures out there are animals, nothing more," Eydian sputtered.

"Idiot," Cyrus said.

"Animals with *guns and steel,"* retorted Dagfinn. "I'd expect you to know, Golden Boy—you're in a sad state."

Reed kicked a pew near Cyrus. "Aye, then what do you propose, *Cyrus*—you, the all-knowing mortal? What say you, *oh, wise one?* What the fuck will *you* do?"

Oh, Me. ...Cyrus whipped his revolver from the holster. "Who's the real animal, Master Mason?" he asked, clicking new rounds into the cylinder, one by one.

What men are we?

"Shh! Listen, you whoresons." The Ram's eyes peeked to the courtyard. *"Listen...."*

"What?"

"Listen, damn you."

The rhythm slowed...*the—the rhythm?* Disharmony turned to an eerie unison, slow and bellowing...breathing as one...*louder... louder still....*

Oh, do listen, Cyrus. You're missing the overture....

*The fears that lie in my heart and mind are tearing me apart...*like a beating drum...*woof...woof....*

It builds, and builds....

No. It grew louder. Wheezing huffs from a thousand shadowy havens, pulsing in slow, heartbreaking tempo. More of them. *Louder still...Woof...Woof...WOOF...WOOF...WOOF!...WOOF!*

Heavy footfalls echoed across the cobbles of the courtyard, thumping over the fire and rain. *What—what creature is this?* Inhuman weight pounded on the stone way with each stride, cracking what lay beneath.

And the drums...

...WOOF!...WOOF!...WOOF!...WOOF!

*The—the roar from before...*the cadence stole his courage with the bawls of the fire whooping behind him. The Furii stood like a statues, frozen solid as the steps—*those monstrous steps*—grew louder. The army of Wolves sang behind them. *WOOF!...WOOF!*

Heavens fucking help us. The Raven darted his eyes from man to man. The Ram furrowed his brow, tightly gripping his blunderbuss. The Sage smiled, unswaying. *Damn you, Deimos, you fucking mad man.* But, Reed and Eydian swayed in their boots, and Cyrus shuddered. *What boys are we?* Cyrus jerked his pistol, the cylinder clinking hard into place as he cocked the hammer back. *I shan't go back to the Prison without a fight....*

The lumbering steps stopped—*quiet.* The fire roared amidst the new stillness. Burnt oranges and yellows flickered on the Furii's faces as the light shimmered in their blood and sweat and the haze of their eyes. *Quiet as the crypt, save for the inferno.* No one moved, nor spoke, nor *breathed.* Their eyes moved over the room nervously, window to window, door to door. *My heart is set to burst....*

The breath pushed forcefully through Cyrus's nose as he held the shakes at bay. *I hear its haunting ring,* he thought, aching. *The bell of the devil and the deep...toll, it rings....*His body trembled with each harsh breath, the blood of the old gods coursing the length of him—body and brain, to the violent beating in his chest...*the drum.*

TOLL.

His addled mind floundered in the heat. *Deimos, help me,* he pleaded, but no words escaped him. The Sage smiled back.

TOLL.

*And so she tolls on me....*He thought of death for the first time since, and leaving without her again. *I've—I've died so many times... what's once more?* He dared not speak her name, for fear of his curse's hold. *With life and death comes great, great cost. It has cost me dearly.*

You honor me with a final prayer?

No, Spirit...not even you could steal her from me here. I fear not your shackles.

TOLL...

"RAH!"

The crescendo!

BOOOOOOM!

The entrance exploded inward, hurling wooden remnants and stone from the archway into the cathedral. Cyrus ducked, his aim fixed under raining splinters and the dust and smoke swallowing the room. An unnatural pause shrouded the room in silence, save for the billowing wind and the rubble clacking to a halt. Thick smoke seeped past the shadows outside. *What—I can't make it out.* The Raven squinted, shaking, stiffening his stance, his hand trembling, revolver rattling.

"*Some—something's moving,*" he whispered.

A figure rose from the shadows. *A silhouette*—Cyrus was sure of it. As if two black hills were rolling under the haze. *Gods no,* he thought. *Not hills—shoulders.*

ROAAAAR!

With a deafening shriek, the beast barreled through the rest of the demolished door, toppling the Ram. *"AGH!"* he roared back. His blunderbuss slipped through his fingers as he barreled into the pews.

The beast towered over Dagfinn, rearing and writhing. Cyrus saw the beast in the burning light, seizing and swiping and shrieking as it swung unsightly, chaotic limbs at the Ram, tearing the pews around him apart.

"Run, you fool, run!" shouted the Sage.

Cyrus dashed away, narrowly missing one of the colossus' errant swings. *A monster among his own*—one of the accursed, but *far* worse. Larger, *hairier*, its hulking muscles were lined with pustules that swathed sinewy limbs, a great bull ape of power and rage. There was something tied to the arm—*nay, chained...a boulder?* Harder than stone—*iron.*

ROAAAARRRR!

Its cries were deafening. Cyrus fired, peppering its swollen, bulking shoulder. *That won't do.* The creature whirled around, shrieking like a banshee, boring the call into the overtaxed ears of the Furii and cracking the stained glass above. Its shattered shards rained down.

SING TO ME, CYRUS....

"FOR GODS' SAKE!" shouted Deimos, dashing forward. With Moonlight drawn and glimmering, the Sage sliced at the leg and haunches. The thing recoiled, wailing and swinging. The chain ball caught him, launching Deimos across the hall.

No.

He crashed through a row of pews, slamming the wall behind. The beast roared again as the smaller Wolves poured into the cathedral. *No, no, NO!*

Yes.

"Dagfinn, get up, you *brute*! Deimos!"

The Ram shouted from the rubble. "*Agh*, shite, the limey bastard!" He yanked the hammer from over his shoulder and caught the nearest Wolf in the midriff. *Crunch.*

"Reed!" Cyrus cried over his shoulder, "Fight toward me! Dagfinn, deal with the giant!"

Reed ignored him, rushing to Eydian. "Come, brother, let's take this bloke!"

"*Reed!*" Cyrus yelled once more, cutting through another. "Fight, *damn you!*"

The beast shrieked and wailed, fixing its grotesque gaze on Mason and Brynjar, swinging its chained arm high in the air, and crashing it down just to their front. The iron cracked on stone, hurling shards in all directions and spraying the youngbloods. Reed's vigor remained as he jumped and dashed away from the monster's frenzy, but not so Eydian. He was sluggish and shaky, and he fell clumsily to a knee, dropping his rapier.

Gods, no....

Great cost, you say?

"Get up, brother!" shouted Reed.

Eydian crawled to his feet, scrambling away, but it pursued. *It's too fast.* Reed heaved his messer high and swung at the brute's exposed leg, catching it above the knee like a cleaver to a roast. The beast wailed and swung, swatting Reed away like a doll. Reed tumbled through the ladder, crashing into the shelves.

No.

"Stonehands!" the Ram hollered, hacking away at the crowd.

*So many....*Feral, ghoulish fiends filled the antechamber from under every rock and shadow.

"Stand up, Mason! There's a good lad!"

Reed lifted himself to a knee but fell back down. "Dagfinn," he wheezed, emptily clutching at his chest. "Eydian—*ugh*—Eydian...."

The Ram swung his hammer through two more, "*Argh*—huh?"

"*EYDIAN!*" Reed choked, pointing.

The beast charged, blundering through pews and splatting frothy drool onto the stonework. The Golden Sun's cutlass gleamed, and he stood his ground. The Ram pushed toward him, but was tackled by two more. They bit and gnawed and clawed at the old Furii's shoulders and neck.

"*AGH!*" the Ram roared.

*Too many....*Cyrus sliced and stabbed at the horde to the front—*the vanguard,* he thought. *They keep coming.* He caught the tip of a rusty cutlass to the rib and lurched. *Ah, damn!* The Raven swatted the blade out and away, replying with his serpentine dagger hilt-deep in the beast's neck.

More pushed past him, hopping onto Dagfinn. He tore a gangly Wolf from over his shoulder and hurled the body into the others. The Ram drew a bowie knife from his kit, slashing at the mob with his off hand as they wrestled his hammer away.

"Where's the Sage?!" Cyrus cried.

"Deimos...," Reed wheezed, graduating to a knee. Three wolves clambered to him. Cyrus pulled his gladius free in time to catch one under the throat, the tip buried in chest and bone while he stomached the others' clubs and claws. *The boy can take a beating.* Reed covered his swollen face with an arm as he wrenched the shortsword loose from the meat, swinging wildly, catching fingers and forearms. They backed off a bit, shrieking, just in time for more to flood from the ceiling and the walls, past the Raven and over the heap weighing down the Ram. *The rat pile grows....What men are we?*

No men here, sweet Cyrus…only Me.

The Raven turned about as they encircled him, thrashing and screaming—their shoddy weapons hailing over him as he dipped and parried. Between wreckage and chaos, Cyrus eyed the glint of brass flickering beneath Reed's boots—*the Ram's blunderbuss.* The youngblood felt it, too, dropping to a knee and swiping it up. *That's it, lad!* The creatures cowered and backed away as the barrel trailed over them. He swung the gun around, pushing each back as they tried to flank him.

The Ram roared, trying to rise under the weight of the dregs. "MASON, THE GIANT!" he bellowed. "SHOOT THE GIANT!"

Stonehands dropped the hammer. The blast punched through the noise, peppering scatter shot across the behemoth's back and shoulder, spattering a red cloud over the pews and the dead. The giant lurched and staggered, its writhing squeals resounding across the cathedral. Eydian lunged forward, his cutlass poised. *Gods in hell!* Cyrus panicked.

Contact—the blade landed, tipping hilt-deep in the beast's throat, poking through and out the back. The Golden Sun held on, one hand firmly gripping the handle. He tugged, but the weapon stayed put. The beast gurgled and sputtered and reared, catching Brynjar with the chain ball and slamming him to the floor.

The monster swatted at the blade softly with his free hand, wincing as it spurted blood. *Stuck,* Cyrus smiled. *We must help him free it.*

Set him free, Cyrus….

Out, damn you!

Eydian crawled backward, but the beast followed. It was standing and swaying over him, the sword protruding from its throat as the blood poured down the front. The giant dropped his arm and grabbed

Eydian's leg, dragging him closer. It stood tall, raising the chained cannonball high above his head. The Brynjar Prince struggled to move, to crawl, but was frozen to the stone as the creature's muscles flexed and tightened menacingly above.

"*EYDIAN, MOVE!*"

BANG! A shot came from the other side of the hall. *THWACK.* The bullet tore through the giant's eye, spewing blood and skull out the back. *Music to my ears.* Cyrus had no time to be relieved as he caught another blow from the crowd. *Damn!* he recoiled. *It doesn't end!*

Nothing ends, Cyrus.

The giant's knees buckled as the creature collapsed forward. Eydian rolled sideways, narrowly avoiding the crashing carcass that slammed the ground where the young Furii formerly lay, cracking the stone. Deimos was kneeling, unshouldering a smoking rifle near the transept. *You beautiful bastard.* He stood, drawing his saber with one hand and clutching his side with the other.

"Aha!" Eydian yawped. He laid his head on the stone.

"Get up, brother!"

Deimos began hacking away at the horde, but more of them flooded into the hall. *More—an impossible number....* A thick haze hovered in the air as the beasts clamored over their slain brothers, clawing, scratching, and shrieking as they came, and came...*and came.* Beneath the Furii's feet, a sludge amassed on slick stone as weapons and limbs blocked their footfalls. The very same sludge layered on their faces and clothing—a dark crimson and black. *We are the canvas, burdened with their souls, streaked across our hearts like our skin....*

Good, Cyrus...but, am I not the painter, then?
So generous with my strokes....

The Ram exploded out from under his heap—bodies hurled in all directions as his iron fists ripped and smashed and swung. *They... ate him*—half-devoured by the look. The Ram's body was marred with chunks ripped from their places, with bite marks and claw cuts, and tethered gore, glimmering in the firelight. He roared like the devil—*not like you, Spirit*—the deep, guttural cry of a brute—*a beast.* He found his hammer, too, and went to work like a sculptor to marble—*artists, one and all.*

They killed them in droves, yet more came. *Through cracks in the walls, the rafters, front and aft doors, and the ground—by gods, the ground—they keep coming!*

Boom...Boom.... Shooting, far off—*from where?* The room was stifling, thick with the rain's vapors like the blood, and the sweat steamed from Cyrus's brow, glistening serenely among the chaos. Devastation stung in Cyrus's eyes—*the sweet nectar flows into them.* They were swollen and full, but a smile curled across his face, and the blood slipped in.

Careful of the drink.

It—it burns, and it freezes.... He crawled hand over hand, pushing through the corpse pile back to the center. *Ugh, the smell.* Reed and the Ram were nearly atop one another, pushing and hacking as feet slipped on the wet stone and bodies below.

Stay up, damn you—you'll be buried! Eydian. *Where's Eydian?*

"EYDIAN?!" shouted Cyrus.

Cacophony.

Reed swung the messer hard through three of them in one swing. *Not the runt, I grant him.* He lifted his head above the crowd but must have seen nothing. He swatted a hand on the Ram's bloodied shoulder, "DAGFINN—*EYDIAN!*" he screamed, pointing to the center.

The Ram nearly swung on him in his rage, but stopped short. *Not lost yet.* He eyed the other side of the room and nodded. Dagfinn lowered his shoulder, charging back into the fight. He barreled through a line of them, sweeping his hammer in a wide arc, thudding and cracking. Reed followed, heaving with his broadsword from low to high. *He nearly dropped the thing.* Cyrus laughed.

The Raven's thrashed black cloak slopped around like a mop made of entrails. It swayed along, heavy and wet with his motions. The roars of the Wolves returned, muting out the Furii.

WOOF...WOOF....

The chorus swells....

Reed looked to the Raven, desperate. *He dared not look to me before.* The boy Furii mouthed his best friend's name, *EYDIAN.* He pleaded with his eyes, and Cyrus felt a decent shred of soul left. He breathed deep, nodding and wrenching his estoc free of recent prey. The Furii pushed together—Reed to the front, hacking in a frenzy, swinging and screaming and thrusting as the bodies fell, settling beneath their feet. *Eydian....*

Deimos's bobbing head appeared, trudging over the heap. They met at the spot Eydian was thought to be. *No sign of him.*

"SAGE!" Reed roared, "EYDIAN, WHERE'S *EYDIAN*?!"

The Sage slashed another. *"HE'S...."* Deimos didn't finish, only shook his head. He pointed behind him and, with the attention of the others, shouted, *"OUT!"*

"EYDIAN!" Reed hollered back.

"DEAD...GET OUT!"

Cyrus's heart sank. Reed turned back to the melee, cleaving more furiously than before. *Poor cricket.* Deimos grabbed at his shoulders, pulling him away, but Reed landed an elbow in the Sage's side and continued to carve and chop. *Like a Blackwood tick, the Burden has its teeth in this one.* He sighed. *Sad for one so young.*

The Sage fell back, and Dagfinn stepped in, wrapping a burly arm around Reed's throat and easing him away from the onslaught...

and away from Eydian. He whispered something in his ear. *What did he say, I wonder?* Cyrus pushed their way, stabbing at the mob as the Ram soothed Reed like a babe. The Sage pointed at something. *Huh?* The Raven looked around, puzzled.

Follow the light you so covet, Cyrus.

Light, indeed. The Sage's finger pointed to the glowing holes in the bookcase, piercing the crumbling wall behind. *I see it,* thought Cyrus, *no Wolves.* His heart jumped.

The Ram dragged Reed that way, but the boy kicked and cried, "NO, EYDIAN! *NO!*" His balled fist thudded into Dagfinn's eye.

"Argh," groaned the Ram, relenting.

Reed freed himself, quickly moving back to the nave and the fray, roaring as he went. *"RAH!"*

No more martyrs today, brother.

BOOM—CRASH.

Cyrus smashed into him with open arms, tackling Reed across the way and into the bookcase. The two smashed through, dragging loose mortar and brick down as they tumbled, spewing stone and timber out into the night air as their broken bodies bounced and tumbled down and down...*and down.*

They slammed and slid, grappled together. The two rolled to a stop down the stone ambulatory causeway, the Raven on top of Reed. *Don't you dare, Spirit.* The rain drizzled, cooling Cyrus's brow as he ached from the spill.

"Remember yourself, damn you!" he shouted.

"I won't leave him!"

His struggling ceased—a sudden, boundless quiet met them. *The fire barely roars at all....* The Raven raised his head—*no Wolves.* He eyed Reed, still struggling under his grip.

"Get off me, you coward!" Reed cried.

"Cyrus, get him up!" hollered Deimos, emerging from the glowing hole they'd made in the church wall. Deimos and Dagfinn sprinted clumsily down.

The Sage reloaded his rifle as he ran. "Hustle, damn ye!"

The Raven pinned the Furii's jaw with his elbow, immobilizing him. He leaned in, and the chaos around them slowed, somehow. "He's gone, brother—there's nothing left for you in there."

"ARGHH!" he roared, thrusting his hips upward, launching Cyrus out of his saddle.

Cyrus reached out. "Reed, please—"

"Speak no more, you snake!" He got away, vying for a weapon.

"Don't!" shouted Deimos, arriving with the Ram.

Reed pushed the Sage. "Away!" he roared.

"Brother, *LOOK and see!*" the Sage pleaded, pointing.

Reed heaved and growled, but his eyes found the hole. The Wolves poured out like ale from a cask.

"Come, brother—*COME,*" Deimos urged. "Look at me—*LOOK AT ME!*" Their eyes met. "I saw him—I *saw* him, I swear it....*I saw him*, and he's *gone....*"

"DEIMOS!" shouted the Ram, cutting down two of the first pursuers. "He comes or goes, but we must flee."

"Come," said Deimos. He put a final round in his repeater and wrenched the lever. The steel rang in the dark to the withering flames and a returning wind.

Reed stood like a statue, staring blankly at the swarming hole. Stone bricks broke and fell as the gateway grew, the Wolves so thick in number that their limbs and mouths and hair melded together, wriggling as one. They pushed and thrashed as they squeezed through. *Gone,* Cyrus admitted. *He must be gone.*

Reed turned his narrow shoulders. With his head bowed, he ran with the others.

XVII

CIRCLES

Marcus—Past

A strange place this is. The strangest, probably, by the mortal man's dial. Time runs together, here, with something betwixt.

This must be...

...the Prison Without Walls.

I shudder. The light lifts, and my eyes adjust. There's grass here, and trees, too, and gentle sounds of an ocean I have yet to see. I see ancient foundations of stone walls and archways, where ruined carvings of hideous beasts dot the land as well as the humans that worshipped them. They are worn and ill-defined, but my heart feels the truth in them, and I begin to fear my loneliness.

"How long have I been here?" I ask.

"Eternity," says the darkness.

"No, I mean, how long since I arrived?"

The darkness offers no reply. I walk for a time or what feels like time, I can't be sure. The world fades in front of me as it does behind, and I turn back. The path is gone, despite my walking. Confusion turns to fear again.

"WHY AM I HERE?!" I scream.

Stillness.

"What will become of me?"

Nothing.

"Is it ended, then?"

"Is what ended?

A voice.

"Life, I suppose?" I say to the darkness. "Who are you? I feel as if a weight has lifted from my chest—"

"No," the voice answers.

"No?"

"The answer to your question...."

A slender, pale hand forms outstretched from the inky black. "I dare not take it," I say. "Where—where am I?"

The hand returned to the shadows. "All things have their beginnings. You were born of a mother's womb, and the cosmos must be born, same as a Crow...."

"I...I don't—"

"But, heed my words, newborn...." The hand returned, holding a ripe red apple in the palm. "Nothing ends."

XVIII

WOLVES IN WINTER

Reed

I…I…I cannot stop. Reed Mason's dogged limbs cramped and shook as he ran—one foot narrowly landing before the other. The creaking pains of cramps tugged at the sinew of his thighs, but he was far beyond ignoring them. *They—they took pieces of me…and Eydian.…*His lip quivered.

Reed's trousers were thickly wet, drenched in blood and water and sweat. *Gods in fuckin' hell, they ate him.…They fuckin' ate him!* His addled mind bounced with the satchel over his hip. *We run now…like we might've before.*

Deimos's rifle clanked on the stone, setting a frenzy upon the others. "Sorry," he said, tipping stiffly with a groan to fetch it from the dirt. "It's—damn, if I can't hold the thing." He winced, dabbing at his ribs.

The Ram swatted his shoulder. "Broken?"

"Aye, I s'pose—*damn,*" he choked.

The Ram leaned over and picked it up. "Come now, brother. You'll be mended by morn." He handed the rifle off, but Reed saw the tremors dancing up Dagfinn's arm. *The skin hangs by threads.…*

They escaped the Wolves by a narrow breadth. *We—we outlasted them. We are Furii, sturdy and…able.…*The trek outside the village went on forever. *Forever,* he groaned, *Eydian's gone…forever.*

The sounds of the Wolves turned to distant murmurs as the wind and the weather waned together. His panicky nerves got the better of him.

THERE—*no, just a shadow.*...His trigger finger itched as the neck hairs ceaselessly rose. *Push the terror out,* he pleaded with himself, *but it digs so deep.*

They forded a gentle stream, scrubbing the scent from their boots and britches as best they could. Reed clawed at his clothes and skin in the icy water, but the blood clung to them like tar. *No, not tar...nothing like it*—*not like anything else in the whole world.* It was a part of him, unpliable and stuck—dyeing his skin, even. He shivered and trudged. *I cannot stop.*...The freezing water squished with each footfall, softly sounding in the wood with the rhythmic cadence of tired breaths, steaming in the dark. *It sounds as if...rah... rah...rah....*

The Sage held up a hand, beckoning them to halt. "A house, just yonder," he whispered.

"We can't stop," said the Ram. "We stop—*we die.*"

"We can't go on, either," said the Raven.

Deimos dropped to a knee. "If we can stop, we must—look," he said, pointing eastward, "sunrise, and soon."

"Aye." Cyrus nodded. "If we hold 'til daybreak, we'll be rid of the Wolves, at least."

"Deimos." Reed shook. "Look." He pointed to the old cottage—*lamplight.*

"*Shite....*"

"Makes no difference—this is their unlucky day," Reed said with a trill in his voice, reaching for his gladius.

"Careful, youngblood," cawed the Raven. "Don't go spring another ambush this night."

"*I...*I will cut out your tongue, and—"

Deimos shushed them both. His eyes bounced from one to the other, then back to the house. His fingers found his cheek and lips, tapping as he pondered. After a long pause, he looked at Cyrus. "A risk we'll assuredly have to take. Come, *clear this house.*"

"*With pleasure.*"

Reed sped forward, the rest in tow. They were tightly stacked behind him, guns and blades at the ready. The Raven ran to the far corner, just under the lanterned window, his revolver high. He held his poniard in the other hand, his balled fist supporting the pistol as he skirted around and outside. Deimos and Reed took their places to either side of the doorway—a dark and mossy thing, with a shoddy iron latch pinning it closed. The Raven appeared with his thumb raised, stacking position behind Reed. Deimos held three fingers high, then two, then one...

BANG.

The Ram barreled through the door, and the others promptly followed. Deimos's repeater was high and pointed, clearing corners and tracking toward the lantern, as the dark empty corner moved.

"Evenin'," came a familiar voice. Then, a metallic click.

Deimos secured the hammer with his thumb and rode it slowly forward. "Swansong...."

"In the *fucking* flesh," Cyrus breathed in relief, collapsing to the floor.

Swansong was perched on one knee, her breechloader long-gun standing near as tall as Deimos against her shoulder, the scratched brass of the scope glistening in the lamplight. Her tattered cape was coated in foliage and camouflage, a distinct rustling of the flora echoing around the cabin as she stood to greet them.

Deimos approached with an outstretched hand. "Tis a welcome sight, m'lady."

No, that I won't allow, Reed thought, his blood curdling. Reed's hand seized the Sage's shoulder, ripping it backward.

Deimos stumbled back. "What the—"

Reed throttled Swansong into the wall, his forearm pinned tightly over her throat. His gladius hovered, pointing just a hair off her unflinching eye. "Where the *FUCK* were you?!"

"Reed!"

"I'll fucking kill you, by the gods, I swear," he spat.

Swansong stood motionless, her eyes fierce, deeply gazing back to his, but nearer to a corpse than a living thing.

"*You fiend—you've killed us!* You could have *helped* us…," Reed pleaded. "You—you disappeared. *Eydian*…he—he died because of you."

"Reed, *please*," Deimos said.

"QUIET, you!"

"Remember yourself, damn ye!" the Ram boomed.

Cyrus let out a heavy sigh. "Nay, brother," he said flatly. "That'd be the Wolves…and *you*, even."

"What did you just say?" Reed turned his head, a violent shake to his voice. *Have I forgotten, then, who my enemy is?*

The Raven shouldered smugly against the wall, holstering his pistol and sheathing his poniard as he pulled his canteen stopper and began to sip. "I said, your *beau* died at the hands of a bloodthirsty mob—you would blame his death on a petty *mortal? Quite* fitting."

"*ARGGHHHHH!*"

Reed threw Swansong to the floor and hurled himself at the Raven, gladius poised. *I will not hear one more word from the snake in the grass. It was him!* Reed writhed. *He's why Eydian's dead, I SWEAR IT!*

"*YOU!*" he roared.

"Careful, youngblood—"

The pistol and poniard appeared in the Raven's hands—*faster than lightning.* He caught Reed's short sword and hurled it away as his revolver's barrel found its place sunk in Reed's eye.

"*ARGH!*" The Furii roared, but stopped short. *No,* he thought— Reed was immobilized, embraced by the Raven with a blade point prodding the veins in his arm as the barrel of his six-gun stayed steady, hard-pressed into Reed's eye socket.

"You see, *dear brother*," the Raven hissed, "that temper of yours will be your *undoing*."

Reed roared again, *"I WON'T SLEEP 'TIL YOU'RE DEAD!"* He struggled against the steel, slicing willfully into the dagger. Cyrus kicked one of his knees out and moved the poniard from arm to throat, pushing the gun *farther* into his eye in the process—*no, no, NO!* Reed fell to a knee with the Raven towering over him, barrel halfway to his brain and his throat naked to the Raven's blade.

"*Ah-ah-ah,*" Cyrus hummed, "don't you see, young Furii?"

Reed lurched and growled, his good eye fixed on the empty ones above him.

"How did you find yourself here? A moment ago, you held the power, no? Swansong was yours to threaten, without so much as a hope from the rest of us...."

Cyrus's face came close to his—Reed broke his eye contact to meet the Ram's, but the old Furii didn't look back.

"But, one small outburst from me, and you find yourself at the mercy of—what was it, a 'puny mortal'?"

Reed's breathing slowed. "*You....*"

"Aye, *Me*. But you—*you petulant fucking child*—are roaring and raging and tempting the wrath of Ares, gambling with our lives. Now, for another query—one for the group, perhaps—"

"I'll fucking kill you—"

"Hush, brother, please," Cyrus said, pressing the revolver deeper. "I am professing, here. What's the difference between us and them? Hmm?"

I'll not answer to you, coward.

"The difference, brothers and sisters, is nothing."

"What?"

"Aye, you heard right—not Wolves nor beasts—people, same as us…hairy, plagued, and pestilent with rage like the devil, but people nonetheless. A tragic species, to be sure…cursed by a bygone age, trying only to live."

"You call *that* 'people'?" the Ram asked.

"As much as I call *us* 'beasts.'" He raised his face from Reed's and continued, but much lower, "What happened back there was an ambush if ever there was one. This was planned. Someone knows—"

"He's right," came Swansong's flat voice from the far wall. *A soothing voice, tempting and evil.*

"Which part?" Cyrus asked.

"'Twas the Banner—I'm sure of it," she said.

The Ram turned. "And how might ye know this, Songbird?"

She stood. "Before sundown, I saw him—the Zealot. Silver glinting from a mile away—nearly mistook him for the church itself."

"Who?"

"The Acolyte," Deimos said, "Father Elatreus."

"*Don't*…call him that," the Raven seethed.

The Ram looked puzzled. "What's it to you, Raven?"

"Weren't you paying attention in the war room?"

"'Tis the Cornicen alright," Deimos said. "M'lady, did you see any other—"

"Yes," she said.

"Come again?"

"Yes, his brother was there, too. The Iron Bull."

"The *Iron Bull*?" Reed sputtered. "He—he's—"

"Not technically his brother." Cyrus smirked. "Searix Uro-Genos is his cousin."

"Shut your gob, swine—*ARGH*," Reed recoiled under the deepening barrel.

Deimos held up a hand to forestall Cyrus. "Was there anyone else from the Tattered Banner?"

"The Witch—the Iomara woman?" the Ram asked.

"I saw no one else," she said, "but the Raven speaks true. They knew we were coming."

"Why didn't you pull the trigger, then, girl?" asked the Ram. "I've seen you put steel through skulls from leagues farther."

Swansong said nothing.

"She tried," Deimos answered for her. "We heard shooting from the steeple. Be glad they weren't waiting for us in the alley."

"*Doubtful*," Reed chided.

Cyrus pulled his revolver and blade from their lodgings and buried his boot in Reed's chest. *The* hit threw him away and down, sliding to a stop on his back, just under the Ram. He lifted his head with tense muscles, as if to bound back to the Raven, but Dagfinn put a heavy boot on his chest.

"I'd stay down if I were you, lad—we may not like the man, but best to pick them battles."

"Dress your wounds," Deimos said with a sigh, his hand tending gently to his ribs. "The sun rises. We rest, only as long as it takes us. Post a sentry. We move by midday."

"I'll take the first watch," the Raven volunteered.

The Ram raised a boot from Reed's chest and offered a hand. He scoffed, shaking his head, but took the meaty palm nonetheless. Dagfinn launched him to his feet with one arm. He wiped the dust from his coat, recovering but avoiding the Raven's wandering eye. *This is far from over.*

Cyrus turned to Swansong, still standing against the wall nearest the window and the lantern, her hair the color of the sunset, burning even brighter in the flames, with eyes like glacier ice in the depths of winter. "I'm glad you're here, darling," he said.

She smiled.

Reed groaned.

The Raven turned back to Reed, who'd since taken a seat near the Ram and began dressing a bite on his neck.

"Don't," Reed said.

"My apologies, sir," Cyrus said.

"I said, *don't.*"

"I mean no insult, brother, but you know as well as I that the Burden has gotten the best of you more than once this eventide."

"Are *you* here to remind me?" Reed asked, ripping the dressing between his teeth. "You're the newest blood here."

"Aye…well, as well as these gentlemen, here—I offer no insult, only my condolences for the loss of your friend."

Reed said nothing.

"You think me callous," Cyrus continued, "but the truth is that more of us are likely to perish before the journey's end. The life of a Furii is a lonely one, to be sure, but I'm sure you know that."

Silence.

"But, I will remind you that *our* survival depends on *your* control, and the same goes for the rest of us."

Reed's glare was palpable, his ripping and tearing of the dressing almost as loud as the gunfire from moments past. The Raven offered a final smug nod—*pompous, ha'p'orth shite.* Cyrus turned back to Swansong, friendly and flirting in the shadows of the Golden Sun's death. *The man knows no bounds.*

"I'm sorry, too," Dagfinn said. "'Tis a shame he was lost to you, but if not him, it would've been you." He began sharpening his buckskin boot knife and cutting strips of gauze, dabbing them on bite marks and open wounds.

Reed nodded but looked away. "There's no chance of catching their defilement, is there?"

"You mean, like, become one of those things? Heavens, nay, brother—despite what the old tales might suggest. Those poor devils are born that way, not *made* to be such things."

"Poor devils?"

"Aye, poorest of poor, to be sure. Doomed to live as they do—hunted for sport in my part of Tara. Smarter than you may think, they are, even cunning, but butchered like wild dogs."

"I shan't pity them," Reed said.

"I wouldn't expect it, but perhaps in time. Say, I've been meaning to ask, what does that-there inscription on your blade say?" He pointed at the carved letters in Reed's messer—*Josey*, they read. "A girl from back home, mayhaps?"

"No."

"A sister?"

Reed threw the rag to cover the name. "No, sir, not a sister, nor any of your business for that matter."

The Ram dabbed at his neck again, "Come, brother, don't be that way. I've seen twice the hardship as your young life—hell, I've *been* the hardship for as many others. What's a tale among friends?"

"A tale not worth telling, I daresay—"

"Oh, is it perhaps something to do with your namesake? Ah, what was it again," the Ram said, snapping his fingers, "That's right, *Stonehands!*"

Reed's eyes rolled far back in his head as he poured water from his canteen on more serrated flesh. Deimos came over, seating himself next to Reed, his hand still glued to his ribs, tenting the looseness of his coat.

"Ahh," he wheezed, collapsing next to Reed. "Please, brother, a tale would do us nicely."

"Please, Sage, I don't wish—"

"*Reed*," he said, "you've lost a friend, same as all of us, and Lord Brynjar has lost his own beloved son tonight, he will soon come to know. You're distressed, same as the rest of us….We beg you."

The Ram nodded agreeably.

Reed looked between the two. "That tale ends only in tragedy," he said, "perhaps not fitting for the circumstance."

"Quite the contrary," the Sage said, "I can think of no better time for a somber tale."

"Not a tale, even—a memento, if anything…."

"Sing to us of your *memento*." The Ram laughed.

"The shorter the better," said Deimos, "we must rest soon."

"Fine," Reed retorted impatiently. "Fine...you wish to know who Josey was, do you?"

The two Furii looked on, eyes wide, ever silent.

"I killed her. My hands crashed down on her head like 'bricks of stone,' they said—unrelenting. I crushed her in the Forge on one of the sparring days. Josey beat me in the first round, as all other aspirants looked on. I was so prideful, so embarrassed. I told myself I'd been going easy, but the next round I beat her senseless—*to death*—with my bare fucking hands for all the world to watch. She—*she*...." He choked. "*Ahem*...she foamed pink at the mouth, and I—I....They cheered me and laughed and clapped, and my fists crashed harder and harder...and *harder.*"

"The Forge?" the Ram asked. "So many perish there, brother, what difference does it make?"

"*What?*" Reed spat.

Deimos simply nodded.

"*Difference?* All the fucking difference!" Reed stood. "Did none of you earn your Ascension as I did? Except you, Raven, of course... *you thankless cunt.*"

"Come again?"

"You fought at the Blacktide, I hear, 'Hero of the Bloodmoat,' right?"

"Aye, *hero*—to be fucking sure. I stormed the beaches with those poor devils, watched as steel and shot peppered boys and men that didn't stand a chance. Thousands survived the beaches only to drown in the fuckin' moat. There was no justice there, only luck. I was lucky to survive—that was my only credit. *I survived.* Heralded for only carrying a rifle far enough inland as not to die, never to fire it...*Hero of the fucking Bloodmoat.*"

"You downplay yourself, sir," said the Sage.

"I thought going to the Forge would separate me from those men—the ones that so wastefully send fathers and brothers and sons to their doom. I thought I could change them—thought I could be better. Keep safe my integrity and honor the chivalry of our fore-bears...but no, I beat a woman to death, for no insult, and instead of punishment or scorn, I was met with only celebrity. Claps on my back and toasts to my fuckin' health. And here, Eydian Brynjar, the Golden Sun, one who earned his title the proper way—with valor and courage—*died like a dog*. They're probably eating him as we speak. 'Tis fitting, I should think, that I kept Josey with me all these years, so that with every swing of my sword or pull of my trigger, I'm reminded of it...my guilt....Reminded that I should have died so long before so many others. Her name survives, ringing in my ears, every moment, sleeping or wakeful...*Josey...Josey...Josey....*"

"They send their daughters, too," said Swansong. Her soft voice was more heavenly than before.

"Aye, I'm sorry." Reed sighed. "Even now—ever prideful."

"We have far more in common than you think, brother," said the Ram.

"I don't doubt it, Lord Einar," he said, "but how often do you *yearn* for death?"

"The Burden digs deep, brother," said the Sage. "Say—Cyrus!" he exclaimed, hopping up to the window. "Well, I'll be damned! If that isn't good ol' Shadow, grazing there!"

"Huh? What?" The Raven perked up.

"Shadow, my black beauty lives!"

Reed looked out, eyeing a black horse in the distance, shimmer-ing in a wet red—*tainted with blood like the rest of us. That looks an ill omen*, Reed thought, dabbing at a wound. He looked to the Raven, who'd since turned a ghostly pale.

XIX

CLOSURE

Reed

Reed hadn't slept since Eydian's death, but he drank. The fortnight since had been a murky fog, bathed in bleakness and booze. *That* night…the one that changed it all—an eventide of shattered hope—couldn't be undone. It survived in his wakeful moments, and he repelled his dark thoughts as best he could. *Another sip.* He shuddered.

What's the point? Why go on? They stole the only friend that he could think of and the only son to a man who couldn't know yet. The King of Norsefyre remained unaware that Eydian was gone. *The Golden Sun is gone*—torn apart by fiends in a dank smoldering pit some place where no one would ever find him. *Gods save the Furii—mortal as they are….*

Few spoke of his drinking, save for the fucking Raven. That man had no filter, no sympathy, nor any kind of real remorse. It was his fault, to be sure—chasing his ginger-haired harlot up the ridge, right into the hands of the enemy. *The fuckin' Banner…FUCKIN' WOLVES…I'll kill that filth before the end, by the gods I swear…to this, I drink…hiccup.*

"How…how did they find us?" Reed asked, nudging the Ram, swaying.

"*Mason,* give it a rest," he scolded. "You're blue as a bruise—let it go."

"But"—*hiccup*—"how did they know? That insufferable *birdman* yonder—he told 'em somehow....I—I just—" He pointed to the far side of the campfire at the Raven, who was running over the map with the Sage and Swansong.

"Brother, you'll drown yourself in the drink if you keep up like this," said the Ram, grabbing at Reed's tankard. He yanked it away with a splash, taking another deep helping.

"*Ah-ah-ah,*" he hummed, wagging a finger. "Let me 'ave this, good sir"—*hiccup*—"I'm *grieving.*"

"You've grieved enough, brother. Don't let it consume you."

"What do you s'pose will happen when Tytan finds out? I 'spect he'll 'ave us hanged...." He took another swig.

"As ye might say—*doubtful,* brother," the Ram said, upending his own canteen. "He'll be devastated, surely, but he knows the risks, same as all of us. If he wanted living children, he never should 'ave sent the poor boy to the Forge to begin with."

"Truer words ne'er spoken." *Hiccup.*

The Sage stood from the huddle and took a few steps toward the Ram, beckoning him to the map. Einar Dagfinn heaved himself to a knee, but winced as he put a hand on his bandaged neck. "*Agh, damn,*" he grumbled, dabbing at the dressing with a couple of fingers. "Bastard won't heal worth a shite."

"We ought 'ave scorched it," the Sage said, putting a hand under his shoulder, helping him up.

"Nonsense," Einar said. "What's the plan, oh, *wise one?*"

Deimos offered a hairy eye. "We believe there's an answer to our infiltration quandary—we're a day's march outside the Eryx, so we'll know more upon a reconnoiter, but the southern portcullis seems our best bet—"

"*Portcullis?*" the Ram puffed. "Pray tell, how do we sneak through a fuckin' portcullis?"

The Sage bit a lower lip before he spoke. "We know the Brynjar will come by sea," he said, pointing, "but we can't know if he means to scale the seawall and the ramparts yonder, *here*, or another route, perhaps....We can't know, but it gives us this side, *here*, to find an entrance—"

"No," Reed's voice echoed across the campsite.

"*No?*" the Sage asked, voice tense.

"A trap, that is," he said, head swaying low between his shoulders.

"Reed, perhaps you'll join us once you've sobered—"

"Agreed," Swansong chimed in, nodding his way, "to the sentiments, I mean—a trap."

"*What?* M'lady, we just spoke of this—"

"*They* knew we were coming, Mister Sage"—*hiccup*—"*they knew*...a trap, too easy...."

"In case you all *forgot*," the Sage said, "the Brynjar initiates the feint *here*—every guard in the city will move east to meet them on the ramparts. We must count on this distraction—"

"The drunkard is right, Deimos," came the Raven.

"*You*, too?"

"They know we're coming. *Someone* knows, or at least, so we should assume. A major thoroughfare isn't feasible—too risky."

"Doesn't matter," Swansong whispered. "Once alerted, they'd bar the gates. We'd need to be inside before then."

"Shite," the Sage muttered.

The Ram dropped a heavy finger on the map, nearly poking a sausage-sized hole through the brittle parchment. "Perhaps we ford the moat, here—could we scale the gatehouse 'round the side?"

"Have you been to the Eryx?" Deimos asked. "'Tis a wide-open outer courtyard and a high stone wall barbican overlooking the drawbridge...lit by torchlight upon the eventide and manned turrets all 'round—no chance we wouldn't be seen. The southern portcullis is the smaller—a gate built into a steep cliffside."

"Guarded nonetheless," Cyrus said.

"Aye."

"We need a way in ourselves," the Raven said. "We *must* be inside the keep when the attack begins; elsewise, we'll have no recourse. Stuck outside a locked down cathedral, stuck *inside* the walls of the Eryx, with ten thousand strong on the hunt...."

"'Tis a suicide mission." *Hiccup.*

"Go to sleep, *boy*," Deimos ordered, pointing an angry finger at a hazy-eyed Reed. "Cyrus," he said, turning back, "how do you s'pose we get into the chapel?"

The Raven hummed. "Grapple our way to the roof, I daresay—a way to the rafters, perhaps...."

"The Bird'll need a vantage point," the Ram said, nodding to Swansong.

"Aye, a reconnoiter will suit the location. You'll—"

"I choose my own position," she said flatly, eyes burning in the firelight.

"But, of course," Cyrus said. He rubbed his chin with a gentle finger. "That doesn't answer the question of the portcullis, though— say we can't get in? What then?"

"Grapplehook the loneliest wall, must be," said Dagfinn.

"Brothers," the Sage said, "and *sisters*, of course—who here has been to the Eryx?"

Cyrus raised his hand. The rest fell silent.

"The outer wall is tall and scarce," said the Sage, "manned by roaming sentry, turret top towers for every half-league—I mean swivel guns and grape shot and sharpshooters all alike—"

"We'll be quiet, then."

"And *that* only gets us to the lower bailey. We're met with an-other wall, another gate, and stair turrets, all standing in the way of the upper ward." No one's eyes met his. Deimos sighed and went on, "The Citadel is only the *forebuilding* of the upper bailey," he said, pointing, "an arsenal of powder and guns, with barracks hiding armies of Eryxian Imperial Guard—grenadiers, fusiliers, artillerymen, and light infantry. Say we get beyond that, only to find ourselves *outside* the Ashen Cathedral...."

"Told ye." *Hiccup.*

"*Gods be damned*," muttered Cyrus, standing up and turning toward the fire.

Reed's glassy eyes noticed but ignored the Raven's melodrama. He found much more comfort in Swansong, her glowing eyes blazing blue in the light of the fire. *She is haunting and far away.* The Swansong wore no vultus, and Reed was glad of it—*here, more than ever*—that he may feast his drunken hunger over the soft porcelain draped across her pointed features. Her soft cheeks met hard bones in just the right spots, where lips rested together, relaxed, in a place between a frown and the ethereal elegance only humans possess—*the horizon of her beauty*, he thought. A strand of auburn hair plunged below to a chiseled jawline like sweet nectar drizzling from the flower above, bunched but sleek, with subtle hints of blonde like a dazzling sunset. *Perfection*, he thought, *and how lonely I should feel because of it.*

"What about the Robber's Entrance?" she asked, eyes ever fixed on Cyrus.

Reed smiled. *She reminds me of Eryn.* A dagger sunk further in, dreaming of her onyx dress next to Eydian's gold coat at Norsefyre all those weeks before. *Never to meet again.* Reed imagined Eryn sitting in Swansong's place. *How—how could I explain Eydian? How will I?*

"Hmm?" the Ram grumbled. "Speak up, girl."

Her eyes moved to his with a crinkled brow. "The Robber's Entrance," she repeated.

The Ram looked to Cyrus. "You know about this 'Robber's Entrance,' Crow?"

Cyrus shook his head, and Deimos turned from the campfire. "Do you know of something we don't, miss?"

She shook her head. "But, every castle of the last millennium has a secret tunnel—the 'Robber's Entrance,' they always call it...and a patrician's way out in the event of a siege...or a Pontifex."

Deimos stood silent for a long while before responding. "Where?"

"She said she doesn't know, brother," Cyrus interrupted, "but the Eryx is old as Tara herself. There must be an entrance."

"How do you expect us to find it, bird boy?" said the Ram.

"You're the Furii, *goat man*," he replied. "Use your powerful *nose* if you must—that is our ingress, to be sure. There is no other way."

The Ram scowled, balling his fist on his thigh.

Deimos nodded. "Yes, that must be our priority. We make for the Eryx at first light—much hinges on the reconnoiter, and mere days we have before the Brynjar arrives. Let us not waste ourselves."

"Do you not know?" Reed smiled, swaying to Cyrus, nodding to the Ram.

"Come again?"

"You two are soul mates now...*linked*." He laughed.

"*The hell*, you say?"

"You'll start *seeing things*"—*hiccup*—"together."

"It's true, brother." The Sage nodded thoughtfully. "In some sense, he's your *father*—"

"Deimos," the Raven hissed.

Reed laughed until he choked. "Call him '*daddy*.'"

"Why do they call you 'Sage,' even?" shot the Ram. "You seem just a dry old spice...."

Reed gasped for breath, weeping. "*Ha*Ha*Ha*HaHa*Ha*HaHa*Ha*Ha-Ha*Ha*HaHaHaHaHa...."

"Would you like to know why they *really* call him 'Sage'? I am old, still, yet I remember," the Ram growled.

What?

"What?" the Raven echoed.

A crooked smile struck across Deimos's face, met with absolute silence from the rest. *His eyes are like tiny suns*, Reed mused.

"Should…should I fear as much?" He forced a laugh. "I could tell you now.…She was—"

"Deimos, please," came the Raven. "No need—"

"Nay," the Sage shot back, "surely, the centuries should blunt the blow. My daughter, she was…well, her name was *Sage*.…"

Reed's heart sank…*to the very bottom.*

The Ram's jaw tightened, but he didn't speak. Reed felt the shame in him.

"They lined the hall," murmured the Sage. "They were alienists back then—with vestals in their stained white.…"

Reed gulped.

"All those my darling girl left behind, and I stood among them. *She is one today*, I couldn't stop saying. I don't remember what day it was…her birthday, but I…*I don't remember.…*"

The Sage sniffled. "She never saw two. She rode the halls in her bassinet, carted through the windy corridors and saluting onlookers—the ones that stood and watched, bowing their graces, never a moment's peace.…They bowed, she bounced down the corridor."

He wiped his cheeks.

"The flies were the first to know. Like rats—like a scourge, they come before the soul of you has left. I saw the flies come for my poor girl before her soul left her body. I shooed them away, but the more I did, the more I cried and spat, the more they came. They lined her bare cheeks, and thighs…they buzzed in her hair, and then in her eyes."

"Deimos," whispered Cyrus.

Deimos spat. "The Furii are not to marry, nor sire, but there is no justice in coveting blood."

"She had strong Furii blood," the Sage persisted. "Her mother made sure of that—*Kathewulf*…but you damned Furii know too well how the Church covets their delights. They took her for my sins… and for her blood. They bowed as they stole her away from me. The soul of her, the mere drops that ran the lengths of her tiny veins… they took it…my dear *Sage*.…"

Reed wiped his eyes. He held up a drunken hand, hanging his sack of wine over the fire. "To lovely Sage." He nodded, taking a sip.

"To...to Sage," said the Ram sheepishly.

"Yes, drink up." The Sage chuckled. "I drank in her name, too—drank myself blind!" Deimos was laughing now. "They'd find me crying, and all I could say was *'Sage-Sage-S-S-Sage.'*" His tears came, too.

...

I...I can't remember what came next. The talking faded away, his memories blurring with the words and the flames and his drunken void. Reed lay awake, sleepless for another night—*so beautiful, and cold.* The fire did little to warm him, the starry skies above his only companions. *Leave a soldier to his stars....*

Cool sea breeze plunged through the trees, battling the warmth. *Uh-oh—too drunk*, thought Reed, as he had been for weeks and would be for a while longer—*least 'til the rum gives out.*

Thoughts swirled around with the wind and flames...*the flames*, he thought. He was referring to those atop Swansong's crown, as much as the campfire. *Swansong*, he mouthed. *Eryn.*

She was cleaning her weapon now, a blackened rag held in blacker fingers rubbing and scraping methodically across the steel bore. Her charging rod punched the barrel over and over, with a thumping and popping that danced between the creaking notes of the firelight.

What a strange journey it's been, he thought. *What a strange journey it will become.* He thought of Tytan Brynjar all those miles away, with all his wants and ambitions. A grieving father yet to know of his son's demise, toting the same pride in his pitiless pursuit for power. *He's just a man*, Reed admitted. *He thinks he can be something more.* His eyes found the brass circlet above Swansong's rifle, and he imagined Cyrus's smug face in the crosshairs. *I'll likely die tomorrow, or the next day perhaps. Maybe by the Raven's hand, even?* He chuckled to himself at the thought.

Uh-oh, thought Reed. *I'm—I'm too drunk....*

Woof…Wolves….

I'm shouting…at—at the Raven, I think…. "Is that a dagger?" I ask. He sways.

"Is that not a dagger there, you point at me?" Reed slurred.

"My hands are empty," replied the Raven.

"So clear it is—*plain as day*…a dagger you hold to my fragile throat, if not with your hand, with your words, at least." Reed drew a dagger of his own, flipping it between his fingers.

"Mr. Mason—"

"This here," he said, "this knife I outstretch is realer than yours—so *hungry* for the throats of those that would seek to betray *Me*…for I am not a man of *figments and fantasy*, nor are my faithful *knights*," he rambled.

"Gods in hell, has he lost it?!" the Ram growled.

"*Here*"—Reed swung back with a *hiccup*—"I sit, writhing under the tall shadows of my *faithless friends*, haunted by the cold of the dead and gone…."

"My heart aches for a drunkard's poetry."

"You mock me, do you?"

"I don't, sir," replied the Raven, "earnest."

"Then you shall sheathe your dagger as I will mine—you shall spit fire and spout rain at my *behest*," sputtered Reed, "and should you *falter*. By the gods, I will set the *dogs* upon you…."

The Raven faded out of view.

"For you know of the darkness I speak, damn you, so full of it you are, tainted between mind and soul. As if I don't know who you really are? *Patrian rat!* I know of"—*hiccup*—"exile…and, I…I know of *cost*…."

"What did you just say?" Cyrus hissed.

"What a fool you've turned out to be, Cyrus"—*hiccup*—"What a fool."

…

Has it been a day? A week? I know not when....

Lost, but I remain...awake, and alone. I consort with myself, and myself alone....I am so alone.

"You are an honorable man," I say to the drunken void. I am no more guilty than the rest, for what should merit my guilt over so many others just like me? Aye, guiltless I must be, for I have never done such ill as the likes of those around me.

Hiccup.

*I may have thought things a time or two—*hiccup*—petty crimes of mind, if not lust of body. But, no, I am an honorable man, to this, I swear. Cate—cape—capable only of the modest versions of the crimes of others. Well, I s'pose my crimes shan't be less than any others, but my intentions are pure, I assure....You are an honorable man, yea, says I.*

But...

Well, you see...hunger makes beasts of us all, like lust...and greed... and soon, I realize that perhaps I am less than an honorable man.

Far less.

I have stolen the souls of people from their vessels....I have bludgeoned and brutalized and mocked and sneered and lusted after and pined for and...and...the mothers of my victims should think me guilty, I expect. Not so honorable to Josey's parents, I gather. Hiccup.

To this, I drink.

"You beat my daughter to death, yet you say you are an honorable

man? You?! How dare you?!"

The darkness re-writes me…page by page…scratching out the sins. I sink to the very bottom….

It is cold, and lonelier. The hands of my victims shackle me to the shore. "I am not an honorable man," I say, suffocating.

No more time—the waves overcome. "I'm sorry," I choke. The ghosts weigh me down as I mourn those I do not know. Mothers I will never meet to children I have butchered like tender poultry meet me in my broken dreams. They scold me so—I am not an honorable man, so what must I be? One word stands above the rest…one that does not satisfy. I struggle to find a man at all—instead, a beast roams the moors of my mind, calling me to Nysa and the cliffside's roaring sea.

But, I will never find those times, nor revert the pain that creeps inside at all my cracks and corners. "There is no honor here in beasthood," says the darkness. Then, what sort of man must I be?

XX

ASCENSION

Cyrus

"I can use this," says the worm.
"Me too," say the grub, the roots, and the archaea we can barely see.

We are weighed and measured in the oldest way here. No more than
the hocks that flay in the butchery, we remain.

"I can use this," they say—the parasites, whatever kind—those that
dine on our bones. "Your meat and your string keep the light of me alive a
while longer," they say, and so they eat. "Good riddance," they delightfully
say between their bites.

And so, must we say, good riddance. Good riddance to want and
desire—to need and greed....

Let my soul die with my body, that I may bid my fears and ghosts
goodbye, for eternity is long—and even Tartarus fails to bar the titans
from my mangled mind....

There's hope for us yet, Cyrus thought. Swansong's shadow interrupted the new beams of sunrise, holding a slender arm outstretched,
thumb raised high. She trudged through the underbrush back to the

rally point. *Reconnoiter successful*, he thought. *She's found the Robber's Entrance.* He stowed his repeater over shoulder as he stood from the bushes, a conciliatory thumb of his own raised high and over his head.

"What say ye, then?" asked the Ram.

"Aye"—she nodded—"seaside cave under the portcullis—spotted a chimney of sorts. Didn't put eyes on the door. We may need to blast our way in."

Deimos rubbed his chin. "Hmm," he said, "Cyrus—how many hand kegs we still 'ave?"

Cyrus put a hand on Swansong's shoulder but looked back to the Sage. "Two powders—the only ones on Shadow's saddlebags."

He rubbed his chin a bit harder. "We'll need to double pack them and fuse them 'fore the eventide."

"Of course," Cyrus said, kneeling again. "Any news from the sea?"

"Not a peep," he said, "but we can't afford to wait much longer." He looked to Swansong. "Did you find your position? An overwatch?"

"Aye," she said, "but not ideal…will take time to reach, and you won't have much to spare."

"Time?"

"*Time.*" Cyrus smiled. "Where will it be—your spot, I mean?"

"A belfry," she said, unshouldering her rifle and resting on it.

"The *upper* belfry? That's a long way off—are you sure?"

Her eyes cut through Deimos.

He nodded.

They picked themselves up in the silence of the morning, edging slowly out of the brush and marching back toward the encampment. Reed and the Ram awaited, a stew broiling over the fire as the marchers unburdened themselves.

Reed scowled at Cyrus. *Sober.* He laughed. The rum had dried up, and he was glad of it. *No way to face one's demons*, thought the Raven. The boy's grief had moved on to misery and shame. *I doubt the Furii keep many friends for long, but a shame to bleed them so young.*

*The Furii.…*His heart sank again. He'd thought of it a few times since, but fought the realization as best he could. *They made me one of them*, he groaned. *I carry my own Burden already, and the Prison lives so deep and dark.…*

I think Myself a friend.

Out, damn you. Such a fleeting thing, life can be. The barrage of violence had hurried the stakes for Cyrus. It was a matter of moments between Eydian's gentle jests as they marched up the ridge and the cruel fate that became him in the end—*the card game that never truly ends…a gambling dance with the devil*—one that Eydian lost.

More will die before the end—many who won't deserve it. The Ram had been a help of sorts, but even he'd lost patience with Reed, Cyrus could tell. If he *had* friends like Eydian in his time, they'd have died in the centuries gone by, this he knew.

Cyrus stepped to his tent nearest Swansong's and unstrapped his pistol belt and powder horn. They clunked on the ground as he took a knee, reaching for a canteen and taking a hearty swig. The sun was peeking through the trees, and warmth blanketed the Furii as they situated themselves. Deimos trudged to a place near the Raven and Swansong, holding out a hand as Cyrus instinctively tossed him the canteen.

"It'll be a hike," he said, "when the time comes."

"Aye." Cyrus nodded and turned to Swansong. "How soon do you think you could be in position?"

"Midday, earliest," she whispered.

"Indeed," Deimos growled. "'Tis a waiting game, yet. The fleet will arrive in mere days—from now on, we keep a spotter over the sea. With sails, we strike."

"With your permission, dear Sage, I say we move our encampment. 'Tis a risk so near the wall, and we need more eyes on the horizon." Cyrus tore a ragged piece of jerky and stuffed it in his mouth.

"Aye, that will do, but the sun rises. We wait for—what was that?"

"Pardon?" the Raven asked.

"Shh!" he said, placing a finger to his lips.

Reed's eyes darted upward. "*Bells?*"

"Aye," the Ram echoed, "bells...."

"*Ships*—a long way off—*hundreds.*"

Cyrus and Swansong wore similar puzzled looks. "How can you—"

"*Haste!*" Deimos exclaimed. "We move for the sea—pack your shite!"

"But...no time to paint?" the Ram groaned.

Deimos pointed at the Ram's helm. "I doubt you'll be taking *that* off today, brother!"

"Ah," he said, "then, today's the day?"

Reed was shouldering satchels and belts in a frenzy along with the others. He hurled his messer over his shoulder, and the hilt clunked the back of his head with a sharp ring. "Ouch!" he rang out.

Cyrus laughed aloud. "Careful, greenhorn," he prodded, smiling.

"Fuck you."

"Reed," the Sage interrupted, "you, Einar, and Cyrus will carry the powder kegs. I doubt you'll need that blasted sword—too heavy."

He scoffed, "Would you say the same to Dagfinn about his hammer?"

Deimos smiled, wrenching his breechloader over his arm. "No, but then, you *are* still a greenhorn."

Reed rolled his eyes and continued to pack, unstrapping one of Shadow's saddlebags and shouldering it.

"Everyone ready?" said Deimos, turning for the path to the cliffs.

"And willing," said Cyrus.

She nodded.

"Everybody else, let us—"

BOOOOM.

A groaning boom echoed across the trees, stopping each of them dead in their tracks.

Toll.

"The siege," said Deimos. "The siege has started—*hurry.*"

They set off, swiftly running and ducking through low-hanging branches and dipping through holes in rock and hill. Cyrus looked to Reed, surprised to see him keeping up with the others. The wayward thumping of cannon fire shook the trees and ground with every step that put them closer to the Eryx. With a few leagues behind them, Cyrus eyed Reed's itching shoulders, struggling under the weight of his messer and the barrel that bounced beneath it.

The powder barrels themselves were clunky and painful, heavily rattling and tearing at Cyrus's own lower back, the rope lines burning into his neck.

A soft sunrise became daylight, where burning rays of summer sun pierced the veil of fog amidst wooded cliffside, scorching the haze from the hills and painting the Eryxian outer wall in dazzling white. The towering architecture was one of precisely layered bricks and blood-red terra-cotta shingles across every rooftop, all jutting from haggard rock and rough seas, swelling and smashing in the tide below.

Cyrus could see the cathedral in the distance sitting atop the layered city with a steeple as tall as the stars. "That's a long fight ahead," he heard himself say.

The path steepened toward the portcullis, but guardsmen had raised the ancient drawbridge from the back gate. Alarm bells clanged as chain links clinked, one by one, the bridge fixed resolutely out of place, leaving a chasm in the way. There was a small crowd standing just across a natural moat, hands raised as they groaned and shouted, pleading for their passage. They were denied, nonetheless.

"*This way,*" the sniper whispered, beckoning the others across the road. Swansong led them to a small rat trail below the rocks on the far side, bringing the company past the small stone shrine stacks that lined the cobbled path to the portcullis under the drawbridge. The volcanic rock between each of Cyrus's steps was porous and sharp—an unnatural path of angles and edges and holes, made doubly difficult by his weighty equipment and the powder keg that ripped at his neck and shoulder with every bouncing step.

They skirted the rock below the moat and cleared it with a couple well-placed jumps between the tide. The Ram let out a boisterous huff, and Swansong hushed him, raising a slender finger to her lips and then toward the guards and their ears not-so-far above them.

Cyrus's face was flat against the marble, palms sliding across smooth stone in hopes of an edge or a hole to position himself in, but a few leagues past the crags, he felt a draft. *Jackpot*, he mouthed as Swansong disappeared into the darkened hole in the cliffside.

The party disappeared one by one into the dank crawlspace, and the Raven was the last to enter. Their path was pitch black, but he could feel the room as the wind passed through nooks and crannies and the Furii's ears.

There's balance here, if nowhere else.

Swansong lit a blinding torch at the head of the formation, stopping short of a plated iron doorway that blocked the path.

"Just as I thought—powder kegs, bring them," barked the Sage.

"Both?" asked the Ram.

"We only have one chance to open it—"

"Both might collapse the cave," Cyrus interjected.

"We try one," the Ram said. "My hammer can do the rest."

"Agreed—Mason, get up here."

Reed shrugged his shoulders in meager relief, moving to the front. He slid past Dagfinn and the others, taking a knee nearest the rusty door.

"It smells like blood," he scoffed.

"It's iron, ye idiot."

"*Cyrus,*" the Sage snapped. "Master Mason—please rig the charge."

The Raven shrugged.

Reed unshouldered the powder from his neck, stretching as he did. He pulled a dainty fuse delicately from his pocket, clutching it with two fingers like the stem of a flower. The youngblood laced it through the hole in the cask. "Get out," he said, shooing the others out of the cramped cave as he waved at Swansong.

She gave him the torch and took her place outside.

"Mr. Mason," said Cyrus.

Reed's brow lowered. "What?" he spat.

The Raven found Reed's shoulder with a gentle palm. Cyrus felt the tightness in his shoulder, but he ignored the youngblood's rigidity. "We can't know what's on the other side," he said. "Light the fuse, hightail out of the cave, but be ready for a fight, should it come to it—you'll be the point man."

"You—*you* wish to tell me how to do my duty? Here and now?"

"No, brother, I mean only to encourage. You're a loose cannon, no need to go dying in the first *wave*."

The Raven clapped him on the back.

Reed shrugged and snarled, muttering his curses as he turned to light the fuse. It sparked, and Reed followed the Raven crouched closely behind as they reemerged in the newly blinding daylight. Reed put his back against the wall nearest the cave and took a knee.

The Sage looked to Reed. "Mason—when you light it, you need to—"

"When? It's already *lit*," Reed sputtered.

"*What?!*"

"TAKE COVER!" roared the Ram, just as the cave boomed from the inside.

BOOM.

The force rushed through the hole, pouring smoke and hot air from the mouth as the others covered themselves up against the seawall. Reed nearly lost his footing under the tremors, but held firm.

The Sage uncovered his face to show his scowling disappointment to the world.

Reed blushed. "What do you fucking want from me, old man?" he retorted, turning back into the cave to inspect the mess. He covered his mouth as the ash powdered his face and hair. The door was indistinguishable from the rest of it—a buried ruin under shattered rock and metalwork. He began to dig, his palms finding loose dirt and iron debris as the weak draft renewed as the others did the same, a thick black soot building layers on faces, fingers, and garb.

"Marvelous, Mr. Mason," the Raven said, pushing a mound of debris aside and wiping his nose. *I pity the pup.* The seaside cannon rumbled the rock around them as they dug, thumping like steady thunder in the wet season, and Reed felt relief. *At least no one's shooting at us yet.*

Once the rubble was clear enough for passage, Swansong moved ahead, never to return. Her footfalls disappeared up the path, tapping on stonework and echoing into nothing as the others headed up poorly carved stairs in the bedrock.

A good sign, thought the Raven.

"Which way?" Reed echoed, coming to a fork between two flowing aqueducts.

"Whatever way is up," said the Ram.

"Nay—the water," suggested the Sage, "follow the water."

Cyrus nodded, turning. He was careful of his footfalls, sure not to slip as he hiked up the mossy gradient. The men wandered the tunnels for a long, anxious while. *The stink alone is enough to kill a mortal man*, thought the Raven. The looming darkness thickened with claustrophobic air.

The walls closed in around Cyrus. *Get me out of here.* "A ladder," the Raven said desperately, pointing.

"*Saved,*" groaned the Ram.

The Sage approached, listening and looking. "Listen," he hushed, pointing. "The grate, just there…we can't know what's on the other side, but…."

The Sage was frozen for a moment. "Cyrus," he said after a while. "You and I will find the Brynjar and his landing party—Reed, Dagfinn, you will find the Pontifex—"

"What?" Dagfinn groaned. "Why must I babysit the youngblood?"

"*Not now,* Dagfinn. Remember, Tytan Brynjar wants the Pontifex *alive*…." The Sage grinned. "Kill him, and you risk your pay."

"When did he say that?" asked Reed.

"Is everyone ready?" the Sage said, ignoring him. "We meet at the Ashen Cathedral—*Godspeed.*"

XXI

REMEMBERING

Marcus—Past

Marcus blew a match, and the sun rose. It turned red with his eyes. *Red…red…I'm painted from head to toe in ominous red. There's dirt and sweat, too, but the blood is indescribable….*

Free. I sail upon a sea of glass. Gentle wind rustles my hair like the thick jungle leaves, far away.

Or, is it just black?

The bright, hot sun burns cool red, sinking into the sea, and so she calls to me….

Her color.

I see the mangroves of home. Their branches grow down, down, down to her—down to the heart of the deepest, blackest ocean there is…inky nothing…knotty, wooden hands reach down, never to root…never to taste the water, only its mirage.

Not nothing….

Truth is a fickle thing, and it's my first night…the oldest of their kind begin to speak to me—old truths and new truths, but all the kinds there are…and dreams, brother, these haunting dreams that keep me from myself.

The red is layered and thick, browning as it dries, crunching and cracking in my hair…

…and my eyes.

I shall go there again, never to return.

There is where time stands still.

The only memory…

…memory…a memor…a mem…

Me…

XXII

REUNION

Aura

For three days, they rode, and Aura schemed. *Plenty of time to ponder—and drink.* She practiced the moment they would meet again. *Tricky Eli, back from the dead.* Her blood began to boil at the thought. *Do not let it overtake you, Aura.* She slid her palm endlessly about Mercy's hilt, rehearsing draws, parries, and the earliest killing blow. *What room will it be in? How many guards? An ambush, what then?*

Aura had answers for them all. *In public and early,* she decided. *No talk, no guile—Mercy needs little breath to sing.* Her muscles tightened. *You're faster than he is, Aura....You're the fastest one there is,* Kora used to say.

"They say the Disgraced Acolyte was the fastest of them all," said Elya one day with the sun on her face. "It goes that Horace Wijnberg was quick—so quick, he could cut bullets from the very air, shooing them away like flies."

She chuckled, shaking her head. "I very much doubt it," Aura was sure to reply. *Absurd.*

The thought consumed her. *How fast is a man that can cut bullets? Like cutting lightning....*Aura thought it impossible, but something deep and sharp weighed heavy in her gut. She knew, deep down, that it wasn't true—*just another tall Furii tale. What of Elatreus, then?* She shook her head. *No, I should be patient and calculating—he shan't be* *overlooked, but remember, Aura...he is not a god.*

They rode through the outer gates, beginning the winding climb to the upper ward and the Ashen Cathedral beyond. Elya would produce the summons, and the guards would bow politely as they showed Aura and Elya the way, saluting. *Strange,* she thought, *am I deceived so fully? These guards know nothing....*Her worry began to cool. *Why should they? It is the Acolyte's sin I carry; it should be a more intimate ambush.*

A valet stabled their horses for them as they took to the steps and dismounted. *My word.* Aura looked to the heavens, searching for the steeple spire atop the Ashen Cathedral. *Unmatched,* she admitted and imposing like a man-made mountain. *Can you get up there?* Far above, it scraped the clouds with the gulls over the sea and stone and surrounding city. *What must it look like up there?*

Nothing like the Fire Falls, I bet....

Steady, Aura. Her eyes returned, finding a great, golden door. It looked delicate, like wood—an image betrayed by its polished, soft edges. *There is but one thing, and a thing only...one big, great golden thing between me and him...him...**Him.***

Steady. An army of painted statuary lined either side of the entrance—twin gardens growing the outside between the buttresses and shrubbery and fountains and the like. Frescoes and polish and ornate branches wrapped every exposed piece of stone, with venerating zealots in dirty, modest robes tending to the grounds as praetorians stood ready. The cathedral was a whitish gray, like the chalky decayed remnants of powdered marble and bonfire dust. The atrium held a burning solitary torch that jutted from an obelisk near the archway, where visible embers floated with the wind, even in the daylight.

She squeezed her fists and gulped her rage back down. *Remember yourself, Aura.* It burned hot in her belly, growing stronger with her thoughts. *Kill the swine, the tricky Eli—tear him apart, piece by piece—revel in his pain,* she repeated.

Steady, thought Aura, working to keep the anger from tainting her face. *Soon.* She envisioned the moment she'd soon lay eyes on Elatreus Cornicen, the Acolyte. *I'll savor it,* she snarled, *the moment I rip his heart from his chest.* She composed her face again. *Soon,* she smiled falsely. *I'll eat it like an apple while there's light still left in his eyes. I'll pull his fingers from their sockets...I'll feed him his toes.* His pitiful tears would pour, and she would laugh. *I'll tear his ears away with my teeth, and I'll be sure to let him taste them....*

Steady, Aura.

Elya's hand touched her shoulder. "No matter the cost, contain yourself, love. He'll die by your hand, I promise you, but it can't be *here.*"

Aura nodded, weaving her fingers in Elya's. *Cost?*

A small man emerged from a smaller door inside the larger, golden one. He wore a crisp white cassock and gripped a scepter in one hand, a parchment in the other. The man wore a shimmering mask that covered his forehead with holes enough for the eyes—*those eyes...eyes like envy, green like grass. Gaze to me, green envy, and pray, gods, let it last....*

The mask was an antique steel *vultus* as ornately cast as the colossal gate behind. Aura knew him to be their envoy, emissary, and escort into the chapel. Aura took instinctive steps toward him and up the stairs, offering something halfway between a curtsy and a bow. *What decorum is there for a woman in pants?*

"Charmed," Elya said, extending her gloved hand.

The man—both hands full—greeted her with a mesmerizing smile of pearly teeth and a courteous low bow, balancing effortlessly on the heel of a buckled shoe. "Most gracious daughters of Ares," he said, "please forgive me, for I do not deserve even the slightest of touches from your goodly...*godly* hands."

Aura rolled her eyes. "Surely not," she said.

The cleric's green eyes glowed. "I humbly welcome you to the Ashen Cathedral of the Eryx, my ladies."

"Easy, love," Elya said. "No need for such formality here—the pleasure's all ours."

"Indeed," he said softly. "If you please, this way. Father Elatreus is expecting you."

Don't fucking call him that.

"Where are we to meet him?" Aura asked, feigning her best smile, given the circumstances.

"He awaits you in the transept," replied the cleric.

These halls are dark...and they hypnotize. Aura marched up the marble staircase to the base of the arched entrance. A worthy tapestry hung on the wall, mixed with twisted metal moldings carved into its depictions. The branches and circlets and statuary were even more detailed at closer look, with minute etchings and fine depth. *What a slavish devotion*, thought Aura, *and built on the backs of them...a masterpiece, but a door.* Aura wondered about the man who made it. *Did he attend?* She thought of Faustus Fabrica and his *Seasons. I wonder if Faustus goes to church.*

Doubtful. Zealots have awfully poor imaginations. She smiled. *Heaven should be pleasant, but hell's more fun,* her father used to say. But, she feared such wholesome faith, too. *I'd hate to be him,* Aura thought, *a man so in love with his fantasy—its magic outshines the emptiness that surely awaits us.*

The man offered his scepter to Elya as he unlatched the rusty portal door. Aura and Elya stood a head taller than their hunching guide, and even he had to duck a bit. Elya passed through, waving her new toy with girlish delight on the other side. Her bashing and booshing echoed across the hallowed chapel hall.

"*Elya, please,*" Aura pleaded. "You're a Furii, for gods' sake."

"You're just jealous he didn't give you his magic wand."

"No need for magic here," the cleric made sure to reply. "The gods need no parlor tricks." He offered another smile, this time quite a bit smaller as he lifted a finger to his lips in quiet deference. Elya lowered her head in guilty bemusement as the scepter stayed behind her back. Aura nearly ploughed into the pews, her gaze stuck to the ceiling. *The Royal Theater is no match for this.* She thought of seeing the Colossi of the Great Mothers for the first time and sleepy Clydae beneath the Fire Falls.

They'd painted the frescoes taller than the clouds, somehow. Soft brush strokes bathed in the gentle lights of shimmering stained glass all around. Ribbed walls, arches, and pillars helmed the mighty vaulted ceiling to the top. She found the tips of the buttresses jutting through the walls just beneath the ceiling, seemingly skewering the building in place. *Two armies could go to war in here*, she thought, *even with the pews.* Her eyes wandered to the treasures and relics, paintings, and a crowd of statues—an endless parade of monuments to sinners and saints.

What's the difference, anyway? Hundreds of statues lined the walls—renditions of gods and goddesses, martyrs and matrons, mixed with pieces of marble, granite, and delicate ironwork.

Sirens of mind...

"Are you from here, sir?" Elya asked.

"Me?" the man whispered. "I'm afraid not. In fact, I come from a land far off. I expect you've never heard of it. They call it Nine Foes. It's—"

"You're from *Nine Foes*?!" Elya shrieked.

So oft, left behind...

The man held up a finger. "Yes. You've heard of it?"

"Of course—*of course* I have," Elya whispered. "I was born in

Nine Foes, myself. What a wonderful coincidence!"

"My dear, there is no such thing," he said. "It is apparent that we were meant to meet."

And fear, ye mighty…

"In that case, I'm happy to make your acquaintance," she said, handing the scepter back. "Beg pardon, holy one, but we never caught your name."

"I'm afraid I didn't offer it," he said. "Not to be rude, assuredly, but my true name is a burden I wish no longer bear. If you please, call me Leon."

…thy fall.

Aura's gaze wandered the room. *Steady.* Their boots echoed noisily out into muted dark. They made their way to the altar. *Steady, Aura.* Unlike the crowd of clerics outside, there wasn't a soul as far as the eye could see on the inside. *What sort of sanctuary safeguards no sinners?*

"Ah, *Leon…*," Elya purred, basking in the name. "'Tis a fine name, sir. It fits you—you're handsomer now than before."

His grin widened.

"Where is everyone?" Aura asked.

"The Acolyte requested a private audience, madam."

"No guards, even?"

"The Fist of the Church thought it best to leave his Centuriata outside—an olive branch, if it pleases you."

"How…*generous*," Elya said.

*The transept…*it approached. A figure sat atop one of the five high seats, offset from center. *Steady.* She breathed, loosening a fist. She couldn't make out the face…*but there's the altar.* She knew that it was him—*Elatreus, himself.* She rehearsed how she'd do it and how she'd get away. *We're to be alone*, she thought. *Now is the time.*

Her eyes panicked, bouncing from window to window, door to door, eyeing the corners amidst a sea of things in the way: pews, candleholders, stone walls, and dead ends that lay beyond. The only exit she knew to be true was the enormous door behind her, where an army of guards and witnesses lay in wait. *He sees through me*, she feared. *He wishes me to draw first.* Her mind was tearing back and forth—*yes*, she kept saying to herself, but then, *no. Go*, then, *wait.*

Her eyes found the floor. *Concentrate, Aura…steady.* Elya's flirting drifted away. No voices or noise, only an Acolyte, glimmering in the dark, his soul ripe for the taking—*and Mercy thirsts*. She gulped down the nerves as her fist balled harder, cracking and shaking as she forced a natural gait. *Steady—do not be consumed.*

They grew closer and closer still. Aura's impatient eyes stayed on the opulent center of the great hall—the detail of the man now quite apparent. She shot her eyes back to the causeway—*I can't, not yet*. Her heartbeat was a galloping cavalry charge, like a knight in a joust. *Steady…steady…now.* She saw him, daring not to look away.

Her eyes met his, one for one, piercing, unyielding, fixed. He was a far cry from the boy she had known—fully bearded now, to say the least. A thick mane of black covered his chin and head, and his armor seemed to dwarf him. A long-scabbarded sword rested in one hand, the tip pointing down to the stone with corded hemp hanging from the hilt. There was a gentle curve to it—a Furii's sword like Aura's, firmly slender folded steel, with a modest scabbard, marred by time and wear. He wore an arbiter's mail—an antique tradition of the Acolyte with a delicate mix of steel plate and bamboo sinew from neck to knickers with equal accolade, but rusted, splintered, and scratched as years of abuse had warped.

He looked starkly different from the Disgraced Acolyte that preceded him. Aura remembered that man from Clydae all those years before. The elder's armor had been a mesmerizing white from head to toe—ghostly clean, nearing haughty. The old man had looked stylish and flamboyant, and completely absurd. This man here, this was the Elatreus she remembered, for better or worse—*disciplined and ruthless*. She wouldn't be fooled by this paltry appearance. *He'll die all the same.* Leon the cleric nodded to the Acolyte and offered a low bow upon the pedestal as Elya did the same. She noticed Aura's unmoving posture and nudged her with a heavy shoulder—Aura didn't move.

"Will you not bow before the gods?" asked Leon.

Aura said nothing, her knuckles the color of the cleric's pearly robes.

"Leon, please," came the Acolyte, "no need."

Leon's green eyes pierced Aura's for another moment, unraveling her. *His eye defeats me, in all ways but one, and I feel beyond doubt something terribly, terribly wrong.* Leon smiled wide, laughing with his eyes. He turned for the stairs and bowed again.

"Aura, *come*," Elya whispered.

Aura stood there for a moment, frozen in the shadows of the Acolyte. She took to the steps slowly, her gaze unflinching. Elatreus slouched in his stone chair, but his eyes stayed with her.

Leon bowed once more at the base. *"Send your wayfarers and gadabouts…"*

"Sorry?"

"Your foul, forsaken, and tempest-tossed…." His pupils were all but gone.

"What?"

Leon wore a newly wide and crooked smile. "Faith is such a strange affair," he hummed, turning. "*Coincidentia Oppositorum*—a coincidence of opposites. To be faithful is to prostrate, and yet to gaze." The priest's eyes burned into Aura's, unblinking.

Steady, Aura. She ignored him, marching past Elya toward the altar and the relics atop the highest of Tara's halls. She moved to meet Elatreus Fabius Cornicen as the Furii do—*face to face*. She halted beneath the tall, carved granite seat at the right hand of the Pontifex's gilded throne, and her hazel eyes blazed through the onyx shade of her vultus. He stared back with a tired gaze, his eyes burdened by black, stifling their color.

"Leave us," he said, shooing Leon away with a steel-clad finger. The cleric bowed deeply, his forehead narrowly missing the ground.

The two were silent for a time, glaring like gladiators at opposing ends of the arena. Elya became scenery. "So...," she hummed.

"Why?" Aura spat. *"Why am I here?"*

"Aura, we spoke of this." Elya pursed her lips.

Aura paid her no mind. "You mean to kill me, don't you?"

Elatreus sat up. *"Kill* you? I—"

"What purpose could this reunion possibly serve? Lull me into service? I think not." Aura unsheathed Mercy. "We do this here and now, *the old way.*"

"Aura, *please,*" Elya begged, "sheathe your sword!"

"If you're half the man Marcus was, you'll fight me the honorable way. I'll wait for no ambush." Aura put her other hand on the hilt, widening her stance.

Elatreus's bewildered look subsided a bit. He lowered his shoulders back to his humble slouch. "I know what you must think of me," he sighed, "but no harm will come to you so long as I am the Acolyte."

"Doubtful," she growled.

"I must say I expected something like this, hence no guards."

"Aura, please!" Elya shouted.

"No," she hissed, *"you"*—she pointed Mercy's tip at Elatreus—"you will unsheathe that saber of yours, or I will cut you down where you *sit.* It makes no difference."

He lifted a hand to his chin. "That won't be necessary."

"I'll be the judge of that—"

"If you run me through with that sword, *inside* the Ashen Cathedral, where, then, will you go? Out the way you came? Come, Aura you've thought of this. Your melodrama is quite wasted on me—"

"AGH!" Aura roared, hurling Mercy at the Acolyte.

"Aura, *no!*" Elya yelped.

SCHING.

He moved in a blur, his blade slipping from its sheath and parrying the tumbling Mercy away in a single motion. He was standing now, tall and ominous—*more like a fist, less like a Father.* Mercy clanged on the stone behind him, grinding to a stop. The snarling lines in his face were drawn deep, but they dissipated. He calmly sheathed his sword.

Aura's breath billowed like fire, wheezing and inflating as her nostrils flared, barely containing them. The bones in her hand neared the crushing point, her eyes swollen and full, twitching in the candlelight. Elya's hand found Aura's shoulder once more. It didn't help to calm her.

"*You...,*" she rasped.

"I...I'm sorry, Aura. Truly, I am."

"You're...sorry?"

"For...*everything.*" He sighed.

"You seem *very* sorry, indeed—sitting on that throne there. How quaint."

"There's no justice in it, I assure you," he said, sitting back down.

Aura shook her head. "Justice? Are those the words you wish to use? What justice is there in this world, pray tell?" She turned away from him as Elya's hand fell from her collar.

"Aura, I mean not to mince words, and I surely don't expect you to forgive me—"

"Where is *my* justice, Eli? Or better yet, what scraps does *Marcus* get? You remember him, don't you? Your *best* friend? The one you so callously—"

"*I REMEMBER EVERY DAY WHAT I DID, AURA!*" he roared.

"What good is that?"

He shook his head, and his eyes wandered from hers. "Not a day goes by that I don't think about how it unfolded—not a *fucking* day. I was a boy then—tis *no excuse*—but I listened to my betters and kept my mouth shut. I thought I was doing the right thing—the *pious* thing, but I was foolish, as were we all."

"Is that a joke?"

"No, of course not. I was weak, and I betrayed the man I *knew* for the powerful one I *didn't*. I regret it every day, and I know that all of this—*all of it*—is on my hands. The blood of Marcus…and others, of course."

"What of Josey, then?" Aura asked.

"What?" he looked up. "Of course not!"

"But, you know who did."

He nodded, "Yes, and I knew then…."

Aura laughed a hearty, fake laugh. "You…you mean to tell me, Acolyte, that despite this supposed '*guilt*' you've carried with you, now you serve this bastard? That *is* who you mean, right? The fucking Pontifex himself, *Vicar of the Gods on Earth*, authority on *all* matters moral, and he raped a girl, not but thirteen?"

"Aura," Elya said, "you can't call the Vicar of the Gods on Earth a bastard."

"I can," she said. "Besides, *fuck* the Pontifex and *fuck* the gods. I'll drink to his bones before the night is over. As I'll drink to *yours*." She pointed at him.

"Indeed, *fuck* them all," Elatreus parroted.

Elya's mouth was fully agape. "Did—did the Acolyte himself just utter those words?"

"What do you mean *exactly*?" Aura snapped. "Is that what I was summoned for, Eli? So that you could feel better? All is not forgiven, you *swine*."

"Nay, I should think not—and surely, that isn't why you are here, Aura, but I may have a small recompense—a sort of *gift*…."

"*You* don't get to do that," she said. "You don't get to unburden yourself so easily."

"I don't mean to—"

"You robbed a friend of life, robbed me of my very innocence, and now you *serve* the filth that raped a poor girl and got away with it. You know she killed herself, don't you? At the *shame* of it all. How often do you think of suicide, Acolyte? For it's all you deserve."

"*Josey*," he said. "Her name was Josey."

"You dare—"

"And I loved her."

"What?!" Elya shouted.

"You did not know her," he insisted. "You probably didn't know more than her name, did you? Just fuel for your vendetta, I expect. Do not lie so quickly to yourself, Aura Westfall, because I knew her. I knew all of her, every bit, and I was hers then, and still."

The last syllable rang out across the pews. Aura felt the welling in her eyes, and she wiped them. The silence was deafening in the chapel. Aura chose her words carefully, savoring them as she chewed them up and spat them out. "A liar once, and evermore—speak plainly, sir, or they shall rename this place the 'Ashen Tomb.'"

His eyes were mirrors to the candlelight and bathed in the stained sunlight rays pouring through the panes high above. "They sent her to the Forge," he said, "in secret. The truth, I promise you. This was her sentence."

"Sentence?" Aura asked.

"A strange kind of penance, isn't it? That the will of our bountiful gods would decide her fate in this world in such a harsh place—whether she be embraced as a daughter of Ares through violence and blood, or cast away like the wretch she was made to be on that awful day?"

"What did you just say?"

He ignored the question. "She died in the Forge," he said tersely.

"No—you...."

"In the same cruel way they all do."

She felt his eyes comb over her face, but she couldn't meet them.

"These are my burdens, and none other's," he said. "It's no matter—I don't expect your forgiveness, nor should I forgive myself for the pain in which I was complicit, but the thing I offer you, madam—it stands far above your ire. In fact, it should only serve to stoke it."

Aura's eyes darted between his features, but she bit her tongue. *Think, damn you.*

Elya piped in, "What—I'm sorry, what's your offer now, love?"

"Revenge," he said.

"Pardon?"

The Acolyte leaned forward and pointed his steel-clad finger toward Aura. "That is why you came, isn't it? I doubt you would've come under any other banner—vengeance is what you seek...against me, for Marcus's sake, and the Pontifex himself, for his enormity. I offer you a chance, Aura—only one—a chance at recompense for all the pain that I have caused you."

"What chance?" she asked.

His voice dropped to a dull whisper. "The Pontifex must die."

Aura was still like the stone. "A lie," she retorted.

"I shan't lie," he said, "and I know how it sounds, I do, but I assure you, this is the truth. The man deserves only torment and death, and you can give it to him."

Aura looked away once more. *The nerve—this is a trap, as it always would be. He's the Acolyte, for gods' sake!* Her mind began to unravel the possibilities, but no answer came to her. Surging thoughts rebounded from ear to ear, whipping through her mind with volatile spurts of potent, thick Furii blood. *A chance,* she thought. *It couldn't be true—but a chance?*

"He's unhinged, if you'd ask my reasons," Elatreus said, "going mad. At first, I thought I could bring him back to piety—*coerce* him somehow, but he's every bit the scoundrel, only now I know how little he cares to hide it. He keeps away in his chambers at all hours—a perpetual orgy of harlots and clergymen one and all, fueled by opium cocktails and some mystifying incense to cloud his sensibilities."

"You swore an oath to protect him," she said, turning back. "Have you no honor?"

Elatreus let out a chuckle. "Honor? No honor here—only honesty. We put so much faith in honesty, yet so much of the world is gray. I learned that the hard way in Clydae, but I know better now."

"Your word means nothing?" Aura asked.

"Once, that sentiment may have spooked me—or inspired, even— but who are we to dictate truth to the masses?" he asked, gesturing to the ornate glass above. "These halls were built by slaves, on foundations of the dead, for men as greedy and malicious as they come. My sword is the one of *truth* and *justice*, entrusted to cut down the enemies of vengeful gods, but in fact I've killed far more *boys* than men...and a few poor girls, to my shame—not very godly, it would seem. Men fight and die on the battlefields of Antigonia for a Vicar who spends his nights whoring himself to an early grave....Where's their truth?"

"How could you possibly expect me to believe...? No, I won't. Elya, come. We're leaving—"

"Have you heard the rumors?"

Aura looked back. "What rumors?"

His head dipped a little. "The Patrian League is fracturing, and the Empire is only as good as its Emperor...."

"They'd hang you at the *smell* of a coup," she said, "and us, too—"

"Aye, they would"—he nodded—"but that won't be much of a concern. You see, Iron Blake Bowman's fleet will be here in a matter of days, and—"

"The pirate?" Elya asked.

"I believe he prefers the term 'privateer' but, yes, one and the same, with something to the effect of a hundred ships."

"How do you know this?" asked Aura.

He sighed again. "I have eyes everywhere, Aura. Bounty hunters loyal to the coin, if not the Eryx herself. My rangers found Brynjar's posse moving through the Tear of Ares, but the enemy was decimated by a horde of Winter Wolves. Such a haunted part of Tara, don't you agree?" The Acolyte's wry smile turned south.

"Who else knows of it?"

"Well, Tytan Brynjar, for starters. It is his insurrection, after all. But none here, none of the Banner nor the clergy. A not-so-secret plot, you see, but I keep the secret all the same."

"For whose benefit?"

"For the betterment of Tara," he said sharply, "to the benefit of all those that live, and to bring about the end of antiquity and barbarism."

Aura's beating heart was thumping back and forth between ribs and lungs and guts, or so it felt. She was unsettled. *Impossible—it's not possible.* The man—the object of her loathing, here and now—one she'd sworn to murder the day he sent Marcus to a shallow, untended grave. *The chance, he said? Remember? But I have another chance, right here, right now.* His bartering built the rage that overtook, clenching her jaw and flaring nostrils as she quelled it with her whitening knuckles. The conversation was almost more than she could bear. Her body swayed as the words came and went with the tide.

She trembled as she spoke, "You mean to tell me, *oh Acolyte,* that *you* are aware of a plot to siege the Patrian Peninsula—one that would destroy all that you hold dear, murder the Eryx's patricians and sell their plebs to the highest bidder, and you now ask *us* to ensure the Pontifex doesn't survive the crossfire?"

"Something to that effect," he said.

Elya's voice rang out, "Mr. Acolyte, sir, I beg pardon, surely, but there are quite a few pieces to this puzzle, love."

Aura rolled her eyes.

"Firstly, how are we to know that this siege will work? In fact, how many failed attempts have come before? Is this city not impregnable? It sits at the heart of the free world, for Agathe's sake!"

"Precisely," he said, seemingly innervated. "Do you know what it takes to lay siege by sea? How many ships and the firepower? The most powerful navy in all of Tara would be hard pressed to find guns, ships, and skill enough to hit our high walls, let alone chip the dusty mortar from their cracks. We'll burn any ship we can hit—and believe me, madam, my Master o' Guns could shoot the wings off a flea at a quarter mile. The siege will never work, not with a thousand ships. Tis a deception, I should think—meant to divert eyes from another operation, a smaller party, perhaps, likely with a similar goal…again, the Pontifex."

"Why us?" asked Aura.

"Insurance," he said, stepping down from his pedestal finally, gripping the ceremonial sword with one hand and hoisting his plated helm with the other. "There's no guarantee that whatever Brynjar has planned will play—but it must at least *look* like it has."

"What about the Banner?" Aura asked pointedly. "Where are your arbiters?"

"If you're the fist," came Elya, "where are your fingers?"

Elatreus shot her a meek glance, deflecting. "Away on assignment—I won't say where."

"But not here?" Elya asked. "And Brynjar? Who's this *Brynjar*?"

"Lord of Norsefyre and the Furies," Aura said flatly, "tired of playing second fiddle to the Patrians, I should think."

"I'm unsure of the intricacies," he said impatiently, "but a plot there is, I assure you, and it *must* be seen through."

"Seen through?" said Aura.

"Yes."

"I want to trust you," she said, after a long while. "I want you to be the man you say you are. Somewhere deep, I want to forgive you for your sins—"

"Sins, Aura? What of your sins, then?"

"What?"

"I know of the company you keep, Aura Westfall." His ironclad finger extended out. "I know all of Rufus Pompey, the scoundrel he is."

"How dare you—"

"What have I said of spies?" he asked. "You were foolish to think

I didn't have my eye on you from the beginning. Why do you think I killed Brandon, but spared Rufus?"

"Why, then?" Elya asked, as if retreating.

"Come again?" growled Eli.

Elya's voice trilled and her eyes began to water. "I—I loved him, but you made me...."

Aura rolled her eyes.

Elatreus curled his lips through flared nostrils. "Spare me your theatrics—*you*, Elya Dair killed Brandon Senn. And you'd gladly kill me, should it be advantageous, you'd kill me here and now, no?"

Elya rubbed her nose clean on her sleeve, snorting. "Aye," she laughed, "it was worth a shot. You give me a chance—an out—aye, I'd kill ye here, love, no offense."

"*Elya,*" groaned Aura.

"Do you think Elya would not have killed Rufus just as quickly? Thoughtlessly?" said the Acolyte. "No, I think you know she would have. And I think you knew it then. You know deep down that you will do what I ask, because you know that, despite my flaws—my failings, in your mind—I'd gladly kill your beau without a second thought, and your closest friends might do the same."

"Damn you."

"How curious? We speak only of Marcus and Patria and Clydae and patriarchy, as if longing for our ugliest days. You speak of Marcus as if he's still here—as if *you* still love him. But Marcus is a dream—a figment. Rufus is all that is real, Aura. You mistrust your feelings perhaps, I won't deny the same of my haunts. My ghouls. My burdens. But Pompey is all the hope you have left in the world, Aura, and regrettably, I am willing to barter for his soul."

Aura paused for a long while. She chewed on her cheeks, if only to keep the words from pouring out. *Steady, damn you.*

I am no enemy to you," he muttered, "I was none to Marcus." His eyes met hers. "If I could go back and take his place, I swear on my life that I would—but I have prayed upon deaf ears. If there were a way to change—I would do anything to give you the happiness I robbed of you, but Marcus is gone, like Josey and all the dead...."

Aura returned the stare. "A fool's errand, Elatreus. I don't care what you offer, nor what you hope for—we do not accept." Aura turned away from the altar and stepped toward the glimmering Mercy beyond.

"Aura, hear the man out—"

"I expected this, too, but I think you can manage what comes next." His eyes hollowed.

He looks so tired, Aura thought. "Speak plainly," she said.

"I don't mean to be...*uncivilized*, but this isn't a choice for you to make. You must understand, there are more parts at play than merely me and mine, or you and yours, for that matter. Something bigger than us—*all of us*—and it must be seen through. For Tara's sake, if not for petty retributions."

"Are you *threatening* me?"

"If it is required," he said sharply, "then, yes."

"What 'parts at play'? What more is there?"

His fingers rolled through the black strands of his beard, and his eyes found a distance beyond Aura and Elya. "There's...*someone*," he whispered.

"*Someone*? 'tha fuck is that—"

"Someone who knows," he hushed, "knows *everything*...."

Her brow lowered. "Everything?" she echoed.

Panic overtook his strength, Aura could see. He spoke in errant and shrill tones compared to the smooth ones from before, as if the words cowered from his mouth. In an instant, Aura's opinion of the Acolyte was brought to its knees. The fatigue that lined his face had suddenly become obvious and sad. A new face took hold that Aura never expected to see. A broken, burdened man sat atop the highest seat in the land, welling in his eyes as the words suddenly struggled to escape. Aura took a step back. *The Burden comes for one and all.*

"I-I-I couldn't explain it if I tried," he stammered, "but *h-he* knows—all of it, past, present, and future. He knew the Brynjar plot, the war in Antigonia—he knew where *you* were and how to get you here....He knew what happened in Clydae all those years ago...and—"

"And what?"

"He knew Marcus...*knew* him...not just *of* him—as if they'd met...in another life...." He began to shake as the words barely dribbled past his lips.

"Who?!" she asked. "*Who* is this man?"

"I...I can't—*my Burden*."

BOOM.

The old cathedral stone groaned and shook as the marble floor rumbled underfoot. Aura toppled as the bellowing, aching boom echoed across the chapel.

"Blimey, what the devil was that?!" Elya exclaimed.

Elatreus snapped, wrenching his helmet over his head and hiding his face behind the abyssal black slits in the steel. His sword rang down the corridor as he pulled it from its sheath. *"THEY'RE HERE!"* he shouted.

Aura's eyes darted between doors and windows both as more booming echoed down the chamber. *One at a time, Aura.* The portal door in the main gate burst forth with a legion of cassocked clergy flooding into the hall, screaming bloody murder.

"TO QUARTERS! TO QUARTERS!"

"Where do you need us?" Aura asked instinctively. *This isn't over,* she thought.

Elatreus stood steady in the quake. "His chambers aren't here," he said.

BOOM.

"Make for the upper bailey, beyond the citadel—take the seawall to the ramparts and climb. For gods' sake, hurry!"

"Elatreus," she said sternly.

"There's no time! Take these," he said, handing down a pair of two long strands of crimson cloth. "They'll know you as the Tattered Banner now. You must go! You *cannot* fail! Promise me!"

She handed one to Elya.

BOOM.

I fear no sea, nor stars or sky, only you, dear brother, and your wandering eye...."You still think me some poor nobody, don't you?"

"Come again?"

"*Where is Marcus—where is Marcus?* Like a widow...or a dolt... or witless Josey."

"What did you say?"

"I am a monster 'cause of you. Mankind trembles in my wake. *You* will see....Oh, Father Elatreus," she croaked, "a god among men—*not by a mile*. If the gods do exist, they should *beg* for my forgiveness."

BOOM.

"Madam—"

"As should you."

XXIII

ELDRITCH TRUTH

Marcus—Past

I've been slumped against this lonely wall for a time. My hands are in my lap, and I can't keep my eyes off them.

He keeps coming back....

Dry cracks line them like hard pan, cracking and dusting as they move...scaled like lizard skin with the hairs like willows poking through the muck.

My memories are so far away—I was hurt, but now? I scrub, and I wipe to no avail. It won't part from me...

...neither will Aura.

I've died so many times....Could it be real? When will my agony end? It's happening so fast now, faster than I can control. My eyes ache to close, and my confusion builds to anger, and I find my breaths harder and harder to take.

"Those fucking beasts," I say.

I feel his presence. The man in white leans against the steeple, gazing out to the great beyond, but his ears are piqued, and his head tilts slightly. He offers a cornered smirk. "And who are the beasts, gentle prince? Them?" He nods to the burning river...Phlegethon.

"No more, Malus."

"Are they not animals as much as men? They wage no wars, conquer no lands...."

His words are poison to my ears, and my blood heats the moment they leave his crooked black lips. I can't stand to hear it, not now.

His gaze is fixed on something far away. "*They rape no women, thieve no coin.*"

"*Shut your fucking gob.*" *I won't listen to one more word. He got me into this mess. He's the one who—*

"*They're animals, darling, creatures of instinct. Ferocious, yet predictable—*"

I am up…and moving.

So fast—faster than lightning.

I have my pistol—she's drawn with that slender hammer back, the way I like. I finger the trigger. I'm not so sure I can keep from squeezing. "*I WILL KILL YOU. BY THE GODS, I SWEAR.*"

The words delight.

He grabs the pistol with a flashing white hand. He pushes it away, effortlessly, and I panic—I wrench the trigger hard, and the muzzle explodes into the wall beside him.

The ethereal moonlight rays shine upon me….

Her rays….

My round cripples the stone, cooling. I swing my free fist at Malus's pale ivory nose.

A mouse to his trap—he catches the fist and brings himself close, the weight of my swinging arm offering the leverage used against me. He rotates me like a doll as a blade appears from the shadows.

Ghosts upon glass and glowing moonlight green, I am contorted against the wall, helplessly entangled in his inhuman clutches.

So grows the delight….

"*Predictable,*" *he says,* "*like a pack of wolves or a gaggle of geese. If they could think or speak, would you not be a god to them? And what kind of god might you be?*"

"*Out, damn you.*"

He pushes deeper, and I wretch and scream. His nose is touching mine, and his lips both soothe and disturb me with a snake-like whisper. "*What, then, lives beneath your waves? Your rage—such hate."*

"Please," I beg to the darkness. "Please, don't."

"It's that squirmy heart of yours." He pokes, his fingernails curling like his smile.

Its smile.

"Your big ol' heart cost you your soul, *darling."*

He brushes his nose on my cheek, and I shudder. He pulls me closer, his lips nearing mine.

"The poor devils outside, the rage fills their hearts, and they fall to your steel in droves, but one man with restraint? Control? He could be a god to them...."

My struggles are pitiless. I hear his voice in my mind as in my ear, layered like a crowd of him torturing my vessel and spirit all at once. His fingers begin to explore....

Then his mouth.

The darkness closes in.

Dear gods, I beg you: kill me, here and now. End my suffering.

"Not yet, darling."

XXIV

HORNSKEWER

Aura

Aura chased behind Elya. *I should tighten these*, she thought, the tiedowns of the sword belt bouncing as she ran. A crowd of clerics began pouring through the small door inside the larger, golden one. *Like a swarm of rats.* The artillery battered the seawall beneath, rumbling the tiles and her feet.

BOOM.

"'Scuse us, brothers," Elya said cheerfully. She held out a stiff arm, thrusting them back out to make way. *She's a Furii, after all.*

They came out to the ivory courtyard, the light blinding like birth. She held up a hand, finding gray streaks of cannon shot that tracked to the sea. *Sails.* Their masts jutted below like a pine grove…*like a forest.*

BOOM.

The Eryx returned fire.

Gods in hell, am I hit? Petals fell all over the garden. *It couldn't be a cannon, could it?*

"Fuckin' hell!" shouted Elya, a finger to her ear. "That one's a bell-ringer!"

"Wh—what?" *I...I hear the bell....It...beckons....*

The mortars came in steady cadence. They thumped in the distance, but the sounds grew closer as they ran. *What chance do the Furii have against gunpowder?* Dots of iron crashed into the base of the seawall with a flash and delayed crack, some in the sea. *An armada....* Black sails lined the harbor, flickering. *Shooting...Elatreus said they wouldn't have a chance.* She ran faster.

"Aura, wait," Elya huffed.

"Hurry—we're a long way off," she urged.

"Why such fervor?" she asked between breaths. "Don't you, *ugh*, don't you hate the man?"

"Aye," Aura said, "but now I have reason to hate the Pontifex *more*."

"Aura, stop," she said, yanking on her shoulder and whirling her around. "This is foolish, Aura—we haven't a hope! We don't know where he is, nor even what he looks like—at least *I* don't."

"I think we'll know him when we see him," Aura replied.

"Even *then*—Aura, if they catch us, we'll be hanged all the same. This crime won't go unnoticed for long, and why *wouldn't* the Acolyte let us go down for this? Darling, he's *trapped* us. We should run—we still can."

Aura's eyes found the clouded ships again as the stone beneath her feet rumbled away. "I...I hear you," she said, "but something, *something* was earnest back there....I can't explain it."

Elya's breathing cooled a bit. "I'm all for *guts* most of the time, dear, but my own are *screaming* at me to run from this place. We don't have a chance. We are no one, even among the Furii. The Pontifex isn't worth our lives."

Aura sighed deeply, her gaze still fixed on the wayward ships. "This is it," she whispered. "This is my chance, here and now.....*There will be no other.*"

"I understand, love, but—"

Aura raised a gentle hand and rested it on the back of Elya's neck. "If you must leave, I'll never blame you...." She wiped a tear.

"This isn't your fight, but mine...if mine alone. I couldn't leave... my boots, firmly planted. I will cut them down, or be cut down, but Mercy thirsts for the Pontifex, and I will, at the very least, drag him to *hell* with me...."

The blood surged through her, electrifying.

The Viper choked a bit, her green eyes glassy. "I...I can't...."

"I know, my love," Aura said.

"*No*," Elya said. "I mean to say, I can't...I can't let you do this by yourself." She sniffed and wiped her eyes as another bomb thumped the ground below.

BOOM.

Elya chuckled, her emerald eyes showing Aura small hints of her madness. "Never forgive, *never* forget." She laughed.

Aura smiled and leaned in. *Her lips...*she kissed her so slightly. "*Never*," she whispered.

Elya reared a bit. "*Aura*," she moaned, "you've smudged my vultus!" Still, she smiled and gripped Aura's neck, too, resting a forehead on hers in a moment all their own, stolen from the chaos surrounding them.

BOOM.

Another blast shook them, and they laughed together. "Thank you for staying," said Aura. "I need you....Besides—if we pull this off, we'll be queens among the Furii. How many lasses get to kill the Pontifex, after all?"

"Too few, I should think." Elya laughed.

They turned, moving faster than before, nearing the stair turret to the high ramparts. *Gods in hell*, Aura thought, clutching to the stone as a stiff sea breeze nearly blew her off the wall. *So...so high.* She gulped. *I don't much care for heights.*

The barrage was heavier with the black sails nearing. Galleons stormed the tide and set loose a steady and unrelenting stream of cannon fire, crashing and splashing in the chaos. The claps of iron on the stone grew louder, ringing in Aura's ears and jerking at her heart strings as she ran.

The bell....

The slams itched at her neck and back. *Like swatting flies*, she thought, strangely. Each boom seemed to flicker the lights of her mind. The roar of soldiers and sentries rang in the air, too—sergeants barking orders to a hustling cannonade.

BOOM.

They returned the heavy iron salutations from the sea, but slower. The seawall battery was booming with shot after shot—*reply after reply*. The larger caliber was far closer and took its toll.

BOOM.

Toll...

BOOM.

Toll...

The guns lurched backward, then came the smoke. The jolting cannon wrenched the sinewy rope taut as the crewmen steadied the tie downs. *One man's in charge*, she spotted, ordering another with a pointed palm. The gunner plunged a baton in a dirty bucket, swathing the pitch-black water from barrel to bore. *Good*, ordered the crew chief with a gesture, beckoning the powder and wadding men.

Then, the round. Three men held them, frenzied by the look. They dropped the ball down the barrel, *but just*. Another followed, plunging his giant ram rod along to the background drum. The chief pointed another hand, a boyish man laid a small light to the fuse and—

BOOM.

Can these old walls hold such a battery? Smoke and flame spewed from the mouths of a dozen cannons all at once, one after the other, shaking, burring, and cracking like a wrathful storm.

"Gods be good," Elya said, finger in her ear as more blasts shook them. "Look there, that's the upper bailey—we're close."

Aura's head swiveled from side to side. "Wait," she said. "Where are the soldiers?"

"Manning the battery, I'd expect," Elya huffed.

"Leaving the citadel to its own? None to protect the Pontifex?" Aura unholstered her pistol at the thought.

"What do you mean?"

The two emerged atop the high bailey courtyard just beneath the rear entrance to the citadel, and Aura turned to Elya. "You heard the Acolyte. This here is the feint, and—"

Thunk.

Something popped behind her—stone and dust. Aura fell to her knees on the stairs. *Impact, then the—*

BOOM.

She grabbed a dirk out of her belt as Elya jumped into a slide, drawing Halcyon, her dainty rapier.

A sniper's taking potshots.

Elya nodded.

Aura nodded back. She hustled up the stairs behind, her eyes darting to the high places.

Where are you?

Thunk.

Another pop. *Fuck*—

BOOM.

"WHERE ARE YOU?!" she shouted.

Aura tripped. *The bodies, gods....*Eryxian soldiers lined the courtyard, sprawled across the stone. Their red and green coats were fine wool once, now slashed and torn, and mixed with the mud and the meat.

Two figures appeared across the way.

Aura thought of the Birdsongs. *Steady, Aura.*

They don't look like friends. She felt a jolt of fear, eyeing the banner wrap on her arm. *Oh no.* Her stomach sank.

Then, a twinkle. *Or, a flicker.* She couldn't be sure. The source appeared above, atop the belfry—*the sniper.* Something faint and black bounced beyond the edge of the stone, breaking its angular silhouette. *I spy with my little eye,* she smiled, *a spider in our midst, most in need of squashing.*

One of the figures was taller than the other—*and wider.* He was pulling on something. It was attached to one of the bodies—*a staff of some kind? No,* she thought, *no, a hammer.*

The tall man unburied the hammer's head from a red and green jacket. It turned redder.

"Gods in fuckin' hell." The words slipped out.

The giant said something to the other, but Aura was too far off to tell. The smaller figure nodded...*or shrugged?* It backed toward the clocktower door behind him.

Elya moved closer, and Aura watched.

Then, another flash from the belfry.

"MOVE!"

Thunk.

BOOM.

"This one shoots for shite!" Elya laughed.

The man turned his wide shoulders slowly toward them. *We're close.* Purple and blue veins lined his shoulder, she could see, like vines swallowing a tree. *So thick,* she thought, *too thick...immortal thick... Furii thick.*

Aura thought of all the books in the Forge about Furian heroes and feared. *I—I think I know who this might be. There's fur and plate, and mail—he's even wearing a helm. He's a Walderman, must be...with one horn missing....*

Flash...

Thunk.

BOOM.

He is Einar Dagfinn the Ram. Her heart sank. *The Hornskewer, they call him.* The stories came back to her—*Einar Dagfinn, the Ram, the Ein-Horn, Hornskewer, the might of the Einwald, and here he comes toward me with fire in his eyes....*

Her feet took three involuntary steps backward. She caught herself, planting them. Mercy slid from her scabbard, but shakily.

"Your business here is yours," called Aura, nearly pleading, "but we mean to help, if you'd call off that shooter, there." She nodded to the belfry.

"Help?" growled the giant. "The Tattered Banner sends its brightest, then?"

"I knew these wraps would get us into trouble." Elya sighed, shaking her head.

"You misunderstand, sir—"

Another flash...

Thunk.

Fuck.

BOOM.

Stone chips sprayed Aura's face. "Call your shooter off!"

He held a halting hand to the belfry. "Youngbloods ye must be," said the Ram, marching forward. "You seek to reassure, yet your sword hisses in the open."

"Sir, I only—"

"No," he growled. "Did ye think this ploy would fool me, child?"

"What?"

"Rest easy, youngblood—the bird will not rob me of this honor, nor you....You'll get a proper death."

A Furii's death. It made her sick. She expected *less*—his hulking arms exploded from fur-sewn shoulders and thick raiment covering his chest. His veins were a nauseating dark blue, pulsating across every inch of exposed hock. They squiggled back and forth like switchbacks winding and webbing over his mountainous muscles, packed tightly together and throbbing as thick Furii blood pumped through the torsion and meat.

*Sweet gods....*Aura looked to Elya. She was calm, prancing almost, despite his thundering steps.

BOOM.

She nearly jumped from her skin. *Just the cannon.*

His hammer shone in the sun—old smoothed carvings of rams' heads and horns, with ornate inlays that had seen more winters than Aura, all tainted by a sickly red brown hue of recent bludgeonings, dangling their green and red wool strands. *His hammer's head is wide as my waist.* He carried it with one hand, swinging it effortlessly, closing the distance with Elya.

Elya didn't waver. "Easy, love," she hummed sweetly. "What's a handsome devil like you doin' in a place like this?" Her heels were glued together, a sultry finger dragging across an enticing lower lip. *Taste me,* they might've whispered, but the Ram drew closer.

Like bait, Aura thought, *but this big fish most needs a harpoon.*

Aura's nerves surged—*he's right on her.* "ELYA, *MOVE!*" she screamed.

No, no, no! she shrieked to herself. Before she knew, she was barreling toward him, Mercy in one hand, a dirk in the other. Her footfalls echoed across the courtyard. *He's there. He's there with her, and she isn't moving and...*

...and I'm the fastest Furii there is. She smiled.

The Ram held his hammer high. It burned black, shadowed by the sun.

Elya extended a hand, diverting his gaze. "Pay attention to me!" she whined, her voice playful like her stance. A small derringer jumped from her golden sleeve and filled her hand—

THWACK.

The noise echoed off the stone walls surrounding them, the tiny barrel smoldering.

"UGH!" the Ram wailed.

The ball had caught his mouth between the steel cheeks of his one-horned helm. He brought a hand to his lips.

Here is my chance, she thought.

Aura jumped into a slide. Her ribs tightened at the weight behind Mercy—*the old girl carves deep!* She rode the sword through the Ein-Horn's unarmored flank.

He swung to retaliate, meeting nothing.

I kill legends by the dozen. She laughed. *Get in line, Hornskewer.*

The stone erupted outward under the crashing hammer. Aura covered her face. The shards sliced her chin like small, searing sparks, but Aura barely seemed to notice. Elya side-stepped, drawing a stiletto from her boot and stabbing it thoroughly through the giant's bicep.

"*RAH!*" he roared, dragging the hammer upward at Elya, narrowly missing her chin.

She dashed backward clumsily.

Steady, Elya.

Elya planted a hand on the cobblestone, her body resting on one knee with the other leg fully extended.

More cat than Viper.

"Aura, look!" Elya chuckled. "I've *skewered* the Hornskewer!" She clapped excitedly and took a bow.

Aura stood motionless, eyes darting from Ram to Viper and back. *He isn't dead yet...and the sniper?*

The Ram rested his hammer on its head, pulling the stiletto from his arm and spitting broken teeth and blood from under the helmet. As for the wound—*he barely seems to notice.*

He snatched the hammer back up and lumbered toward Elya. She raised her other derringer, firing.

THWACK.

BOOM.

Toll.

The giant turned, catching the bullet in the shoulder, unflinching. Elya dropped the pistol, her posture panicking.

He rushed, crow-hopping into a mighty swing. Elya darted forward and slid beneath the hammer, her sword tip slitting the mail of his leg.

No contact. She cleared the swing and jumped up behind him, thrusting Halcyon between the plates at his shoulder.

"ARGH!"

Aura rushed toward them both, but his swing had brought him around to face her. She missed another hammer strike by an eyelash, side-stepping as the stone and sparks erupted again from the floor below, splashing rubble into Aura's face and eyes. She swung Mercy in kind, but his gauntlet caught the blow.

CLANG.

BOOM.

A shrill clang, then the cannon. Then, his fist thudded into her gut.

UGH. The strike hurled her across the courtyard. It slammed her insides—*rattled my cage...what the—?* She lost both sword and dirk, her body crashing to a halt in a heap of green and red.

Aura writhed, recoiling from the bodies. *He's broken me with a single punch.* Aura heaved and gasped for air that wouldn't come. Her insides burned as she gripped her stomach with both hands, curled into a weakened ball. *Elya's all alone.* She winced.

Her hand found the stone. She pushed, getting to a knee, but falling. *Mercy...where is Mercy?*

"Come, Aura," chided Elya, "you mustn't go easy on 'im."

She was strafing the giant, her rapier still painted with a thin coat of his crimson.

Dagfinn was panting, spitting blood and remnants of teeth from time to time.

He's far from dead. Aura wheezed.

"You're a feisty one," Dagfinn said with a nod, "but certainly not the first whore to treat me so."

"Nay, sir, I should hope not." Her eyes fluttered. "Merely the *last.*"

The Ram smiled sickly red, rearing his hulking hammer one more time. Elya bounded forward, rapier poised.

The Ram's shoulder jerked low to swing, hurtling toward Elya's legs. The Viper dodged deftly, jumping into the air and turning wide. Her sword pointed out, its edge wonting for the fleshy neck of Einar Dagfinn the Ram as he heaved his great hammer too slowly.

Wait—no—a ruse—Elya—

"ELYA!"

Too late. The hammer swung high, changing course. The speed overtook Elya.

Heavens, help me.

The hammer face caught Elya Dair, mid-chest.

CRACK.

No.

BOOM.

The cannon rings like the bells of my wake...of Marcus's wake...

Of Elya's...

The sound was nauseating—a pulpy crunch and a violent, unnatural halt as Elya's body plummeted to the stone floor. *The wind is taken from her sails.* Her sword clanged to a stop beyond where her broken body lay, her mouth sputtering and gasping as her hands grabbed at the buttons of her reddening coat. Her chest was a deep, concave basin under her clothes. Blood dripped from the sides of her mouth and down her chin as she gurgled.

And—and her nose....

Dagfinn stood, hammer cemented in both hands—*redder than before.* He eyed the dying girl as he stepped toward her, his red snarl spread across wine-colored teeth.

Gods, please!

Aura knelt across the courtyard, gasping for breath. The Ram's eyes were like sunken black holes behind his one-horned helmet, but Aura could feel them.

I've felt such hate before, she cried. *I dare not watch.* She thought of Acheron Petronax and the Pontifex, but then, Lucy...*oh, Lucy!*

The giant removed his helmet, exposing the misshapen upper lip that Elya's derringer had torn wide open. The thing was bisected into two pieces, hanging by gory scarlet threads connected just below his nostrils. Dagfinn ran his tongue over the mess of tendered meat and tapped it with a finger.

His gaze was fixed—misshapen like his mouth, and paralyzing. He smiled again, a distorted, disgusting smile.

Please, she pleaded through her tears.

The giant froze. The courtyard grew cold and quiet with nary a sound but the flapping of a battered flag above a nearby rampart—*a tattered banner.*

Frozen. She knew what came next. Aura saw it already but dared not accept. She saw it in the shape of Elya's chest. *It's—It's crushed.* Aura shook her head. *I—I can't....*

The courage left her, too. *She's already dead, just like me.* The flag flapped on.

BOOM.

The Ram raised his hammer with stained hands over Elya's gasping pale face and brought it down.

BOOM.

BOOM.

Toll...

Aura wretched her guts out onto the stonework. The nausea came and went so suddenly. She wiped the sides of her mouth, recovering in time to fix her shaky gaze on the last laborious breaths of Elya Dair—the mallet face finding her skull squarely, her slender cheekbones and soft lips disappearing under a shadow of steel, the bones in her pate blossoming outward as a bright red scarlet rose painted the ground around her shoulders and neck.

Gone. It collapsed the upper part of her ruined skull, making a bowl of her mouth.

Aura hurled again.

Dagfinn's hand rested delicately on the leather handle as the billowing flag withered in the wind, tormenting Aura with every crackle and snap. The cannons continued, unrelenting.

BOOM.

Like the unsinking bedposts of old....

She was a statue, sewn to the stone like threadbare burlap draped across a cork—nothing to do, no hope, no prayer. She was curled in a heap of weakness and regret.

All this, she thought, *only to die here, under the thumb of a barbarian, near the defiled corpse of a dear, dear friend. How apt.* She thought of Rufus. *How pathetic.* He was no comfort, just more shame.

The Ram's gaze found Aura in her pile of pity. *I did nothing for Elya—surely, I owe myself the same.* She felt away, like an onlooker outside the body. She'd slaughtered before, but here she failed to prevent it. Aura clutched her stomach, hurling like a child again.

BOOM.

Toll...

Soon, now. Elya fearlessly fought, but Aura could see the backs to one of her eyes. *Those—those green eyes.*

Doubt began to drown her. *I've already lost.*

The Ram ripped the hammer out of her friend. The head gushed, the hammer dripping blood and fragments. Some of them dangled. The sound was a meaty tearing, like wet, dead underbrush. *That's what he's made her...worm food.*

Aura's breathing slowed, pulse waning. Her clammy skin turned white like winter wood. The Ram's eyes stole her warmth as he slowly approached, lumbering like before. She had learned to fear his steps.

Aura was weaponless and getting faint. She began to accept. *Death has come early—and oh, how I've wished for you before.* The pain subsided, and could subside further, to her mind. *Let go,* she told herself. *Give up the suffering. It could be quick—painless,* she reckoned, like Elya's swift execution. One last hammer swing, and Aura could be rid of this mortal coil—free from the cowardice, drudgery, and crippling sham that she felt so often.

Her tears dripped down, caressing her pale, unwrinkled cheeks. *Closer now.*

BOOM.

She closed her eyes. "Just take me," she whispered. It was a sweet relief, to accept and transcend—to be at peace before the fall of his mighty hammer.

"Do not cry, my dear. I'll be quick."

His voice was warm and welcoming. She hadn't noticed that before—fatherly and kind. A sweet and genuine tinge pervaded the syllables, rhythmic and bouncing like the hearth in Marcus's chambers. *Marcus. Must I remember him, even here? Perhaps I can go to him, I s'pose.* Aura wanted nothing more than to fall into a violent embrace—*a short walk into the void, arms outstretched.*

But then, a voice...one from deep inside: *"Why are you crying, Aura?"*

He said that, didn't he?

I'd nearly forgotten. She opened her eyes, saw the Ram standing over her, a black giant blocking the radiant red sun, hammer raised like Antigonus himself.

"Close your eyes, child," he said.

"'I'm...I'm a flower on a vine,' he used to say."

"Hmm?"

"*If I'm not growing*," she said, cutting her eyes, "*I'm wilting....* There are wonders yet in your dark horizons. I see the color still."

Warmth flooded her cheeks. Aura's vultus dripped with the sweat returning to her brow, her hands lifting free from their invisible chains.

It's not over, she breathed coolly, *and so, I plant myself.*

"It's not over."

He reared and swung the hulking hammer down.

I was ready all this time—the fastest one there is. She slipped to the side, delicately past the mallet. Her elbow smashed into his knee.

"*RAH!*"

The steel crashed on the stonework behind her.

BOOM.

*The bell tolls on, and on, and so it tolls for thee….*The crack of the giant's knee rumbled, tickling her.

The Ram roared back.

Oh, how this swine squeals! She rolled away, the man swinging wildly around, aimless and clumsy. She was up, sprinting toward Mercy. She didn't slow to pick her up, merely jumped into a slide and grabbed the handle. She kept her momentum, barreling toward the Ram, each footfall louder and louder.

"*ARGH!*" she roared.

Her boots screeched on the stone, feinting low. *No rams here, only a raging bull.* She lowered her shoulder with her utmost.

He'd slowed. *Stopped.* His stance was wider, both hands tearing at the leather. Elya's pieces still painted the hammer's face.

BOOM.

The giant leaned forward, lowering his weapon behind him. His reddened mouth was sputtering and growling like *a rabid fucking dog.*

High, then. She flew toward him. Her toe dragged on the ground with Mercy mirroring her murderous eyes.

He swung—*sideways.*

Aura dropped, crouching beneath the swing.

CRACK.

She smashed headlong into his bum knee. Aura bounced harshly backward, breathless and disoriented. Her brain rattled as she lifted herself off the stone, Mercy clutched just between her fingers. *No.*

The Ram fell back, too, gripping at his knee as he let out another howl.

Now.

BOOM.

Now...

Toll...

Now, now, NOW! She brought herself up, bounding—Mercy outstretched.

SCHING.

The blade rumbled in her hands, deep through the giant's knee and out the back. Aura turned her hands—*heave!* She rowed it over as she tumbled, the knee cracking and splitting, Mercy buried to the hilt. She yanked and sawed, Mercy bound up between tendon and bone.

"*ARGH!*" he shrieked, his fist crashing down.

BOOM.

It caught Aura's face, knocking her flat. *Urgh.* Her body plummeted to the stone, sliding to a stop. Her eyes were glued shut, pouring tears as her nose spewed hot red down her front. Her face seared—the salt and iron tickled her tongue.

*My, my nose....*It was likely broken. *Is it—is it more? He—he hit me so—so, so hard*, she rattled deliriously.

Aura's shaky hands wiped the blood from her eyes. She then put them on the stone, dragging herself. *No, no—no....*

"*RAH!*"

The Ram was crawling toward her, hand over hand. His hulking arms extended out like monstrous claws, tearing at the stone as he dragged his mangled carcass toward her.

Heavens fucking help me.

BOOM.

The cannon fire shook the stones, the smoke and dust spraying in her eyes. The Ram was writhing and screaming as he closed the distance.

Aura was weaponless—Mercy still firmly lodged in the Ram's leg. *Elya*, she thought, *just there, close enough to touch.* The Viper's dirk rested on the stone just outside the cadaver's open palm.

Mercy's bloody tip clinked across the cobbles, stuck in his leg. The Ram roared, turning around.

What—what the...?

The veins of his arms thumped beneath his sinewy shoulders, tightening as they wrenched Mercy free, severing the lower leg from the upper.

SCHING—Thump.

The booted calf flopped to the stone, a spurt of red shooting from the stump.

He—he doesn't seem to notice....

The Ram dragged his mangled knee, waddling and clawing and gnawing. It bled all over.

Aura watched in horror. *He's—he's picking it up.*

The Ram snatched up his *own* amputation, *laughing* as he did.

"*Ha*Ha*Ha*Ha*Ha*Ha*Ha*Ha*Ha*Ha*Ha*Ha*Ha*Ha..."

Gods in fucking hell.

BOOM.

He threw it at her.

"UGH, FUCK!" She recoiled.

The hock of meat thudded into her shoulder, spattering the Ram's blood on her face.

"COME BACK, GIRL! HAVE A TASTE OF ME!" The Ram sputtered, crawling closer. *"I WILL MAKE A MEAL OF YOU!"*

Aura slid backward—*no.*

He was there, his claw wrapped around her ankle, dragging her back. *"COME NOW!"*

BOOM.

"RAH!" she roared, turning and smashing her boot into his mouth.

"ARGH!" he shrieked, swinging wildly for her as she crawled desperately on, elbow over elbow toward Elya's corpse.

Her fingertips tasted the cold steel. *Come on, damn you.*

The Ram clubbed her hard in the lower back.

THWACK.

"ARGH!"

BOOM.

The Ram's fingers were raw to the bone, now curling between her coat and webbing. His spit sprayed her face.

"I'LL FUCKING KILL YOU!" Aura kicked hard again, reaching high and behind. *Gods, if there is one feat left in me, let me stick*

this fucking pig!

Then, a miracle. The dagger came to her. *I—I got it. It's in my hand*, she thought.

BOOM.

Aura punched hard, pushing up. She rolled to her back. The Ram dropped his fist.

THWACK.

Aura swallowed the punch. *"Come on, Hornskewer!"* She stabbed—

SCHING.

The dagger poked hilt-deep between the Ram's knuckle and fingers.

"RAH!" he roared, rearing back.

She slid it out, thrusting again, this time deep into his planted forearm. The Ram let out another harrowing cry. The brute reared his head and slammed his forehead into hers, clobbering it into the stone.

"ALL THAT POWER AND NOWHERE TO PUT IT!" she roared back, ripping the blade free and dragging it across his fleshy throat.

SCHING.

Sing to me, goddess.

The blade passed through veins and skin like a hot knife through butter. Dagfinn staggered backward, clutching at the irredeemable part in his neck. *It hangs wide open.* The color of his face dissipated as his muscles slackened on top of her, his weight pinning her down.

Aura cried and screamed and stabbed all the more, but his hulking body and armor weighed her in place like an anvil. *Gods, no.*

The Ram gurgled and choked as thick, Furii blood poured into Aura's face, eyes, and mouth.

She roared again, pushing and pulling to free her bladed hand from under the beast's belly. She stabbed aimlessly at the Ram's shoulders and neck as she tried to lift him.

Aura stabbed blindly, shrieking the last of her wind into his face, the blood running over the corners of her mouth. *No, not the blood.* She thrashed in a frenzy, desperate to avoid its touches, but it covered her.

My eyes—my nose—and my own blood, too. The coppery aroma filled her nostrils, and she tasted something salty and sweet in the back of her mouth. *I s'pose, just a taste couldn't hurt.*

Its warmth blanketed her like a bath. *It pours over me like the waters on the rocks, all those years ago...oh, how I feel it...so much...*

*So much **Power**...*

The sickening delight took hold—*the Burden lives so fucking deep.* She urged and wanted and needed...

Oh, how I need it....

I need it....

I need you....

Aura began to laugh.

XXV

ASHES AND THE ACOLYTE

Aura

Aura listened to the flapping of the banner above. It was the only sound. She'd raised to a knee over the Ram's fresh corpse, bleeding its last onto the stone. Her insides hurt, churning and brewing, ready to spill.

Our bloods have mixed. She felt a cold sense of dread. *I feel them fighting inside me.* Searing pain shot through her body and head. She winced.

Aura wiped at the blood in her eyes, but it hued her world in scarlet. She writhed, shouldering the moments like they were hours—*torturous hours, waiting to die by that damned sniper's looming trigger.*

Her fingers were the color of moonlit snow, with a near twinkle under splotches of blood that dryly tugged at the skin of her hands, now shaking outside of her control. *Take me,* she pleaded. Her breathing steadied in quiet acceptance. Her blood-red view faded to the distance, lost to walls and the cannon and the green and red jackets in piles all around.

How am I still here?

No one answered but the banner.

Where is Elya? she asked herself. *She's gone, remember? Never to return....*

"Not all that is gone is lost," came a voice.

It startled her, but she stayed put. *I have naught courage for another battle.* She kissed those soft lips but a moment ago, and she chose to think of them now, forming the words.

"Elya?"

"No, dear, but a friend."

I know that voice. "Kora," she breathed, relieved.

Aura opened her eyes, finding the gleaming mask among Kora's black feather shadows standing over her. She looked around, eyeing the tower where the scope glare had flickered and muzzle flashed just before the fight.

Where—where did—

"You have come such a long way, child—I'm so very proud." Kora's words were honey.

"How—how did you get here? And, where did the...?" Aura's mind clouded the rest.

"*Shh*, no need for that, dear....Come—be with me, but for a moment." Kora the Crow held out a gloved hand. "Take it," she hummed.

The hairs on Aura's neck began to stand. "I—I don't think I should...." She noticed the raw, pink skin between Kora's glove and sleeve. *Is—is this real?* "Are you—are you here? Your skin, I—"

"Ah, have I told you how I lost it?" she asked, purring.

"Lost...lost what?"

"Well, my skin of course!" An unfamiliar laugh rumbled out from under her steel vultus.

I fear no sea, nor stars, nor sky....

Kora removed the glove, showing stumpy pink sinew and bone.

Aura's stomach tightened. *I trust not what I see.* She gulped.

"Ares swam the fiery Phlegethon—she lost the beauty she cared so little for." The steel-carved lips of her mask began to shift and move. "The fires left the stringy bone and muscle, like rot iron." But then, the mask itself—

CREAK-CREAK-CREAAAAAAAK.

The steel lips stretched and cracked, the warping metal screeching and panging as they opened, flooding scarlet red gurgling down the front as the laughed through the blood.

Gods in hell....

"Take my beauty," she purred. "I give it *so WILLINGLY...*"

This isn't Kora....It can't be.

Kora began to cackle.

*"Ha*Ha*Ha*Ha*Ha*Ha*Ha*Ha*Ha*Ha*Ha*Ha*Ha*Ha...*"

No, please. Her eyes fluttered, as if to sleep, but the light of the sun caught her eye, fading quickly away, leaving only a sudden, unnatural deep dark that blanketed all but Aura and the Crow. Black tar poured up through the mortar and cracks of the cobbles she knelt on.

Hearts like oceans, deep and dark.

Kora was shrieking now, gleefully.

*"Ha*Ha*Ha*Ha*Ha*Ha*Ha*Ha*Ha*Ha*Ha*Ha*Ha*Ha!*"

Remember yourself, damn you! Aura slapped her own face. *Wake up, damn you! Where's that sniper? I'm right here. Just do it!*

Kora stepped toward her.

Aura thought of the Ram's blood that gushed into her face and eyes—*his Burden is becoming mine…not Kora, just the boogeyman.*

The Crow held out her mutilated hand, reaching to Aura's chin and jaw, grabbing a handful.

She's so strong. The skinless fingers forced past her lips, poking at the back of her throat. She choked and spit, but Kora's apparition held her with an iron grip.

"RAH!" she choked, but the darkness set in. *Steady, damn you!*

BOOM.

Toll…

No bullet came. She squirmed under the grip, eyeing the corpse of the giant and the remnants of the gold of Elya's coat.

She closed her eyes.

"I'll *die* when it's over," she whispered.

XXVI

THE STRANGER

Reed

Reed staggered up shoddy wooden stairs and planks of clumsy scaffolding. It wrapped the inside of the clock tower, winding up and up. The dust shook from the cracks and the mortar, the walls swaying under the weight.

Heat from the fires below steamed in through the murder holes. It blurred the horizon. Reed held his gladius shortsword in one hand and the Ram's scattergun in the other—*heavy bastard.*

Take this, he'd told him. *Catch him, and kill him early, and get this deed done.* He heard the batteries below, blasting red hot iron to the ships in the sea, fiery to the touch. *And so, the Blacktide follows me.*

The Ram would cover the outside, he trusted.

He smashed that platoon, hardly with my help. Reed focused on his climb and the clumsy stairs beneath his feet. His footfalls felt unsure, his guts, mistrusting.

Don't go, came the tiny voices raised on the back of his neck. They plucked at his nerves, playing with their food. The top drew closer.

Reed arrived. He looked up to find hulking metal cogs to a golden door, their teeth interlaced. He didn't make a sound, but they began to move, cranking in synergy.

Click-click-click…

Rust squealed from the springs and sprockets, colliding and contracting. The booms of Reed's heartbeat rattled his ribcage...*like the howitzers outside.*

The thumping battered the stone beneath, rumbling lowly. Ships popped in the distance. He stopped for a moment, eyeing the rays of sun that punched through the clock face, painting the wood around with warm yellows and cold browns. *The door.*

Planks creaked beneath Reed's feet as he approached the precipice. The cogs clicked together, and the clock clicked, too, out of time.

Click...Click—Cl—Click...

Out of time.

Reed's thumping heartbeat boomed with the cannon. He began to drool. *I—I—I have such a hunger for these things, you see...I must....*
*Well....*His blood began to cool. *I shan't spoil it, shall I?*

The cogs stopped, the lock sliding open.

Reed simmered with delight. *Oh, these things that I will do.* The tears welled in his eye, rage then joy, on and on. *It is more than to be robbed of innocence—the guilt was thrust upon me.*

Reed wiped them along with the spittle that dotted the corners of his mouth. He looked at his hand and found it smeared with the sickly black of his *vultus. Onward.* One of his boots found their place in the rusted bolt and launched the door completely from its hinges.

BOOM.

It tumbled inward into the dimness, splintering across the floor. Reed was inside, standing over modest furniture and the figure of one man crouched over another in dim sunlight.

And then, those green eyes. *Eyes like oceans, deep and dark...it's him,* he gulped. *It's him.* He lifted the blunderbuss and clicked the hammer back.

The crouched man's eyes glowed through his shadowy face.

"Welcome, my child."

I know that voice. I swear I do...

He wore a ruddy smock stained with putrid browns and yellows, and his skin was much the same. Reed's eyes adjusted, making out a single ring that shone in the dark on a finger.

What ring might that be?

Reed found no other adornments in the whole of the room. Two lonesome candles burned near their wicks' end on a matching table, but Reed could see the man clear as day—the poorly-shaven face covered in soot and blood, a stringy and thinning silver crown amidst eyes glowing so green that they might have muted the vibrance of the candlelight.

Sickly...stern. He looked down to find a corpse—*a corpse*—a similar-looking fellow, but with nicer white robes and humble heraldry and embroidery soaked in a browning red mask. *He's—he's eating him.*

"I expected someone like you," garbled the crouching cleric, chewing. "Tell me, what did you expect?"

"What have you done to the Pontifex?!" Reed cried, raising the barrel of his blunderbuss.

"This must look quite poor, surely." The man smirked. "You think"—*burp*—"you think this here is the Pontifex?" He swung the cadaver's arm limply at Reed, the way a child might gesture with a doll. "Nay, I should think not."

You—you are an honorable man, Reed reminded himself. *By the gods, what the fuck have I come upon?* The man stood from his victim, away enough to expose the remnants of the corpse's face—butchered meat cascading pinkish white cheekbones. *No nose...he...he ate him.*

"You...you—"

"I—I—*I'm* the Pontifex," he imitated. "Likely shocking, I concede, but true, nonetheless. Tell me, *brave Furii*, what brings you to my lonesome holdout? *Supper isn't for some time....*"

Reed's eyes darted to the corpse's face and back to the stained one of the supposed Pontifex and back again. Chunks of viscera dangled from his smock like it were a bib.

"Nay, don't tell me. You wish to kill me, of course—*obvious*—but why, I wonder? And perhaps, for *whom?*"

Reed froze, finding no words. He thought of a conversation with the Raven, in the days before.

"Why do you wish to kill the Pontifex?" I asked.

"Because he wronged me," cawed the Raven. "What do you say for yourself?"

"Servitude," I drunkenly admitted. "Then, perhaps I am a slave. Like Eydian...young blood for the Blood God."

"To Eydian, then...for planting his boots...."

"To planting his boots..."

Reed planted himself.

He held the barrel calmly to the cleric's chest and leaned into the trigger.

"No quarter."

BOOM.

The shot tore through the bed and the wall—sun rays came in behind the holes. The debris clouded the room along with Reed's vision.

Ah, he reared. *I—I can't see him....*

"Here, darling."

THWACK.

The old man's fist slammed Reed's chest, cracking and hurling the Furii back through the door and down the stairs, taking a few with him. His body tumbled, crashing through the wood and toppling the staircase. The pieces fell far below.

Reed halted himself against a wall, balancing on a sturdier platform, swaying. He clutched a small piece of the leftover floorboard.

Steady, brother, the Ram might've said.

Yes, mum, I'd say.

He picked himself up and brushed himself off. *Why shouldn't an old man kick my arse today? Strange eons, indeed.*

Reed wrenched his gladius free, ready.

Silence.

The shape of the old man glided to the edge of the stairs. He was feasting on his fingernails. "Dear *Me,*" he said, "you look as if you've seen a *ghost.*"

"*Who* are you?!" Reed shouted.

"*Me?*" he said, "why I'm *you,* of course. I'm *all* of you, in fact—the Furii, the layman—the pious and the sweetly *deranged.* I'm what's waiting for you in the deepest of darks—the one you pray to in your hour of need. I hear your sorrows—oh, how they make me smile."

The Pontifex flew down.

CRACK.

The old man's open palm smashed Reed's ribs. The hit propelled him through the stone, the clumps of wall and broken bricks following him to the courtyard far below.

XXVII

THE BURDEN

Aura

I…I must be in a fever.

The blood…

So much blood…

K-Kora?

She's gone. I am…I am alone…

In the dark.

I'll die when it's over…

…is it over?

BOOM.

The cannon shook the stones beneath, violently rousing her. *No—no Crow,* she thought, looking about. *No…no sniper?* Aura rose with keen eyes, but then winced and shut them. *Damn!* She held a hand to the pain, delicately dabbing with her fingertips to a clean, round hole just between her neck and shoulder, the dry blood sticking at her open, frayed collar.

Gods in hell, the sniper hit me. But, when?

Aura stayed low, snatching up a stricken Mercy and sliding her home in the scabbard over her back.

She crawled toward Elya, fearing another shot. Aura swallowed hard and wiped her eyes, carefully opening her dead friend's coat as she slid her hand to Elya's back. Her eyes watched nervously to the high points and the sniper's former perch. *Relief.* She felt the handle of the sawed-off shotgun, still holstered.

But Aura's hand slid across Elya's clammy skin, jolting her. *It's not her*, she said to herself. *She's gone.* She wrenched the weapon free, jerking the corpse a bit...*like—like a doll.* Aura's eyes glanced over the basin in her head, and she nearly choked. *It's not her.*

She picked up the rest of her things and eyed the stair turret, yonder—the one the Ram's friend had taken. *I'll kill the rest of them, by the gods, I swear. I don't care whose side they're on.* As far as Aura was concerned, every soul in the whole of the Eryx was now her enemy, and vengeance would be hers. The errant shots and shouts and meaningless noise of the bombardment struck her chords again as the outside sounds came back to her, cannonballs slamming hard into rocks below.

A few errant mortars landed very near, spraying debris from time to time, but she paid little mind. After stepping toward the stairs, she caught a glimpse of the carnage below—landing boats had departed their vessels, en route to the beach and the gate. She eyed the splashing of cannonballs that peppered the sea all around, and she could hear the far-off screams of gun crews and soldiers in the heat of the crossfire. There would be a clash quite soon, she could see, and those screams would worsen as they always do.

Make haste, Aura.

The eerie loneliness of it all gave Aura pause. She'd found piles of the dead even on the way up those bastille stairs, not a soul left to twitch or wriggle or squirm. Scores lined the courtyard she'd only just skirmished in, but she heard not a grunt or even a whisper. Perhaps she'd be a corpse, too.

Let me kill the swine, she prayed. *One last time, let me bring my justice—let me drag them to the abyss.* She had no doubt she would die in this place, but a final barter with the gods couldn't hurt, even if it was the Pontifex in her sights.

She remembered his features, but under shroud and veil. His hair and his eyes were the staples—a sleek silvery gray top with eyes green enough to punch through the fog of his face. He was handsome but strange, somehow—an ethereal presence that floated more than walked and pondered far more than spoke. She had seen him only the once at the Ball, and it was toward the end, well after her dealings with Marcus at the Falls. She remembered his scarcity that night but found him in the drawing room before the festivities began.

He asked me to dance, she recalled. *Will I remember his face?*

The cool wind prickled her cheeks and jaw as ocean air rocked and cradled her tears. She wiped at them with a shudder, opening her eyes to the sun's imposing rays and the gleaming of steel approaching from the nearest stair turret. *Tricky Eli.*

"Too little—*too late!*" called Aura, dragging her face along her sleeve.

"By the gods," he muttered, surveying the sea of bodies strewn across the yard as he approached. "Did he—your friend, I—"

"She's gone," Aura spat, drawing her sword. "And I will be, too, if I don't move—"

BOOM.

An ear-splitting *ping* erupted near the Acolyte and bounced around the square, followed by the resounding crack of a rifle in the distance. *The sniper.* Her eye caught an unnatural twitch jerk Elatreus's chest sideways as he fell to one knee. His eyeline was still high and alert, dancing between steeple and perch as the flowing steel branches of his inlaid helm shimmered in the sun.

Aura sprinted to the man, shouting, "GO BACK, GO BACK!" with every echoing step as she closed the distance.

Elatreus unsheathed the ornate, curved sword dangling from his hip.

SCHING.

"Get down, fool!" she shouted, clapping a free hand on his back as she half-pushed, half-dragged him to the stairs behind.

Aura eyed the slim puncture hole just between pauldron and center chest, now oozing a steady stream of red as the Acolyte leaned heavily into Aura's shoulder. She moved her arm further under his, bearing as much of the broad Furii's weight as she could whilst propelling him to cover, her steady hand vying for a better grip on his weighty gambeson. The back side showed another hole—*a bigger one*—flowering strands of torn steel outward.

BOOM.

Another pang echoed before another crack.

"Argh—SHITE!" she hollered, swatting at her collar like she'd just had a bee sting. She faltered and tripped, careening off the ledge and barreling downward. Her body went limp as she toppled over the armor-clad Acolyte, whose clanking and crumpling raiment echoed not far behind.

Aura came to a stop a few stairs lower, dabbing furious fingers at the flesh between her clavicle and collar, finding the hole and plugging it as deep as she could. *Damn.* She winced, forcing her fingertips deeper into the wound, the warmth running past them.

Cool air tickled from the far side—*through and through.* She breathed a sigh of relief. Warm spurts of blood enveloped her trigger finger as she pushed it further—*come on, clot, damn you.* The Acolyte was dressing his, too, pushing through the shilling-sized hole in his chest piece as his face squirmed and strained.

"*Damn it all,*" he muttered, loosening his gorget.

Aura found his eyes when Eli wrenched his helmet off, gulping a few greedy breaths. She turned over, crawling the few steps up and gripping his collar with her free hand. "Can you breathe?" she asked, pulling him forward and inspecting the blooming rose on his back. "Lungs intact?"

"Aye, I think so." He coughed. "You? How's the bleeding?"

Aura tugged, yelping, "*How*—how's it look?"

Elatreus leaned forward, cringing himself. He put a soft hand to Aura's jaw, rotating her head sideways as he inspected the wound intimately. "No arteries," he said.

She pried his hand off her face. "We need to keep moving. The sniper's up in the belfry with plenty of cover—can't go back that way."

"Agreed." He nodded. "We—we need to find the Pontifex… before…before—"

"I know, I know," Aura replied. "The Ram was covering another Furii. He went up the clock tower while Elya…*Elya*—" She stopped short.

"Aye, the clock tower," Elatreus said. "There's—there's another way 'round," he huffed.

She looked him in the eye, pressing a hand to her neck once again as she paused for a small moment. Deep breathes metered her gaze. "You're the *fucking* fist of the Church," she chided. "Where are your soldiers? Where are your *civilians*?!"

He wheezed a sad laugh through gritted teeth and nodded. "I—I didn't want to be *conspicuous*," he replied, "and why would I want civilians? The whole point was to—"

Aura let out a giggle.

"Laughing at me, then?"

"Always." The wound stung with her smile, and she recoiled. She nodded firmly and began to stand. "Shall we?" she asked.

"Yes, let's," he said, dragging his armor along the wall.

XXVIII

HUMAN GODS

Reed

What—what men are we?

What honor have thee?

Ocean breeze rapped at the sweat of Reed's brow, rousing him. The rest of him lay buried under a mound of bricks and dust. *Ugh— ugh.* He was choking. Reed worked an eye open but saw little. He wriggled his fingers under the rock and found his sword missing. *Still up there someplace, with—with the fuckin' devil himself.*

His head hurt. *I need to move.* Reed tried to roll, but his shoulder wouldn't budge—broken and trapped as the blood leaked out, pooling in his sleeve. He lifted with the other, shrieking on the inside.

It crumbled loose. The rocks shifted and fell, exposing most of his back, but Reed failed to rise. *Come on, damn you. Get up.* His head came out from the rocks, catching a breath and looking to the tower above. Reed found the Pontifex leaning lazily on a gargoyle stationed at the top of the tower. The old man grinned wide, taking another bite of his fingernail and licking the remnants from his curled lips. With a small step, he dropped from the tower, landing just in front of Reed, crashing like an anvil on the courtyard floor.

BOOM.

Through settling smoke, Reed found the emerald gaze and the crooked smile of the Pontifex, unblinking. *Those—those green eyes.* The tails of his nightgown flapped in the sun. A rumbling siege raged on below as Reed looked for an exit. He saw the trails of towering smokestacks hovering above the lower ramparts, clouding the city limits and the lower bailey. He could feel the trickles of blood on his forehead as he tried to raise himself.

His head was like a boulder on his neck. *I need a weapon,* he thought drowsily. With his good arm, he reached to his back—*the messer.* It was still there, Josey, so faithfully strapped in her scabbard.

My guiding moonlight....

Reed tried rolling harder this time, getting over. He buried his face in the dirt and pushed. *Argh.* His good hand unclipped the scabbard and shakily yanked at the handle.

*Breathe, my love. Just breathe...*Reed charmed the blade as if it were a snake.

"Dear child, please lay down your arms. I mean you—of *all* people—no harm." The old man smiled.

"What have you done to the Pontifex?"

"How many times must I say it? I *am* the Pontifex..."—he giggled—"or perhaps, someone else. Another name, you know?"

"What?!" spat Reed.

"Was it Leon? Roy? Or perhaps...*Saul*...another name, another lifetime...another *world,* even...another...*time.*"

I must fell this beast, Reed vowed, forcing himself the rest of the way up. His ribs seared. *I fear no thorns along the path.*

They draw only mortal blood.

The beast in Reed roared like billowing hellfire. *The Bloodmoat and the Silver Church and the fiery tide of the river Phlegethon, scalding the dark on shores of the underworld.* He felt his muscles tighten into reeds of ironwood as he gripped his messer with the hands of a living god. The pain was gone—*the hate remains.*

"*RAH!*" he roared, lunging at the old man.

His great sword swung high and fast.

SCHING.

The old man was still, but the blade had met its mark.

I…did I?

The cleaving blow landed between neck and shoulder, sinking to the old man's mid-chest. His blood poured by the bucketful as Reed dragged Josey out of him, leveraging his heel on the Pontifex's stomach as he dragged Josey free. He came apart, but…

*The smile stricken on his face…*the red rained down.

I—I got him, Reed thought in relief, unfazed by the man's blood and severed pieces.

The old man's eyes were open. *Those eyes,* he thought, *still shining.*

I—fear…only you, dear brother…and your wandering eye.

BOOM.

Tolling, on and on…

The red covered him again. Reed grinned, mirroring the madman's contorted face. *Silly, isn't it?* He began to laugh aloud. *So much blood in this one, gushing his last.…*

Reed's chest tightened. *Ugh,* he wheezed, *I killed him, I s'pose. Let's just sit for a moment.*

He pried his hands free from the hilt and sat on the rubble. *Easier than I thought*, he admitted, the pain shooting up his back as he sat. *Damn.* He winced and sighed, dabbing at tender ribs with one eye closed. *Fuck*, he agonized, *this won't do.*

The Ram and the Raven won't have shite to say now, will they?

Reed heard their footsteps approaching. *And others…many others.*
He looked up.
The Raven's black feathers peeked over the stairs.
No, he noticed, squinting, *not the Raven.* "Who—who are you?"
A woman's low voice returned behind a shimmering steel mask. "Why, brother—you've made a grave mistake," she answered.

BOOM.

The carronade blew hot iron violently to the sea.

Toll…

"The cosmic clock strikes twelve," she said, pointing an outstretched finger. "You shoulder a burden not your own."
"What—what burden?"
"Sin is absolute," she whispered, peering behind empty steel eye holes. "Do you know what you've inherited?"
"Inherited?"
"You said it yourself, young, brave soul…*what sort of man must you be?"*

BOOM.

Toll…

The sun faded away, spilling to eclipsing black.

Like a Blackwood tick…the Burden has me.

"Do not fret, child…for all things die. All things end."

No, Reed closed his eyes painfully. "No," he whispered. "Nothing ends."

"Mason…," she said.

"Huh?"

"Mason!"

"What say you, specter?"

BOOM.

"Mason!" came Deimos's voice from down the stairs.

Remember yourself, damn you. "I'm here!" Reed shouted back. *Where is Dagfinn?*

The Raven followed Deimos up the stairs, then another man. *Holy hell.* The stern bald head became Tytan Brynjar leading his veteran guard up the causeway, fully armored.

How did he get here?

Reed shifted beneath the clock tower but failed to rise. *I don't have the heart for this—not here, not now.*

The shadowy woman is nowhere to be found.

The troopers behind carried grappling hooks and tightly tied ropes that slung over shoulders, their short rifles and swords bloodied and bouncing on their hips.

How did they get here?

"Is—is that *him?*" the Sage demanded.

"Aye," Reed said. "I—I found him…*eating*—"

"What in the name of Tara have you done…?"

"Pardon?"

"You *fucking* fool," cursed the Raven. "He said capture, not kill!"

"Capture, not kill!" echoed the Sage.

Reed's eyes found the Raven's just in time for his tattered cloak to whip sideways, exposing the red of his revolver barrel, now peering odiously his way.

"I *know* you aren't pointing that blasted thing at me—"

"You have no *FUCKING* idea what you've done," he shouted, gnashing his teeth. The gun was rattling in his hand.

"*Gods in heaven*," Deimos whispered, "what have you done?"

"*What?*"

A long pause before the Brynjar stepped forward. He was smiling. Reed wiped the blood from his eyes.

Tytan nodded politely at the Sage and the Raven, yet his boots clopped closer and closer to Reed. "My boy!" he exclaimed, opening his arms wide and embracing him.

Reed's heart sank. "Sir, I—Eydian—" he choked.

"Be at peace, Master Mason. I've heard the news—my bereavement: *mine own*, and no place for the battlefield."

Tytan's sly smile was casual and nearly convincing—*but he's betrayed by the mist in his eyes.* "Now then—as mine own son was a casualty of this mission, let me embrace you as another."

"An honor, sir," Reed said, "earnest."

"*Sire*…gentlemen, I cannot convey a more solemn pride," Tytan said, snorting. "The wheels of change turn here and now, and with the fall of the Pontifex comes new opportunity." He turned to the others.

Cyrus's six-gun was still fixed on the young Furii.

A traitor, he must be.

"Cyrus, brother, what's the matter?" said Tytan.

"You have no idea—"

"Calm yourself, sir, and holster that piece before—"

"We're *DOOMED*, you fucking fool!" Deimos shouted. "You set *him* free."

"Set whom free?" Tytan asked. "This whoreson here?" He kicked at the body's top half. "The plan to capture was for Kora's sake, but I must say…don't you prefer to see him like this?" He laughed, kicking at the grinning face.

Reed smiled, too. *For Kora's sake? I—I hear something, do I?*

A horse neighed in the distance.

Ah, he nodded, *ol' Sphinx sounded just like that. But…but only when she was startled.*

Then, a horse. It smoldered at the nostrils, appearing on the stairs.

Black as night.

BOOM.

Toll…

…and red.

It clopped up, gliding behind the Raven.

A crown…a kingdom…a Crow…

And a horse…

…the Night Mare cometh.

"*You honor Me, darling…*"

XXIX

DREAMS THAT SPEAK

The Raven

Is this real?

Surely, you have escaped no prison?

But I...

All is possible within her walls, beyond the shackles of time...

I've escaped nothing...

Divine...malign...our worlds will align...

"What have you done?" asked Cyrus earnestly.
"Capture, not kill," recited the Sage.
"Capture, not kill," Cyrus lamented.
Tytan turned to the Raven. His face turned stiffly south.
"Is that a dagger, there?" he asked, pointing to Cyrus's poniard, the blade coming over his other arm, parallel to the pistol.

A what?

"Is that not a dagger there, you point at me?" Tytan said again.

The Raven nodded. "Not to you, sir—"

"So clear it is—plain as day…a dagger you hold to my fragile throat…."

"Mr. Mason—"

"Raven…."

BOOM.

The bell, oh, how I hear it…please, for the love of all, Tara and Aura, and light itself….

Show me thine eyes….

"I am not a man of figments and fantasy, nor are my faithful knights," rambled Tytan. He cast a wide arm to his guards behind, giggling cruel delights.

"Gods in hell," said the Raven. "I've heard these words before."

"Here, I sit," said Reed, "haunted by the cold of the dead and gone…."

"Huh?" barked Tytan. "Shall you sheathe your dagger, then? Shall you spit fire at my *b-b-behest?*"

Gods, Brynjar's stark raving mad. Run, the Raven's guts shrieked from their depths.

Run, dear.

BOOM.

"I think," sputtered Tytan, getting close, "should you falter one more time, Raven—should you fail me one more FUCKING time… by the gods, *I-I-I* will set the dogs upon you…."

The Raven did not answer.

"For you know of the darkness I speak, damn you," croaked Tytan. As if I don't know who you really are?" A grin contorted the Brynjar's face. "I know of exile, Ghost of Clydae."

The sun turned an inky black before the Raven's eyes, stifling out the light. He closed them, the words too painful, burning somewhere deep below the surface. *Fucking titles.*

"And I...I know of cost."

"Enough," croaked the Raven.

"What a fool you are, Marcus Petronax...what a fool."

BOOM.

Cyrus heard the voice before he saw, but he could feel it coming. *He is coming,* he recoiled. *He—he said my name....*

The cosmic clock strikes twelve.

The Raven kept his eyes shut, fearing what might appear. *And yet, I—I feel him.* With the soft sea breeze came the ethereal whispers and dreamlike shadows. *Stay out of my head.*

"You can't leave me locked away in there forever, dear."

Shut up. The words were low and far off, but the Raven pried his eyes painfully open. *I hear him in my ears, not just my head. He—he... he is here. The Night Mare is here.*

"Indeed, *I* am," came the low rumble of the stranger's voice.

Cyrus shuddered. *I heard him in the words of Tytan Brynjar the Torchbearer. I hear him still, taunting me. I feel him.*

Pale white fingers curled like spider legs out from the shadows, ghostly free. Long white hair flowed down to match the stained robes of a stranger appearing out from behind the rubble pile. *Not a stranger.* Old, wispy strands stained amber at the tips fell combed from a golden crown, like silver curtains to the emeralds peeking through the shadows of his face. *A king.*

Sinews in his antique armor creaked between square, ceremonial shoulders and chest. His arm guards matched the gold of his toothy, alien crown. Brick red sleeves bled beneath the dirty white of robes and ashen hair that fell straight and pristine to his mid-back.

But, his face...*his face*...a hollow thing and pale like the moon with gaunt cheeks that met a line of black paint that covered his mouth and plunged down the rest of his neck. The shade around his eyes was a similar pitch—a dark, wrinkled mess, as if scorched to each corner, the emerald of his eyes blazing through.

"Salutations," said the stranger, folding his ghostly fingers together as his footfalls echoed slowly closer.

"Who—who are you?" Tytan asked, reaching for his pistol.

"I might ask you the same," replied the stranger.

"I am Tytan Brynjar, the Torchbearer—"

"*Torchbearer?*" he mimed. "And what torch? What flame do you bear, oh, king?"

"Is this your doing, Raven?" Tytan scoffed.

"What? Of course not! The youngblood, there—"

"As if I do not know?" Brynjar shouted over him. "*Evil is mud upon the hill,*" he recited, "*slippery and entrenching; it worsens as it slowly swallows; it buries your light as it sticks....*"

The man's glowing green eyes glared blankly at Brynjar for a moment. Then, without a word...

SCHING.

The Night Mare is here. A pale white hand shot upward and seemingly through Tytan's head, faster than the Raven's eye could follow. His fingers flashed across the Brnyjar, freezing in place in a hover over the lord of Norsefyre's head.

A gut-wrenching pause glued Cyrus in place. *What...what the...?*

The stranger's fingers were painted red, dangling loose viscera, dripping the Brynjar's own humors into the Furii's face and mouth. The stranger let out a laugh.

"*Urgh,*" Tytan choked, his throat gushing open.

"I care naught for your fictions....Here, have a taste—"

SPLAT-SPLAT...

The stranger wrenched a loose handful of Tytan's meat into the poor bastard's own mouth. Cyrus's courage was snuffed out like a candle. *He—he's...he's shoving it—shoving it in his...in his m-mouth.*

The blood of Tytan Brynjar spilled out by the bucketful, and he collapsed.

"*Shite!*" hollered the Raven, turning the barrel away from Reed as he fanned three quick shots at the stranger.

Each missed.

Each. He was everywhere...

...and nowhere.

He stood firmly still, but then...

WHOOSH.

The stranger moved like lightning, jumping without a sound through the light and the air, and through the Raven's fingers and the falls of his revolver's hammer.

Nothing but open air.

"*Mhm,*" hummed the man in white. "Cyrus, *my love,* won't you introduce me to your friends?"

"*ARGGH!*" roared the Raven, throwing a wild punch.

THWACK.

He—he caught it. The stranger moved it aside, effortlessly. He attacked, bludgeoning the Raven's stomach with an iron fist, curled in ivory white.

BOOM.

The hit launched the Raven.

"My *dear* Cyrus," he purred, "come now. This is no way to treat an old friend…a riding partner…."

The Raven crashed into a heap of loose stone.

"We sang of this, do you remember?"

"You had to fucking do it, didn't you!" the Raven spat at Reed.

"Come now, Cyrus…*Cyrus!*" The stranger laughed, enunciating. "Cy-rus…oh, how I *hate* that name…."

No.

"It's not the one *I* gave you." His black lips curled.

"You—you killed him!" shouted Deimos, lunging forward. "You killed Brynjar?!"

The Sage swung sideways with all his weight.

Air. The stranger slid beyond the blade, slyly missing.

Deimos wheeled Moonlight to a point, thrusting.

Wind. The stranger dodged Moonlight's shimmering steel, dropping another iron fist on top of the Sage's shoulder, crushing it.

CRACK.

The old Furii collapsed quickly—*pitifully*—wheezing and dropping the saber to the stone.

Tytan Brynjar hacked and gagged in a pool of thick Furii blood, splashing over cobbled courtyard by the pint. He grabbed and pinched at severed skin folds, splayed distressingly apart.

"Darling," hummed the stranger, "who's this one? Sorry, old boy—*I* didn't wish to kill you, there...*my mistake.* I'm more powerful than I remember, it would seem."

Reed Mason lunged, too, dropping his good shoulder and charging forward. *"RAH!"*

Seabreeze. He barreled into nothing, falling clumsily flat, but rolling through it. He looked back up to see the stranger.

BOOM.

The carronade continued.

The bell tolls on.

Tytan's guardsmen jumped forward, but far too late. The first two ran to their lord, snatching frantically at his collar. They rested hands under his head, but the blood spilled out through their fingers, nonetheless. The Torchbearer's color drained from his cheeks and lips as his sunken eyes closed, never again to open.

His veteran guardsman cradled his neck. It was all the man could do.

The rest looked on, watching as the throat came together and apart.

Gods in fucking hell.

No gods here, sweet Cyrus.

The man in white smiled, holding his hands together. "Perhaps *I* can teach another lesson," he said.

...only Me.

His fingers became daggers again.

SCHING—SCHING…CRACK…

He darted amongst the rest of Brynjar's cohort, slashing his long nails across their throats and bellies, like white comets tailing red. The man in white tore them apart, one by one.

Cyrus halted himself, as if retreating. He took a knee, burying his face in an open hand. *Out…out, damn you….*

Oh, I'm out, brother….

The stranger froze upon one of the victims, and Cyrus opened his eyes. He found a twisted snarl, beading saliva from the corners of putrid yellow. The stranger motioned his outstretched fingers to the Raven, and he got a better look. White, stained skin fell away, exposing long, jagged bones that came to clawed tips.

They're…they're growing. The Raven swallowed hard. *His damned claws are growing.*

They dripped viscous red as he spun and jumped, slitting open the belly and spilling the entrails of another guard, this one merely trying to run.

The Raven could feel the color leaving his cheeks, evaporating with his courage. *They—they barely have time to scream.*

The stranger's hands—*white iron spiders*—clawed through the rest, ripping them wide open. The man in white did so delightedly.

He killed their Brynjar….He killed them, too.

What makes you think I won't kill you?

His fingers were glowing, now. *They're—they're fucking red hot….* They steamed and hissed as blood boiled off them. The claws dragged scorch lines into the cohort's blue and gold coats, each slice like lighting a match. The screams quit before the embers could catch.

"Gentlemen, do not raise a hand to your *lord*...." His voice got deeper, bellowing over the cries of the dying. "*I* mean you no harm.... Cyrus—tell them."

Breathe, damn you. His boiling blood began to cool. *We must be cool to handle him here.*

You will say my name before the end.

The Raven felt an urge—*revenge*, he thought, clenching his fist. *Revenge against this damnable Reed, for releasing the King of Battle... and ruining my chance.*

You...yes, you...

Cyrus rested on his knee, his eyes rooted in the stone underfoot. *Steady, damn you.*

"Cyrus," sighed Deimos, "he's...he's released the beast...."

You, there...I see you....

"You," said Reed, pointing at the Raven.

"Me?!" roared the Raven. "*You*—you hateful wretch, you had to kill him, didn't you?! I warned you—"

"*Cyrus*," the man in white hissed. "Dear, this shade doesn't suit you...but I suppose neither does that name, does it?" He laughed. "Ugh, tis so *splendid* to be free from you and whatever's going on between your ears!" He clapped his hands together, his crooked black lips curling over his yellow teeth. "So dark and dreary in that mind of yours...so sad, Cyrus....How shall we make you feel better?"

"*WHAT DID YOU DO, CYRUS?!*" Reed roared.

A deal's a deal.

The man in white's mouth didn't move, and yet the Raven heard him. Cyrus turned to Reed, *"You,"* he growled. "You did this, you stupid child, not me."

The stranger shushed the Raven. *"Mmm,* no, darling, it's my turn to speak for us." He pointed delicately at Reed. "You there—*Mason,* is it? Your mind must be an addled mess." He laughed jovially. The man in white slapped his reddened hand on a stunned Reed's shoulder. "I'm sure it didn't need to begin this way. *Violence begets violence,* after all...but not for *Me.*"

"Damn you," Reed snarled, hurling a punch, hitting only air and dust.

"Darling, you mustn't blame the boy—you couldn't have kept me cooped up in that head of yours forever." The stranger turned to the Raven.

"Who the *FUCK* are you?!"

The stranger looked back at Reed, cocking his head, "Good sir—did you not hear me before? I do so *hate* to repeat myself. You think lightning might strike twice with that sword of yours?" He nodded to Josey.

"You're—you're the Pontifex?" Reed asked shakily.

"Heavens, no!" The stranger laughed. "Not anymore, brother. Thanks to you. Now I'm just *Me*...

"Me...

"Me...."

"What?!"

"Ah-ah-alas, I shan't expect you to solve this yet, Master Mason...tis all too new, surely." He swatted the bloody stumps of his fingers on Reed's cheek. "But, if I may, please be silent—I have

much to discuss with the Ghost of Clydae, there."

He glided toward the Raven, now kneeling, defeated.

BOOM.

Fuck this cannon, fuck this bell...and, gods, fuck me. Cyrus lifted his gaze. Glowing green, pitiless eyes stared back. His crown shone in the sun.

"What shall I call you?" asked the man in white. "Cyrus? Raven? Ghost of Clydae? Or perhaps...your *true* name...."

Cyrus gathered himself, lifting his tired body from the stone. He met the white one's eyes, one for one. *Those fucking eyes, oh, how I wish to shut them.*

Deimos spoke up. "It matters naught what ye call him, specter— what, pray tell, shall we call you?"

The Raven groaned. *I—I know his true name.....*

Say it.

BOOM.

I hear you, Spirit...but tell me, where's that bloodied horse of yours? It wouldn't be a revelation without—

She comes to you, beyond the moon.

Does she, then? Your nag that just won't die?

Your visions are your own—perhaps, something more you might remember...

That—that was the deal I made so long ago, now...lifetimes gone by, nameless like the seasons and the true gods.

But, a deal, nonetheless…

I don't wish to—

What, your love didn't last as you thought it might?

Shut up.

The man in white's green gaze shot to the Sage with a raised eyebrow. "But of course," he said, "darling—would you introduce me to your friends?"

"Burn in hell," spat the Raven.

He frowned. "Poor form, dear."

The King of Battle's white hand thrust out, catching the Raven's jaw. His bloodied fingers curled into Cyrus's mouth, prying it open. The Raven choked and struggled, but the iron grip held him firm, cutting off the breath as he gagged on the King of Battle's deepest fingertip. Cyrus tugged at the hand, clawing out from under the King of Battle's clutches, his blue eyes swimming in red.

"You see," he said, "I've been here since the beginning….*I* helped make it! *All of it…*the sea, the city…*the stars.* I've had *many* names over just as many lifetimes. And so have you, *black-feather bird!* But, you will not survive this crossfire, I'm afraid….*I* saw Tara's birth….*I* shall see her end."

The Raven's vision turned to black behind his eyes. His blood began to boil. *I'll swim the Styx. I don't care….Her spectral soul would be with me 'til the stars flicker out.*

BOOM.

Toll…

He threw one last balled fist in desperation. It *thunked* on the man's forehead, knocking the crown off his head, dropping to the stone.

CLANG.

Say My name, sweet Cyrus...

One eye was swollen shut, the Raven could tell, but Reed was nodding. The Raven sputtered and choked. *That's it—kill me, you swine.*

"*My crown.*" The man in white frowned.

Mason reached for the crown, snatching it up.

Uh-oh, thought Cyrus.

Reed held it out, in parlay—*defeated.* "A crown for a king," he offered. "Tell me: what are you the king of, Spirit? Tara? The Furii?"

His mustard smile stretched from ear to ear. "Furii?" He laughed. "Nay, little one, *I* am far above that abomination coursing through your veins. You *apes* were never meant to have it...too young, you are...like the cosmos." He turned back to the Raven.

Out—out, damn you.

In, brother! IN...

"B-Battle...," Cyrus hissed.

"What?" asked Reed.

"*King of Fucking Battle.*"

"*I* believe I've been a parasite for far too long—robbed of my... *status.* Weaker gods with weaker stomachs, eh, Cyrus?" The man in white kicked at him facetiously. "As *I* am bound no longer, neither shall you be, friends..."

...nor you.

BOOM.

Cyrus heard a horse neighing in the distance. *Gods in hell.*

The man turned to Reed. "*I* am *the devil to your pitiful souls*—the first god of all the eons and, one day, the *last*....*I* am Master of Chaos and Saint of Despair—Harbinger of every retribution and the Reclaimer of your weakening world."

My light fades—he steals it away from me.

"I am god of the shadows…"

BOOM.

"I am lord of the dark…"

BOOM.

*"…*Death, *the Boatman, and the King of Battle, hark."*

BOOM.

The stone groaned beneath them.

"Mark my words, all you accursed sons and daughters of Ares—*the Prison knows no Walls…"*

…and neither shall you.

XXX

FLOATING

Cyrus

Reed sat up, disrespectfully.
Stay down, fool, Cyrus thought.

"What do you desire, *oh king?*"

The King of Battle whirled around with a vexing green gaze. "I shall start with the *soul* of this world. Tell me, Master Mason, are you familiar with the Prison Without Walls?"

Gods, kill me.

Not yet, my sweet...

"Aye."

BOOM.

A burning hot ball blasted through the weakened side of the clock tower. Sparks and debris sprayed into the courtyard, followed by a heap of pulverized stone—the wall cracked and heaved, tipping forward. Confusion and chaos came with the cannonball.

"Uh-oh." A stone smashed into the Raven's shoulder. *Urgh,* he croaked, coughing and staggering his way to Deimos and Reed. "You've killed us, you stupid child!" he choked.

"Where is he?!" cried the Sage.

"Where is he?" echoed the Raven.

Deimos turned to Reed, snatching at his jacket. "Capture not kill, you remember?! You remember what they said?!"

Reed yelped. The Sage's hand gripped a stern handful of the youngblood's shoulder, twisting the beading fabric, tightening it like a tourniquet across the wound. "Oh, *fuck off*, the both of you," Reed shouted, "he was fuckin' *eatin'* him! Munchin' on his—"

"Munchin' what, ye say?"

"Oh, piss off."

"Small beer for the gods, *ye jackass*. You've done it now—set the beast upon Tara."

Reed shook his head, looking down. "Where—where is he?"

"I don't see him anywhere—"

"Don't look—*run!*"

They sprinted toward the stair turret. *We must run.* Cyrus ran with the others, scrambling down stairs and over clutter and through the dust and the noise, daring not to look back. *Just run.*

CRACK…CRACK…

The last of the tower wall tipped and fell, smashing onto the courtyard behind them.

BOOM.

The causeway appeared through the cloud. *There's dust in my bloody eyes,* the Raven winced. He wiped, but the dirt of his gloves did far more harm than good.

CRACK—CRACK…

The stair turret collapsed over the side behind them. Loose

stones thundered down the cliffside, slamming into the sea beneath.

"Run, you fool!" Deimos shouted, grabbing Reed by his tattered shoulder.

Run, run, run—fast as ye can...

Cyrus shuddered.

"Gods be damned!" Reed squealed, prying the Sage's hand from his injury. "Watch the wound, ye cunt." Reed rose, stumbling after the others.

The blood was soaking through the armpit of Mason's jacket, the Raven saw. *Give him the youngblood if it comes to it*, his gut told him. "Brothers, *left*!" Cyrus cried. "The egress, there!" He pointed to a small opening under the near rampart—*the Portcullis*.

They turned doggedly to another alleyway, dodging strewn boxes and bushels obstructing the street. Deimos had pulled his breech-loader from its case and fitted a long shell between the groove and lock, slapping the mechanism and cocking the hammer. He turned over his shoulder with a ready rifle, but the King of Battle was gone.

BOOM.

It rings—it rings...on and on....

"What are the sailors shootin' at?!" shouted Reed. "The Brynjar's dead, for gods' sake!"

"They couldn't know," grumbled the Sage.

"Where's *Malus*?!" cried the Raven.

WHAT?! WAS THAT WHAT I THINK IT WAS?!

Shite—

*Oh, HOW I LOVE TO HEAR IT—I CRAVE, AND I HUNGER—
TO HEAR MY NAME IN THAT MIND OF YOURS! To hear it
from that mouth…*

Out, damn you!

Deimos clapped him on the back. The Raven unsheathed his estoc.

I so wish to be inside…

I'll tie you up by your guts…if you have guts….

The cries of battle blighted the Raven's ears like the bells and the booms. Shot bounced from the wall, rattling his ribcage. The Eryx's clapping carronade lit the sky. The Raven followed the red-hot balls to the sea, splashing high spouts or disappearing in splinters and smoke as the shrieks of the wounded stretched eternally. They flooded through the corridors and thoroughfares as the heat rose with the sound. The breeze billowed between the palls, churning pockets of anguish and heat, burning at the dry wood and thatch of the city and the street.

Where is everyone?

"Where is he?" shouted Reed, wiping the sweat from his eyes.
"I—I don't know…."
They descended under the final archway, spilling out to another lower courtyard. The Raven saw a small steeple overlooking the sea—a gutted bell tower with holes beaming light through the internal wooden scaffolding—*and the portcullis, just there…a stone's throw beyond.*
"Hurry!" the Raven shouted, wrenching open the cast-iron gate.

He looked over his shoulder and back, finding something new—a new man standing on the other side with another figure. *Silver armor, shining in the sun....*

This silver Furii had stepped out of the shadows accompanied by a woman painted red.

The Raven's heart sank, and he spat.

Fuck.

The ancient armor—*absurd* – was hued with a red sash, draped over the silvery branches etched in his fine raiment—*the tabard of the Tattered Banner.*

"*No,*" he groaned.

"Oh, gods be *damned*," Deimos huffed.

"Who's that? We don't have time—" Reed said.

"Damned, indeed," muttered the Raven. "A...a wild *Acolyte*," he said hungrily. "He appears before me: a wounded wolf, lone from the pack."

Oh, child...look closer...

The Raven's heart dove down to his soul.

BOOM.

The King of Battle appeared up the way, coy, coquettish—*cunt*— leaning against a near archway stained black.

Something glows, thought Cyrus as he peered at the shadow, holding out a bright red orb caressed between both hands.

An apple.

Shimmering emeralds twinkled above, blinking toward Cyrus before raising the fruit to the ebon mouth, taking a bite.

The Raven's mouth began to water.

Yellow teeth sank sharply into the ripe red skin. Juice and spit spilled down the pitch-dark vultus that swallowed the bottom of his face. The King of Battle held the apple out, pointing.

Look…

He was waiting for us.… Cyrus looked back the way they came.

Not me, brother, not me…look.

"*I don't care, you miserable serpent!*" shouted the Raven. *Unbroken and unbridled*, he nodded to himself, *perhaps, I am the Night Mare?*

"Oh, dear," said the man in white. "*I* felt your power, just then, Raven.…Oh, is that—yes, *My* word, there's hate in them eyes!" He laughed. "Splendid."

The Raven's world turned to ash. Tara burned out around him— the shooting ceased in his ear; the stone slipped away beneath his feet. Marcus Petronax shut his eyes.

The flaming chaos pours through me…the color.

Perchance, her color.

"Is—is that *the Acolyte*, yonder?" said the King with a crooked smile. "Why, dear Cyrus, do you know that woman with him, then?"

BOOM.

It thumps through my veins.

BOOM.

Enough to shatter my walls.

BOOM.

It's…it's her.

> *Her…*

"*Her,*" he whispered.

"Who?" asked Reed.

"Gods in fuckin' hell," spat Deimos, both exhausted and astonished.

"My Prison Without Walls," the Raven whispered.

Her chestnut hair glows in the light, unkempt and…

Aura…

> *So close, Ghost of Clydae…*

He furrowed his brow, swallowing. *Only a knight and a stranger,* he affirmed, but the moments blurred, and he saw them for who they were in Clydae all those years before. *Both? And together….*

No, he pleaded, *not here…not like this…not my—not with him.*

The Raven's jaw creaked and ached as he clenched. Every vein from neck to forehead coursed thick atop a thin surface of his brittle skin as his heart rebounded around his chest.

The Sage's gentle hand came to his feathers. "Cyrus, brother, *please*, we can't—"

The Raven stepped away, closing the distance. *My blood boils*, he snarled. *It hurts.*

TOLL.

The small belfry rang above them, stirring him to terror. *Gods, no.*

The Acolyte was gripping the collar of his cuirass. Beneath a shiny gorget, dried blood browned on the plate from a hole near the center.

He's hit.

She was—*she's.…*Blood was all over her, in her hair and eyes.

Someone else's blood.

The Raven edged closer.
"WAIT!" Deimos shouted.
The Acolyte raised a hand. "Brother, I—"
"Brother?!" the Raven roared.
"Marcus?"

TOLL.

Huh?

"Hmm?" murmured the Acolyte.
The man in white interrupted, bellowing so deeply that it rattled the rafters in the rooftops all around and shook the very stone.

"HAHAHAHAHAHAHAHAHAHAHAHAHAHAHAHAHA-HAHAHAHAHAHAHA…"

The Raven stopped. *No, please…not like this…*

Not like this.

"Marcus?" she said again.
The Raven winced. He came up short, seeing her fully, closely…

Intimately.

The chestnut brown of her hair still shone through the blood and the grit. *She is still beautiful.* He could never deny that. He felt a deep breath ease the pressure in his chest, unwinding him with overwhelming sadness. *She suffers…they—they killed me, and I wasn't there to—*

TOLL.

"*I know that face,*" he whispered. *Those eyes….*

"Marcus—Marcus *Petronax*?!" Elatreus exclaimed.

The Raven's eyes glowed like sapphires through the silence, spilling a few tears over their lids.

He let them.

The Raven saw through the blood of her cheeks and brow, her eyes like gems of autumn.

My—my autumn goddess…Lady Ares…

With…with the Acolyte….

"Hmm"—the stranger hummed over his fingernails—"do *Mine* eyes deceive? Or, is that Aura Westfall with Elatreus Fabius Cornicen—the Fist of the Church, is it?" His brow dipped menacingly over his eyes. "They look quite cozy…."

She stepped toward the Raven. "Marcus…," she said, "Marcus, listen to me—"

Stop saying it.

"Marcus, *please*," rang the Sage from behind.

TOLL.

Not you, too. It stung the Raven's ears. *Stop—stop saying it.*

Elatreus stepped forward. "I mean you no harm, Marcus, only to—"

He was cut short. *"THAT IS NOT MY NAME!"*

BOOM.

The Raven barreled into the Acolyte, tackling him through the cast-iron gate and down the stone steps below. They bounced and crashed and tumbled and brawled to the very bottom. The Raven wrenched his poniard free in the chaos, slashing down.

"ARGH!" roared the Acolyte. He blocked the blow, sacrificing his hand to save the more fragile neck. The dagger sunk deeply into his palm, nearly tearing the thumb away altogether.

"Bleed, you pig! I want you to bleed, and I want you to SQUEAL!"

TOLL.

"Marcus!"

"Marcus!"

"RAH!" roared the Raven. His elbows, fists, and knees clouted and punched the Acolyte all the way to base of the bell tower. The Acolyte reached for his own sword, but the Raven's clawing fingers dragged it back into the scabbard. The Raven wrestled to free his own.

The Raven felt the searing hot iron in his cheeks. *I'm boiling.* His hands were more talons than barreling fists, crashing and clawing over Eli as his elbows joined the barrage. Elatreus bounced limply under the salvo.

TOLL.

Toll for me, you fucking curse! I care not for deals or petty you, or her, the harlot of my nightmares. ... Is that what your blasted fucking horse was meant to show me, spirit?

The Raven heard no reply. *If I am to return to hell, then I shall bring him with me…*

Dear Cyrus, you cannot die here! We are bound, you and I…

"MARCUS, NO!" Aura wailed.

Yes…

Yes, I think I will die here.

XXXI

LOST LAMBS

Aura

His neck…

His throat…

…the frays of his coat.

Aura leapt down the stairs, recognizing the one called *Raven*. She saw his shoulders, black and stringy, curled in a ball, mauling at Eli like an ape. She was almost to them—

SLAM.

An anvil crashed into her lower back, hurtling her into the front-facing tower wall. The one the others called *Reed* pinned her to the stonework and shouted in her ear.

"Where's the Ram?! Where is *SWANSONG?!*" He punched her in the gut.

BOOM.

"Who the—"

THWACK.

A fist crashed down on her forehead, slamming the back of her skull into the stone. *A Furii, then.* She groaned. *They're all brutes and Birdsongs, aren't they?*

She threw an elbow that caught his face, smashing him backward. She turned tightly, grappling her hand to his neck, then her shoulder to his. *He's wide open,* she smiled, throwing a high knee.

CRACK.

Ah, the drums. The knee crashed into his ribs. With one hand, Aura cradled his head, weaving his silky brown hair between her fingers...*and now, the strings.* Her other hand slipped the dirk from her scabbard.

"*RAH!*" she roared, plunging it into Reed's chest—*to the hilt.*

Reed staggered back. "*Fuck,*" he groaned. He gasped for breath, tugging at the handle.

Tug all you like.

With both hands, he eased it slowly out.

Aura laughed.

The King of Battle laughed, too.

Blood poured through Reed's duster, running long stains down the front. The scarlet dagger trembled in his hand, but he wrapped his shaking fingers around the leathery hilt, pointing the tip toward Aura, wheezing meager relief.

A strong Furii, perhaps, but not a smart one.

"*RAH!*" she roared, dashing toward him.

He jumped up—Aura's sword flashed.

CLANG.

Mercy's edge glanced across the dagger, cracking sparks out of Reed's narrow parry. Reed followed with a dropping fist, slamming hard into her neck and the wound there.

SLAM.

The hit knocked her hurtling into the wall.

Damn ye, whoreson! She looked to the Acolyte—*the Acolyte? Think of Marcus! Has he killed him?!*

"Has he—has he killed him?" she huffed, wincing.

Eli, she saw. He had broken free—sword drawn, the frayed cords of the ceremonial hilt dancing in the breeze. The blood-drunk Raven was unyielding, stabbing and swinging.

That's not Marcus, she told herself. *It couldn't be....He's—he was....*

The Raven howled a bellowing war cry. *That's not Marcus.* She shook her head. *That's an animal, there, on the loose....*He was getting *faster* somehow—*stronger*—each strike blurring together as his tattered coat rippled and tore in the wind. *That's not Marcus—that's a Furii.*

"Marcus, *listen to me!*" pleaded the Acolyte, blocking the barrage.

The Raven roared again, *"LET THAT OLD, DEAD BOY'S NAME SPILL PAST THEM CUNT LIPS ONCE MORE, I SWEAR—"*

It—it couldn't be. "M-Marcus?" Aura choked, *"Gods—"*

"N-N-No gods here!" the Raven sputtered over his shoulder. *So... so fiendish*—his lips curled wickedly. *"Oh, oh-oh-only Me."*

The King of Battle leaned on the shattering wall. He cackled and coughed, curling over.

"...HAHAHAHAHAHAHAHAHAHAHAHAHA..."

BOOM.

The stone rattled beneath them as the wall crumbled behind.

The Acolyte's stance turned wide, his boots sliding across the grit and the cobbles as his sword rose high overhead.

Too late.

SLAM.

The Raven smashed Eli's chest with the steely hilt of his estoc, throwing him. Eli crashed across the way, tumbling with the sparks of his armor as the corners dragged a trail of debris. He slid to a stop, huffing.

Aura turned, flashing Mercy. *"RAH!"* she roared, hacking at Reed with all the speed she could muster.

CLANG—CLANG...

He parried the first of Aura's attacks, but the frenzy overcame him...one by one, Mercy met her mark.

You're faster than he is, Aura. You're the fastest one there is.

BOOM.

Pay it no mind.

Mercy's long, seeping gashes beaded through his coat. Aura didn't relent. *I won't.*

"Argh!" Reed cried, trembling as he stepped backward, faltering. The red spilled down the tails of his duster, dripping into deepening pools.

The tang of copper turned her stomach. *It stinks.* She could smell it everywhere on him—blood drained from his pale face. *All that Furii blood...this one was just meant to hold her dagger for her—a second sheath.*

Aura breathed firmly through her nose. Mercy was poised, dripping. "Submit," she growled.

Reed's face had little color left at all. His arms shook, and his eyelids fluttered over sunken eyes.

I hear his heartbeat, she smiled, *so weak....*

He threw one last pitiful swing.

Poor form, dear.

SCHING.

Mercy eased it away, rounding into an uppercut that dragged up the length of him. Aura's fingers felt the flesh and the muscle and the defenseless bone rumbling down the handle as Mercy's razor edge erupted up and out.

Reed's wilted body lifted from the stone, barreling over the wall to the sea, and down, down...*down.*

Down, by the gods. She didn't wait to watch him smash on the rocks. *More fish...there's more fish in this barrel.* The dagger had fallen from Reed's hand, clanking on the ground in front of her. Aura picked it up, twirling it between fingers and sliding it home in the scabbard.

"That's two—*TWO FURII, just today!*" she roared. "*Who will be next?!*" She planted herself.

"*NO!*" the one called *Sage* cried. He shouldered his rifle at the top of the stairs, firing.

BOOM.

Aura dashed aside, covering her face. The shot panged across the way, narrowly missing her as stone chips and grit dusted Aura's front.

Moving target, Aura—moving target. She reached instinctively for a pistol she no longer had.

Fuck.

The Sage loaded another long round into the breech, slapping up on the bolt and down on the hammer, taking aim once more.

The Raven stood over Elatreus, the Acolyte still sprawled out in the rubble. A rust-red revolver extended out from the Raven's black hand, fixed on the Acolyte's bloodied face.

No time.

The Acolyte put his hand up to the mouth of the barrel. The Raven swatted it away, taking aim.

Damn—damn it all to hell. There's no time.

BOOM.

You're the fastest one there is. She caught him in time, lunging and kicking the pistol from the Raven's hand and away from the Acolyte's servile eyes. The revolver fired, blasting into the cobbles just behind Elatreus's head, showering him with chips.

Aura snagged her arm around the Raven's neck before he could crack another shot, wrenching his body over in a violent embrace. *Fancy this!* her cruel mind mocked, *you and your beau, reunited.*

Steady, Aura. She whirled him away from the Acolyte, bringing Mercy to his throat. Aura faced the Raven toward the Sage, shielding herself in the process.

The Sage was granite—a motionless black shadow in fading sun.

"Drop it," she whispered.

The Raven's revolver rattled in his hand.

It—it isn't Marcus, she swore. *There is no Marcus—not anymore.* "PUT IT DOWN," she shouted to the Sage, "OR THE RAVEN—"

"Is that what *I* am to you?" said Marcus softly.

Her heart sank. She could hear it—rolling deeply in his words. *I—I know that voice. It calls to me.*

"*No*," she spat, letting Mercy taste a bit more of his neck, letting the red dribble. *It—it's not Marcus*, she thought, tightening her choke hold. *It can't be.*

The Acolyte was sprawled behind her on a pile of red and gray rubble.

"So close," squirmed the Raven, straining under Aura's hold.

"*Quiet.*"

"I...."

She tightened Mercy to his throat.

"*Argh.*" He winced. "I—I almost had my vengeance."

"*Shut up.*"

"But, here I am, thwarted by another ghost."

"I'll kill you—by the gods, I swear," she hissed.

"No gods here," laughed the King of Battle...

Only you, *Aura.*

Her walls came crumbling down. *Spare me, please....Spare me my name, if only from his lips.*

What is it they say of visage and piety?

His lips aren't moving....He's—he's in my head. I can—I can feel—

I shan't sugar on the devil.

The Raven loosened under her grip. "Peace," he soothingly

said, "*peace…*thy will be done, *oh, goddess.*" His throat gulped past Mercy's edge.

Think, Aura, think.

"I—I s'pose," choked the Raven, "I suppose you wouldn't let me take *that one* with me?" He nodded to the Acolyte. "He's the bastard, Aura—you know it. If I am to die, let me take him with me."

"Only revenge, is it? That's what you came for?" Aura's blade loosened. *Get out, damn you. You have to get out. I didn't come this far….*

"What's it goin' to be, love?" shouted Deimos, muffled behind his shouldered gun. "There's nowhere for ye to go."

She dragged the Raven slowly backward, their boots sliding together away—*the tower,* her gut told her. *Get to the tower.*

The Sage's barrel followed her.

The doorway was just behind Aura now, the one leading to the bell tower stairs. The breeze cooled her brow in the tower's shadow.

"There's no way out that way—"

"*I* think that's the point, dear."

Her fingers reached blindly backward, finding the loop of the latch. She dropped her fist hard, and it clanked open, creaking the old door forward, exposing the shadows that she began forcing the Raven's body toward.

"*Quiet,*" she hushed, dragging him inside.

The Sage was out of reach, but he began closing the distance. "Cyrus! Cyrus, don't let her—"

"Give them a moment, Sage! Such a prude, you are!" The King of Battle laughed.

But do be quick, Aura. A siege is on, after all.

His motionless lips were swallowed by the black and overpowered by the haunting, beaming emerald of the King of Battle, disappearing behind the heavy door. She slammed it shut, kicking the lock firmly into place.

Deimos cursed her from the other side. "You think I can't break this door down, girl!"

Aura spun the Raven around, hustling him up the stairs. She jerked the revolver from his hand, avoiding his eyes as she did. He handed the pistol over willingly, to her surprise...*but those eyes.*

That's enough. Her thumb clicked the hammer back, and she pressed the barrel to his chin. "Move," she said, nodding the tip up the dark stairs.

"They'll be through that door in a minute—"

"Move!" She kicked him.

He didn't budge. "Look at me."

"Move," she snarled.

The Raven planted his feet. He leaned his chin harshly into the barrel, lowering his gaze to hers, forcing her to meet it.

Eyes like oceans, deep and dark....

"If I am to face the abyss again," he hummed, "let me bring this small memory of your loveliness—"

THWACK.

Aura thumped him across the head. *"Move,"* she repeated. "I won't say it again."

"What about your *precious* Acolyte?"

"To hell with him—and to hell with you. Now *MOVE.*" She butted Mercy's handle across the Raven's temple.

THWACK.

The Raven winced, turning.

XXXII

CLOSER, STILL

Marcus

These colors…

…these perfect colors.

She guides me…my travels, far and wide—so far…so far, indeed.

I have trekked so many lifetimes. I've seen my share of the sun….I bask in her warmth, outnumbered by the dark days that torment me without her light. But here—here she is…glowing.

She finds me now, guiding me up these stairs. I have seen her, immaculate Ares, shimmering in the mirror of Aura's blade, thirsting for me…

BOOM.

…and I have seen you.

Sun streaks peek through the broken wall at the top of the winding tower, illuminating the bell, coppery green, like haunting moonlight.

BOOM.

There are no words—fuck them.

BOOM.

The guns rumble beneath a hand-painted sky…

A man could miss it by a thousand years…

But not me…

…not now.

Ah, I rejoice. A raven comes to us, silky black and flapping to a pose in the setting summer sun. The mark of Ares, I remember well. She caws beautifully.

Ah, my heart begins to sink…why a raven, then? Some symbol?

Aye…

A symbol indeed.

BOOM.

Toll…

Ah, I sink deeper. I feel the answer coming to me, but I cannot bear the thought of it.

"No," I say. "No, it's not possible."

What have I told you?

"It's—it's real. I swear it is—"

What of the Prison and her hallowed halls?
Do you remember, dear Cyrus?

I shudder at the thought. The words and the thoughts lock themselves deep inside, but the damage is done. I feel its biting truth, rusting at the hinges of my fragile mind, unshackling itself.

Aura shoved at his knee with Mercy's hilt, and Marcus tripped up the stairs. His feathered coat was heavy with sweat, blood, and fatigue. *I am Marcus, after all.* He nodded. *The ghosts have played their tricks.*

Here is my reunion—here, my reclamation…here, my deal…what is owed, like property…like a dowry…like a fucking aurochs.

Aura is no aurochs. This transfiguration is dangled in front of me only to torment. My ghosts have shown me her scars and exposed my own. My love marches me up this stark tower at gunpoint.

BOOM.

It happened not at all the way he might've hoped. *I lost my temper*, he thought. *The sight of Cornicen and Aura…Aura…*

"Aura," he whispered. The name felt so foreign here and now, or perhaps it was him. "Tell me"—he gulped—"I—I know that I am dreaming, but…but what kind of dream does this end up being?"

She tightened her hold.

Marcus choked out a laugh. *How 'bout you, eh? What do You have to say, then?*

…Coward.

"The Sage will kill your Acolyte, you know it—"

She silenced him. "Good riddance," she said.

They marched on. The Raven's footfalls creaked up each wooden step, replacing the tolling bell and the blasts below with the simple cadence of his breath and heartbeat ringing in his ears. Aura followed just behind, her steps landing in unison—*but only at times.*

Together, at least. Marcus wheezed as he climbed…and climbed… *and climbed.*

They poured out to the top.

WE CLIMBED

Aura

We...

We climbed...

We...Marcus and I, like we used to climb before...

I...

You climbed and climbed, did you?

"What—who said that?"

REVERSAL

Marcus

Leave Aura out of this, you coward! Marcus was shouting, but only in his mind.

The man in white didn't answer.

The summit came, where cool, twilight rays of sun poured through holes in the stone of the wall and the roof. The bell at the top was missing entirely, with only remnants of the gable and scraps of a tattered belfry bathing in the last of the daylight hiding behind the hills.

The Raven's icy blue eyes found the light. *A setting sun strikes upon me, its light of life gone by…*

My light of life.

Cool breeze and blue sea met a fire-red sky above city steeples and long-shadowed hilltops rounding above the cliffs, the city, and the sea. The sea was a toiling deep blue with a glossy top layer of crimson rippling in the mounding waves, crashing and retracting on the ancient rocks below. They called to him.

"The color," he murmured.

She said nothing.

He turned to find the cold eye of his own revolver staring back at him. *Cold, like the moon.* Marcus sighed.

Aura pushed him through the demolished doorway.

Marcus went gladly, withdrawing.

She put Mercy to his stomach.

He reared, but the tension in his shoulders eased again, his shameless eyes moving along her. Marcus had seen her before—*I...I remember*—her elegance, energy, and last ethereal bit of sunlight painted across her face—*her vultus.* The light hid the blood, and Marcus hungered for the soft skin beneath.

She said nothing, merely stared.

Not nothing, Marcus insisted. Her hazel eyes opened like shutters to her soul. *Ah,* he relieved, *I see it now...her color.* Her gaze welcomed him in—soul-deep—and he graciously entered. He tied himself to her spot, fully planted.

I loved her then, and always...

Once, and still...

I love her here, at gunpoint.

Forever, and in hell...

Marcus found the lines of her...*her*—he dared not speak her name, *not yet.* Soft lines—*barely lines at all*—dimpled from her lips to her nose and up. Some of them he remembered. Most, he did not.

She thrust him forward.

She touched me. "I prayed for this," he spilt.

BOOM.

The cannon shot below.

Aura moved the barrel slightly. "I—I need to think," she said. "I—*you*—"

"*I hoped*," panted the Raven. "I imagined….I *dreamt*…."

Her revolver rattled. "What…? I don't know what to—"

BOOM.

Aura staggered.

Marcus ignored the rumbling ground, leaning in.

"How?" she broke. "*How?* You died—they *killed* you. I saw it with mine own eyes."

The Raven smiled warmly. "Thine eyes…," he whispered.

"You're an imposter," she said, pushing the barrel back to the Raven's throat.

"I wish"—he gulped—"I wish I were that….I wish I were that, or nothing at all…."

"How did you come back?" she choked. "No one ever comes back."

"Aura, I—"

"Tell me," she said, leaning in. "Is this a dream? Are you some hateful hunter? Am I a puppet to some vengeful gods? Which is it?! Is it—is it the Burden?"

Marcus sighed. "How pitiless…to think—in this moment we could be *us* again—"

"What?"

"I just mean—"

"What in the name of Tara could you mean?!"

He gulped.

BOOM.

The cannons boomed their last. Shots faded from the ramparts as the sun simmered behind a wall of smoldering, shadowy smoke.

Aura looked the Raven in the eye, and he recognized her less.

"I...," he hummed.

"Huh?"

"*I*...,"he restated. "I'm *not* Marcus, am I? Not anymore."

Her hold loosened.

"Marcus *did* die in the Prison Without Walls...a hundred life-times ago, even. I've tried to be him—to keep him alive somewhere inside. For so long, I *hungered* to be here with you—*here,* or at the Fire Falls with a kiss, or our hidden room in the loneliest corner of that library in Clydae, where I became the man I was supposed to be, away from parents or politics or expectations all alike—a place for us to finally be—to *be*...to be...*together...to be together*...."

He choked.

She choked.

"*I*...I yearn for it...."

Aura lowered the piece.

"But...."

A tightness came.

"*I*...I am *Marcus Furius Petronax* no longer," he said, "no more than Cyrus, or the Raven, or the Ghost of *fucking* Clydae. I was robbed of that life, same as you."

She gulped.

"We're just killers now," he said, shaking, "murderers and brutes no better than the *beasts*—tainted by the thirst of it—never to recover."

Her eyes found his.

The Raven gazed back, struggling not to blink. *I dare not miss a moment.*

Aura's eyes were shadowy and far away, and the King of Battle's cackles rang in the distance.

I see the clouds, now....They cloud her hazel eyes. The Raven saw anger, not light—her barrel pressing deeper into his throat.

"We love to think ourselves the saint, don't we?" he said. "Nay, no gods will come for us—"

"What are you on about?" she spat.

He laughed strangely. "I fear the end, don't you?"

"The end?"

"Aye," he said. "Aye, the end—the end of this. All of it...."

The Raven motioned his arm in a wide arc. "All of us...no gods," he choked, "no righteous *other* will come to smite us for our secret villainy. Him? *It?!* He is the King of Battle and the Lord of War...."

Say it...

"Just titles," she hissed.

The Raven smiled. "That's just it." He laughed, then. "King of what? Lord of who? It makes no difference...." He looked down.

Aura loosened Mercy.

"We...we...*we*...."

"*We,* what?"

"We will destroy ourselves," the Raven said flatly. "Demons? Beasts? They are small noise and pithy grunts as compared to the shrieking bloodthirst of man."

"I am no man," she replied just as flatly.

"Nor am I," he said, grinning, "but you've heard the cries of this battle yourself, haven't you?"

What wondrous, wild warmth I find in your eyes, my lady....I won't deny this to myself.

Do not be greedy with your spoils, Cyrus.

Out, damn you.

She said nothing.

"Damn you, then, if you'd say otherwise. You've seen it like me—human war with human cries and mortal tolls beyond our reckonings."

"*Tolls?*" she said.

"Cost, Aura."

"I've—I've heard it," she muttered, looking down. "I've felt it, I mean. I've felt the cost."

"Then, help me," he pleaded. "Help me take him....You've heard him. I—I doubt...I doubt you could even *imagine* it...his power and his presence. He has haunted my lifetimes—"

"Lifetimes?" Aura asked.

"Yes, I...," the Raven stammered. "I don't know that I should survive today, if I am alive at all—"

"Marcus...."

"There...there is your first mistake, my love." He gulped. "Let me take him with me. Let me drag this scale-less serpent back to hell...."

BOOM.

Aura was silent and cold.

"I wish to take these moments back," said Marcus. "Please," he said, his fingers retreating the length of her arm, the small hairs perfectly in place. *"Please,"* he whispered, gripping her. "Please," he said again, dragging rough hands along her scrapes and cuts.

She winced.

BOOM.

The Raven recoiled. *"I am a lonely winter,"* he sighed, *"impervious to spring...."*

"Speak plainly."

"No," Cyrus hummed.

"From the Epitaph? Is that it? Found the gods, have you?"

*"Never...*I'd quote its little truth for the sake of a life lost, if only lost in living it."

Aura didn't reply.

"A life that has amounted to nothing…yet, a *something* in this simple place…."

"Simple place?"

"I dare not trust myself. You are a specter, most likely—a spirit and a ghost like all the rest…like me. But, if I am stuck in this elaborate nightmare, at least in this modest corner do I find you here with me, close enough to touch and taste, and without the sheep that seek to separate us."

"Marcus—"

"Please." He stopped. The Raven heard his shame, retreating further. "Please…I miss you—that is all, I swear it. I miss you—now, like ever."

"Where—where were you?"

Marcus felt the tears. "Pardon?"

The words spilt past her lips, dribbling out like the tears burning at the whites of her eyes.

The Raven counted the moments.

Aura's jaw clenched, her nostrils flaring. "Whatever *this* is," she spat, waving an arm between them, "it's gone. Dead. And has been for some time. You miss an idea, Marcus. A myth—a fantasy we made together, but a dead one."

"I had a feeling you'd say that." He gave a fleeting smile. "And perhaps in some place you'd be right—here we are, top of the Eryx— *top of the world*—with guns and steel at each other's necks like the brutes and the beasts we are…." He leaned into the sidewall, and his eyes met the cooling tide of the horizon.

"And?" she said.

"And," he parroted, "we are slaves in our errands."

Aura stood in silence.

The Raven smiled. "So many have we killed and likewise watched die for the simple sake of others. Feeble *others*—pompous fools in the petty pursuit of power. Many with their necks torn out all over the stone, yonder." He laughed.

Coppery silt scorched the Raven's nostrils. The blood, the banging, the pounding blasts of black powder on salt and sea—all descended on his senses as the war waged on far below. His warmth drifted with the wind, and he savored the last light of color as the sun sank low.

The color, he thought, *always by my side*. His eyes found Aura then, illuminated by yellow gold...

...*a goodly paint brushed by godly hands*. Her eyebrows glinted blonde tips with matching lips, bathing in the light. The red fell away to muted browns and unimposing darkness peppered across porcelain cheeks and eyes like the unyielding moonlight. *Those eyes*.

"Those eyes," he whispered.

REBIRTH

Aura

Aura loosened her menacing brow. She had to force herself to do it.

Marcus's glowing blue eyes made her skin crawl. *A demon there—one I do not recognize.* The Raven's mangled body rested bleakly under her saber and his borrowed pistol, featureless to her disinterested heart.

The tangled rags corded down from his shoulders, strewn over his arms. *Not much here*, she decided early, *I've outgrown this.*

But his face, she thought, *his face, I know*—rounded high cheek-bones nearing gaunt, with a narrow nose and thin bristling hairs at his lips and chin. That face was welcoming—the eyes a living warmth in the darkness, despite their haunting glow. His smile enticed her then, as she imagined her lips upon them like so many times before.

"Why are you here, Aura?" he said. "How could you? With the Acolyte?"

"I didn't," she said, pleading. "I sought to kill the man, I swear."

"Why?" he asked.

"What? Wh—"

"Were you doing it for me?"

Her hands began to shake. "I—well, yes," she admitted.

"Aura," he said, pushing away from the wall. "You don't owe me anything."

"No, I don't," she said, but not with her eyes. "What of this King of Battle? What comes next?"

Marcus paused, shaking his head for a moment.

This is how he thinks—I remember that—steady, damn you.

"He's the devil," said Marcus, "and now he's *awake*."

BOOM.

Her eyes felt heavy, like the arm doggedly holding Mercy to Marcus's throat. Aura felt uncomfortable, holding the man, embracing him with longing as well as bite. *He does not feel like Marcus,* she swore, *but then, I don't feel much like Aura....*

I don't feel much like anyone.

Anyone?

These are your powers, then, stranger? Playing parlor tricks? Smoke and mirrors in my mind?

You shall see soon enough, my dear.

What good is a name? Nay, our lives are not moments but songs... melodies...long and winding, full of slowing, soothing, and swelling... like time, the sun and her stars...like crashing crescendos that just can't seem to stop crashing.

We are Antigonus...lonely winters, impervious to spring, I see.

Agathe, we are...frivolous and fertile...gardens to be planted with growing vines rare to wilt.

Ariston with his scheduled suffering...spears poked from his back, symbolizing his sacrifice...the spirit of summer.

Aura felt something deeply more. *I finally see.* She nodded. Her gaze was drawn to the thirst of the sunset, spilling too quickly for her liking. *Oh,* she wondered as she gazed, *oh, Ares...come to me.*

I could stay for a million moments. I could stay for just one more.

Her blood felt full, rushing to her corners with vibrant warmth. She feared not for the soul of Elya—*ancient history.*

I'll see her again, she agreed. *I must. For here stands Marcus Petronax, despite my efforts to forget...so full he is of his unmatchable self.*

Aura's muscles hardened. *I wonder what hardens him, these days.*

Her tired muscles shook, and Aura liked it. *Like rattling jitters in a rainstorm, I survive.* Her muscles shook, and Aura felt alive. *These muscles here rumble like the thundering Fire Falls.* She smiled.

Aura was calmly enraged. *In tranquil rage do I find patience.*

Me, too...

I feel it deeply—more than welcoming its hurt and its hate.

"You cannot imagine my hate," *I softly say. For I have the hate of Ares, no?*

I felt her here.

I've felt her before.

Marcus's hands grew cold and white. His knuckles cracked and crunched with a curling fist. The veins lined his face—no white left in his eyes, only red.

Another vision—another monster.

The Raven shook. His features sank beneath the surface, muddled in the swelling. The bones began to poke through the bloodless peaks of his knuckles.

"*Gods....*"

Gaunt skin lined the valleys of his hands, the bladed bones bleeding through. The arms were longer—longer than before. His face grew crooked and warped, where...

...*where—where the hair grew long, even, whitening and singeing...* silvery auburn turned like autumn leaves before her. Aura feared Marcus like she feared the ghosts in the room, numerous and far away. She backed toward the ledge.

The beast before me smiles—a toothy, mangled grin. She yearned to recognize the Marcus there was left, but none could be found.

Crack...crack—crack.

The body broke and cracked beneath her grip. Marcus curled over, ghostly white. He groaned and roared, the creaking resounding beneath him. His brittle bones moved beneath the skin, poking holes, even, breaking and expanding outward. Marcus's spine cracked and grew, lengthening his midsection to something slenderer...*more bestial.*

A hacking laugh groaned in the deep. Its guttural chugs rumbled Aura's insides.

"Ha*Ha*Ha*Ha*HaHa*Ha*Ha*Ha*Ha*Ha*Ha*Ha*Ha*Ha*Ha*HaHa..."

A demon is here where an old friend has been—a madman with a mad face and the cruelest gaze since yore or aft—unlike any animal or man that walks the earth.

Aura's brow turned downward.

"I am a figment—of you, among you…and sometimes, you yourself."

Confusion painted itself across her blanching face. Then, dread.

Aura heard her soft tones in her ears, plucking at strings far away. *My anthem—*thumping with the waves and the battery, the tones of Fabrica's melody—*shining…pristine…*

BOOM.

Serene…

She smiled absurdly.

Bang…BANG.

Metal clanked on stone from the shadowy stairs behind her. Aura faced the door, finding groans and grunts behind the panging, coming closer in the dank, dark air.

"Marcus," Aura mumbled, "you aren't yourself."

"I'd say not…"

The mangled Raven lifted to show the ivory white of the King of Battle's cheeks. "You'll—you'll forgive me," he snarled, "but what I need to say—*I*…I must wait for the others."

The King of Battle's posture straightened up—the feathers draped vertically over slender black arms folded behind the frays.

She saw the King appear before her very eyes, but Aura felt something—*something inexplicable.* It was him—*Marcus*—someplace deep down. She could feel him, like his soul was trying to tear itself free beneath the stranger's slimy exterior.

I feel his power, still. Aura couldn't figure how, but Marcus lay buried somewhere far beneath. *Perhaps we only need uncover him.* She pointed the pistol at the ivory King, backing toward the ledge of the tower.

He's quite deep, dear.

Get out of my head.

"Alas"—the King smiled—"while we have a minute—"

WHOOSH.

The stranger lunged forward, the lightning white of his hair dashing past her as he snatched Aura's cheeks together.

"'The fastest one there is,' you say?" He laughed, gripping her harshly by the face.

The Raven's fingers curled tightly over her jaw and cheekbone, creaking and popping as he squeezed her face together.

Aura writhed under the mounting pressure, tearing fruitlessly at the Raven's hand as her other hand held up the revolver.

He swatted it away. *No chance.* It flew from her fingers, and she shrank under the weight of his hand. The rust-red revolver thudded in the corner.

Aura keeled and shook under an inhuman grip. He arrested her with one hand, squeezing her face agonizingly together under his palm. She jabbed and swatted and swung.

THWACK—THWACK—THWACK.

Mere dust from his coat. His limbs were iron, unyielding.

"I can see why *he* likes you," said the King of Battle. His nosed brushed her forehead, then her cheeks…and on to her lips. "Aye, I see it," he purred, "*plain as day….*"

A forked tongue slid past his saffron-stained teeth, and it began to…touch her.

They're all fucking Birdsongs, then. She was a child again, fearful like the first time, all those years before. The bobbing bedpost floated to the surface with the Ram, but here—*with Him*—it came to kill her. He was stronger—*far stronger*, beyond Aura's mortal reckonings.

Mortal! She laughed absurdly. *Big talk, killing gods, but here you are, Aura.* The Raven was gone, but there…a soul and proper body left something eerie and uncanny—*something similar, but wrong…an imposter with his look and sound.* Her heart sank further.

"You'd have me feel small," she sputtered out from under his palm. Her glare was honest and fierce, and the soul of her one exposed eye overpowered, despite the malignant glowing green that met them. "You are a sad sort," she huffed.

He squeezed slightly.

"*RAH!*" Aura shrieked.

"Oh? *How so?*" he asked, a grin knotting up his face.

"So what if you *are* a god?" she choked. "You're still just a *man.* A sad one—"

He squeezed harder.

She lurched from under his hold. Her toes lifted from the stone, but she swallowed the pain.

Sink, damn you.

"You—you have unlimited power by the look of you. You've taken Marcus—if what you say is true, you'd have us worship you like a god."

"I *am* a god," he purred.

"Mhm," she forced out. The lines of her face broke and tightened, but she stomached his torments. "Some *god* you are," she whispered, "all that power, and nowhere to put it."

"Careful, darling," he whispered.

"All my life, men have made death howl with all sorts of ghouls," spat Aura. "I fear not death. I fear no ghouls."

The King of Battle let Aura go, relinquishing her face with his last hissing syllable. She fell to a knee on the stone with a choke.

BOOM.

*And so, I plant myself....*Aura looked up, finding his gaze with equal opposition. *I am no slave to you, spirit, if it is here that you can hear me.* Her brow relaxed, contented.

I hear you, child.

Aura feared naught. Her eyes overflowed with their malice.

The King of Battle's black lips stretched wide, exposing the crooked yellow smile, spanning from ear to ear.

"What of Marcus?" she asked flatly. "Will he die with you?"

"I do not believe you understand who Marcus is, child—you do not understand *Me*...."

"Tell me," she pleaded. "I will do what you ask—"

"He will return...like before...*and again*...like the winter and the summer...and the *fall*."

XXXVI

PARADISE WITHOUT WALLS

The Raven

The Raven clawed. He scratched, and he squirmed, his fingers turning to talons, ripping at the threads of the inky dark. His feathers rustled in the shadows of himself, his eyes glowing through.

He shrieked and roared to the still darkness.

The darkness roared back.

I will have my vengeance....

I will have my reward....

Reward?!

The spirit laughed.

That is surely fine, dear Cyrus, but will she have you?

I will show myself to her—I will show my color*...if for the first and only time.*

Dear Cyrus, it's all well and fun, but hardly fun at all, the way you sow your own suffering.

I stand by my oaths, the Raven begrudgingly bargained.

Come again?

I will be your harvest—

You take me for a fool, do you?

The King of Battle's voice rumbled low.

Shall I return to your shackles, Marcus?

I only mean to barter for Aura's—

You think Me tamable, do you?!

The King of Battle's fingers tugged the Raven down, deeper into the dark.

"The cosmic clock strikes twelve...."

"Huh?" said Aura.
"Look closer, dear," hummed the King of Battle, leaning in.
Cyrus watched on, helplessly stuck. *AURA! AURA!*

She can't hear you, child.

"I see nothing," she said.
Please, not again. The Raven slipped further away. *Don't take her again.*

XXXVII

SAINTS AND THEIR STATUES

Aura

Something came from nothing, reaching out—*not nothing.* The shadows were black and empty, but...*but they....*

"Merciful gods."

The shadows grew long as the light left the hills. Firm darks struck the floor, clashed by rays that began to move, bending together, meddling in waves—*inconsistent and shattering.*

Trickery, Aura thought. But they warped and danced in the nothingness, speaking in their way, whispering Aura's name and beckoning with pitch-black tendrils like they were fingers.

And so they battle...on and on....

BOOM.

The Ram's blood, she shuddered. *It's on the move...coursing and creeping its way through me, finally to my brain.* The darkness was muttering its mysteries, and she was listening so intently. *It'll be over soon.* She watched the shadows like they were flames dancing in some humble hearth on the side of the road. Aura surrendered to them. *Their coldness welcomes me.*

The shadows warped the light and the room, distancing her from the rest—from herself, even. *Give him to me*, she pleaded in her loneliness. *Please…no more cruelty…*

…no more pain….

The hairs prickled up, one by one. She reached out.

Please, she pleaded. Then, the icy cold curled between her out-stretched fingers. It was black, but she could feel him. *It* must *be him. I feel it—I feel his gentleness.*

The darkness welcomed her.

I…I could stay….

Aura's eyes itched when she saw…*something*, a wisp or a shadow. She shut her eyes, not daring to look.

Aura reached deeply down into a cold, dark peace. Its icy song froze her with her name—*Aura*, it called. *Come home, Aura.*

"Aura, don't you see? Don't you recognize Me?"

"What have you done to him?!" she cried, her eyes still closed.

BANG.

Aura's eyes burst open with the door behind her, where a bloodied Sage had already dragged Elatreus across the threshold. He held a buckskin knife to the Acolyte's throat, his breechloader balancing delicately over Eli's shoulder, the eye of its muzzle staring Aura down.

"*CYRUS?!*" he roared.

"*Not quite,*" hissed the imposter, rushing toward the Sage.

"*Shite!*"

He was there in a flash, the Raven's eyelashes brushing the blood of the Acolyte's cheeks. "What a lovely ornament," he growled, dragging a stumpy finger over the Acolyte's brow, then cheeks. He moved it over Eli's lower lip, leaving a thin trail of red.

Elatreus squirmed, his eyes crunched tightly closed. He twisted under the touches, so desperately fruitless.

The Sage turned slowly, guiding the barrel away from Aura as the muzzle's black eye stared toward the Raven.

He peered back with his haunting blue eyes, brightly white but bathing in a bloodshot brandy. The Raven smirked, gliding backward.

"Cyrus," the Sage huffed. "Cyrus, brother, you in there?"

"He's alive, darling," hummed the Raven, "but, alas, we must be patient."

"What have you done with him?!"

"Deimos, Aura—this one here." The Raven laughed, knocking twice on the wounded Acolyte's armor plate as he recited their names. "Please, you *all* misunderstand *Me*—you most of all, Sage! Tempers are high, but *I* assure you, you'll have your answers."

"What answers? And how do you know my name?" Aura asked.

"Why, *all* the answers," he hummed with another grin. "And, your name? Why, Aura, I know you as well as the Ghost of Clydae does."

Aura said nothing.

"Better, in fact. I've been with him his whole life," he continued, "and don't think I don't know you too, *Mister Helicon*? That is your true name, right? *Deimos Gaesorian Helicon*? Of the Blackwood?"

"Who the fuck're *you*?" Deimos said flatly, more statement than question.

"Your daughter fares well in the sun," the King replied.

"*What?*" said the Sage.

A gurgling wheeze came from Elatreus as he cleared his throat. "Don't listen," the Acolyte croaked.

"*SHUT UP!*" the Sage roared, bashing Eli over the head. "*You…* what did you say about my—"

"*Sage.*"

A tear came briskly to Deimos's eye. "I—I care not for your tricks, Spirit."

"It's a trap," garbled Eli. "He's the one who—"

"Oh, yes, dear, *I AM THE ONE*…."

"You're the *White Death*, then?" asked Deimos, "the Epitaph's *Winter Reckoning*, is that it?"

The stranger's eyes lit up where Marcus's had been, "Aye," he nodded happily, "so many names…*so many lifetimes.*"

"Lifetimes?" asked Aura once more.

"Do you see, Aura? *'White Death,' 'King of Battle'*…I'm a prophecy, even—that's how much of a *god* I am."

"Leave," she said.

Come again?

"I don't care who you are, who you were, or what business you have here." Aura snorted and spat on the mangled floorboards.

SPLAT.

"Kill us if you can," she snarled, "or step aside."

"Aura, dear, your cruelty is beyond my reckoning," the Raven whispered. He paced between them—his steps were careful and light. He rubbed his chin with the same bloodied fingertips, staining skin and lips a browning scarlet turned to burnt orange in the distant light beyond the horizon.

Just another ghost, she thought.

The cannon fire slowed. Ships skirted black above the glittering horizon and disappeared altogether in the veil of depleting twilight.

"You see, as Aura only knows, we're running out of time…."

Her hairs bristled. *Out—out of time?*

"Who am *I*? *You ALL* seem not to know, still—despite my countless answers…not that *I* answer to *you*.…"

You—yes, you.…

"*You*…those that serve to inspire piety and fear, *but not much else,* as Aura so kindly put it." He winked at her. "Nay, this here is bigger, and *we* must be better."

"*We?*" the Sage asked.

"Yes," he replied sharply. "Where there was only *me*, thanks to our dear Marcus, there must now be *we*."

"What?"

"*Time,*" he said, "and the stars above and those pesky things betwixt. A balance, it is, but broken like your rattling clocks with their ill-fitting cogs.…"

"Speak plainly," Aura spat.

"We speak of the cosmos," he hummed. "We speak of *celestial* balance, of the stars and her children and the gods of this plane and the next. But, here and now, we must speak of the Prison Without Walls—a place we all will undoubtedly come to know."

"We're out of time," Elatreus wheezed, nodding. "He…he showed me."

Aura sighed deeply. Her fist uncurled itself as cool wind calmed her blood. "So many," she said, eyeing the Acolyte's innumerable wounds. "*So much.*" She stepped toward him. "The dead out there, they line the streets.…They line the shores and the sea."

Aura took another step, this time toward the Raven. "I could be a slave in this moment"—she nodded—"I feel an urge, so sick and sweetly deep.…I wish to hack and to cut—to swallow and swing. I feel this urge so deep to butcher you all—all you fucking bastards and beasts—*brutes and Brigands.…*" Aura stopped. "I do not know of what you speak, spirit, but I feel it, somehow. Same as you two,

I'd wager," she said, nodding to the others.

"The Prison Without Walls, my dear—"

"I care not of the stars or the gods or balance. Where is Marcus?" Aura's gaze was bleak.

"Patience," said the stranger. "You know only of this world—your beloved Tara and her rules and slipping time, but she is a small vessel, boiling in the cosmic sea. You will be *consumed*."

"Consumed?" she said.

"The Prison," the stranger repeated, "it is a place outside of this one…a world between worlds, yearning to be set free—yearning to exist."

"Enough," said Aura. "Where is Marcus?"

XXXVIII

NOT YET

Marcus

He tore himself from the shadows, nearly free. I feel the sun! He yearned, leaning forward. The blackness overtook bits of his skin, bringing the red rage to the whites of his eyes.

A damned beast!

The King of Battle cackled in his ear.

Out, damn you!

BOOM.

The Raven reached out, pleading with his eyes, muzzled in his agony.

Aura backed away.

I...I am the beast, then. He pulled harder, resisting the clutches of heaven and hell—*all the gods' false promises.*

Marcus's arms were stained black with smoke and soot. Heat steamed off him, singeing the tips of his feathers. *"I'LL KILL YOU!"* roared the Raven.

"Marcus...." He heard Aura's voice, but it was far away.

"...*rooooooooo*OOOOOOOOOO*AAAAAAAAAAAAAAAAAAA AAAAAAAAAAAAAAAAAAARRRRRRRRRR!*" He shrieked in the darkness, but couldn't hear himself.

"Marcus," he heard again.

He was a black, smoking ruin, crawling agonizingly out. The shrieking shrank to a dull wheeze as Marcus returned to his bestial self—*the reliable self.* He crawled hand over hand between the fabric of the cosmos, pulling himself away from swallowing black. *The Prison pulls me back.* Shadows tearing around him relented to something else...*the gateway—the portal...to...to the abyss....*

Not again.

BOOM.

ONE MORE MOMENT, PLEASE—

—No need to beg, dear.

He's here before me. Marcus shuddered Marcus. *More than a voice.* The King of Battle snarled his toothy mustard smile, spilling his stink over Marcus.

Come now, dear Cyrus...you'll work yourself sick!

"Marcus?"

Her voice is getting louder.

That is your name, isn't it, dear?

My soul smiles. She returns to me. The Raven snarled back at the man in white, inching forward. "You—you...*you....*"

Me.

BOOM.

"You—you think," growled the Raven. "You think you could beat me, do you?"

Come again?

"I...I s'pose you could," strained Marcus, laughing. He inched closer to the light. "But I—I need not beat you—"

—you couldn't...

Marcus laughed all the more. "*HaHaHaHaHaHaHaHaHa-*Ha..."

The King of Battle's nightmare smile turned to a frown.

A ghostly Aura stepped out from behind the man in white, her ethereal hand outstretched.

Is—is this a dream? Is this—is this the Burden?

"*Stay,*" came her soothing voice.

Her tones are brandy sweet. I could stay forever.

BOOM.

The noise tore Aura's visage away, leaving Marcus alone in the dark.

"*NO!*" The Raven cried. *I...I see the tower. I—I can get back if I... if I can....*

Keep crawling. Each handful felt like the weight of the world as he dragged himself agonizingly across whirling dark and color and time, washing over him in the shadow of the King of Battle, who laughed as Marcus crawled.

Crawl, damn you.

He could see the tower's details in the distance, fading within the swirling chaos. He made out the Sage and Eli and Aura....

What hope do you think you have?

The revolver. She'd dropped it, now glimmering on the floorboards. "*I...I—I need not beat you,*" Marcus said. "I need only beat myself."

You are bound to Me, dear....You will be beaten no sooner than I say.

"*You know,*" the Raven choked. "I—I have been a slave to you...a slave to you, and so many others." He wrenched slowly forward. "I—I s'pose I've...I've never been a very good slave...."

Get cozy, dear, for you are bound—

"*No,*" growled Cyrus.

BOOM.

"*You—*you miserable serpent!"

BOOM.

"*You must not know WHERE YOU ARE.*"

"What?"

"You…you…you're locked in here with me, didn't you *know?"*

Suddenly, the shadows loosened their hold. The Raven felt a smile stretch the length of his face as power filled his bones. *"This darkness rewrites me,"* he growled, *"page by fucking page."* He began to laugh. "Ha*Ha*Ha*Ha*Ha*Ha*Ha*Ha*Ha—"

What—

"You mustn't know where you are! You think these shadows on your side?! They have swallowed me over a thousand lifetimes."

You—you….

"I am the god of all the eons"—the Raven laughed—*"not you, snake….I made you, I did. I can destroy you."*

XXXIX

COST

The Raven

The abyssal black tendrils loosened, and Marcus took a breath. *What need have I of breath in this place?* The black turned from a suffocating restraint to the extensions of his limbs, creeping out, contorting with the shape of arms and feathers. He lunged forward, flying through the unending void, approaching the gateway and the tower and the body and...*the color.*

BOOM.

The tower nearly toppled—the sound, unlike any cannon or man-made munition. The darkened rift had closed behind him—*but I, I crossed the plane.*

It cracked like lightning, jolting him alive, searing at the tips of his fingers as he felt them again. *I've—I've returned to my body.* He fell to his knees, hacking and wheezing and spitting black tar upon the wood.

"Marcus!" Aura knelt.

In the same manner of the King of Battle's ghostly arrival, the man in white faded out from under the Raven's feathers as his true self, too, stumbling and rattling in his absurd white armor as he clapped and hooted.

"HAHAHAHAHAHAHAHA."

He's…he's mocking me. Marcus caught Aura's eye, shaking his head.

She crinkled her brow.

Concern, he realized with a smile. He spoke to her in this small moment, if only with his rage and his tears and perchance the shape of the abyssal resin he was whooping onto the floor. *I'm out of time,* he lamented.

In another life, perhaps….

She nodded.

Ah, there you are, precious. The Raven scooped up his trusty revolver. *Always by my side.* He was gunning for the edge of the tower and the cliffs far below. *There's only one way. Only I need die.*

"Come now, Cyrus."

THWACK.

The King of Battle snatched the Raven from the air with his sickly strength. He held him close.

"Not yet, child, but soon…."

Now—now—now is my chance. The Raven wrenched the revolver up toward him, the stranger laughing and swatting it away.

"You'd try to kill Me, with that?"

"No," strained the Raven, "…*me.*" He held the barrel up, beneath his own chin. His eyes found Aura.

*Gods, look away, please! Look away....*The revolver rattled under his hand—*more than it did for the cleric.*

Aura never looked away.

I'm sorry, he pled with his eyes.

I know. She nodded.

CLICK.

Don't you know?

Fuck. The Raven's heart sank. *No rest. No relief.*

The sun rises at My behest.

"Then who, pray tell, makes it set?" asked Eli. His blood-stained hand hovered over his long, arching hilt. "Should only the Raven get a good death?"

Tricky Eli....

The Acolyte smoothly slid the edge from its long sheath, slashing in a wide arc at the weak stone around him.

He's...he's taking the tower down. "SAGE!" the Raven cried. "The tower!"

The Sage followed, unleashing Moonlight on the rotting wood and chalky corners.

The King of Battle hurtled toward the Acolyte, smashing forcefully into him.

BOOM.

"Stop this now."

Elatreus crashed into the far wall, bringing a few stones tumbling down.

"Bring it down!" cried the Raven.

Aura caught on, slashing Mercy in long, wide arcs, hacking sparks and splinters as she cut away the brick and the mortar, the tattered belfry collapsing all around.

NO!

"It's working!" the Raven shouted, smashing his shoulder into the nearest wall.

The floorboards were giving out beneath him as dust and debris rained down, the tower swaying with the wind. *It's—it's time.*

"Marcus...."

"I...."

"NOW, BROTHER!" roared the Sage. *"GET OUT!"*

The Raven nodded firmly. "I love you, Aura," he said. "I loved you then—still...*forever.*"

"Forever." She nodded.

YOU WILL NOT TAKE THIS WORLD FROM ME!

In another life.

The Raven leapt from the tower, plummeting to the sea below.

XL

FRIENDS OF DEATH

I...

I...

I...

AM...

I.

AM

DESPAIR

Aura

The words horrified—so deep and loud, groaning in her ear, rippling under her skin. She could feel them yanking the hairs out of her neck.

The King of Battle was frozen white, shrieking in the center as icy cold blew ferociously out, stinging Aura's face. The dark, cold emanations froze tiny crystalline icicles in her hair and eyebrows.

"*MARCUS!*" she roared.

He...

He fell....

The King of Battle's bellowing cries rang in her head and her ears, everywhere and completely.

Gone, she sank, *stolen again.* The tears came, and Aura retreated. *What's the difference?* The tower collapsed around her. *We're all to die anyway.*

Eli and the Sage had quit their abolishing, but the tower was ruined, falling apart piece by piece beneath them. Aura stood tall, guiding her feet to a stable ledge, missing the falling rocks. The Sage held a clumsy foothold, worsened by the loose rock above. It broke and split, crashing onto him and dragging him down to a bare ledge of scaffolding.

"*AH, SHITE!*" he roared.

There's no way down. She took a deep breath. *All this...just to die here.*

CRACK—CRACK, CRACK.

The aching stones of the tower clapped together and apart, descending.

The bell tolls on. Aura thought to make for the ledge, but she couldn't find the foothold. *Please,* she pleaded, *take me with you.* She wished to leap herself, but another blast of freezing cold air knocked her back.

BOOM.

The ivory white, statuesque King of Battle exploded, blasting shards of broken ice and cold. *He's done it, then. He's gone.*

Marcus is gone.

The frost nicked at her cheeks and nose, painting the rocks frosty white as the shattering stone was thrown out and down. A stray stone smashed through the Sage's platform, dropping him down and through the wooden stairs.

Gone.

The King's long howl waned, ringing its last to the night air, leaving Aura's bones. *"Good riddance,"* she whispered.

Marcus dragged him back to hell.

Stone crashed down, cracking and breaking. *Let it end.* The errant bricks thudded into her back and shoulders. She covered her face, shielding herself with a vicious growl. She saw Elatreus nearby, his footholds crumbling like the Sage's beforehand.

"Aura," he said, "I'm sorry and—and…thank you."

She shook her head at first, but then, Aura nodded.

Elatreus nodded back. He smiled for what felt like the first time.

He—he looks almost happy.

Without another word, Eli let his fingers slip from the rocks, letting his body fall limply backward and down.

Down goes the Acolyte.

She smiled and laughed a bit, too. *The queen of the hill—the last one standing.* A rock smashed her shoulder.

"DAMN!" She recoiled.

Aura thought of Marcus's eyes, then. *Marcus.* She laughed, *Marcus Petronax killed a god today…and so did I.*

But the god of death had bested her, too, she reasoned. Standing alone among stars and smoke, now—the last light of sun burnt out, Aura smiled in the face of her demise. The tower ached beneath, ready to topple, and she wanted it to. She was ready. *Only one way down.*

Take me, she called to the abyss. *I'm ready.*

But then, something stirred.

A voice? No, a whistle?

Flapping. Aura heard distant flapping, but it was getting closer. She spotted the source—a small silhouette floated up from the sea, flapping to a perch above her.

"What's this?" *A gull, must be, or a pelican.*

No, it's a…a raven. She knew it from the sound. *Like the ones in Clydae.*

The raven's caw was sweetly soft, like a cooing baby. *"That is the mark of Ares, that is,"* her mother would say. *Gods, the Burden has me, even here. Even now.*

The raven cawed again, louder this time.

"Wh—what?" *I can take no more tricks.*

"T-tay…puh…."

Gods in hell, it speaks. "I…I don't understand," said Aura, losing her footing.

The raven cawed again, pointing its ebony beak out to sea, bobbing.
"I don't understand."
"Take..." cawed the raven. *"Take...the..."*
"Take—take the what?" Aura replied, clinging to the stone.
"Take...the...plunge."

WALLS

Marcus

Not here…not here, again.

Not again.

Anywhere…anywhere but here.

Where am I?

When am I?

I've awoken to a dark hand, its strangling grip tightening inside my chest. Dread strangles the mind equally, and I am terribly afraid.

I—I saw her. She was there. I saw her in the sun, with the ships and the sea….

My breath overtakes as more comes to me. No, not again…

Not the Prison…

Not again.

I panic. I squeeze my eyes tight in hopes of unhinging myself from the reality I wish to forget, and I fear all the more. Dark shadows swirl and tantalize, smothering the light of me...again.

"My hands are far away," I hear myself say. Their blood bubbles beneath the skin, coursing like spurts of oil, heavy and hot.

Oh, how the fury builds...it builds, on and on. It builds, still.

I'm not sure what more I can take.

My fingers lust for my own throat.

I'm shouting now. "I WILL SHOW YOU FURY!" I shriek in solitude. "I WILL SHOW YOU DESPAIR!"

The darkness never responds. It lurks and persists, like a plague and a pall. It skulks through the infinitesimal nooks and crannies, corrupting the cracks and the corners we can barely see.

My cracks.

My corners.

I wish only to die, but the tendrils tether me to ashen, petrified earth.

"Be still, child," a shapeless voice comes.
My blood cools at the soft, motherly tones. "Please," I beg. "Aura— promise me she will be safe from him—"
"Him?" her calming voice replies.
"Yes, the...the King of—"
"No kings here, child...just you."

A light shines in my abyss—a footprint.

Then, another.

Soundless and gentle motioning burns the dark away in a quiet corner as a fair, ghostly hand unshadows itself. The fingers reach toward my chin, and I let them.

"Be still, pilgrim. This place is not your end."
"Spirit, I beg you—"
"Words can be so...fragile," she whispers, "...and faint. But here, look...."
"What—what is it?"

A pair of ghostly green orbs hover over wisps of cheeks and lips that curve to a smile, showing her dim, spectral loveliness.

Almost as lovely as Aura.

"In time, you will learn your truest potential."
"Leave me to my weakness, Spirit."
"Brave champion," she softly sings, "as those before were flesh and blood, you are shaped in salt and stone and the stars above. Carved deep into the heart of Tara by my hand alone. Where weak men fail, you will triumph. Where others will destroy, you will reclaim and rebuild. And where evil lives, you shall cast it out. Do you accept this charge?"
"I...."
"You doubt?" she purrs.
"I fear for the things that I have done...for the things I will do."
"Brave champion," she says again, retracting the ghostly white palm to the shadows.

It returns with an apple.

"So many things you have done...."

Her apple shines red, sweetly ripe.

"So many things you will do."

"Let my soul die with my body," I beg, *"that I may bid my fears and ghosts goodbye."*

The eyes of Ares meet mine. "Eternity is long, my dear."

"Aye," I say. *"Save me, Spirit....Save me from the shackles of my mangled mind."*

"You will come to save yourself, brave champion."

EPILOGUE

Malus

Ah…

What's this?

A lost lamb, so far from the shepherd and the path…

So far from those that keep you safe and from you, yourself.

You, dear reader—I do mean you.

How did you come to find such a place?

"So convincing, is it not? This dream of ours?"

Is that what the Sage said?

"Why not wade a little further? It could be no worse than what came before…."

HaHaHaHaHaHaHaHa…

It can be far worse.

You shouldn't have come.

Shall I show you something?

Just there…can you see them?

Shining in the sun, look!

You see him, don't you? There's Marcus…

…and Aura, just there…and simple Reed…

…so beautiful they are, as they were meant to be.

Preserved here, if nowhere else…

Where they can live and die as we all do…

Toys in my box…

Or perhaps, cats…live, or dead…

Their vibrance spills out across the land, across Tara…

…their color…their paradise.

One without walls.

HaHaHaHaHaHaHaHaHaHaHaHaHaHaHa…

…Poor, poor steward.

Worthless wretch…

…shameful peasant that you are…

…it can be far worse.

You must not know of where we are.

Xibalba…

Tartarus…

Hel…

Tis no matter what you call it, for I…

I am…

I…

Am…

KING…

Here, in the dark…

Have you heard my hissing whispers?

Felt my tongue caress your ear when no one else can see?

"You are not safe," *I softly say,* "not here."

Not here—you have no friends here in the dark…only Me.

You—you have something…so dearly special, and I…

I so hunger for it.

You—yes, **you** *—the only kind of* **you** *there is. In dreams you hear my whispers, no?*

Have you always heard them?

The cold voice that haunts you…

…that which plucks at your loneliness…laughs at your sorrows.

Ha*Ha*Ha*Ha*Ha*Ha*Ha*Ha*…

Does it drown you*?*

I think you know, deep down. I've watched you grow from birth 'til now—so far you've come. No longer a child, yet…

…I remember your shrieks in the dark.

I know of the intimate imaginings of your nightmares, so focused and fixed…

I am their architect.

And yet, my soothing tones disarm you. My dread doesn't come for you here.

No.

No, the dread is still to come.

For I am the weight...

The Burden.

The trouble of your past and present...

...and one day, your eternity.

I watched you in those ugly moments you thought were yours alone—
you thought no one was there to witness your sins?

No gods watch over you—of that I have made sure—nor spirits of the
loved or lost. Only the darkness lingers, listening to the sweet melody of
your loneliness.

I am the feeling that someone is watching. My fingers pluck at the
hairs of your neck. I am the dying smile, sapping the warmth from your
hollowing soul.

The ghost of your portraits...
wilting their petals.

My touches are the gray, yanking at your youth, and the wrinkles that
come as I steal the ones you love. Your sufferings are slow—
my goal is decay.

Entropy...

I so ache to watch....I've seen your wickedness and your secret filth. I
will pull it from you, so that all the world may see as I do.

With the softest stirrings of your addled mind, I feel myself between your ears as your eyes dance nervously about.

Where am I?

I think you know.

Yes, a tugging stone that drags down, down, down...

Come down with Me, lost lamb...

that's it...

come down...

For I...

I...

I...

I am the devil—the swallower of souls—lord of the four true *gods...*

Master of Chaos.

Saint of Despair.

Harbinger of Cruelty.

Reclaimer of Woe.

I am god of the shadows.

I am king of the dark.

I am Death—*the Destroyer of Worlds...*

The King of Battle...

Without equal...

Without end...

Mark my words, all you accursed sons and daughters of Ares...

...the Prison knows no Walls...

...and neither shall you.